D0210001

"*Starclimber* is an intriguing read, with lots of space adventure (possible and impossible), a smattering of romance (Kate and Matt Cruse), and plenty of suspense. . . . Promises to be another bestseller."
—*Winnipeg Free Press*

"Once again, Oppel has assembled intriguing characters, especially Matt's fellow astralnauts, who populate a fast-paced narrative that features enough unpredictable plot twists to keep readers riveted to Matt's story to the finish."
—*Kirkus Reviews*

"Fans of the earlier novels will find more of the same here—breath-stopping predicaments, narrow escapes and two resourceful heroes who can't quite feel secure in their affections."
—*Toronto Star*

"To Oppel's significant credit, he makes [the] love story an integral aspect of the novel without slowing the action or alienating mush-averse readers. They will be far too enraptured by this gripping tale, which delivers fast-paced fantasy and rich psychological drama."
—*Quill and Quire* (Starred Review)

Starclimber

Kenneth Oppel

Starclimber

HarperTrophyCanada™
An imprint of HarperCollinsPublishersLtd

Starclimber

Copyright © 2008 by Firewing Productions Inc. All rights reserved.

Published by Harper*Trophy*Canada™, an imprint of HarperCollins Publishers Ltd

Originally published in a hardcover edition by HarperCollins Publishers Ltd: 2008

First Harper*Trophy*Canada™ trade paperback edition: 2009
This Harper*Trophy*Canada™ digest paperback edition: 2011

HarperCollins books may be purchased for educational, business, or sales promotional use through our Special Markets Department.

HarperCollins Publishers Ltd
2 Bloor Street East, 20th Floor
Toronto, Ontario, Canada
M4W 1A8

www.harpercollins.ca

Library and Archives Canada Cataloguing in Publication
Oppel, Kenneth
Starclimber / Kenneth Oppel.

ISBN 978-1-55468-521-9

I. Title.
PS8579.P64S73 2011   jC813'.54   C2010-907238-3

Printed and bound in Canada
HC 9 8 7 6 5 4 3 2 1

For Philippa

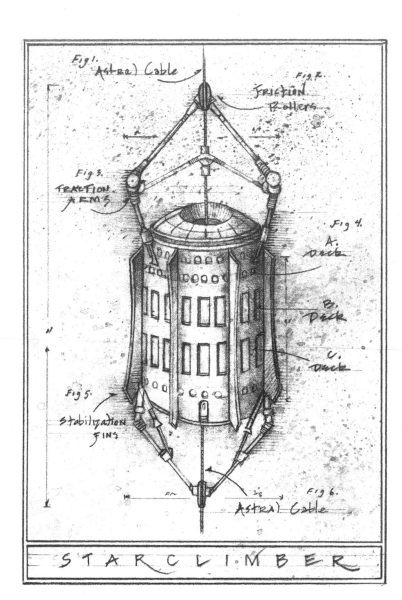

Fig 1. Astral Cable

Fig 2. Friction Rollers

Fig 3. Traction Arms

Fig 4.
A. Deck

B. Deck

C. Deck

Fig 5. Stabilization Fins

Fig 6. Astral Cable

STARCLIMBER

1 / The Celestial Tower

RISING INTO THE WIND, I flew, Paris spread before me.

For the first time in my life I was at the helm, though my ship was a humble one, and not my own. Aboard the *Atlas*, we didn't even use terms like *captain* or *first mate*. This was no fancy airship liner or private yacht; she was just an aerocrane, forty feet from stem to stern, but she was mine to command for the summer, and I loved every second of it.

"Elevators up five degrees, please," I told Christophe, my co-pilot. "Throttle to one half."

As the drone of the engines increased in pitch I put the ship into a gentle starboard turn. We climbed, and I brought the *Atlas* about so that we faced the construction site. Though I had gazed upon it almost every day for two weeks now, the view still filled me with awe.

Rising two miles above the earth was the base of the Celestial Tower. Massive metal piers and arches supported its platforms, each one large enough to hold a city. The third platform had just been completed, and work on the next level was well underway, great spans of metal jutting skyward. Gliding over the site were dozens of aerotugs, delivering materials and prefabricated sections of piers to waiting work crews. From all across the tower came the flash of welders' torches, fusing together girders. Already the structure was ten times higher than the Eiffel Tower, but it had much farther yet to go.

It was meant to reach all the way to outer space.

There was so much airship traffic around the construction site that it had its own harbourmaster. His voice crackled over the radio now, giving us our approach instructions. Hanging from the *Atlas*'s winch was a three-storey-tall section of support pier to be delivered to the tower's northern side. I turned the rudder wheel and brought us onto our proper bearing, circling the tower in a wide arc.

"Did you hear," said Christophe, "that already they have named it the Eighth Wonder of the World?" Christophe was a Parisian, and extremely proud of the tower. He seemed to have an endless supply of information about it.

I nodded. "I saw it in the *Global Tribune* this morning."

"How high you reckon they're going to build this thing?" asked Andrew, coming forward from the cargo area, wiping his greasy hands with a rag. He was the winch operator, a hefty, red-faced fellow from Angleterre who'd moved to Paris, like so many others, to find work on the tower.

"I heard about sixty miles," I said.

Christophe sucked his tongue in disagreement. "*Non, non, ce n'est pas vrai.* I heard at least six hundred."

"Suits me," said Andrew. "The higher they go, the longer I have a job. At these wages, I'll be retired with me own castle before long."

I too felt lucky. Piloting an aerotug for the summer would fund my final two terms at the Airship Academy. The French had hired tens of thousands of workers from all around the world. It was the greatest construction project in the history of mankind. The French boasted it made the Great Pyramids look like an afternoon garden project. Nothing, they said, would topple it. It was designed to sway, to bend with the elements, but never break. I hoped they were right, because if it ever did, it would fall over half of Europa.

"I thought it was meant to go all the way to the moon," said Hassan, our Moroccan spotter, coming forward to peer out the windows of the Control Car.

"How could they do that, you numbskull?" said Andrew, whose tone was often a bit bullying. "The moon orbits around us, doesn't it? We can't go tying ourselves to it! We'd get all yanked about."

Hassan nodded amiably. "Yes, I can see that would not be desirable."

"At the summit of the Celestial Tower," said Christophe with patriotic confidence, "I read, they will launch a fleet of ships to travel into outer space, first to the moon, and then beyond."

This certainly seemed to be the government's plan. All over Paris, buildings were plastered with posters—PARIS TO THE MOON! or THE MARTIAN RIVIERA!—and showed chic ladies and gentlemen strolling through crystal lunar palaces or along red Martian beaches. Another poster proclaimed, OUR BRAVE SPATIONAUTS! and had a group of fit young men in silver suits, fists against their hips, staring arrogantly into the heavens.

"What I'd like to know," said Andrew, "is where they're finding these fellows daft enough to go to outer space."

"They've set up some kind of special training facility, haven't they?" I said.

"I have heard this also," said Christophe wistfully.

"I think our Christophe here wants to be a spationaut," Andrew sniggered.

"I am desolate I do not have the skills," said Christophe, and he did manage to sound quite desolate when he said it.

"What about you, Matt?" Hassan asked. "If they asked, would you go?"

"In a heartbeat."

"You're a madman," said Andrew. "Couldn't drag me up there, not in a million years."

"Of course, they will only be selecting Frenchmen," Christophe sniffed, "so no need for you to worry."

"The French are welcome to space," said Andrew, "the entire black puddle of it."

I didn't share Andrew's disdain. As cabin boy aboard the *Aurora* I'd spent lots of time in the crow's nest, staring at stars. Their constellations blazed with myths and legends. I'd always wondered what it would be like to go farther, to get closer. At the Academy last term we'd studied celestial navigation, and now the night sky beckoned me with even greater intensity.

But for now, space was for the French, just as Christophe said, and I'd have to be satisfied with helping them achieve their dreams. I didn't feel too sorry for myself. My own dreams at the moment didn't live in outer space anyway, but much closer to Earth.

"We're almost in position," I told my crew. "Let's get ready, please."

Despite the fact that I was the youngest aboard, the others never questioned my command, not even Christophe, who always gave the impression of knowing everything. My crew didn't call me Captain, or Sir, or Mister, but I didn't expect it. They knew I had authority of the ship, and I think they trusted me. We'd worked well together so far.

Andrew and Hassan went aft. The aerotug's gondola was a single long cabin, taken up mostly by the cargo area, where the powerful winch was positioned above the open bay doors.

It was Andrew's job to control the winch and Hassan's to make sure we were positioned perfectly before lowering our cargo. From his caged spotter's post on the underside of the gondola, Hassan had an excellent view of what was directly below, and he gave me directions via speaking tube. His job might have sounded lowly, but it was vitally important.

"Level off, please," I told Christophe, and throttled back, swinging us in towards the tower's north edge. I saw the waiting work crew below, the signaller guiding us in with his orange flags, and then we were almost overhead and Hassan was the ship's eyes.

"Slow ahead, slow, we're almost at the mark," came his voice through the tube.

I cut the engines right back so that we had just enough power to keep us dug in against the headwinds. Then I let

Christophe take the throttle so I could concentrate on the rudder wheel for the final manoeuvres.

"Nudge her to port," said Hassan. "Too far—bring her back a bit, you're drifting astern . . . We're on the mark!"

I heard the winch's motor hum as it unspooled. It was always a tense time, lowering the cargo, because we had to keep the ship as steady as possible. Some days the crosswinds gave us a terrible shake.

"They've got hold of the guy lines!" said Hassan. "We need another twenty feet, slowly."

Andrew unspooled more cable. I knew the workers would already be shunting the tower segment into place. Welding torches would flare to life, red-hot rivets would be swiftly hammered home. The tower had just grown another fifty feet.

"They've cast us loose," Hassan said through the speaking tube. "Winch up!"

I put the throttle ahead a quarter and pulled us away from the tower. Behind us, the next aerotug was already waiting to deliver its own load.

"That's us done," I said. We'd delivered our last load of the day, and our shift was over. I was looking forward to a break—and to seeing Kate this evening. I had a special surprise planned for her.

"What about this one?" Andrew asked from the cargo area.

I glanced back and saw a single wooden crate secured against the rear wall. I'd not noticed it until now.

"I thought we'd made all our deliveries," I said to Christophe, reaching for the clipboard that held our manifest.

The sound of boots hitting the deck made me turn. A man had dropped from the companion ladder that led up to the gas cells. In his hand was a pistol.

"Back against the wall!" he shouted at Andrew, and at Hassan, who'd just climbed out of his spotter's cage.

Two more men dropped from the ladder, guns clenched in their fists. All three wore construction coveralls. On their backs were bulky rucksacks.

Before I could radio a distress call, one of them, a pale fellow with a gaunt face, strode over and put a bullet through the transmitter. Then he levelled the gun at my head.

My first thought, absurdly, was: *I'm going to be late for Kate.*

"What the hell's all this?" Andrew roared.

"Easy, everyone," I cautioned. I didn't know who these fellows were, or what they wanted, but it would do no good to anger them. Christophe seemed calm enough, though his cheeks were flushed. I was most worried about Andrew, for he had a brawler's temperament and I feared he might do something rash.

I doubted these men were pirates, for we had nothing of value aboard. Maybe they were escaped convicts and needed speedy passage out of the country. They must have been aboard my ship the entire afternoon, waiting.

"We are going down to the southeast pier," Christophe told me. "The first platform."

I looked at him, confused, before realizing what was going on.

No one was pointing a gun at Christophe.

"You understand?" he said.

"What's going on?" I demanded.

"We fly normally. Do not try to attract attention. We shall begin now."

He was keeping me at the helm, which meant he didn't know how to fly the ship alone. I took the rudder wheel and eased the throttle forward. "Elevators down three degrees."

I would not say *please* any more. My heart beat wildly and I was glad I had my flying to keep panic in check. The back of my head burned, as if the pistol projected deadly heat.

"Why're we going down there?" I asked.

He ignored me.

"Christophe, you great gaseous frog!" Andrew roared. "What d'you think you're doin'?"

"Shut your pie-hole or we'll gag you!" one of the other men said.

I guided the *Atlas* down towards the first platform, watching carefully for other airships. Our flight was unauthorized and right now the harbourmaster would be trying to raise us on the radio. Frightened as I was, it irked me to know that the harbourmaster and other pilots in the area would be thinking me an incompetent menace.

The southeast pier was one of the four cornerstones of the tower, a massive fortress of interlocking girders that supported not only the first platform, but all above it. We were approaching it from the south at three thousand feet. I throttled back, not wishing to draw too close. I had no idea what Christophe's intentions were.

"Level us off," I told him.

"No. We will go underneath the platform."

"Underneath?"

"Correct. Inside the pier." He pointed through the window at the close weave of girders. "There."

"I'm not sure there's room," I said.

"There is room," he said with complete assurance.

"You've studied this, have you?"

"A great deal," he said.

We were headed straight for an opening that looked no larger than the *Atlas*. A cross-gust shook us off course, and we both struggled with elevators and rudder to keep us on target, for there was little margin for error. In we went, nearly grazing the underside of the platform. Stray ten feet to either side and our engines would be sheared straight off. We glided deeper inside.

Christophe reached for the throttle and killed the engines. "Tie up the ship," he shouted back at his men.

The gaunt fellow who'd had his pistol trained on me strode aft to help.

"Your work is done," Christophe said to me, pulling a pistol from inside his jacket and grabbing my arm. He marched me into the cargo area, where his men had thrown open the gondola's side hatches. They held grappling lines, and let fly. The hooks caught hold amidst the girders, anchoring the *Atlas*.

I looked down through the open bay doors and saw the ground through a criss-cross of girders, three thousand feet below.

"You two!" shouted the gaunt fellow at Andrew and Hassan. "Bring the crate over here."

Glaring hatefully at the hijackers, Andrew slowly walked over to the crate with Hassan. The two of them released the straps and pushed it across the deck towards Christophe.

"That's far enough," he told them, when it was within ten feet of the bay doors. "Back against the wall. You also," he said, giving me a shove.

"I never liked him," Andrew growled to me. "Always so full of himself."

I looked over at Hassan, who was very quiet, and I saw his hands shaking.

"Open it, Pierre," Christophe said to the gaunt man.

The fellow obediently holstered his gun and pushed back the crate's lid. Inside was enough dynamite to knock the face off the moon. I felt sick, thinking that this had been aboard my ship all day without my knowing. A complicated tangle of fusing sprouted from the dynamite and fed into some kind of archaic-looking device that seemed half steam engine, half grandfather clock. The clock face had two hands, both pointing at twelve o'clock, and underneath was a large winding key.

"You're Babelites!" said Hassan in disbelief.

All Paris had heard of these fellows. They hated the Celestial Tower and were dead set against its construction. They took their name from the Tower of Babel in the Bible.

That tower was a giant ziggurat meant to reach all the way to heaven. But God was angered by the Babylonians' arrogance and made all the workers start talking in different languages. They couldn't understand each other, and the ziggurat was abandoned and fell into ruin.

The Babelites had already made one attempt to sabotage the Celestial Tower. They'd tried to kidnap the chief engineer but had botched it, and some of them were caught and jailed. I looked at Christophe in astonishment.

"I can't believe you're one of them," I said.

"It is not for man to build a gateway to the heavens," he said. "God meant heaven for those good souls on Earth who've *earned* it. The tower is an abomination and must be struck down."

"You lunatic," said Andrew, "you'll kill thousands of people!"

"If we do not topple it now," Christophe said, "it will be toppled by God's own hand. We have planned our explosion to make the tower fall away from Paris. We are trying to minimize the loss of life. You may think us mad, but we will be remembered as herocs."

I doubted this very much, but said nothing. Christophe and his followers acted with a zeal I couldn't comprehend.

"Set it going," Christophe told Pierre.

The gaunt fellow pushed the clock's long hand back to ten minutes before twelve. He gave the winding key several complete turns. A dreadful sound emanated from the contraption, more a gasp than a tick.

Hunh-unh-hunh-unh-hunh-unh-hunh-unh . . .

"And what about us?" Andrew shouted.

"I am, of course, desolate," said Christophe, "but sometimes these things are necessary."

"You mean killing us!"

One of the other Babelites tossed Christophe a bulky backpack, which he caught with his free hand and slung over one shoulder.

"Yves," Christophe said. "Go now."

Yves wasted no time stepping to the open bay doors and jumping out. I was close enough to the edge to see narrow parawings explode from his pack. They were extremely manoeuvrable, for the man made a sharp turn and went soaring out of the pier through a set of girders. He had enough height to sail a safe distance from the tower before the bomb exploded.

"You cowards!" spat Andrew, and Christophe levelled the gun at his head to discourage any last-minute heroics.

"Pierre, go!" said Christophe.

Before Pierre could take two steps to the doors, the ticking stopped with a wheeze, like a dying man's final exhalation.

Hunnnnhhhhh . . .

My eyes flew to the clock. The minute hand was still nine minutes from twelve.

"What is wrong with it?" Christophe demanded.

Pierre gave a shrug and said, "It is temperamental."

"It's run out of tick," snapped Christophe. "Did you wind it properly?"

"*Mais oui,*" said Pierre, "but with the mediocre materials you give me to work with, what can you—"

At this Christophe exploded into an angry torrent of French, which his compatriot returned with much gesticulating and shrugging. During all this, the other Babelite kept his pistol aimed at Hassan, Andrew, and me, nervously glancing between us and his fellows.

"*Mon Dieu!*" Christophe said, throwing up his hands. "Just wind it up some more. Imbecile!"

Pierre stepped towards the clock, but before he could touch it, the wheezing tick resumed.

Unh-hunh-unh-hunh-unh-hunh . . .

He turned to Christophe. "*Ça marche.* It's good."

Christophe's face was rigid with contempt. "Perhaps I should make you stay behind, to make sure it is, as you say, *good.*"

Pierre gave a shrug. "It will work. I have tested it many times."

For a few seconds Christophe stared at the timer as it wheezed on. Then he blew air noisily through his lips. "Pierre, go. You too, Jules."

Looking grateful, Pierre jumped out the bay doors and deployed his parawings. Jules followed.

Christophe turned his pistol on the rest of us, shrugging

his parawing pack onto both shoulders. "Would you prefer that I shoot you, or would you like to go down with your ship?" he asked me.

"Down with my ship," I said, though I had no intention of dying today.

"Very well," he said. "I am sorry." And as he clipped together his chest harness, the pistol fell from his nervous hand.

All three of us sprang at him, Andrew with a savage roar. Christophe lunged for his pistol. We landed atop him in a heap, kicking and punching. The pistol spun away across the deck towards the open bay doors and I launched myself at it, snatching it up just before it went over the edge. I leapt to my feet.

"Get up!" I shouted, aiming my pistol at Christophe.

Breathing hard, he stood.

"Shut it off!" I yelled.

He shook his head. "Unfortunately, only Pierre knows how."

"Bollocks!" shouted Andrew, striding towards me. "Give me the gun, Cruse!"

He snatched it from my hand, fumbled it, and it fell to the deck.

As Andrew scrambled to pick up the gun, Christophe ran for the bay doors. Hassan and I grabbed him from behind and we all struggled on the very brink. Christophe punched me in the face and jumped towards the opening, but Hassan had him firmly by one of his shoulder straps and pulled back with all his weight. Christophe spun around, the parawing pack flying off his body and onto the deck. He staggered off balance, arms windmilling, then with a cry fell through the bay doors—to his death.

The three of us stood panting, staring at one another.

The bomb wheezed in its crate.

"How much time do we have?" Hassan asked.

I ran over and looked. "Seven minutes."

The tick faltered a few seconds, then resumed. I had no idea whether this meant we had more time, or whether the infernal device was still keeping track of the seconds and meant to surprise us.

"What if we just rip out the clock?" Hassan suggested.

"That might set it off," I said. I knew nothing about explosives but didn't fancy my chances tugging at wires.

"I want off this ship!" bellowed Andrew.

"There's no point!" I said. "We can't climb down in time."

"Who said anything about climbing!"

At the same moment all eyes fell on Christophe's parawing pack.

"Sorry, lads," said Andrew, springing on it. "It's only good for one." He looked at me, a little shamefaced. "And captain goes down with the ship anyway, right?"

He still had the pistol, and though he did not point it at us, I didn't trust him. Hassan and I watched as he buckled on the pack.

"You know how to use that?" I asked. I couldn't bear him much ill will. Someone might as well get clear in time.

"I'll take my chances. Good luck."

He jumped out the open bay doors. I saw his wings deploy, and he careened crazily around the girders before colliding with one, hard. The blow seemed to knock him out, for his head lolled and his wings crumpled, and then he fell, bouncing from one girder to the next on his fatal plunge to the earth.

I wasted no more time. "Cut the grappling lines," I told Hassan. "There's a knife in the emergency locker."

I ran forward to the helm. Even from up front I could hear the bomb's wheezing. I started the engines, and the propellers quickly accelerated into a satisfying drone.

"We're cut loose!" Hassan shouted, running up front. "What's our plan?"

"Dump it in the drink." On the southern fringe of the Bois de Vincennes was an ornamental lake.

"Will we make it?"

"We'll make it. Take the elevator wheel."

"I've never flown!"

"There's nothing to it."

I pushed the throttle and gripped the rudder wheel. There was no time to try to ease out backward. Our only way out was straight through. Before us was a narrow passage that would bring us out the far side of the pier. I opened the throttle. Girders hurtled past us, the underside of the platform streaking overhead.

"Just hold her steady, Hassan, you're doing very well."

He stood, shoulders hunched up around his ears, staring straight ahead with wide eyes.

I saw the opening coming up, a narrow slat of brighter light. We were straying a little too high, but before I could ask Hassan to correct our altitude, an awful ripping sound came from the ship's back. Warning lights flashed on the ballast board. We'd torn most of our gas cells but there was no time to worry about that now.

Suddenly we were through the pier, but still underneath the tower's first platform. I reached over and gave the elevator wheel a swift turn so that we dipped sharply and shot beneath one of the tower's colossal arches, and then—we were out!

"Bring us back up now, Hassan," I said.

Aerotugs glided all around, seeming to move incredibly slowly. I weaved through them, banking sharply and climbing as I took us out towards the park and lake.

"There it is!" shouted Hassan.

"How much time's left?"

Hassan ran aft to check. "Two minutes and a bit!" he called. "Wait, it's stopped . . . no, it's going again!"

My heart was beating madly now. The wind was light, and I lined the *Atlas* up so that we'd pass directly over the lake, then tied off the rudder wheel and hurried back to help Hassan.

Together we shoved the crate gently to the edge of the bay doors. I had no idea how sensitive the thing was and held my breath, fearing we might set it off. We peered down at the parkland—people sitting on benches, children playing—and waited breathlessly for the water. *Where was the lake?*

Unh-hunh-unh-hunh-unh-hunh . . .

Silence.

I looked over at the timer. The minute hand had stopped altogether, just a shade before twelve. Then, as if making up for lost time, the clock started ticking with surreal speed, gasping like a marathon runner in his final stretch.

Hish-a-hish-a-hish-a-hish-a hish-a-shhhhh . . .

With horror I watched the hands swirl around, as though the insides of the clock were uncoiling.

"There's the water!" shouted Hassan.

"Heave-ho!" I bellowed.

We put our shoulders to the crate and pushed it over the rim. It plunged down and hit the lake with a mighty splash.

"Grab hold!" I yelled.

"Maybe the water'll put out the—" Hassan began.

Then a colossal fountain burst from the lake. The blast tossed us to the deck. Cabin windows shattered. Hot wind shrieked past, creating a hellish symphony in our rigging. Then, finally, silence.

"It's spent," gasped Hassan.

"Good work," I told him, struggling to my feet and back to the helm.

We were losing gas swiftly, and the rudder must have been damaged, for the *Atlas* was sluggish to turn. But we would make it safely back to the aeroharbour and, with a bit of luck, I might even be on time for Kate.

2 / The Stars from Montmartre

THE NEIGHBOURHOOD OF MONTMARTRE is the highest point in Paris, and by the time I'd jogged up all the stairs to the park at the top, I was already an hour late for Kate. She was nowhere to be seen.

Dejected, I sank down on a bench. Probably she'd left long ago in a fury. Which wasn't entirely fair, since this was the first and only time I'd ever been late for her—and I did happen to have the best excuse imaginable.

After bringing the *Atlas* in, Hassan and I were interrogated by the police for a very long time. I was worried they'd think we were the bombers, but luckily, Pierre had already been caught. His parawings had snagged in the girders and he'd been recognized by the police as a known Babelite. Jules and Yves had gotten away. Christophe was dead, as was Andrew. The gendarmes clapped us on the backs, commended us for our bravery, and told us to keep our mouths shut.

Of course, I had every intention of telling Kate—but she wasn't even here to listen to my story. I'd been rehearsing it the whole way on the Métro. I shook my head. She could've waited a *little* longer. I'd once added up all the time I'd waited for her and it came out to something like six days.

I was just about to head back down to the Métro when a motorcar pulled up. The driver hopped out and opened the back door.

"I am *so* sorry," Kate said, stepping out. She was all dressed up, like she was expecting a night at the opera. "You won't believe the day I've had. Have you been waiting long?"

"Just got here, actually."

"You look a little bedraggled," she said, concerned. "Are you all right?"

Usually when we met, I dressed up in my Academy uniform, but this time I'd scarcely had time to change out of my ship clothes, I was in such a hurry to meet her.

I gave a world-weary chuckle. "Did you hear that huge explosion a few hours ago?"

She frowned. "No . . . well, I might've heard something. I thought it was a motorcar backfiring."

"No. That was me. I'll probably be quite famous by tomorrow morning."

"Well, that's nothing new for you, is it?" she said with a smile. "You'd better tell me all about it."

As the twilight deepened we sat down on a bench overlooking Paris and I told her about the Babelites and their bomb plot. As always she was a very satisfying audience, for she listened, rapt, interrupting only when she wanted more details.

"You're going to be a hero when the morning papers come out," she said when I finished. "You kept a cool head. You've always been very good in a crisis."

I'd seen Kate in some tight situations, and knew how capable she was too, and told her so. "Anyway," I said, "heroism has nothing to do with it. It was sheer luck Christophe dropped his pistol."

"What a complete scoundrel that man was! Still, I hate to say it, but the Babelites do have a point." She gazed off to the east, where the base of the Celestial Tower was clearly visible, outlined with twinkling construction lights. "I do think it was foolhardy to build it so close to Paris. It's tempting fate. They could at least have built it off in the countryside. That way, if it falls, it only crushes some cows and chickens."

"Maybe one or two farmers," I added, grinning.

She took my arm. "I'm so glad you're safe."

"And I *still* managed to get here before you." I nudged her playfully.

She looked a little embarrassed. "Well, my day was nothing compared to yours, of course. But remember the talk I was supposed to give about the aerozoans in two weeks?"

I nodded. Last October, during a high-altitude salvage expedition, Kate and I had encountered a bizarre and deadly airborne creature. It was like a combination squid and jellyfish, with electrocuting tentacles. She'd named the creatures aerozoans.

"Well," Kate said, "they moved my talk up. To tomorrow!"

"But why?"

"I suspect Sir Hugh Snuffler's behind it. He thinks I'm a huge fraud, and he'd love me to make a mess of it in front of the Zoological Society. Anyway, I was in a frenzy all day trying to prepare."

"Don't worry. You'll be brilliant," I said.

"I don't want to think about it tonight. Now, tell me about this special treat you've got planned."

"I hope you weren't expecting a night at the opera," I said, eyeing her evening gown.

"A night at the opera can be very nice once in a while."

My spirits flagged. I'd been worried she wouldn't like my surprise. For a girl like Kate who was used to the finest things, maybe it would seem paltry.

I took a breath. "I thought . . . you might like to watch the stars with me."

"Ah."

She didn't seem disappointed exactly, but certainly surprised. I watched her carefully. By now Kate's expressions were well known to me, and I was hugely relieved when I saw that thoughtful look in her eyes. She lifted her face to the sky.

"Well, I see why you suggested Montmartre. The stars are much clearer up here, aren't they, away from all the city lights?"

"It gets better," I said, taking her hand. "Come on."

Behind us, rising from the summit of Montmartre, was the Paris Observatory, an imposing white stone fortress with observation towers and a large central dome for the telescope.

"But surely it's closed now," Kate said.

"Not for us," I said with a wink.

"Really?" Her eyes widened. "Do you know the director?"

"Someone much more useful," I said. "Night watchman."

I led her around back to the loading doors and rapped

three times. After several long minutes, I heard the bolt being shot back, and the door opened.

"I thought you weren't coming," said Richard.

"We both got held up," I said.

He ushered us inside. "Come in, come in."

Richard was a fellow student at the Academy and this was his summer job. He was an American, and the two of us got on well.

"Thanks so much for this," I said.

"Your timing couldn't be better," he said. "The staff's all in Zurich at some sort of top-secret meeting. The place is all yours. Promise you won't break anything."

"We promise," said Kate.

I could tell she was excited, looking all around. I felt relieved that my surprise was working out.

Richard led us down a wide marbled corridor to a grand set of doors and pulled them wide. Total darkness greeted us, for the room was windowless. Richard flicked a switch and several sconce lights dimly illuminated the vast circular hall that rose to a soaring dome. Occupying the chamber's centre was the famous Paris telescope. It was one of the world's most powerful, the size of a small house. Its central cylinder was tilted towards the dome's underside.

"Shall we open it up?" I said.

I'd visited the observatory once before at night, and Richard had shown me how the dome retracted by a simple system of ropes and pulleys. Working together now, we managed to slide the roof open along its oiled tracks. Moonlight and starlight spilled down on us, silvering the room, making everything strange and magical. Overhead we saw the running lights of ornithopters and airships passing over Paris. Everything seemed amazingly bright and sharp, as though the domed portal itself was some kind of lens, magnifying the night sky.

I looked at Kate and saw the utter delight on her face. That look alone was all the reward I needed.

"Are we going to look at the moon?" she asked.

"Much better than that, you'll see."

Richard and I walked over to the great wheels that moved the telescope itself. I took a piece of paper from my pocket and showed it to him. Then, under Richard's direction, we began moving the vast cylinder into the proper position.

"That should do it," said Richard, when the telescope was angled up, deep into the night sky.

The eyepiece of the telescope was quite high off the ground, and a special chair had been built that slid up and down a kind of slanted ladder fixed to a track in the floor.

"Please be seated, Miss de Vries," I said, gesturing to the chair.

"You're going to join me, I hope," she said, moving over as far as she could.

The seat was just wide enough for the two of us. I sat down beside her. Kate's fragrance was most distracting—her perfume and the smell of her hair and skin intermingled and I found it entirely intoxicating. It was all I could do to keep my hands off her. There was a lever to one side of the chair, and I pumped it up and down, jacking us up off the floor towards the eyepiece.

"I think you two can take care of things now," said Richard from below. "I'll have to leave you for a bit to do my rounds."

"We're grand, thanks."

"Thank you very much for your help," said Kate. As he left the hall, she said to me, "This is awfully nice of him."

I leaned into the eyepiece and adjusted the focus with the little knobs. I gazed at the view. Good. I was in the right place.

"Have a look," I said, sitting back.

Eagerly she put her face to the eyepiece, and then went very quiet, staring.

"I'm not sure you've ever been silent so long," I said after a while.

Her voice soft, she asked, "What is this I'm looking at?"

"That's the Draco constellation."

"It's so beautiful!" she exclaimed. "They look so close! And it's much more crowded up there than I thought! They're everywhere! And they're all quite different . . ." I saw her eye flicking from place to place. "Not just their size, but colour too! And some seem to twinkle more than others."

"They don't really twinkle, you know," I said. "It only looks that way to us down here. It's the atmosphere distorting the light."

"Is that right?" she said, looking at me.

I nodded. "It's called stellar scintillation."

"What a wonderful phrase," she said. "You seem to know a lot about stars."

"It comes from long hours in the crow's nest," I replied, pleased I'd impressed her. It felt good to be explaining things to her for a change. It turned out I did have a bit of a flair for celestial navigation.

Kate put her eye back to the telescope. "I wonder if there's life out there."

"Who knows," I said.

"There's a Bulgarian fellow, Dr. Ganev, who just last year published a pamphlet on lunar life."

The name sounded vaguely familiar. "Hold on, wasn't he the fellow who spent some time in a lunatic asylum?"

"No more than a year. They say he's better now."

I laughed, and Kate looked at me severely.

"You know, Matt, people talk about me that way. 'That poor lunatic Kate de Vries. Cloud cats, aerozoans, what will her diseased little mind think up next!' What makes you think Dr. Ganev's any different from me?"

"Well, for starters, you never tried to eat a banana through your ear."

She blinked. "Did he really do that?"

"No, but that's the kind of thing that gets you tossed into a lunatic asylum."

Her nostrils narrowed in annoyance. It was a unique skill of hers, one that tended to have a withering effect on the person at the receiving end.

"Considering all you've seen, Mr. Cruse, you're not very open-minded about life beyond Earth."

"I'm sure you're right," I said apologetically. "You've never disappointed me yet. Twice I've nearly been eaten by new creatures you've discovered."

She stared back into the telescope. "We don't really know anything at all about outer space. I suppose the French will be the first to find out, next year when they finish the tower. It's quite something, isn't it? A stairway to heaven."

"I think heaven's just a bit higher up," I said, "but I'm sure they're already thinking ahead."

"Draco, the dragon. So where's the tail?"

"Look for the big stars slanting across the sky."

"Yes, I think I see it!"

"Now," I said, "there's something else I want to show you. Just off the dragon's tail, on the lower right, there's one star that has a blue twinkle to it."

"I see it! Which star is that?"

"That," I said, "is 'Kate de Vries.'"

She looked over, confused. "What do you mean?"

I pulled the piece of paper from my pocket and showed her. "This is a document from the International Astronomical Union, verifying that this star will hereafter bear the name Kate de Vries."

"You did this for me?" she said in astonishment.

"Happy birthday," I said.

Her few seconds of delighted silence were wonderful, I must admit. Then her arms were around me in a tight hug.

"This is the best birthday present I've ever had," she said decisively. "How did you know? How did you know I'd like this better than a visit to the opera, or a silly bit of jewellery?"

"I know you pretty well."

"Better than anyone, I think."

I smiled. Her compliment was like a gift in itself, only more precious than anything that could be bought.

She gazed in satisfaction at her star. "Mine's the twinkliest."

"Well, I spared no expense."

She looked at me, concerned. "Was it awfully expensive?"

"Surprisingly affordable. Apparently there're billions of them."

She laughed, then frowned, her mind already busy again. "What if tonight had been cloudy? How would you have shown me?"

"I suppose I'd have had to entertain you some other way," I said, and kissed her.

"What a perfect birthday," she murmured happily against my lips, and pressed herself closer.

By nature I was restless, but when kissing Kate, there was nothing more I wanted, nowhere else I wished to be. The world evaporated entirely; it was a surprise afterwards to find it was still there, going on without me. I would have traded it all away for another kiss.

"We lead a charmed life, you and I," Kate said after a few minutes. "We both get to chase down our dreams. Me at the university, you at the Airship Academy. And thanks to Marjorie, we get to see each other all the time."

She was referring to Miss Marjorie Simpkins, her chaperone. Miss Simpkins didn't really approve of Kate spending her time with a former cabin boy, but she and Kate had a little agreement. Marjorie had a new beau, and Kate let her see him whenever she wanted—as long as Marjorie let Kate see me whenever *she* wanted. Marjorie would never tell Mr. and Mrs. de Vries about me; and Kate would never tell her parents what a negligent chaperone Marjorie was.

"I wish we could just stay in Paris forever," Kate said.

I nodded, knowing exactly what she meant. Back home in Lionsgate City we wouldn't have had this kind of freedom. Kate's family was extremely wealthy, and they would never tolerate our romance. *Romance*—only in my head did I use that word. Kate and I didn't even dare utter it. We were both afraid, I think, that if we named it, others would see it and try to stop it. We never talked of engagements or marriage either.

But in less than a year, I'd be graduating from the Academy with my officer rating. My job would almost certainly take me away from Paris, and from Kate. And once she finished her own studies at the Sorbonne, she'd doubtless sail away from me. I worried very much what would happen then. I could no more be parted from Kate than from the sky.

One day I hoped to wear a captain's insignia on my collar, but if I didn't have Kate, it would be small consolation. Secretly I'd decided that once I had my first position aboard a ship, I'd ask her to marry me—but part of me was terrified that she'd say no. Or that her parents would.

I pressed my nose against the back of her neck and breathed in her scent. "We've got lots of Paris left," I said. "The summer's hardly begun." I heard her sigh.

"I didn't want to mention it tonight, but . . . my parents want me to come back home for the holidays."

"But what about our plan?" I said, shocked. "I took a job here so we could be together!"

"I know. But my parents have been very insistent. You should've seen the letter. 'Your father and I wish you to spend the summer among your family, and in the society which will be yours for life.'" Kate paused. "Sounds like a jail sentence, doesn't it?"

"Tell them you . . . you *have* to stay here!"

"I did! Then I got a telegram from Father that just said: 'You sail June 26th.'"

"That's in less than a week!"

Kate sighed. "They pay for everything, Matt. And they didn't want me to come here in the first place. If I say no, they might call me home for good."

July and August, just hours ago, had seemed to stretch out with such promise. Now I felt all my happiness drift out through the open dome and evaporate in the night sky. Kate was going back to Lionsgate City. Her parents probably wanted her to start thinking about marrying. She'd attend society balls and galas and clink champagne glasses and dance with dashing men—and what if she met someone she liked better than me?

I slumped back in my seat. "I hate this," I said savagely.

"Me too," she said. "But what else could I do?"

I shook my head, for there was no solution, but knowing that made it no easier to bear.

Kate took my hand. "I love my star," she said.

"You can take it home with you," I said, feeling completely discouraged.

"I'll watch it every night." She put her eye to the telescope. "Matt?" she said.

"Yes?"

"I think someone's stealing my star."

"What?"

She leaned back so that I could get to the eyepiece. I quickly found the bright blue light near the end of the dragon's tail—and blinked in amazement. Slowly but surely, the star was moving to the left.

"Can't be right," I mumbled.

"But you do see it moving," Kate said.

"I see it! Maybe an airship or something . . ." But it was too high to be an airship.

Suddenly the light disappeared altogether.

"It just went out!" I said.

"What do you mean, went out?" Kate demanded. "You paid good money for that star!"

"No, wait, there it is again!"

The intense blue light was back, still moving slowly across the heavens, though on a slightly different trajectory.

Kate's cheek was against mine, her shoulder shoving me off so she could get to the eyepiece.

"It's stopped moving, but it's flashing now!" she said. "And there's another one!"

"There're two?"

"It's moving towards the first one!"

I craned my neck to look out through the open dome. I wondered if some fireworks display was playing tricks on us. But no pyrotechnics flared in the Paris sky.

"They're *both* flashing now!" Kate exclaimed.

"Let me see!"

Reluctantly she made room for me. I'd never seen anything like it. A second star, flashing green light every three seconds, was slowly gliding towards the first, which pulsed its own blue light like a beacon.

"What's happening?" Kate said, pounding on my arm.

I described it to her as I watched. The flashing became more frenetic and irregular as both stars converged on each other. I stared, transfixed, as the lights merged into one of even greater intensity. Then it simply disappeared. No interstellar flare, nothing. I stared for a little longer, but nothing reappeared.

I sank back, letting out a big breath. "Gone," I said. "Both of them."

She leaned in to check. "Stars aren't supposed to carry on like that, are they?"

I shook my head.

"Some kind of shooting stars?" Kate suggested.

"I don't think they can change direction like that," I said.

"We'll have to tell the astronomers."

I winced. "Difficult, without admitting we were playing with their telescope."

"But this might be important!"

"We can send an anonymous note," I said.

This seemed to satisfy her. I looked back into the telescope. "Your star's still there, by the way. What we saw was something else altogether. Here, look."

"Oh, good," Kate said, smiling. "Yes, there she is."

"We should get going," I said.

"Thank you so much for a thrilling birthday," she said.

"I always get more than I bargain for when I'm with you," I teased.

"Would you want it any other way?" she asked.

3 / A Little Schooling

IF I'D THOUGHT I WAS GOING to be famous the next morning, I was sadly mistaken. The Saturday newspapers didn't even mention the Babelites' bomb plot. After paging twice through the *Global Tribune*, I spotted a tiny story about an engine falling off an aerocrane and exploding in the park, but nothing about how the Celestial Tower had almost been destroyed—and saved by me and Hassan.

"I can't believe how mean they are," Kate said angrily when I told her. "You should be on the front page, with a big medal around your neck!"

We were backstage in the lecture hall at the Sorbonne where she was about to give her talk.

"They must be covering the whole thing up," I said. "They don't want anyone to know the Babelites nearly wrecked their tower."

"Well," she said, "*I* know you're a hero."

"I was kind of hoping for a medal," I admitted.

"I'll have one made for you," she said. "Now, look, go find a seat. I'll be starting soon."

"Good luck," I said. "You'll be fabulous."

Kate needn't have worried about a poor turnout. The lecture theatre was packed; every seat was already occupied and people were standing two deep at the rear. I wedged myself into a space against the back wall. Near the front was a big group of grey-haired gentlemen in dark suits, hunched forward expectantly like a murder of crows. I wondered which one was Sir Hugh Snuffler.

On the wood-panelled stage was a screen, and before it a table with a Lumière projector. The noise in the room was considerable, but dropped off quickly when the lights dimmed and Kate walked out and took her place beside the projector. She did not seem at all nervous there on the stage, before what must have been two hundred people. Her voice was calm and steady.

"Ladies and gentlemen," she said, "thank you for coming. Last year I observed a new form of airborne life, which I hope you will find of interest."

She touched a switch on the Lumière projector, and the first image appeared on the screen: a detailed scientific drawing of the aerozoan. A great rumble of amazement swelled from the audience. Kate took a pointer from the table, stepped closer to the screen, and began to itemize the creature's anatomical components. As she spoke, complete silence finally fell over the audience. They listened, rapt. Kate pointed out the balloon sac, the intestines, the beak.

"And here," Kate continued, "long, whiplike tentacles, with eye spots for detecting light, and olfactory sensors for locating prey. Two of these tentacles can discharge a high-voltage current, enough to electrocute a full-grown man."

It was odd watching her there on stage, bathed in the dusty shaft of light from the projector. She was both the Kate I knew so well and a complete stranger. She seemed a cool, highly intelligent woman, one who'd never have anything to do with the likes of me.

"Where's your proof?" sniped one fellow from the audience.

I looked over, trying to spot him, but the voice might have come from any number of gentlemen near the front.

"During my expedition," Kate said, "I managed to collect an aerozoan egg, which was in a state of anhydrobiosis."

"Nonsense!" came another voice from the front.

Kate was a marvel of composure. When the audience grew too noisy, she simply paused and waited for the ruckus to abate.

"Anhydrobiosis is a well-documented state," Kate continued. "Without water, the organism goes into a torpor to conserve energy. It can survive like that for years. When it's returned to a more hospitable environment, it revives itself. My companions and I saw several adult aerozoans do just that. We also witnessed the hatching of several eggs, which had been floating in wait for some forty years."

Her projector now showed a photograph of the aerozoan egg inside a large glass jar. Through its translucent shell you could see a tightly bundled coil of intestines and glimpse a beak. I felt the preternatural chill of the ghost ship shiver through me.

"As you can see," Kate said, "the egg contains enough hydrium to keep it aloft until it hatches."

"But where is your proof?" cried yet another gentleman.

"There is no proof!" one of his cronies grumbled.

I could see Kate give a sigh, bend down, and lift a large

case covered with a velvet cloth. She set it on the table beside her.

"I couldn't decide whether to dissect the egg and study its embryonic anatomy, or let it hatch . . ."

Kate paused for a moment, and the audience fell attentively silent. I could see that she was actually enjoying the drama of her presentation now. She gazed out into the audience.

"I let it hatch."

She whisked the velvet cloth off the case and there, inside, was the aerozoan hatchling, flexing its small tentacles and jetting vigorously against the glass. It was larger than the ones we'd seen on the *Hyperion,* some eighteen inches in length.

I smiled at the satisfying gasps and cries that gusted through the audience.

Kate stood beside the case and beamed. "Ladies and gentlemen, I give you *Aerozoania deVriesus.*"

I couldn't help chuckling at the name she'd given it. But really, I'd have expected no less from Kate. Even though I'd seen it before her, and nearly been electrocuted by the thing, she had taken the liberty of naming it after herself.

"This specimen is only two weeks old, but in time will grow to eight feet in length. It's thrived on a mixed diet of insects and small rodents, which it can already lift with its tentacles to its beak. After electrocuting them first, of course."

"No! No, I won't stand a moment more of this nonsense!" said a balding gentleman, standing up in front.

"Sir Hugh," said Kate calmly, "I'm happy to take questions when I'm finished."

So this was Sir Hugh! Usually, when you hear a lot about someone and then meet them for the first time, they look quite different from what you expect. Amazingly, Sir Hugh looked *exactly* as I'd expected. He was large, fiftyish, with a big pompous head. What little hair he had started about half-way back on his skull and tufted out slightly at the sides. He didn't just look pleased with himself—he looked *immensely* pleased with himself. He turned his back on Kate and faced the audience.

"Ladies and gentlemen, it wounds me that this fine institution even hosts such a carnival sideshow! But to have it passed off as science is too much."

"Sit down!" someone cried.

"I can't see!" another irritated viewer shouted.

"Let her continue!" I called out.

But the outraged Sir Hugh worked his way out to the aisle and strode up onto the stage.

"Sir Hugh," said Kate, "this is most inconsiderate. Please take your seat."

"Not a moment more!" Sir Hugh said, swishing his hands through the air. "Won't stand for it, no, no." He turned to address the audience. "This young lady is a distinguished charlatan. First, as you may remember, there were the so-called cloud cat bones that she exhibited widely. More recently we learned she has a yeti skeleton to show us. What's next? Perhaps a dragon? No, no, ladies and gentlemen, don't be taken in! Some of you may think this creature genuine, but it's little more than puppetry. You can pay a penny to see such things at the freak shows of Montmartre."

Kate's face was flushed with anger now. "Sir Hugh, I must ask you—"

But the eminent zoologist strode past her to the case.

"Show us the strings, Sir Hugh!" one of his cronies called out.

"Make it do the cancan for us!" another hooted.

"Leave my specimen alone, Sir Hugh!" Kate said.

"This is no *specimen*, Miss de Vries."

With a flourish the zoologist swept his hand over the case, probably hoping to find strings. He frowned. The conceited oaf was having his first doubts. He passed his hand several times more over the case, like some magician's assistant. The audience gave a great burst of laughter. He turned and glared at Kate.

"Humph! Clockwork and a bit of balloon, then, is it? It looks as real as a wind-up toy! Look here!" He fumbled with the case's latch.

"Sir Hugh, don't—"

Before Kate could stop him, he had opened the door and thrust his hand inside.

I winced.

Incredibly, nothing happened. Sir Hugh closed his entire fist around the hatchling. Its balloon sac went limp and sagged against his hand.

"Ha ha!" cried Sir Hugh. "Another charlatan debunked! It's

nothing but a bit of silk and thread!" He gave it a good shake.

"What have you done to it?" Kate cried. "Put it down, you'll harm it!"

"Miss de Vries, I think I speak for the entire scientific community when I say that we've tolerated your tawdry kind of scholarship—and I dignify it by even calling it *scholarship*—long enough-f-f-f-f—"

Sir Hugh was stuttering. His face was going red. His clenched fist and arm shook as though he had a terrible palsy.

"F-f-f-f-f—"

"Oh, for heaven's sake!" said Kate in irritation. "He's being electrocuted. Can someone lend a hand?"

None of Snuffler's colleagues seemed terribly keen to help, so I started pushing my way towards the stage. Snuffler was now making a high-pitched squeal, an odd sound to come from such a snooty old gentleman. But I'd seen what those aerozoan tentacles, even the young, slender ones, could do. In his agony, the zoologist tried to wrench his hand out of the case, and knocked it off the table. It tumbled to the floor, glass exploding across the stage and into the audience. Snuffler staggered back, cradling his singed hand.

"That was a very foolish thing to do, Sir Hugh!" Kate said.

I was near the stage now and my eyes were on the aerozoan, which was hovering, stunned, a few inches above the glass-strewn floor. Without warning, its balloon sac inflated, its apron flexed, and it jetted out over the audience.

Panic seized the entire theatre as the aerozoan bobbed

about overhead. There was shouting and screaming and a wild scramble as the people in front fled their seats, climbing over one another in a most uncivil manner to reach the exits.

"Don't let it escape!" Kate cried, hurrying off the stage.

I snatched a top hat from a gentleman's head.

"May I borrow this?" I said, and sent the hat spinning through the air towards the aerozoan. It was a lucky shot, for the hat dropped right over the hatchling and took it straight down to the floor.

"Well done!" Kate said beside me.

"Fantastic lecture," I said.

"A shame no one's staying for question period."

We rushed over to the hat, which was taking little hops along the carpeted aisle.

"I don't fancy picking it up," I said.

"We'll need something to slide underneath first," Kate suggested.

The hat suddenly leapt off the floor and sailed above our heads, the tentacles flailing about menacingly. We ducked, then dashed up the aisle after it, hoping it would come to ground again. But it only jetted higher. Bobbing beneath the timbered ceiling, it headed towards one of the open windows.

"Oh no!" cried Kate.

The top-hatted aerozoan bumped against the window frame several times before sailing out over the rooftops of the Sorbonne.

"I'm sorry about your specimen," I said to Kate.

"That thing nearly electrocuted me!" thundered Sir Hugh, striding towards us, still nursing his hand.

Kate turned, eyes flashing with anger. "You have a great deal to answer for, Sir Hugh!"

"Look at my hand!"

"Dear me," Kate said tartly. "I'm awfully sorry. But you know, that's what sometimes happens, Sir Hugh, when you shove your hand at wild animals. They tend not to like it!"

"There may be permanent scarring!" Sir Hugh bellowed.

"But the good news is, now you know it's a real creature."

Sir Hugh paused. "I know no such thing."

Kate's nostrils narrowed. "You held it in your hand. It attacked you. You saw it fly."

"The work of wily accomplices, perhaps," he said. "And where is your proof now, eh? Conveniently disappeared!"

"*You* set it free!"

"I mean to have you removed from this institution," said Sir Hugh. "I'll be speaking to the provost about this. In the meantime, I'll also speak to my attorney—about grievous bodily harm!"

"And I shall talk to *my* attorney about how you injured and lost my priceless specimen!"

"Ha!" said Snuffler as he stalked off, taking nervous glances overhead.

"Do you really have an attorney?" I asked.

"No, but I should get one," she said, staring forlornly out the window.

"I don't think it's coming back," I said.

"No, but if it does, I hope it has another go at Sir Hugh. Poor Phoebe. I hope she'll be all right."

I laughed. "You gave it a name?"

"Of course I did. She and I spent a lot of time together."

"I'm sure she was very affectionate."

"Oh, be quiet, Matt."

"Nothing like a tender little zap when you're feeling low."

"Ha ha ha!" she said. "I'm glad you're so jovial about the end of my career."

"Sir Hugh can't do that, can he?"

"He's a very powerful man. There're enough rotting old carcasses like him around here. They can have me thrown out if they want."

Near the front, Miss Simpkins poked her head up between two rows of seats, where she'd been cowering under her parasol. I hadn't even noticed her earlier. Cautiously she stood and brushed herself off.

"Well, I could've told you it would end badly," she said. "Bottling freakish little creatures and bringing them home. You're lucky no one was killed."

"Thanks for your sympathy, Marjorie," said Kate.

"It was rather diverting, though," she said. "I'd never seen anyone get electrocuted."

"Is there to be no question period?" someone asked politely.

For the first time I noticed two gentlemen sitting far back in the theatre. The house lights were still dimmed, so I couldn't see them properly.

Kate turned to them. "I'm sorry, gentlemen. Of course I'm happy to take your questions now."

"Do you think there are any limits to the heights at which life can exist?" one of the shadowy gentlemen asked.

"I certainly know life can exist in all sorts of unlikely places," she said. "But how high, I don't know. That's an area that needs a great deal more study."

"Would you consider joining an expedition that would allow you to do just that?"

Kate blinked. "Instantly."

"Well then, perhaps we should talk further."

"Excuse me, sir," said Miss Simpkins primly, "do we know you?"

As we all walked closer, the two gentlemen stood and moved out into the aisle, where they were more visible.

"My name is John McKinnon," said a slim man in a finely tailored blue suit. "I'm the Canadian Minister of Air. And I believe you already know Mr. Lunardi."

I was surprised enough by a cabinet minister, but now I stared at the second gentleman in astonishment. He was most familiar to me from newspapers and newsreels. Mr. Otto Lunardi was the airship magnate who owned the *Aurora*. Two years ago, when the ship had returned to Sydney Harbour after escaping the clutches of Vikram Szpirglas, Mr. Lunardi had greeted the crew. He'd even shaken my hand.

He seemed large, even though he was surprisingly short. He had a boxer's physique, compact and barrel-chested, with powerful shoulders and a large head. His body appeared barely able to contain all its energy. Even standing still he seemed in motion, rocking back and forth, his quick, curious eyes darting from face to face, missing nothing.

"Miss de Vries and Mr. Cruse, it's fine to see you both looking so well," he said, shaking our hands heartily. "And Miss de Vries, what a fascinating lecture that was."

"Why, thank you, Mr. Lunardi."

"Precisely the kind of thing Sir John and I are looking for."

"You're involved in some kind of zoological research?" Kate asked curiously.

"Much more than that. Much better. You'll be interested too, Mr. Cruse. Or at least I hope so. It's a bit stuffy in here, isn't it? Let's go for a walk. It's a lovely day, and we have a great deal to talk about."

4 / Kepler's Dream

OUTSIDE, WE CROSSED the street to the Luxembourg Gardens and strolled along its shady paths. Through the trees I caught glimpses of the honey-coloured palace, and the fountain where children sailed toy boats. All around, people sat on benches and chairs and read or chatted. We walked along, the four of us, with Miss Simpkins trailing behind.

I felt quite tongue-tied in the presence of Mr. Lunardi. It wasn't just his fame. Seeing him woke my memories of his son Bruce. We'd sailed together on the *Aurora*'s fateful voyage. He'd helped save the ship from pirates, but Szpirglas had killed him. When Lunardi had met the ship in Sydney, it was to collect the body of his boy; and when he'd shaken my hand, the grief in his eyes had brought tears to mine.

Sir John McKinnon led us down a set of steps to the fountain terrace and ushered us towards a grouping of empty chairs.

"Let's enjoy the sun here, shall we?" he said, inviting us all to sit.

Above the trees to the east was the Celestial Tower, reaching ever higher into the sky. There was virtually nowhere in Paris from which you couldn't see it. The sight of it made me think of the god Atlas, shouldering the weight of the entire world.

"You're familiar with the work of Johannes Kepler, I'm sure," said Mr. Lunardi, following my gaze.

"The German astronomer," I replied. "The Laws of Planetary Motion. We studied them last term at the Academy."

"The fellow was a visionary," said Lunardi. "Must've felt he lived three hundred years too early. His eyes always on the sky, but he never had the ability to go there. Did you read the letter he wrote to Galileo?"

I shook my head.

Mr. Lunardi smiled and cleared his throat. "Kepler wrote, 'There will certainly be no lack of human pioneers when we have mastered the art of flight. Let us create vessels and sails adjusted to the heavenly ether, and there will be plenty of people unafraid of the empty wastes. In the meantime, we shall prepare, for the brave sky travellers, maps of the celestial bodies—I shall do it for the moon, you, Galileo, for Jupiter.'" Lunardi chuckled. "Fabulous stuff, eh?"

"It's very stirring," Kate agreed.

"Here's the matter at hand," said Sir John, lowering his voice and leaning in towards us. "What I'm about to say is a matter of great secrecy, you understand, and I know I can trust the three of you, as patriotic Canadians, to respect that."

Kate and I murmured our assent. I felt a prickling of gooseflesh across my neck.

"Our government," Sir John resumed, "has entered into a joint venture with the Lunardi Corporation to explore outer space."

I leaned forward so quickly I nearly toppled out of my

chair. I looked at Kate in amazement, then back at Sir John. "I didn't even know the Canadians had a space program!"

"We've been keeping it all hush-hush. We're in the lead and we intend to stay there."

"But the French—"

"Forget about the French," said Mr. Lunardi. "They haven't a hope. That tower will never make it through the stratosphere. It's sad, really. One almost wants to say something— but there's no arguing with the French."

"You have a ship, then?" I asked.

"We have a very fine ship," said Sir John. "Mr. Lunardi and his team have taken care of that."

"We've been working on it for almost two years now," Lunardi said, his eyes alight with enthusiasm. "The ship is built, and ready to fly."

"We're assembling a group of people we'd like to be on her maiden voyage," said Sir John. "We want the best people in their field. And you came to mind quickly, Miss de Vries."

"Did I?" she said, trying to sound surprised, but I don't think she'd ever sounded more delighted.

"We've been following your work," Mr. Lunardi said. Even sitting, the man crackled with energy, his hands aloft, gripping the air for emphasis. "And your lecture just now convinced me you're exactly what we need—a pair of fiercely inquisitive young eyes. If there's life up there, you'll find it."

Kate seemed to positively blaze at these compliments. And I was burning just as brightly—with envy. They'd just invited her to take part in the first voyage into outer space! I would've given anything to be on that ship.

"Well, it's very kind of you to think of me," Kate said modestly.

"Will you join us then, Miss de Vries?"

"I'd love to," she said, without a second's hesitation.

"Your parents," chimed in Miss Simpkins, speaking for the first time.

"Oh, my parents," said Kate carelessly.

"We'd ask their consent, of course," said Lunardi.

Kate waved her hand. "I wouldn't bother, they're terribly busy."

"They'll never consent," said Miss Simpkins. "And you'll not have me as a chaperone this time. Nothing could convince me to travel to outer space. I've had quite enough of your absurd adventures."

"I won't be bound by my parents' wishes," Kate said frostily. "Anyway, I don't see why they'd need to know—would they, Marjorie?"

She gave her chaperone a bright and terrifying smile.

Sir John cleared his throat. "Well, I'm afraid this isn't something that can be kept secret, Miss de Vries. Once we announce the expedition and its crew, your name will appear in every newspaper in the world. Your parents will have to be told. And since you're technically a minor, we would need their consent."

"Shouldn't present a problem," Kate said breezily.

"I've met your father several times in Lionsgate City," Mr. Lunardi said to Kate. "He seems a reasonable fellow, and I wager he'd appreciate the historic magnitude of our venture. Let me speak to him."

"I can't see it making any difference to Mr. de Vries," Miss Simpkins said.

"If it's propriety they're worried about," said Sir John, "there will be another woman aboard ship, so you'll be properly chaperoned."

"I *do* so like being chaperoned," Kate murmured.

"And as for your safety," Lunardi added, "I can assure you I've never built an un-skyworthy vessel in my life. The captain and crew will be unrivalled in their expertise."

"They're lucky fellows," I said.

"Indeed," said Lunardi. "The first astralnauts."

"The French are calling them *spationauts*," I remarked.

"The French can call them whatever they wish," said Mr. Lunardi. "I'm sure their uniforms will be splendid. But they won't be the ones in space. Which brings me to you, Mr. Cruse. How high would you like to fly?"

I felt a smile soar across my face. "As high as I possibly can."

"An excellent reply. We're starting the training program next week, and we want you to take part."

"Next week!" I said.

"You have a more pressing commitment, perhaps, Mr. Cruse?"

"It's just . . . I have a job here for the summer."

"At the Celestial Tower, yes, we made some inquiries," said Sir John. "That's not a problem. You can give notice immediately. The Ministry of Air has arranged very generous compensation for all the astralnaut trainees. Twelve hundred dollars, I believe."

I almost gasped. It was triple my salary for the entire summer. I knew what my mother would say, though. Once you accept a job, you should finish it. But only a fool wouldn't seize this chance. I would've done it for free.

"Not bad, eh, Mr. Cruse?" said Lunardi. "And that's just for the training. If you're selected for the expedition, there'll be additional remuneration."

My smile faltered. "So there's no guarantee I'll make it on?"

Lunardi shook his head. "Afraid not. But you're an extremely promising candidate."

"You came highly recommended," said Sir John. "And space travel is for the young. We shan't be looking at anyone over thirty for crew. We reckon it requires an entirely different set of skills than sky sailing."

"I can't imagine they'll find anyone more able than you," said Kate with an encouraging smile, and though I smiled back, it irked me that she'd simply been invited, while I had to prove myself.

"I mean to be on that ship," I said to the two gentlemen.

Mr. Lunardi nodded. "Excellent."

"The last century belonged to France," said Sir John, "but

this new one shall be Canada's. We're about to make Kepler's dream come true—"

"May I see your chits, please?"

With a start we all looked up to see a uniformed park attendant looming over us, his little silver whistle dangling from his neck.

"Pardon me, our what?" asked Sir John.

"*Chits.*" His exasperated gaze strayed past us, as though he couldn't bear our stupidity.

"We have no chits," I said.

"To *sit,* you will need a *chit.* Do you know what a chit is, monsieur? A token, a ticket that allows you to sit in one of the park chairs."

"And where would we find such a chit?" asked Lunardi, sounding impatient.

"That must be bought at the *chit counter.*" He pointed across the park, and I saw a small kiosk that was shuttered.

"It looks closed," I said.

"Of *course* it is closed, monsieur," the attendant said. "It is three o'clock. Therefore, you will have to purchase your chits from another counter. I believe the one in the Champs-de-Mars is open."

"But that's miles from here!" Kate protested.

"Yes, mademoiselle."

I looked around the park, at all the happy people sitting on benches and chairs. "All these people—they have chits, I suppose?"

"Of course. And if they do not, I will ferret them out and they will be dispersed."

"This is incredible," I said.

"I direct you, monsieur, to the park rules, located, *ironically*, not ten paces behind you."

I turned to see a tall wrought-iron post on which was framed a large, impressive notice. REGLEMENTS DU PARC, it said in bold black letters. Underneath, in print almost too small to read, were six columns of rules.

"This is absurd," said Kate. "We do not have chits. We will not *get* chits."

The attendant clucked his tongue. "No, no, mademoiselle, I am very sorry, you must have chits."

Kate gave a disdainful wave of her hand. "I pooh-pooh the chit."

The attendant looked stunned. "You cannot pooh-pooh the chit!"

"I do," she said solemnly. "I do pooh-pooh."

"We'll walk," I said, standing.

"Normally, monsieur, that would be fine, but now that I have exposed you as *chit delinquents*, I must ask you to leave the park *immédiatement*."

"Look here, do you know who you're talking to?" said Sir John, whose face had taken on a scarlet hue.

"I do not care, monsieur. These are rules that must be obeyed by all. We are not lawless hooligans like you Americans."

"Canadians, actually," said Lunardi.

"I see little difference between you."

Behind us, someone started shrieking. We whirled around to see an elegant middle-aged woman swatting in terror at Kate's aerozoan hatchling. It had ensnared her little poodle with its tentacles and was doing its best to pluck the stunned dog off the ground.

"Phoebe!" cried Kate.

"*Quel monstre!*" shrieked the woman. "*Assistance! Gendarme!*"

"I think someone needs your help," I told the warden.

He turned in time to see sparks flying from the aerozoan's small tentacles. He turned back to me and, without even lifting an eyebrow, said, "This is not my responsibility. Your name, monsieur. You leave me no choice but to write you a chit delinquency ticket—"

"May we borrow your jacket?" Kate asked, already yanking it off the warden's shoulders. "We may be able to catch her. Come on, Matt!"

"That is my jacket," said the bewildered warden.

We ran towards the distraught lady, who'd just received a zap and was now whimpering under a bench. Phoebe was still struggling to lift the dog off the ground, but it was proving too heavy.

"We're coming, Phoebe!" Kate called out.

But Phoebe did not want to be caught. She seemed to sense our approach, and as Kate threw the jacket, Phoebe released the dog and shot high into the air, narrowly avoiding getting tangled in the branches of a chestnut tree.

"Oh dear!" Kate said.

A few people in the park watched the aerozoan's escape, but must have thought it was just a fancy balloon. They looked away, unimpressed.

"My jacket, monsieur," said the warden frostily, coming up behind me. I picked it up, dusted it off, and held it out to him.

"Are you all right, ma'am?" I said, offering my hand to the lady under the bench.

She ignored me as she emerged and rushed to her poodle. The dog was whining piteously, but he seemed all right, just a bit singed. The warden peered severely from the dog to its owner.

"Madame, may I see your dog's chit, please," he said.

Kate and I took this opportunity to rejoin the others, and we all walked on. Kate kept peering up through the trees, hoping to catch a glimpse of Phoebe.

"Your aerozoan seems to have a taste for Paris," Lunardi remarked.

"Well, who doesn't like Paris?" Kate said.

"You'll both have to say *au revoir* to the City of Light for the time being," Lunardi said to us. "We want you in Lionsgate City by Thursday."

"Lionsgate City?" I said. "Is that where the training is?"

"I thought that would please you," said Mr. Lunardi. "You're going home."

5 / Lionsgate City

I ARRIVED WITH THE DAWN, the spires of Lionsgate City already aglow as our ship came in to land. I'd forgotten just how high and glorious the city was, its skyscrapers straining to compete with the mountain peaks that encircled them.

Stepping down the gangway onto the landing field, I suddenly realized how much I'd missed the sea and mountains. Almost two years had passed since I'd been back, and when I got into the hired car with my luggage, I gave the driver the wrong address, automatically thinking of the old Gastown apartment where I'd grown up.

"Sorry," I said, "we're going out to Kitsilano." The new address sounded strange to me, and I realized this was the first time I'd spoken it aloud.

"Very good, sir," said the driver.

I was glad our route would take us through downtown. It was Thursday, and the city was wide awake and already in a hurry. Paris, with its beautiful old boulevards and buildings, was like an orderly symphony, but Lionsgate City was all ragtime and jazz. Carts and lorries unloading at markets and factories and the grand department stores, and the honking and shouting and motorcar fumes and cigarette smoke and the smell of wet pavement and horse manure and the clanging of the streetcars . . .

"Oh-oh," said the driver, "looks like trouble up ahead."

I peered past him through the windscreen and saw a crowd coming our way down the middle of the street. There seemed to be a great many ladies' hats and bobbing placards, though I couldn't yet read what was written upon them.

"Is it a parade?" I asked.

He snorted. "Of sorts. It's those ladies who want to vote, sir."

"The suffragettes?" I said.

"That's the ones. We had Mrs. Pankhurst in town last night giving one of her speeches and she's got our Lionsgate women all riled up now."

I'd seen the suffragettes marching in Paris earlier in the spring. All across Europa and North America women were banding together and demanding the right to vote.

"They'll get bored soon enough," said my driver. "It's a serious business, voting. They wouldn't want the responsibility. We're doing them a favour, don't you think?"

"I don't see why they shouldn't vote," I said.

"You're young yet, sir, if you don't mind me saying. Let's see if we can take a little detour and—blast, they've blocked off Cordova! We'll just have to wait them out, sir."

He pulled over. Before long the motorcar was completely engulfed by women shouting "Votes for women!" and "Equality not slavery!" My driver sat hunched over his wheel, waving his arm as if trying to scatter midges. The women ignored him, parting around his car and flowing by in their dark skirts and white blouses and summer hats. A few thumped merrily on the car's hood as they passed, which made my driver's fists tighten on the wheel.

"You're blocking our parade!" came a familiar voice to my right, and a hand slapped imperiously on the car's roof.

I looked out the window and straight into the face of Kate de Vries, a placard in her hands. She stared back at me in astonishment.

"Hello!" she said brightly, as I rolled down the window. "Welcome home! You must've just got in!"

"I was on my way to my mother's."

"You should've taken a different route."

My driver gave a hollow laugh.

"What does your sign say?" I asked.

She sighed. "'New Laws for a New Century!' I wanted 'Equality or Death!' but they were all taken."

"Do your parents know what you're doing?"

"They think I'm at the library, reading morally improving literature for young ladies."

The driver was watching us in his rearview mirror. The tide of women continued to flow past the car.

"There're certainly a lot of them," I remarked.

"Not *them,* Matt. *Us.* I heard Mrs. Pankhurst last night. She's very inspiring. I simply couldn't resist the chance to march. Care to join us?"

"Maybe another time."

Kate nodded. "You don't want to be late for your mother. But I should get back."

"When will I see you?" I asked, as she hoisted her placard high.

"Oh, I've already taken care of that. Give my best to your mother and sisters! See you soon!"

She marched off, her voice ringing out above the rest: "New laws for a new century!"

The driver looked back at me. "If you don't mind me saying, sir, she seems a right handful."

"You've no idea," I said.

"Ah, I can see the end of the parade now, sir. I'll have you in Kitsilano in a jiffy."

The driver let me off in front of the house. There was a new log road, but no sidewalks yet. To the north, across Burrard Inlet, the mountains rose magnificently. I stood looking at the house. This was a strange homecoming, since the home I was coming to was altogether new.

It was a fine little clapboard house, two storeys, freshly painted blue with white trim. My father had always wanted us to have a house. Last year, after salvaging the *Hyperion*, I came away with some gold. Four bricks was my share. I'd sold them and given most of the money to my mother, so she could finally buy her own place.

Mom had taken months to agree. She'd hemmed and hawed and said she couldn't accept the money. Then she had said she was too busy to bother moving. But in the end she'd bought the little place in Kitsilano, an easy walk from the tram line on 4th Avenue. She and my sisters had moved in May. I'd read a description of the house in letters, but this was my first time standing before it. I must say, I did feel proud.

I stepped up the little path to the front door and banged the knocker. My telegram had told my mother I'd be home for breakfast.

I heard a flurry of footsteps inside, and then the door swung open and there was my mother, with Isabel and Sylvia close behind.

Mom took me by the hands and smiled, and as usual her eyes filled with tears.

"You look *very* well," she said, giving me a hug, and then my sisters pressed in on both sides and I was wrapped up in everyone's arms.

"You look quite fine, Matt," said Sylvia.

I'd dressed in my Academy uniform, for I wanted them to be impressed, and I could see Sylvia's eyes taking in every detail from cap to shoes. She'd always had an interest in what was fashionable.

"You look too strapped in," said Isabel, wrinkling her nose. At eleven, she was two years younger than Sylvia and hadn't yet transformed into a young woman. "It looks too tight round your neck."

"It's meant to be worn that way, Izzie," I said.

"Of course it is," Sylvia told her little sister, and I remembered how well they could exasperate each other.

Isabel smiled with menacing sweetness. "You don't know *quite* everything yet, Sylvia."

"Enough, you two," said Mom, and ushered me into the house.

"What do you think?" Isabel demanded excitedly.

The height of the ceilings was the first thing I noticed, at least half a foot taller than our old ones. In the ample sitting room, light and fresh air streamed in through the open windows, and you felt you could really breathe here. The floors were oak, and the plaster walls were painted a pale apricot.

"I don't think I've seen a nicer, friendlier house in my life," I said. "You chose very well. Do you all love it?"

"It's utterly charming," said Sylvia, very ladylike.

"It's a lovely house," my mother said. "But, you know, it was hard—surprisingly hard—to leave our old place."

"Not for us," chirped Isabel with a smile.

"No more cigarette smells," Sylvia said.

"Or neighbours fighting," added Isabel.

"And we've got our own rooms," Sylvia told me. "Finally."

Our old apartment was on the third floor above a Gastown tobacconist. It had only two proper bedrooms, one toilet with sink, and a parlour with a tiny kitchen off it. It hadn't seemed small to me before I started work as a cabin boy, but after I'd been aloft and my eyes had widened to the horizons, I returned to find it cramped and airless. The last time I stayed there I had been ready to make a rope of my bedclothes and climb out the window.

But standing here, looking at our old and slightly shabby furniture in this new, fresh room, I knew what my mother meant. This house was a completely new space, with none of the memories that had filled our old apartment. The old place hadn't been very nice, but it had contained our lives: our meals and birthdays and all the other happy times—and sad times too. It was the place where Isabel and Sylvia were born; the last place where we'd all been together as a family. This new house would never hold my father.

"Come see my room!" Isabel cried, grabbing my hand and starting to pull me towards the stairs.

"After breakfast," Mom told her firmly. "Let's sit and eat now. Everything's ready. You arrived at exactly the right moment, Matt."

The girls led me through the sitting room to the cozy little dining room. Delicious smells wafted in from the adjoining kitchen. The table was all laid with a freshly ironed cloth and our finest cutlery and glasses. Mom had prepared a bang-up breakfast. She and the girls brought in platters of bacon and scrambled eggs and grilled tomatoes, and fresh rolls, and biscuits and dewy butter, and little dishes of jam, and a pot of tea, and even some freshly squeezed orange juice.

"This is better than first class on the Lunardi Line!" I said, and Mom beamed.

We all sat. Sylvia daintily helped herself to food, while Isabel slopped things onto her plate. I smiled when Sylvia glowered at her younger sister.

"Honestly, Izzie, your manners!"

"I'm *very, very* hungry!" Izzie protested.

"I hope I didn't keep you all waiting and starving," I said.

"Not at all, not at all," said Mom.

"We've been waiting *ages*," said Isabel.

"Tea?" Sylvia asked.

"Yes, please."

"That was a mysterious telegram you sent," Mom said, sounding amused. "A masterpiece of vagueness. So what brings you home? You were to be working all summer in Paris, I thought."

"Yes, but I was offered another job. A better-paying one," I added hurriedly, for I knew she wouldn't like the idea of my quitting any job. It wasn't respectable. "And with this one I'll get to spend a bit of time with you all."

"What will you be doing, then?"

I'd thought a great deal about how I would tell her. Slowly, was the only brilliant idea I'd had.

"It's an advanced training program sponsored by the Lunardi Corporation and the government."

I thought my mother would like the idea of more schooling. As she'd had little herself, she put great stock in classrooms and diplomas.

"Not a job, then, exactly?"

"No, but I get paid very well for my time."

"What is it you're to be trained for?" she asked.

I choked back a little piece of bacon. "Well, there's going to be an expedition, quite an important one. But there's no guarantee I'll be selected. This really is *tremendous* orange juice! How many oranges did it take to make this?"

"And just what kind of expedition would this be?" my mother said patiently.

My hand trembled slightly as I put down my glass. "A bit of a high-altitude test flight really."

She stopped chewing. "*How* high?"

There was no avoiding it. "Outer space," I said.

"Ah," she said. She put down her fork.

"Mom, you mustn't go worrying about it!"

"Just outer space," she said.

"They won't choose me. They've got lots of fellows trying out. I haven't a hope."

"Then why are you even bothering, Matt?"

I saw the humorous light in her eyes and chuckled. "Because I want to go. I surely do."

"I've heard it's very dark in space," said Isabel sagely.

"I don't see why," Sylvia said. "There's the same sun and moon and stars up there."

"Well, it seems pure foolishness to me," said my mother.

I wasn't sure this was the best time to launch into the wonders of the stars, and the canals of Mars, and the dark side of the moon.

"It's going to be the first voyage beyond the sky!" I said. "A lot of people want to be first. A lot of people want to see what's up there."

"Will you be visiting the moon?" Isabel inquired.

"Not this time. And look, all this is still secret. You're not to go gossiping to your little friends."

I caught a glimpse of scorn in Sylvia's eyes. "I'm sure my *little friends* and I have better things to talk about."

"I'm sure," I said.

Mom sighed. "You must want to go badly enough, if you're willing to spend the summer away from your Kate."

I cleared my throat. "She's already been invited on the expedition."

My mother's eyes flashed. Even though I hadn't been home much in the past five years, it was a look I remembered well enough.

"Is it her you're doing this foolish thing for?" she demanded.

"It's awfully romantic!" piped up Sylvia.

"I'm going for my own reasons," I said firmly. "If Kate weren't going and I had the chance, I'd still go. You mustn't think she's dragging me into it, Mom."

My mother shook her head. "It's bad enough you want to make your life the sky; but I don't see why you want to go embarking on something so treacherous. I couldn't bear it if something happened to you, as well."

She looked so bereft that I was tempted to say I wouldn't go. But I didn't. How could I? What sky sailor, given a chance like this, wouldn't grasp it with all his might?

"I'm sorry," I said. "I don't want you to worry. And look, even if I'm chosen, the ship's going to be safe. It's built by Lunardi, and no one builds better ships." I turned to the girls to avoid my mother's hard stare. "There're going to be lots of famous people aboard, you know."

"Will Sarah Bernhardt be going?" asked Sylvia, referring to the movie star.

"No," I said. "I meant famous *scientists*."

"Oh," she said, and wrinkled her nose.

"Of course it's your decision," my mother said, but she looked downcast.

She did have a way of making you feel guilty, with those big sad eyes of hers. I wondered if she was doing it on purpose. Kate had taught me about the things women could do to show their disapproval.

"If I get chosen," I said gently, "I'll need your consent. Mr. Lunardi won't take me on without it."

Mom hesitated a moment, and then said firmly, "You'll have my consent."

I blew out a breath. "Thanks, Mom."

"How long is the training?" Sylvia asked.

"Just two weeks."

"Two weeks staying with us!" said Isabel.

"Well, no," I said, hating to see her face fall. "I'm here for the weekend, but then I've got to stay at the training facility. I can't even tell you where it is; it's secret. They won't let us off the compound, except Sundays. So I'll come see you then."

"When you're not off with your sweetheart, you mean," said Sylvia.

I gave her a stern look. "Kate and I are just good friends. And I'd appreciate it if you didn't use terms like *sweetheart*."

"He's madly in love with her," Sylvia told Isabel.

"Is he?" Isabel asked.

"It's so obvious."

"Girls, show some consideration, please." But my mother was looking at me, every bit as unconvinced and amused as my sisters.

"When will we meet her?" asked Isabel.

"Well—"

"Your Kate's already taken care of that," said my mother. "This arrived today."

From the sideboard, she handed me a thick cream-coloured card with a gold border and script swirled elegantly across the front:

Mr. and Mrs. Charles de Vries request the pleasure of your company at their 12th annual Summer Garden Fete.

Kate hadn't mentioned anything to me about a garden party, but she'd obviously convinced her parents to put us on their invitation list.

"It's this Sunday!" said Isabel.

"I can wear my new shoes!" said Sylvia. "They're perfect for summer."

"I don't know what I'll wear," said Isabel, with a little puff that would have done justice to a Parisian socialite.

"I'm not sure we should all go," said Mom.

"What?" cried Sylvia.

"It's very kind of the de Vrieses to invite us," said my mother, "but we hardly move in the same circles. I'm just not sure we'd feel comfortable."

I was worried about the same thing. I wished Kate had told me she was planning this. I had an idea what her parents were like, and wasn't sure they'd be thrilled rubbing shoulders with a seamstress and her children. I didn't like to think of my mother being snubbed. Kate had never really understood the divide between our worlds—she thought the divisions were silly. But she was unusual.

"I want to go!" said Isabel.

"Mother, if they've invited us," said Sylvia carefully, "isn't it rude *not* to go?" She turned to me. "Wouldn't Kate be hurt, Matt?"

I chuckled at her persistence. "I know she'd be very disappointed. She really wants to meet you all."

"I'm not sure I have anything nice enough to wear," said Mom.

I smiled. "I hear you're handy with a needle and thread."

"Well," said Mom, "it is very nice of Kate's parents to include us. Mrs. de Vries wrote me that very nice letter, you know, two years back."

I remembered it. Mrs. de Vries had told her how grateful she was to me for helping take care of Kate when the *Aurora* was shipwrecked. And since then, my mother seemed to have a much steadier flow of work from fancy people. I wondered if Kate had had an invisible hand in this, though she'd never mentioned a thing.

"So we're going?" Isabel said.

"Very well, then, yes, we're going," said Mom, a bit reluctantly.

"Hurray! Shall we take a walk?" Sylvia said. "We're so close to the beach now!"

"I think that's a fine idea," I said.

6 / The Garden Party

"WHAT A DIVINE HOUSE," said Sylvia as we approached the de Vries mansion.

"Why are you talking in that fancy voice?" Isabel demanded.

"This is how I talk."

"No it isn't. You sound all snooty."

"You two," said my mother, in such a way that they both fell silent.

The mansion was set well back from the tree-lined boulevard, on a hill, which made it look even more impressive. There were more windows than I could count. We walked up the path to the front door, which was flanked by high fluted columns. It was the Sunday of the garden party and we were all dressed up. I wore my Academy uniform.

I took hold of the brass lion's-head knocker and rapped it against the heavy oak door. I'd sooner have been knocking at Hell's gates. I wasn't at all sure I was ready to meet Kate's parents.

"Good afternoon," said the butler, with a look that let us know he'd never opened this door to us before.

"The Cruse family," I said.

"Of course, sir. Please come straight back. Everyone's in the garden."

It was strange to walk through the grand house where Kate had grown up. She'd toddled along this marble hallway, and run up and down that grand swirling staircase, and played on this sofa with her dolls—or more likely her microscopes and tweezers and bits of mangled bugs. Thinking of it made me smile as we made our way to the conservatory, where a bank of French doors was flung open to the garden.

And what a garden it was—vast, with great leafy trees and winding paths and trellises with climbing roses and sunken terraces, and a big gazebo where a string quartet played. Lavish tables of food were set out under a great marquee tent. Uniformed staff circulated with trays of champagne and hors d'oeuvres.

"How charming," said Sylvia, as though she'd been to dozens of these.

The party was well underway, for there must have been hundreds of people here already, the ladies in their white summer dresses, the men in pale linen suits. I stood with my mother and two sisters, as rooted as the chestnut that shaded us. I knew no one.

"I did that dress," whispered my mother, surveying the crowd. "That's Mrs. Mackenzie. And that's Mr. Vanderzalm over there; I altered a suit of his."

"Let out the trousers, I bet," said Isabel, a little too loudly.

"Shh," I said.

"Perhaps we shouldn't have come along, Matt," said my mother. "No one wants to meet their seamstress at a party. We don't fit in."

"Of course you do," I said, wanting to reassure her.

I could see my sisters, especially Sylvia, carefully watching all the other young ladies, taking note of their outfits.

"You're all dressed more elegantly than anyone here," I told the girls quietly. "You can thank Mom for that."

"She can do anything," said Isabel proudly. "I feel utterly fashionable."

Across the wide lawn I spotted Miss Simpkins and almost didn't recognize her, for she was laughing, and was on the arm of a man. Could this be her Paris beau?

"That's Kate's chaperone," I said, nodding.

"Really?" said Isabel. "I thought she'd be an old crone, the way you described her. She looks nice."

"Don't be fooled," I said.

"She's quite striking, you know," said Sylvia.

I had to admit, Miss Simpkins did look fetching. It wasn't often I'd seen her smile. Probably she was just happy she wasn't on another expedition with Kate.

"Let me get you all some punch," I said.

"You're leaving us?" said Isabel, sounding panicky.

"I'll be right back," I promised. "If anyone comes near you, just scream and run."

I walked towards the refreshments tent, where an enormous crystal bowl sparkled with ice and floating berries. As I was filling cups, a soft voice behind me said, "Well, aren't you just the most dashing fellow in the garden."

I turned to see Kate. She was dressed in a long, white summer dress, with her auburn hair up, little tendrils curling down past her cheekbones. She was utterly beguiling, and I very nearly leaned in to kiss her.

"Mr. Cruse," she said in a formal voice, extending her hand, "how nice to see you again. Thank you so much for coming."

"Miss de Vries, I'm very pleased to see you," I said, and politely shook her white-gloved hand.

Kate's eyes quickly surveyed our immediate surroundings, making sure no one was close by. "It's not like Paris any more," she whispered. "Do you understand?"

I nodded. "How much do your parents know about us?"

"Nothing."

I knew this was for the best, but couldn't help feeling hurt.

"They know you're a student at the Airship Academy in Paris," Kate went on, "and our paths cross from time to time at various society functions."

Her eyes were scarcely on me, they were so busy making sure no one would overhear us.

"And what about salvaging the *Hyperion* together last year?" I asked.

She shook her head and smiled. "Forgot to mention it to them."

"And Miss Simpkins hasn't let anything slip?"

"She's been good as gold."

"So you and I are just acquaintances," I said.

"Nothing more."

I sighed. "This is going to be difficult."

"Just pretend we're in a play."

"Well, there's always plenty of drama when you're around."

"It is exciting, though, isn't it?" she whispered. "Pretending we're practically *complete* strangers."

The way she said it made me blush. "Have you told your parents about outer space?"

"They know *of* it."

"But have they agreed to let you go?"

"I have no worries on that count," she said. She tapped her temple. "I have a plan."

We heard a buzz of excitement across the lawn.

"Ah," said Kate. "That would be Phase One."

Everyone was turning to look at the entrance to the garden, where none other than Otto Lunardi had just arrived, arm in arm with his wife, Anna. The newspapers always described her as statuesque. She wasn't really very tall, but compared to her husband she did seem to tower.

"You invited him, didn't you," I said.

She nodded, beaming. "My parents are terribly impressed by magnates. I asked Mr. Lunardi if he wouldn't mind popping in. He's going to put in a good word for me. Look, my mother and father have just latched on to him."

I'd only ever seen Kate's parents in a photograph. They were certainly a fine-looking couple. Mr. de Vries was tall and broad, with a slightly lupine face; Mrs. de Vries was beautiful in a languid way, with heavy-lidded eyes and a full, sculpted mouth. Both were now smiling and chatting with the Lunardis.

"This is going very well indeed," said Kate, watching. "Exactly as planned."

"Is there anything you *don't* have planned?"

"A few things," she said. "Now, we've talked for long enough. People will start to chatter. Where's your family?"

"Over there."

I saw her eyes lock on to them. "Take me right over. I *must* meet them this instant."

"Don't frighten them," I said.

"Do I look frightening?"

"You do look a bit carnivorous."

"I'm just enthusiastic!" she protested. "I've been looking forward to this for ages."

We walked over together carrying the cups of punch.

"Mrs. Cruse," said Kate warmly, "thank you so much for coming. I simply cannot tell you what a pleasure this is!"

"It's lovely to finally meet you, Kate," said my mother, taking her hand.

My sisters both did pretty curtsies to Kate, and then their eyes widened as she embraced them lightly and kissed them on both cheeks.

"That's how they do it in Paris," she informed them.

"Is it?" said Isabel with delight.

"Absolutely. They can't stop kissing each other."

Isabel laughed, but Sylvia looked suspicious.

"What a pretty garden," my mother said.

"Yes, it is nice. It's also a graveyard, you know," Kate said to my sisters.

"A graveyard?" Isabel repeated.

Kate nodded and lowered her voice. "Not many people know this, but there are several corpses beneath the soil. When I was eight I buried Franz Ferdinand, my cat, at the back, right under that silver maple. And when I was ten, Teddy, my beloved cocker spaniel, died. His tombstone's right beside Franz Ferdinand. They got along famously."

Isabel went off to have a look, but Sylvia was too grown-up to want to see.

"We've got a garden now too," said Sylvia, who I could tell was wary of Kate but also fascinated.

"So I hear," she said. "What will you plant?"

"I've not had time to give it much thought," said my mother. "I wouldn't mind a bit of a vegetable patch."

"Except that vegetables are so boring to look at," said Kate. "Do promise you'll plant some roses or peonies, won't you? They're so glorious."

I looked at my mother, wondering if she'd think Kate was completely frivolous, but she just smiled back pleasantly, and then the two chattered on about their favourite plants and flowers. I realized I hadn't been breathing properly, just sucking in little bits of air like someone in his final stages of drowning. I'd been so tense about Kate and my mother meeting, but they seemed to be getting on pretty well.

Kate was a marvel. I'd never met anyone who was better at talking, and she never let a silence stretch on for longer than a second. She talked so easily to my mother and sisters that I started to relax—and even feel a tad left out. I decided to let them be for a while and take a walk around the garden. I only hoped my sisters wouldn't say anything embarrassing.

At the gazebo a waiter offered me a glass of something fizzy, and I stopped to listen to the string quartet.

"I hope you and Kate are being discreet," said Miss Simpkins, appearing at my side.

"Of course," I replied. I'd never been fond of Miss Simpkins, and it made me uneasy that she knew about me and Kate.

"You want to see the future?" she asked me.

"I didn't know you were clairvoyant, Miss Simpkins."

"That tall fellow over there," she said, ignoring my joke, "do you see him, in the green blazer with the crest? That is James Sanderson."

"Let me guess," I said, "the heir to the Sanderson fortune."

"Ah, so you *have* heard of him."

"No. But whenever someone gets pointed out, he's usually filthy rich."

"And so he is—or will be. And that, young Mr. Cruse, is most likely the man your Kate will be calling husband before long."

I wasn't prepared for the fury that seized me. My pulse hammered at my temples. I felt sick. The expression on my face must have been unpleasant, for Miss Simpkins looked away.

I watched Sanderson, who was talking with some of his chums, smiling and laughing with all the presumptuous, easy grace I'd seen so often aboard the *Aurora*. I'd served many young men like him, who scarcely noticed their food was prepared for them or their clothes pressed every day. They had little idea where their money came from, and had done nothing themselves to earn it.

The thought of this fellow calling Kate his wife, touching her, made the garden tilt on its axis. I stared at him, and everything else seeped away off the sides of my vision. I imagined terrible fates for James Sanderson.

"Well, he looks like a pleasant fellow," I said, forcing myself to smile. "I hope he won't be disappointed when Kate turns him down."

"I know you think me cruel," said Miss Simpkins, and her tone was almost kind. "But I'm trying to make it easier for you in the long run. You mustn't entertain notions that you and Kate have a future together. You'll only be disappointed. You must be sensible."

"Thank you for your advice, Miss Simpkins," I said stiffly, and walked off.

I was about to check on my mother and sisters, but before I'd gone twenty paces I saw Mr. de Vries walking straight towards me, smiling.

"Mr. Cruse!" he said, hand extended. His grip was tight. "I'm Kate's father, Charles de Vries."

"How do you do, sir."

"I've been looking forward to meeting you. You're a remarkable young man by all accounts."

I was completely unprepared for his enthusiasm. "Well, uh, thank you, sir."

"That business with the pirate Szpirglas was quite something. Kate tells me you're in your final year at the Airship Academy. How're you making out there?"

"It's hard work, but I'm learning a great deal."

"You must be one of the younger students, no?"

"I am, but I think I'm holding my own."

"What are your plans after graduation?"

It was like being interviewed for a job, but somehow it made me less nervous. Answering questions was easier than making polite chit-chat.

"I'd hope to find work as a second officer to start with, sir."

"And then?"

"Work my way up to captain."

"You've got your eye on the future. Excellent. Having a plan is halfway to success." He leaned in closer and lowered his voice. "It's quite a secret you're keeping."

An icy tingle coursed down my spine. He *knew*. He knew what was going on between me and his daughter. I didn't know what to say, I was so mortified. Luckily I didn't lose my head and start blubbering a confession.

I tried to look perplexed. "What secret might that be, sir?"

He chuckled and gave me a wink. "Kate told me."

"Is that so?" I said weakly. This made no sense. Why on earth would she tell him?

"Otto Lunardi let it slip too," Mr. de Vries said. "You know, the airship tycoon. I was chatting with him just now. Charming fellow. That's quite an honour to be chosen as a candidate."

I smiled, my anxiety evaporating. Mr. de Vries was talking about the astralnaut training program. "And I understand Miss de Vries has been invited to take part too," I said.

"Indeed." He nodded, eyebrows lifting, and I could tell he liked the idea.

"She must be a very accomplished scientist," I said, "if Mr. Lunardi wants her aboard his ship."

"Not really the sort of thing suitable for a young lady, though, is it," said Mr. de Vries. "But perhaps allowances can be made, given Mr. Lunardi's involvement. One wouldn't want to offend a man of his quality. No doubt Kate will settle down afterwards. A woman can't carry on like this once she's married, eh?"

I said nothing.

Mr. de Vries leaned in still closer, and I could smell the alcohol on his breath.

"We've indulged our daughter terribly, of course," he said in a confidential tone, "letting her study abroad. We've let her have a long holiday from the real world. But this is her world, right here in Lionsgate City, and she'll come to realize that before too long."

I wasn't sure Mr. de Vries knew his daughter terribly well. The mansion and gardens were all very nice, but I couldn't see Kate settling for such a view when she had the whole world to choose from.

"Next year," Mr. de Vries continued, "she'll be back home for good, and she'll likely receive several proposals of marriage. I have no doubt she'll make an excellent match."

When he said this, he looked directly at me and his eyes had a sudden piercing clarity that made me uneasy. Did he know how I felt about Kate, after all? His words seemed meant to warn me off.

"Hello, you two," Kate said, strolling over.

"Ah, Kate, I was just talking with Mr. Cruse," her father said. "A capital young fellow. He'll go very far indeed. Splendid, splendid. Now if you'll excuse me." He hailed a gentleman across the lawn and walked off.

Kate grinned at me. "So what did you and Daddy talk about?"

"You, mostly. Apparently you'll be married off by next year."

She chuckled. "Gosh, I had no idea. I should talk to my father more often."

"Rumour has it James Sanderson is the lucky man."

"The heir to the Sanderson fortune?" she said, eyes wide with mock amazement.

"Yes."

"My father didn't tell you that, did he?"

I shook my head. "Miss Simpkins."

Kate waved her hand impatiently. "She's just making trouble. Don't give Mr. Sanderson a second's thought."

"That's a shame. I've already thought of three ways to kill him."

Her eyes glowed. "Really?"

"Two of them were quite good. The third would've been messy—it involved chopsticks. So you haven't heard of this plan?"

"Oh, my parents may have mentioned it once or twice."

I looked at her. "This might be funny to you, but it's really . . ." I didn't know how best to finish my sentence. "Very painful for me."

"I'm sorry, Matt. Can you really see me marrying someone for their fortune?"

"No."

"Then that's all you need to know." She gave me her warmest smile. "Your mother and sisters are delightful. You never told me your mother was so beautiful. I hope she liked me."

"How could she not?" I said, happy that it mattered to her.

"Did she say anything about me?"

"I haven't had a chance to talk to her yet."

"No, of course not."

"I think your father's going to let you go on the voyage," I said.

She nodded, beaming. "I have no doubts at all. But I should move on now," she said abruptly. "We've talked long enough. I can see my mother staring at us."

"When—?" I was going to ask her when we could see each other again, but she was already gone, floating away across the manicured lawn in her white summer dress.

I was on my way to find my mother when I spotted Sylvia talking to none other than James Sanderson. He was standing too close to her for my liking, talking and smiling and every so often touching her forearm. Sylvia's cheeks were unnaturally bright, and she kept laughing gaily. I hurried over.

"Oh, hello, Matt," she said, not looking altogether thrilled to see me. "This is James Sanderson."

"Pleased to meet you," I lied.

He was not quite as handsome as he'd appeared from a distance. And I was happy to see I was slightly taller than him, even though he must have been three or four years older. He had rather pronounced shadows under his eyes; no doubt he stayed up late, carousing.

"So you're Matt Cruse," he said. "I saw you talking to Miss de Vries and wondered if it was you. You're quite a hero around here, you know. That whole pirate Szpirglas incident. That was sensational."

His tone, I realized, was genuinely admiring and not at all mocking.

I wondered if he was going to ask if I'd killed Szpirglas with my bare hands; luckily he didn't.

"You're studying at the Airship Academy, aren't you?"

"I graduate next spring."

"What brings you back to Lionsgate City?"

"Just visiting my mother and sisters." I turned to Sylvia. "You should check on Isabel."

"But—"

I smiled at her, and she knew from my expression that I meant business.

"It was very nice meeting you, Mr. Sanderson," she said.

"Enchanting, Miss Cruse," he said. After she'd left, he smiled at me. "Charming girl. Say, you're not here because of the astralnaut training program, are you?"

This took me by surprise. "The what?" I said.

"The city's all abuzz with rumours. They say they're choosing astralnauts for the first space voyage."

I let my eyes widen. "Is that right?"

"Bet you wish you were part of that, heh?"

"That would be something."

"Ah well, maybe when you're more experienced. So, do you know Miss de Vries very well?"

"Not really. I see her in Paris from time to time."

"She's quite lovely, isn't she."

I followed his gaze to where she stood across the garden. The fellow seemed smitten.

"I find her a bit plain," I said, and had to bite my lip so I wouldn't laugh.

"I don't think so," he said, sounding surprised. "But it's odd, don't you think? All her studying, and in foreign parts too."

"That's not the half of it," I said.

"Really?" He seemed simultaneously intrigued and alarmed.

I lowered my voice. "She's notorious in Paris."

He stepped closer. "Is she?"

I nodded. "Rumour has it she's opened her own secret circus. All sorts of freakish things she's gathered up."

"You don't say . . ."

"They say she punts along the river at night, dredging up dead things from the bottom. Then she sews them back together, all mixed up, and *zaps* them with high voltage to revivify them."

He gave a little jerk and looked at me queasily. "That does seem unnatural," he murmured.

"Just rumours, though, old boy," I said, slapping him hard on the shoulder.

He looked across the party at Kate, a puzzled expression on his face.

"Well, nice chatting with you," I said, and walked away, feeling mightily pleased with myself.

Riding home on the streetcar with my mother and sisters, it seemed they'd all had a good time. Isabel had devoured three bowls of ice cream; Sylvia had been complimented on her dress and shoes several times and been invited to a tea party next week; and my mother, to her surprise, had not been snubbed at all. In fact, she'd been offered enough new work to take her through the winter.

"What did you think of Kate?" I asked.

"I liked her," she said carefully.

"But . . ." I prompted worriedly.

"She's a beautiful girl, and very bright and confident, and I can see why you think so highly of her. But I wonder if she thinks rather highly of herself too."

"She can be a little exasperating sometimes," I said. "But that's just her way."

"I just wouldn't want to see you get hurt," my mother said.

She was sounding alarmingly like Miss Simpkins. It seemed everyone today was warning me away from Kate. I started to feel foolish. Even Kate herself had scarcely spoken to me, so we could play our parts as polite friends. Or maybe she too was beginning to realize how impossible our "romance" was.

Paris suddenly seemed a long way away.

"Are you going to marry her?" Isabel asked me.

I chuckled, but uncomfortably. "It's too soon for me to marry anyone," I said. "Anyway, first I've got to go to outer space."

7 / Training Begins

MY HEART SANK when I entered the gymnasium and saw all the other astralnaut trainees. There were easily a hundred, all men, and most of them looked older than me by ten years. I couldn't be sure what any of them did, for Mr. Lunardi had given us instructions not to wear any kind of uniform. Still, it was easy enough to tell the military men by their short-cropped hair and the way they stood so straight. Some looked like weightlifters, others had the lean and fanatical look of mountain climbers. As my nervous eyes moved over the crowd, I imagined everyone else as a fireman, or engineer, or world-famous athlete. I was amazed Mr. Lunardi had even asked me to try out. Surely they didn't want someone so young and inexperienced.

No one was talking much. We were all strangers—and competitors—and we stood restlessly with our duffel bags at our feet, waiting for things to start. It was seven o'clock, Monday morning.

Last year, Lionsgate City had hosted the Olympic Games. Playing fields and arenas and residences for the athletes had been built hastily along the shores of False Creek. The buildings were mostly vacant now, and it was here that Mr. Lunardi had set up his secret training facility. He'd chosen well. When the cab driver had dropped me off, the site was eerily deserted, and it took me a while to find the right building.

All eyes went to the stage as Mr. Lunardi walked out now to greet us.

"Gentlemen!" he said. "I am delighted to see you all safely arrived, and looking so eager and fit. You know why you're here, so let me introduce you to the man who will oversee your training for the next two weeks. Some of you may already know his name. He's one of the finest sky captains of our time, and will be the commander of our first voyage to outer space. Do your best, gentlemen! I hand you over now to the care of Captain Samuel Walken."

I had a big smile on my face as he strode onto the stage. I hadn't seen Captain Walken since leaving the *Aurora* to start my studies at the Academy. Three years I'd served aboard his ship, and happy years they were. He'd always encouraged my ambitions and done all he could to advance me. I wanted to wave at him and shout out a hello, but of course didn't.

He stood for a moment beaming down at us, as though he couldn't imagine any finer company in the world.

"Gentlemen, good morning. You're all here because you're exceedingly skilled at whatever it is you do. Look around this hall and you'll see soldiers and surgeons, submariners and sky sailors, gymnasts and high-altitude construction workers. Working in extreme conditions is commonplace to many of you, but our new venture will require unusual skills, some of which have never been taught. My task is not to question your expertise, but rather to find out who has the peculiar combination of skills necessary to pilot a vessel in outer space."

His kindly eyes travelled over the assembly, and for a moment I thought they came to rest on me.

"It might give you some comfort to know that I myself have already undergone this training regimen, and if a grizzled fellow like me can get through it, so too can you! Some of the tests are gruelling, I'll admit, but I can't imagine they'll pose any problem to the excellent candidates I see before me. Now—you'll be divided up into groups, given a tour of the facility, and then to work! Space awaits, gentlemen!"

A great cheer rose from the crowd, and my voice with it. Captain Walken had always had a way of encouraging men to give their utmost.

The gymnasium was suddenly filled with athletic-looking fellows with clipboards, shouting out names. I heard mine called, grabbed my bag, and stepped smartly over. Our leader looked a proper Viking, with flowing red hair, a full beard, and large biceps bursting from his shirtsleeves. He had a wide, but slightly sadistic, smile.

"You are Group Four," he told us, "and I am Grendel Eriksson, but no doubt you will call me other things as the training progresses. Grab your things and follow me— you've got a busy day ahead of you."

There were ten in my group, and as I looked around I spotted a fellow around my own age. He was a bit shorter than me, compact, with dark, wavy hair. His blue eyes were quick and intelligent, and though his face was frank and open, his thick eyebrows hinted at a temper.

"Matt Cruse," I said, extending my hand.

"Tobias Blanchard," he said, and we shook.

There was no time to say anything more, because Eriksson was already marching us out of the gym. Without stopping, he barked out his commentary.

"Refectory through there. Delicious food, no one's ever survived to complain. Breakfast at six a.m., lunch at noon, dinner at six-thirty. Half an hour for each. Chew quickly. To the right is Disorientation Training."

"What happens in there?" someone asked.

"Don't want to spoil the surprise. Through that door is Celestial Recognition. Off to the left is Low-Gravity Familiarization."

"What about that door there?" Tobias asked, pointing to what looked like the entrance to a vault.

"That's the bathroom, in case you need to be sick," Eriksson said. "Up now!"

We jogged up two flights of stairs and were shown our dorm. We were assigned cots and lockers, and handed two fresh sets of training kit. Then we were shown the toilets and showers, and told when we could use them. We were also told when to get up and when to sleep.

"Check the notice board bright and early every morning, gents," Eriksson said. "If your name's on it, congratulations, you're free to leave."

"You mean we got the boot," said one of the trainees.

"Correct. You can't all go to outer space. Only a small

number of you will make it to the final trials at the end of two weeks. Now get into your kit and assemble on training field number two immediately."

"I like him," Tobias said to me from the corner of his mouth.

"He'll make a fine jail warden one day," I replied.

We stripped, quickly pulled on our training gear, and hurried after the others. Everyone seemed awfully keen.

"I've read about you," Tobias said, as we jogged downstairs. "You killed the pirate Szpirglas in a swordfight—and all you had was a butter knife."

"Don't believe everything you read," I said, pleased he'd heard of me.

"You didn't have a butter knife?"

I sighed and said, "He slipped, actually. Fell to his death."

He raised an eyebrow. "Oh. Well, that's still something. What do you do now?"

"I'm a student at the Airship Academy. You?"

"Underwater welder," he replied, a bit sheepishly. "Seems most of you have high-altitude experience. I'm not sure why they wanted me to have a bash at it. I couldn't go swinging around in the air."

"I'm not sure I could suit up and dive under water."

"Sometimes it's a suit, sometimes it's a diving bell. I do ships and bridges mostly. I work in Victoria."

I'd flown over Victoria enough times on my way to the Orient. It was a pretty city, filled with tourists who promenaded along the Inner Harbour and drank tea at the Empress.

"I feel like a little kid here," Tobias said, nodding at the other men in our group.

"You and me both. How old are you?"

"Nineteen," he said.

"Seventeen," I admitted. "So you've got a hankering to go up into space?"

He reached into his shorts pocket and pulled out a small stone. "Ever since I got given this."

It was an ordinary enough looking bit of rock, though intriguingly flecked with black and silver.

"What is it?"

"Bit of the meteorite that made the Badlands Crater. My uncle was prospecting out there and brought it back for me. They say it's got stuff in it that's never been found on Earth. Minerals and the like."

He let me hold it, and it was amazingly light—like holding nothing at all.

"It feels warm," I said in surprise.

"That's just 'cause I rub it."

I chuckled, but the glamour of the rock was undiminished. Where had it come from? Before it struck the earth, it must have passed through countless worlds. Was it a bit of a planet that had met its doom? Had other galactic creatures touched it, as I did now?

"Bit of a lucky charm," Tobias said, shoving it back into his pocket. "I take it down with me whenever I dive. Figure I'll need it now."

Grendel Eriksson ushered us through a set of doors and across a plaza towards the coliseum. It looked twice the size of the one in Rome. We entered through one of the enormous archways.

"Welcome to trial by fire, gents," Eriksson said with what sounded like delight.

"What the hell is that?" said Tobias, gazing up.

In the middle of the open-air coliseum, hovering at one hundred feet, was a lightweight metal platform, held aloft by a hydrium balloon at each corner and tethered to the earth by ropes. Dangling from an opening in the middle of the platform's underside was a wispy rope ladder. Safety nets had been strung beneath it.

"This is Altitude Familiarization," said Eriksson.

"You want us to climb up there?" Tobias muttered, looking queasy.

"For starters," said Eriksson. "Let's go, gents, one at a time. Douglas, you're first, you lucky devil. Further instructions when you're topside! The rest of you form a line. No pushing. Everyone gets a turn, I promise!"

I was second in line, with Tobias right behind me. We all moved under the shadow of the platform to the rope ladder. Douglas took a breath, gripped the rungs, and started climbing purposefully.

"You do this all the time, I suppose," Tobias said in a low voice.

"Are you afraid of heights?" I whispered back.

"Not until now. What're we supposed to do when we get up there?"

I shook my head.

Douglas was now halfway there. The rungs were baggy, so climbing was no easy thing; the ladder swayed with every step. He seemed to be getting on all right, though he did falter for a moment after looking down.

"Cruse, you're next," said Eriksson.

I grasped the rope and started up. The climbing was difficult but I felt no fear. After a while I glanced up to see Douglas clamber shakily through the opening in the platform's underside. I checked on Tobias below me, doggedly hauling himself up, staring straight ahead, and hoped he wasn't scared. I was almost at the platform and was wondering what was going to happen next, when I heard a cry of pure terror. I saw Douglas plunge earthward, arms and legs flailing as he passed me.

I froze, staring. When he was no more than twenty feet from the ground, Douglas miraculously slowed, hovered for a split second, and then bounced back up. It was only then that I noticed the slim cord trailing from his ankles. He soared halfway back to the platform, bounced a few more times, and was then lowered gently to the ground. Two attendants removed his ankle harness, and the line was winched back up.

I swallowed and kept going, pulling myself through the opening and onto the platform.

"Good morning, Mr. Cruse."

Captain Walken stood there, grinning as if our paths had just crossed in the town square.

"Sir," I said, "I'm very, very glad to see you again."

"As am I." He grasped my hand in both of his and gave it a warm squeeze. "I'm delighted Mr. Lunardi was able to lure you away from Paris. I understand you've had some interesting adventures since we last spoke."

"Yes, sir."

"I look forward to hearing about them. But for now," he said, nodding at the platform's edge, "how do you fancy a little land diving?"

"Douglas seemed to enjoy it," I said.

Captain Walken chuckled. "The first time's always the hardest. But you've jumped off higher things, Mr. Cruse."

I smiled. Over the Pacificus he'd seen me swing from a rope into the gondola of a sinking hot-air balloon. And he knew how Vikram Szpirglas had pushed me off the *Aurora's* back and I'd flown and grabbed hold of the ship's fins. "Lighter than air," they used to say about me.

"I think I can manage," I said.

"I have no doubt. Hugo and Walter will rig you up."

From one side of the platform a narrow gangplank jutted into thin air. Two assistants quickly fastened the elastic rope to my ankles.

"The Pentecost Islanders were the first to do this, apparently," said Captain Walken. "They use vines. Oh, here's a little puzzle they want you to solve while free falling." He tossed me a kind of cube, with coloured segments that could be rotated and turned. "Just get all the red squares on the same side. It's fairly simple."

"I'll do my best, sir."

"Jump on the count of five," said one of the assistants. "Five, four—"

But I saw no point in waiting. I leapt, arms out, putting on a bit of a show and giving a whoop of delight as I soared through the air. I'd never feared heights. Funny, how time can stretch out so long when you're moving that fast. Each second was like a little room I could explore. Clouds through the coliseum's open roof, one in the shape of a blue whale. Light on the tiers of arena seats. The faded chalk lines of the racetrack. The ground attendants watching my fall, hands raised to shield their eyes from the sun.

I almost forgot about the puzzle. It was pretty simple; you just had to turn the cube segments a few times. I think it was just to see if you could concentrate on something else while free falling. I got it done before my second bounce.

If I was expecting any praise from Eriksson and the other attendants, I was disappointed. They silently unfastened my diving line, checked the puzzle, and scribbled on their clipboards.

"Back of the line," Eriksson told me. "You've got another dive ahead of you. But this time we'll be moving the platform higher."

I took my place and watched Tobias do his land dive. He made no noise at all, but when he joined me a few minutes later, his eyes and hair were wild.

"I didn't like that," he said.

"You did it, though," I said, clapping him on the shoulder.

"I dropped the stupid puzzle," he muttered.

"You'll get another shot at it."

He grimaced. "Can't wait."

I was good at the land dives, but my confidence quickly evaporated on the obstacle course. The Airship Academy had us all on a regular exercise regimen, and I'd thought I was fairly fit, but I was no match for some of the other fellows. They left me in their dust as I jumped hurdles, scrambled over piles of logs, and scaled brick walls. Tobias and I kept pace through most of the course, but towards the end he pulled ahead. By the time I crossed the finish, I was drenched, my chest and throat burning. I staggered about, hunched and gasping. I was ninth place. I watched Eriksson check his stopwatch and silently jot notes on his clipboard.

"Don't worry, gents," said Eriksson when everyone was done, "you've got time for a nice shower before lunch."

What Eriksson meant by a "shower" was cringing naked in a wooden tub as icy water poured down on us. The water slowly filled the tub until it was at our knees.

At first it was almost blindingly painful, like a vise around my legs, but after a few minutes, a seeping numbness took over and I started shivering violently. A rubber-coated assistant kept shoving a thermometer between my teeth and checking my temperature, writing on his clipboard.

"Can you feel your fingers?" my assistant asked.

"Yes," I said, teeth chattering.

"Toes?"

I looked down at my submerged feet. "Think so," I gasped.

Beside me, in his own tub, Tobias shuddered, arms tight across his chest.

"Can you feel your toes?" his assistant asked.

"No!" he shouted. "No, I bloody well can't! I haven't felt my toes in ages!"

"Some blueness around the lips," his assistant noted.

"Yes, I'm blue!" said Tobias. "You'd be blue too if you were in here!"

After lunch, Eriksson led our group down to a large hall in the basement.

"Welcome to Centrifuge Training," he said.

Crouched in the middle of the room like an enormous tarantula was a fascinating piece of machinery. Radiating from its circular hub were ten many-jointed wooden arms, each of which ended in a single-seat open cockpit.

"It looks like a fairground ride," said Tobias warily.

"That's exactly right," said Eriksson. "Just a kiddie ride. Pick a cockpit and strap yourselves in, please."

I hopped into my seat and was surprised to see both a lap belt and shoulder restraints. I buckled up. In front of me was a panel with a row of coloured buttons.

"This one's a piece of cake, gents," said Eriksson. "Just sit back and enjoy the ride. The coloured buttons will flash in various sequences. Red, green, blue, or what-have-you. Then, when they pause, you just press the buttons in the same order. Simple, yes? Let's get to it."

"What are all those buckets along the wall?" one of the trainees asked.

"The ride used to be called Buzzy Bee," Eriksson said with a wolfish grin, "but we've made some modifications. We call it the Scrambler now."

Tobias and I exchanged glances. I tightened my belts. Eriksson disappeared inside a little control booth. Through the smoked-glass window I saw him turning a large crank. A motor spluttered to life.

Gently the machine began to turn. A peppy carousel tune crackled over hidden speakers and I couldn't help smiling. A couple of the men laughed. My father had once taken us to the Summer Exhibition, and I had a sudden and very clear image of him watching me, smiling, from the sidelines as I whirled on a merry-go-round.

The Scrambler picked up speed and my lights flashed blue, red, blue. This was too easy. But within seconds the sequences grew longer and more complicated—purple, yellow, yellow, red, purple—green, red, yellow, red, purple, blue . . .

We were going at quite a clip now, and suddenly my cockpit was yanked out of its circular orbit into a jerky figure eight. I looked up and saw that all the Scrambler's jointed wooden arms were flexing and extending, hurtling everyone's cockpits towards one another, though always veering clear at the last moment. Faster and faster we careened about. I hoped that whoever had made the modifications knew what they were doing.

Yellow, purple, green, green, yellow, red, blue . . .

The lights gave you less and less time to respond, and then launched right into the next sequence.

We weren't just spinning now but rising jerkily up and then plunging down. The carousel music grew faster and more desperate-sounding.

Red, green, green, purple, yellow, yellow, green, red, white, orange, yellow . . .

Was it purple after the first green, or yellow . . . ?

Without warning, my cockpit twisted upside down. I gave a shout, and heard it echoed by the others as we whirled crazily about one another. Now I understood the shoulder straps. My buttons flashed away, heedless of my discomfort. The Scrambler's music was all but drowned out by the shrieking of its wood and metal joints. We whirled so fast that my body was pressed hard against the side of the cockpit. My cheeks felt like they were flapping.

I was having trouble focusing on the lights. They smeared together into a rainbow. My body felt terribly heavy, my hands clumsy as anvils as they struggled to hit the right buttons.

Just when I thought I might black out, abruptly my cockpit spun right side up and the Scrambler began to slow. When the machine had been going full tilt, I hadn't felt sick, but as its movements became deliberate and sluggish, my stomach gave its first queasy lurch. I wasn't sure if closing my eyes made it better or worse. Some of the men didn't even wait for the machine to come to a complete stop before jumping out and rushing to the metal buckets along the wall. There they retched miserably, between curses.

I stayed seated, breathing slow and deep, and gradually my stomach unclenched. I glanced over at Tobias. Though he looked a bit green around the gills, he gave me a thumbs-up.

"How'd you do with the lights?" he asked.

"I missed a lot towards the end," I said.

"I could barely *see* by the end," he said. "But at least we didn't throw up."

"All right, gents, everyone out," Eriksson said. "The next group wants its turn."

They worked us right up to dinner, and after that we were left to ourselves. The dormitory had a rooftop terrace, and Tobias and I joined a large group of other trainees, smoking and chatting as the sun sank into the west. My legs ached pleasantly from all the running. I felt good about my land dives, but knew I'd have to do better at the obstacle course. As for the icy shower and the Scrambler, I had no idea how I'd done. Our assistants never told us anything.

Tobias and I found a place near the balustrade, on the fringe of things. I think both of us still felt self-conscious about being the youngest.

He offered me a cigarette, and I shook my head.

"Don't know about you," he said, lighting up, "but I could use a drink." He gazed longingly in the direction of downtown. "'Course, that's impossible, since they've got us all locked up like chimps."

Mr. Lunardi didn't want any of us leaving the facility, except on Sundays. I think he was worried we'd blab about the space program. And the city already seemed alive with rumours. This morning's paper had a story about the Canadian space race, and suggested there might even be secret goings-on in Lionsgate City.

"Will it be like this every day, you think?" Tobias said. "Jumping and spinning?"

"Scares off the weak ones," said a fellow to my right. "Standard first-day tactics. It's the same in the Aero Force."

He wasn't in our group, but I recognized him as one of the military types I'd spotted earlier. He was in his early twenties, a strapping, tall fellow with a big, but slightly aggressive, smile.

"You're a pilot, are you?" I asked.

"First Lieutenant Joshua Bronfman," he said, extending his hand. "And this is Captain Chuck Shepherd right here."

Shepherd was leaning against the balustrade, staring out over the city. He had a thick moustache and high forehead. He turned his cool, appraising eyes on us and gave the smallest of nods. I put him at no more than twenty-five. And already a captain. Confidence wafted off him like heat from a tar roof.

"We're both test pilots," said Bronfman smugly.

I was impressed, but Bronfman already seemed so impressed with himself I refused to show it. Test pilots were usually considered the best of the best. Any new ornithopter design the Aero Force came up with, these fellows put it through its paces.

"Have you flown the new Avro-class machines?" I asked, for I wanted to show them I was a sky sailor myself.

Bronfman grinned and nodded over at Shepherd. "Sure, we've taken them up for a few spins. We've got 'em working pretty good, eh, Captain?"

"We have indeed," Shepherd said laconically.

"The Avro is one fast machine," said Bronfman. "Some people said she wouldn't even stay up, but she stays up just fine. I worked her so hard once, I thought her wings would come off—but she's built strong. And no one's taken her faster than the captain."

"She's got a bit more speed in her," Shepherd said, and looked back out over the city.

He was a man of few words, Captain Shepherd. But Bronfman more than made up for him.

"You hear eight people dropped out today?" he said with a smirk. "The land dives and Scrambler finished 'em off."

"Maybe I've got a shot after all," said Tobias, looking cheered.

"Of course you do," I said.

"How many astralnauts you figure they'll pick?" Tobias asked. "I heard six."

"I heard nine," I said.

"They're not telling," said Shepherd.

"Well, you better hope it's more than two," Bronfman said smugly, "'cause that'd be Bronfman and Shepherd."

He looked over at the captain, as if for approval. Shepherd didn't laugh, but his right eyebrow lifted ever so slightly in amusement.

"I'm planning on being on that ship," I said, hoping I sounded cockier than I felt.

Bronfman clapped me on the shoulder. "That's the spirit, kid, but the competition's pretty stiff. I wouldn't get your hopes up."

My back stiffened. I hated being called a kid.

Bronfman looked over at Tobias. "And you'd have a better shot if you knocked off smoking."

"I'll keep that in mind," said Tobias, lighting another cigarette off his last.

"Good luck," said Shepherd, walking off across the terrace. I guess he figured he'd spent enough time talking to kids.

"Nice meeting you two," said Bronfman, following his captain. "See you tomorrow—if you're still around."

"They're quite a pair," I said to Tobias after they'd gone.

He shook his head in disgust. "I don't know which one I hate more. No, I do. Bronfman."

"He's just full of hot air," I said. "Shepherd's the scary one. The way he just stares at you, like you're a waste of space."

"I heard he got almost perfect on the Scrambler."

"How would anyone know?" I said irritably.

"He probably didn't even turn blue in the shower," said Tobias.

I grinned. "He probably just stared straight ahead and said, 'That's mighty refreshing.'"

We had a good laugh over that.

"You think I should quit smoking?" Tobias asked.

"They say it's bad for your lungs," I said. "Didn't stop you from beating me in the obstacle course, though. Maybe I should take it up."

We wandered over to some fellows from our own group and sat down. Most everyone seemed tired, but as the stars brightened, they got more talkative, their voices rising up into the darkness. Reg Perry said he wanted to see the canals of Mars. Tim Douglas said he was bored with being a fireman and wanted a new challenge. One fellow, a surgeon, said he'd seen a picture when he was a kid, of a train leaving the station on a track that tilted right up to the moon—and he'd never forgotten it. Still another trainee said he wanted to see his name in the history books.

"What about you, Captain Shepherd?" someone asked the test pilot as he passed by on his way inside. "What brought you here?"

He shrugged. "They asked. And it's my job. To fly the farthest, the fastest. Someone's got to do it."

I actually felt a bit sorry for him then, as irritating as he was. It didn't seem like being an astralnaut held any romance for him. He wasn't curious; he wasn't an explorer; he was just a pilot, and he saw this as a chance to fly a new ship. I wondered if he even cared what was beyond the cockpit. I liked the idea of the ship well enough, but it was where it might take me that excited me.

From Earth, from this very terrace, the view of the sky was wondrous enough. Imagine how much more you could see thousands of miles beyond it. I tilted my head back and looked at the stars, now shining in full force. I found the tail of Draco, and with a smile my eyes settled on Kate de Vries.

8 / Under Water

THE SIGN ON THE DOOR said ROOM F.

Normally the signs were more helpful, giving you at least some idea what you might expect inside.

"Room F," said Tobias. "I don't like the sound of that."

It was day three of training, and last I'd heard, we were down to eighty-three candidates. My name hadn't appeared on the board yet, and neither had Tobias's. It was the first thing you did every morning: check the board, give a sigh of relief, send a sympathetic glance to the fellows who got chopped. Then hit the showers. Maybe I should've felt proud of myself, but some of the tests were so strange, it was hard to know how well I was making out. So far I'd managed to hold on, but it was early days yet. And now we had Room F to reckon with.

I took a deep breath, stepped inside, and stopped short.

Room F was a lecture theatre, with a chalkboard at the front and rows of little desks with astralnaut trainees squeezed inside. It seemed that all the groups were being brought together for this session. Some of the other fellows looked as confused as I felt. We were used to diabolical machines and endurance tests.

Standing down at the front was Captain Walken and a small, dejected-looking man with spectacles who was leaning on a cane.

"It's just like school," said Tobias with a hint of terror in his voice. "I think I'd rather do another land dive."

We found two desks at the back, each of which had a notebook and two sharpened pencils waiting for us.

"Let's begin, please," said Captain Walken. "Ah, welcome, ladies."

I turned around to see Kate and Miss Simpkins entering the classroom.

"Gentlemen," said Captain Walken, "allow me to introduce Miss Kate de Vries and Miss Marjorie Simpkins. Miss de Vries is an expert on high-altitude zoology, and I'm very pleased to tell you she'll be joining our expedition."

So Kate's plan had worked! Her parents had given their consent. I can't say I was surprised. Kate was almost supernaturally skilled at getting what she wanted.

"Good morning, everyone," said Kate, sitting down in the desk beside mine without giving me a glance. "Mr. Lunardi has very kindly allowed me to sit in on some of your sessions."

The other trainees didn't seem to mind at all. They were smiling and sitting up straighter in their desks. But I was surprised by my own contrary mix of feelings. I was always hungry to see more of Kate—but I didn't want her *here*. This was my testing grounds, and I didn't want her to see me if I looked foolish, or too young, or if I failed. It was bad enough that she got to be part of the expedition without lifting a finger to prove herself. So why did she have to come and gawk at us like a tourist? Why couldn't she keep clear?

"Now, to business," said Captain Walken. "Without the know-how of this gentleman beside me, we wouldn't be going to outer space. This is Dr. Sergei Turgenev and he'll be chief science officer aboard ship. Our expedition will take us into a new world, and Dr. Turgenev has a great deal to share with you now."

After all my months at the Academy, I felt quite at home behind my desk. But I could see that the other fellows were ill at ease, already rearranging their bums on the hard seats and playing with their pencils.

Dr. Turgenev limped forward, leaning on his cane. He wasn't old—no more than forty—but he gave the impression of being crumpled. His long face was made even longer by his goatee. He sighed deeply.

"I am very excited to be here among you," he said, in mournful, heavily accented English. "And so I am here to tell you about outer space."

He turned his back on us. Splinters of chalk exploded from his hand as long strings of numbers and symbols scrolled across the blackboard.

I saw Kate eagerly copying everything down in her notebook. The other candidates stared at the board in horror. I knew how they felt. I'd never seen some of the symbols that appeared there like malevolent hieroglyphs.

"Now someone complete equation for me, if you please," said Dr. Turgenev, turning to face the class. "I am sorry this is insultingly simple. I promise we get more challenging. Anyone?"

I glanced over at Kate, but even she wasn't going to take a whack at it.

"No one?" said Dr. Turgenev. "I am very disappointed." He stared at us dolefully.

Then something strange happened to his face. At first I thought he was having some kind of seizure, but then I realized he was trying to smile.

"I am just *kidding*. This is *joke,* what I have written on board. Is meaningless. Complete gibberish."

We all looked around at one another uncertainly.

"Captain Walken told me it is good idea to begin with joke. So that is my *joke.* And now I think we are more relaxed, and I begin to tell you about outer space."

He wiped the chalkboard clean with his brush and drew a circle.

"Here is our planet. Around it we have sky. And above sky we have outer space. Where does it begin? We must find out. What is this outer space? What is it made of? Is it liquid? Is it gas? Now, thirty-five thousand feet is highest humans have gone. At this height, air pressure is much lower. I calculate it gets even lower, higher we go. Is possible that in outer space, there is no pressure at all. But we will see."

When Kate and I salvaged the *Hyperion* last year, we'd been as high as twenty thousand feet—and I knew what a hostile place it was: airless and extremely cold. I could scarcely imagine what it would be like beyond that.

"Ship will be pressurized," Dr. Turgenev continued, "and supplied with heat and air, but when you venture outside ship—"

"We're going *outside* the ship?" Reg Perry asked in alarm.

"Yes, certainly. Not me, of course, I have weak lungs. But astralnauts will be first men in space. And so we create special suits for you. They bring one up now . . ."

There was a knock at the door.

"Ah, here it is," said Dr. Turgenev. He opened the door. "Front of class, please," he told the assistant.

We all watched as a mannequin wearing an enormous puffy silver suit was wheeled into the room. The suit was extremely shiny and reminded me of an oversized Christmas tree ornament. The mannequin beamed at us, obviously very pleased with his spacesuit.

"I'm not wearing that," said Bronfman, and some of the other trainees laughed.

"I am very sorry to hear this," said Dr. Turgenev. "Because without suit, you die. First, lungs explode. Then, gases in your tissue expand and you swell to twice normal size. Water on your eyes and tongue boils and then mouth and nostrils freeze. After that you lose consciousness and die within seconds. Oh," he added with a yawn, "there is also possibility blood boils."

There was a moment of heavy silence.

"That is one fine-looking suit," said Bronfman, to more chuckles. "And I have a feeling it comes in just my size."

I glanced at Tobias and rolled my eyes at Bronfman's arrogance.

"Outside ship," Dr. Turgenev continued, "we get extreme temperatures. Very hot in sunlight; very cold in shade. Suit is your astral skin. It keeps body at right pressure and gives you oxygen."

"Excuse me," said Chuck Shepherd. "But when do we see the ship?"

Dr. Turgenev gave a weary sigh. "Oh, yes, yes. Ship. Everyone is curious about spaceship."

"I think we'd all like to have a look at it," Shepherd said.

Murmurs of agreement rose from the audience. The other trainees, I'd noticed, paid close attention when Shepherd spoke. He was a man of few words, but already, even on the third day, everyone looked to him as the standard we were all trying to achieve.

"You do not need to see ship yet," said Dr. Turgenev, glancing nervously at Captain Walken, who stood off to one side, listening.

"So far," Shepherd said, polite but persistent, "I have been dropped, spun, iced, poked, and prodded. But I thought I was here to fly."

"We know you can fly, Mr. Shepherd," said Captain Walken. "The purpose of this training is to determine your overall fitness for outer space."

"Yes, sir," said Shepherd respectfully. "It just seems funny we can't see the actual ship."

"We're hankering to take her for a little spin," said Bronfman.

Captain Walken nodded patiently. "I'm sorry to disappoint you, gentlemen, but the ship isn't here. She's undergoing final preparations at the launch site, which, for obvious reasons, is being kept secret. Now, please listen to what Dr. Turgenev has to tell you."

The gloomy scientist continued his lecture, relating each fact like a great tragedy. All the same, he gave us plenty of information about gravity, and atmospheric composition, and pressure and vacuums, and orbital velocity. I can't say I understood all of it, but I got the gist of it—or so I hoped. Whenever I glanced over at Kate, she was listening intently, her busy little pen whisking across her notebook.

I started to wonder if the lecture was actually just another test—this time to see who could stay awake longest. The sunshine poured through the windows and the room became awfully warm. Some of the men, I noticed, had propped their heads on their hands and kept lurching forward.

A little paper ornithopter touched down on my desk, and I looked over to see Kate innocently staring straight ahead. Luckily Miss Simpkins was dozing, and we were both in the last row of seats, so I didn't think anyone else had seen. I glimpsed some handwriting on the ornithopter and quietly unfolded it. In Kate's neat penmanship was a short message.

I'm coming! Told you my plan would work! Aren't you pleased?

I gave her a quick nod and wink, then pushed her note under my book and turned back to Dr. Turgenev's drone. But I was aware of Kate's eyes boring into the side of my skull. I couldn't believe it—she wanted a message back! Maybe *she* could listen to the lecture, take notes, and chat all at the same time—but I knew I couldn't.

I dragged out her bit of paper and quickly wrote:

Very pleased! Let's hope I'm coming too.

I didn't bother refolding the ornithopter, just crumpled the paper up and tossed it onto her desk when no one was looking.

Paying attention in class would be a good start, she wrote back.

I looked at her in annoyance and she smiled sweetly.

Sitting up straighter, I focused on Dr. Turgenev. Down near the front one large fellow was flamboyantly asleep on his desk, and as I watched, he began to slide out of his seat. Just before he spilled out onto the floor he woke with a shout.

"Hell's bells!" he said.

"I know, I know," said Dr. Turgenev, turning from the chalkboard, "these equations are very exciting for me also. But I am done for moment. Now I think some of you go for swim."

I thought Dr. Turgenev was joking, until Grendel Eriksson appeared at the door of the lecture hall and told us we were going to the pool. Dread settled over me.

"Enjoy your swim, Mr. Cruse," Kate said.

"Thank you, Miss de Vries. Good day."

"You know her, then?" Tobias asked as we headed off with our group.

I grunted. "I met her a couple years ago aboard the *Aurora*. What happens in the pool, have you heard?"

He shook his head, then looked at me closely. "Are you all right?"

In a low voice I said, "I can't swim."

"Not at all?"

"I can thrash about for a while before I drown."

"Just stick close to me," Tobias said.

I felt awfully grateful to him, but I didn't want to spoil his chances of doing well. Anyway, if we had to do laps or some kind of endurance test, I didn't really see how he could help me.

In the change room, we stripped off our clothes and donned the swimming gear we were handed.

"What're *they* doing here?" Tobias muttered.

I followed his gaze and my spirits sank even lower. Bronfman and Shepherd must have joined our group. Every day, as the number of trainees shrank, the groups were evened out. I'd be competing directly with these two every day now. I sighed. At least Kate wasn't here to see me humiliate myself in the pool.

Captain Walken and a team of assistants were waiting for us on the deck. I was tall and I'd started to fill out, but I still felt boyish beside all the other, bigger men in their swimming gear.

"One thing you'll experience in outer space," the captain said, "is reduced gravity. Dr. Turgenev predicts complete weightlessness beyond a certain height. Moving about inside the ship will be one challenge; moving around outside will be quite another. Here on Earth we can't perfectly simulate weightlessness, but we can come close under water. So suit up, gentlemen, and let's take a walk in outer space."

Eleven spacesuits hung from the wall like the skins of silver giants. Resting on a shelf above each suit was a helmet with a mirrored visor.

I didn't like the idea of getting inside one of those, but I was hugely relieved we weren't actually swimming. Maybe I wouldn't end up making a fool of myself after all.

Though the suit was flexible at the joints, it had a rigid layer of rubber insulation inside, and getting it on was a struggle. Last year, while working aboard the *Hyperion* at twenty thousand feet, I'd donned a snow leopard sky-suit that felt as comfortable as a second skin. But in this astral suit I was heavy and clumsy—and uncomfortably hot. An assistant had to help me pull on my boots and gauntlets and lock the airtight metal collars into place. All that remained was the helmet.

On the edge of the deck was a huge machine sprouting lengths of narrow hosing. Captain Walken took hold of one and held it up.

"This is your umbilicus," he told us. "One end's connected to the ship, the other to the back of your suit. It supplies you with oxygen and carries away the carbon dioxide you exhale. It also keeps your suit pressurized."

The assistants led us over to the air pump and starting attaching our umbilicuses.

"Once your helmets are on," Captain Walken said, "we'll be lowering you into the pool. Your boots have metal soles, so you'll sink quickly. When you touch down, we'll inflate your suits a little to make you as near weightless as possible. You each have three very simple tasks to complete."

Now that I was close to the edge, I could see the pool's deep bottom. All manner of machines and hulking bits of equipment had been bolted down there. It looked like a strange underwater factory.

"You'll each see a closed hatch in front of you," said Captain Walken. "It matches the main hatch on our spaceship. To open it you'll need to turn the wheel to the right. Then you'll need to pass through the hatchway. On the other side you must pick up a red box, come back through, and return to the surface."

"That's all?" asked Bronfman, with his usual cocky grin.

"That's all," said Captain Walken. "But I think you may find moving down there quite challenging. When you're ready to surface, or if you have any difficulties, place both hands atop your helmet. We'll inflate your suit and you'll be buoyed to the surface. Each of you has a knife in the pouch at your hip, in case of emergency. Good luck, gentlemen."

"Let's get to it," said Shepherd.

I glanced over at Tobias. "You'll feel right at home down there," I said.

He sent me an encouraging wink, and then an assistant approached with my helmet. I felt a hot flash of panic. I'd never liked things covering my face.

"Ready?" the assistant asked.

I nodded, not at all ready. The helmet came down. I swallowed as all sound was suddenly muted. I heard the clamp snap shut against the metal collar of my suit.

Almost immediately there was a low hiss. My ears popped and I felt cool air from the umbilicus playing against my back. My mouth was dry. I felt sealed off from the world, the voices on deck dull and distant. My heart pounded in my ears.

My assistant guided me beneath one of the many little cranes that jutted out over the pool, and a line was hooked to the back of my suit. He gave me the thumbs-up, which I repeated back to him, and then I was hoisted up and swung out over the water.

Slowly I was lowered. It was strange to see the water rising over my legs and waist without feeling any wetness at all. For a moment I bobbed up and down, then one of the safety divers unhooked me from the crane, and I sank swiftly. The water rose over my visor, and as it passed my nose I held my breath.

I saw Tobias sinking beside me, along with the other trainees, their white umbilicuses trailing from their backs. I was used to the open air and I didn't like being surrounded by water. My visor was steamy from my panting.

I landed clumsily on the pool bottom, teetering. The hatch was before me, no more than ten feet away. I felt my suit inflate, giving me more buoyancy. My feet still touched bottom, but scarcely. I tried to walk but just slewed about uselessly. Guide rails had been bolted to the pool floor. I grabbed hold of one and dragged myself forward. To my right I saw Tobias moving like a silver aquatic animal, already at his hatch. Darting around in the water, watching over us, were several safety divers. I knew Grendel Eriksson was among them. They didn't have clipboards, but I was sure they were busy taking mental notes.

Laboriously I hauled myself closer to the hatch and seized the wheel in my puffy gauntlets. I gave it a turn, but the only thing that turned was me. My legs swirled up off the floor and kept going till I was upside down, still clutching the wheel. I felt a complete fool: of course the wheel wasn't going to turn unless I was anchored in place. Now that I was upside down, I could see, on the pool bottom, numerous metal footholds. I pulled again on the wheel and managed to get myself right way up. I hoped none of the safety divers had seen that.

Across the pool I could make out several trainees with their hatches open, Shepherd and Bronfman among them probably. But Tobias, I was happy to see, was ahead of all the rest; he had already skimmed through.

With difficulty I managed to wedge my clunky boots into two footholds. Despite the cool air in my suit I was already drenched with sweat. Legs tensed, I turned the wheel, pulling with my whole body. It was amazing how difficult it was to do things when weightless.

Now to get inside. With one hand I grabbed a handle beside the hatch; with my free hand I pushed it. Slowly it moved back and to the side.

The opening was none too large, and I felt bulky as a whale. Feet first or head first? I decided on feet first. Still holding on to the handle, I slipped my boots out of the footholds and managed to get my legs up and aimed at the opening. Then I pulled.

It was going well and I was halfway through, when I felt the back of my suit scraping against the hatch's rim. It brought me to a halt. I gave another hard pull on the handle, trying to get my body clear—and felt something give at the back of my suit.

I twisted round sluggishly as I drifted through the hatchway and saw the severed end of my umbilicus, undulating like an eel and spewing great bubbles of oxygen into the pool. I felt water on my back, then on my legs and feet.

I was filling with water! I felt it glugging coldly down each of my legs and pooling in my boots, weighing me down.

I made a grab for my umbilicus, but it was thrashing about over my head, out of reach. I tried to push off from the bottom and grab it, but was already too full of water. It was up to my waist now.

I looked about wildly, but everyone I could see was still intent on their tasks, their visors turned away from me. Tobias was nowhere to be seen. Where were the safety divers? I put both hands atop my helmet, then churned the water with my arms.

"Hey!" I shouted. "Help!"

The water was at my lower ribs. Soon it would be at my neck, and then it would fill my helmet. I would drown inside my suit.

I needed to get out of it. My clumsy gauntlets clutched

uselessly at my suit, and then panic mastered me and I was shouting and raging.

All at once two safety divers were alongside me. They took hold of my suit and tried to haul me to the surface, but I was too heavy. I saw one shake his head, and the other fellow streaked up to the surface. Maybe he was going for the winch line, but by the time he returned, it would be too late.

The water was at my neck, then my mouth. I tilted my face, trying to keep my nose clear. I sucked in one last breath, and then the water gurgled above my nostrils and filled the helmet to the top.

The water blurred my vision, but when my severed umbilicus suddenly jetted past, I managed to grab it. Air bubbled from its end. I wanted it. Despite my terror, I had a sudden, small moment of calm. I knew there was no point trying to plug the umbilicus back into the suit. It was full of water, and the water had nowhere to go.

My knife!

I clutched the umbilicus tight in one hand, and with my other, tugged the knife from its pouch. I didn't know how much longer I could hold my breath. Without hesitation I plunged the blade into the neck of my suit, cutting deep through the rubber lining, and in the process jabbing my own flesh.

Then I dropped the knife, took the umbilicus in both hands, and jammed it into the gash I'd made. I held tight. It wasn't a perfect fit, but it was good enough. I heard bubbling as the pressure from the hose started pushing the water out through the torn umbilicus opening at the back of my suit. I tilted my head and could see the water dropping in my helmet. I strained, lifting my face as high as I could, needing to breathe. My forehead was clear, and then my nose, and soon I snorted back air. The water dropped to my chin and stopped, but I knew I was all right now.

The other diver appeared with his line, hooked me, and I was hauled up. The moment I broke the surface, they had my helmet off and hoisted me, gasping and spluttering, onto the deck. Captain Walken and Chuck Shepherd caught hold of me and helped me onto a bench. Bronfman and Tobias rushed over to help.

"Are you all right?" the captain asked, taking me by the shoulders, his forehead creased. "You're bleeding."

I looked and saw a rivulet of watery blood running down over my silver suit. For the first time I felt a narrow throb of pain. "My neck," I said. "I had to cut a hole."

Shepherd swiftly opened up my suit and checked my wound. "It's not deep. Won't even need stitches."

"What happened?" Captain Walken asked me.

"His umbilicus tore," said Grendel Eriksson, hauling himself out of the pool. "Suit filled with water. He had the sense to grab his hose and cut an opening for it. Gave himself enough air to breathe."

"That was quick thinking, Cruse," said Shepherd.

"Lucky you didn't slit your throat," said Bronfman.

"I'm sorry, Matt," said Tobias, looking pale. "I didn't see. I was just coming out."

"There must've been a flaw in the suit," said Captain Walken, and he sounded as angry as I'd ever heard him. "It shouldn't have torn so easily. I want all the suits checked again before anyone else goes down. See to it, Mr. Eriksson."

"Yes, sir."

I was grateful to the captain, for I felt what had happened was my own fault. I'd seen Tobias swishing through the hatch like a sea lion, and I'd hurried, not wanting to fall so far behind. I had been careless.

Shepherd gave me a sympathetic clap on the shoulder, but I wondered what he really thought behind that inscrutable expression of his.

Eriksson got the first-aid kit and patched me up. As I saw more of the trainees emerge from the pool, some holding their red boxes, I couldn't help feeling like I'd failed.

"Don't blame yourself, Matt," Tobias said later in the change room. "Your gear let you down."

I nodded, but wasn't convinced. Under water, I didn't think clearly. I'd felt my panic, always crouching like a tiger, ready to leap.

"How do you do it?" I asked him. "Concentrate down there. I saw you, the way you moved about."

"You want to know my secret?" he asked quietly.

I nodded.

"I pretend I'm a shark."

"Really?"

"No," he said, laughing at the expression on my face. "There's no secret. I've spent a long time down there, that's all. It feels like my element. Just like being in the sky doesn't bother you. More practice, that's all you need."

"The helmet makes me feel like I can't breathe."

"I bet you were holding your breath."

"I'm sure I was, on and off."

"Don't," he said. "Your body has enough air. You just have to tell your mind that. Now, any tips for the parawing jumps coming up?"

"Yeah," I said. "Just pretend you're lighter than air."

9 / Evelyn Karr

IT WAS DAY SIX, and I was standing beneath a stuttering light, trying to assemble a small machine from a pile of junk.

All around the room, astralnaut trainees—and Kate—stood hunched over their tables, frantically sifting through mismatched nuts and bolts and bits of scrap metal. All I had to guide me was a picture of the machine I was supposed to build, without any instructions on how to build it. I was no mechanic, but I'd made my fair share of shipboard repairs, and I reckoned I could handle this—if only I could find the right parts! I squinted and bent closer, for Grendel Eriksson was flicking the lights on and off to simulate dire conditions aboard our vessel.

"Twenty-five minutes left!" Eriksson called out.

It was distracting, knowing Kate was here, and I wished Mr. Lunardi would stop letting her drop in. I wondered how Shepherd and Bronfman were making out, but I refused to waste time looking around—I'd let my thoughts stray enough as it was. I wanted to be first.

The room was very quiet for a while, except for the sound of clinking metal and the occasional curse. But the flickering of the lamps was like a maddening mosquito drone in my head . . .

"Ten minutes left!"

I kept at it. I was very nearly done. I just needed to find one more set of washers and—

"Finished!"

I looked up, and I think everyone else did too, for the voice didn't come from one of the astralnauts.

"I'm all done over here, thanks!" Kate said, holding up her machine and beaming.

"Excellent, Miss de Vries," said Grendel Eriksson. "Just leave it on the table, please. You may leave. Keep working, gents, you've still got six minutes left!"

Everyone got back to work with fiercer determination. But I must've been flustered—how could she beat us all like that?—because I was having trouble putting the last of my machine together.

"Done," I heard Shepherd say calmly. And then, moments later—

"Me too!" That was Tobias.

"Three minutes left!" Eriksson called out. "Clock's ticking."

With trembling hands I fastened the last bolt, checked to make sure the machine worked.

"Done!" I called out, my heart racing.

I wasn't first, but at least I'd beat Bronfman! I could barely keep the smile off my face as I walked past him and out of the flickering room.

Outside in the corridor I found Kate chatting politely with Tobias and Shepherd, as Miss Simpkins looked on.

"Hello, Mr. Cruse," Kate said, "you did well."

"Not as well as you, Miss de Vries."

"Sheer luck, really," Kate said modestly. "It was a lot like a bug trap I built once."

To my surprise, Shepherd was grinning. "You put us all to shame, Miss de Vries." He looked at me. "Apparently she flies ornithopters too."

"Is that right?" I said, hating that I had to pretend not to know. I looked down at my shoes, not trusting the expression on my face.

"Maybe you can convince my fiancée to let me take her up for a spin," Shepherd said to Kate.

Fiancée? My jealousy gave way to utter astonishment. Who on earth would want to marry Chuck Shepherd?

"Oh, it's great fun," said Kate. "She doesn't know what she's missing."

Kate seemed to find Shepherd perfectly charming, and so he was—to her.

A few other candidates trickled out from the hall, looking flushed, and then I heard Eriksson's final whistle blow. Everyone else filed out, including Bronfman, who wore an angry scowl.

"I didn't even have the right parts," he said, shaking his head. "Can't do it without the right parts!"

Shepherd nodded but said nothing, fixing Bronfman with that inscrutable stare of his. I was glad to see that even Bronfman got the stare sometimes.

At that moment Mr. Lunardi came around the corner with an intent look on his face. He headed straight for me. I swallowed, worried that he was going to give me the old heave-ho. After all, we were down to sixty-eight candidates now, and I'd just been bested by a young lady who wasn't even training to be an astralnaut.

"Ah, good," Mr. Lunardi said, smiling. "Mr. Cruse, Miss de Vries, I need to talk to you both. Will you come with me, please?"

Tobias stared at me strangely as I turned to follow Mr. Lunardi down the hall. Probably he was wondering if he'd ever see me again.

"We've hit a snag," Mr. Lunardi said quietly, "and I was hoping you two would help me out."

"Yes, of course," I said, and Kate nodded. It didn't sound like I was about to get cut from the program, so I started to relax.

"One of the experts we've invited on the expedition is having second thoughts. Evelyn Karr, the photographer."

I'd certainly heard of her. She was famous for her brooding pictures of rainforest and Indian totems and villages. She was also an accomplished journalist, and her stories and photos appeared in magazines and newspapers the world over.

"Evelyn Karr?" Kate said, enthralled. "I'm a huge admirer of her work! She's coming?"

"That remains to be seen," said Lunardi. "She seemed agreeable at first, but she's notoriously temperamental. Right now she's saying she no longer wishes to go to outer space."

"Can't you just find someone else?" I asked.

Mr. Lunardi shook his head. "The Minister of Air has his heart set on her, you see. He wants a Canadian, and he wants someone with an international reputation. You'd be hard pressed to find anyone of Miss Karr's calibre. She's our reporter and photographer both. She's also the only other woman on the expedition."

Kate looked stricken. "Meaning that if Miss Karr doesn't go, I'll have no chaperone—and can't go."

"*I* certainly won't be going," said Miss Simpkins.

"We know, Marjorie," Kate said.

"You couldn't force me aboard a spaceship for the world," the chaperone added.

"No one's *asking* you to go," Kate said, silencing Miss Simpkins with an angry look.

"Can't you offer Miss Karr more money?" I suggested.

"Tried that," said Lunardi. "Money's of no interest to her. What I want is for you two to talk to her."

I blinked. "You think *we* can convince her to come?"

Lunardi nodded. "She doesn't much care for old men in suits," he said. "Last time we spoke she called me a parasitic little weevil."

Kate sniffed. "How absurd."

"Thank you, Miss de Vries," said Mr. Lunardi.

"Weevils aren't parasites at all," Kate explained. "They're a snout-headed beetle. Quite destructive to crops, but technically not parasitic. She could call you a weevil *or* a parasite, but certainly not both."

I stared at Kate, horrified by her tactlessness, then back at Mr. Lunardi. To my huge relief, he chuckled.

"Well," the magnate said, "if I had to choose, I suppose I'd take the weevil."

"Gosh, I'm sorry, Mr. Lunardi," Kate said, blushing. "I didn't mean to suggest you were either. It just really annoys me when people confuse their species."

"You're quite a species yourself, Miss de Vries," I told her. "No one could mistake you."

"How kind of you to say so, Mr. Cruse."

"Miss Karr hates most people as a rule," said Lunardi, "but she likes the sound of you two."

"She's . . . *heard* of me?" Kate said, clearly pleased.

Lunardi nodded. "I told her about how you nearly electrocuted Sir Hugh Snuffler. Miss Karr thought it wickedly amusing. And, Mr. Cruse, she was very interested in your pirate adventures. I'm hoping you two can charm her into signing on. We'll go visit her tomorrow in Victoria. I thought we'd take her to the Empress for lunch. Who doesn't like lunch at the Empress, heh?"

"Victoria?" Miss Simpkins said.

Mr. Lunardi turned to the chaperone. "Just a hop across the puddle. But don't worry, Miss Simpkins, we won't be interrupting your Sunday plans. Mrs. Lunardi will be joining us, so Kate will be well taken care of. I'm sure her parents won't mind."

"Not at all," Kate said.

Sunday was my only day off, and I'd told Mom and my sisters I'd spend it with them. But how could I refuse Mr. Lunardi?

And I certainly didn't want Kate to lose her place because of Miss Karr.

"Excellent," said Lunardi. "Let's meet down at the marina at nine o'clock tomorrow morning."

It wasn't often I got to travel by boat. There simply wasn't much call for them any more as passenger vessels, not when you could sail the skies faster. But what a wonderful feeling it was, skimming over the Georgia Strait in Otto Lunardi's elegant yacht. Off to starboard were the Gulf Islands. The Olympic Mountains rose on our southern horizon. I began to understand why mariners felt such passion for the sea.

Mr. Lunardi had a small crew, but because he liked to pilot the boat himself, he was up on the bridge, a captain's hat sitting jauntily on his bald head. Mrs. Lunardi was conferring with the purser about some new decor for the main cabin, and Kate and I were left alone to enjoy the sunshine on the afterdeck.

"It's so nice to be away," said Kate with a contented sigh. "Practically everywhere I go in Lionsgate City there's someone who knows my family. I feel like a lab mouse. All their silly questions about what I'm up to in Paris, and when I'm coming back home for good. And have I called on so-and-so or seen what's-his-name yet."

"Has your future husband come calling?" I asked jokingly, but I watched her carefully.

"Who?" she said, then, "Oh, you mean George Sanderson."

"I thought his name was James."

She winced. "Right. James. He just looks like such a George to me. Gosh, I hope I haven't been *calling* him George to his face. And yes, he does come calling. Every day, actually."

"Really?" I said. This was alarming.

Kate looked at me sternly. "What's all this about me digging up corpses in Paris?"

I shrugged. "Just a bit of fun. I thought I'd scare him off for you."

"Well, it's done the opposite. He seems awfully keen on me. He keeps telling me these ghastly stories about freaks of nature, and dead things brought to life."

"I can't believe it backfired," I muttered. "He comes *every* day?"

"What's even worse, my mother thinks he's a perfect gentleman." Kate shook her head. "By the way, you never told me what *your* mother thought of *me*. Did she like me?"

"Oh, very much," I said breezily.

I could feel her looking at me hard, and I wouldn't meet her eyes, afraid of what mine might give away. Her gaze could be like a crowbar.

"What *exactly* did she say?" Kate persisted.

"What a well-bred young lady you were. How pretty you were. Things like that."

"She didn't like me, did she."

I forced myself to meet Kate's steely gaze. "Why do you say that?"

"You sound completely unconvincing."

"I do not," I said.

"You're a bad liar."

"She's just not used to girls like you," I said lamely.

Kate's eyes widened. "Girls *like me*? Oh, you mean the fast, disreputable kind?"

"Of course not." I was scrambling now, wondering how to haul myself out of this mess. "I meant girls from high society."

"So she thinks I'm a snob."

Kate's eyes were blazing. It drove her crazy that my mother hadn't been utterly smitten by her.

"She doesn't think you're a snob. She just worries you might be a bit . . . determined."

Kate was speechless, but only for a split second. "Of course I'm determined! Everyone should be determined, or else what's the point of living? When a *man's* determined it's wonderful, but if it's a woman it's horrid and unattractive." She shook her head bitterly. "It's bad enough *men* judge us unfairly, but when our fellow women—"

"I don't think my mother was judging—"

"I don't see the other mothers of Lionsgate City warning their sons away from me," Kate said haughtily. "In fact, they seem to find me highly desirable."

"I'm glad you're so certain of your charms," I said coolly.

"Oh, so you think I'm conceited now too, do you?"

I gave a laugh. "Of course you're conceited! That's hardly a surprise to me."

I was worried someone might overhear us, but Mrs. Lunardi was up on the bridge with her husband now, and the wind and waves made enough noise to drown out our talk.

"Your mother *did* think I was snobby, didn't she!" Kate demanded. Then she frowned uncertainly. "Was it what I said about the roses?"

"What?" I said, confused.

"You know, about how roses were so much better than a vegetable garden. I worried about that afterwards. It was too frivolous. Sometimes things just come out too quickly at parties."

She was biting her lip, twisting at one of her fingers, and suddenly seemed so full of doubt and regret that I felt sorry for her.

"My mother liked you," I said gently. "I think she just saw us as . . . mismatched."

"Well, that's a bit presumptuous, isn't it?" Kate said, flaring up again. "Mismatched. It's not like we're engaged!"

"No," I said, hurt by the disdain in her voice. "She knows how I feel about you, that's all."

At this, Kate seemed to soften. "I'm sorry, Matt," she said. "I'm being beastly. I'm just nervous about meeting Miss Karr. What if we can't change her mind?"

"You *are* pretty persuasive," I said, smiling.

Kate looked at me gratefully. "Do you really think she'll say yes?"

"If it stops you talking, absolutely."

She chuckled. "It's good to be just the two of us again."

I glanced around to be sure we weren't being watched and

gave her hand a quick squeeze, wishing I could kiss her.

"But look," Kate said, reaching into a large wicker basket and pulling out a sheaf of pamphlets and books. "I thought we should read up on Miss Karr."

She seemed insistent, so I took the book she held out and began flipping through it.

"I was reading madly all last night," said Kate. "A lot depends on this, you know."

"I know."

"Don't just look at the pictures. Read!"

I couldn't help laughing.

"What?" Kate said.

"You are so *bossy,*" I said.

"Yes. Now read!"

I must say, I was relieved when Mr. Lunardi came down and asked if I wanted to take a turn at the wheel.

It was a quick walk from the Inner Harbour to the quiet, tree-lined street where Miss Karr lived. Gulls cried out over James Bay; from the busier streets came the occasional *clip-clop* of horses drawing carriages and the sputter of motorcars. Mr. and Mrs. Lunardi walked along arm in arm, chatting happily. I wondered if Kate and I would ever be able to stroll like that in public. I glanced over at her, but she was lost in thought, no doubt worrying about what she was going to say to Miss Karr.

"Here we are," said Mr. Lunardi.

Beyond the picket fence, a path led through an overgrown garden to the veranda. For such a famous person, Miss Karr was obviously not vain about her house. The windows had an unwashed look, and the gutters needed mending. Paint flaked from the gables.

Mr. Lunardi held the gate open for Kate and me, and then stepped back.

"You're not coming with us?" I asked.

He gave a quick shake of his head. "I think I'd just annoy her. Inflame her artistic sensibility and all that. Last time I came she set her dog on me. Her guinea pigs too. You'll have much better luck without me. We'll wait here. Holler if you need help."

Kate and I made our way up the path. "Guinea pigs can be quite fierce," she said, and we both had a chuckle.

I rapped on the front door, which after a moment swung open by itself. It took me several seconds to realize that a monkey had opened it.

He was a tiny thing, not more than a foot tall. Dressed in a sailor suit, he had large grey sideburns and looked like a very short, very old British admiral. He peered up at us expectantly. I glanced over at Kate, not knowing what to do.

Speaking very slowly, Kate said, "Good—morning. We—are here—to—see—Miss—Karr."

The monkey gazed back at her pensively.

"You're talking to the monkey?" I asked.

"Well, he does look quite bright," she replied.

The door swung open a little wider and the monkey

scampered back, as if inviting us inside. We hesitated, but the little fellow chattered so insistently that we stepped into the hallway.

"Hello, Miss Karr?" I called out.

There was no reply. I peeked into the parlour—or what I thought was the parlour. It was hard to tell because there was so little furniture in it. Then I looked up and saw that all the chairs were dangling from the ceiling by ropes.

"Oh, I read about this," Kate whispered. "She hates visitors, and only lowers the chairs if she wants you to stay."

I nodded. "Makes perfect sense."

The monkey barraged us with more chittering, and then scampered deeper into the house, periodically looking back to see if we were following.

"He seems to know what he's up to," Kate said.

The backroom of the house was enormous, with a high, pitched ceiling. Sunshine streamed through the skylights and large windows. This must be Miss Karr's photography studio, I decided, for there were large lamps on stands, and umbrellas with silvery undersides, and several large cameras on sturdy tripods.

Hung carelessly on the walls were some of Miss Karr's most famous photographs. There was the Prime Minister, sitting on the cowcatcher of the first train through the Rockies. There were our Parliament Buildings, encased in ice and glittering like a fairy palace after a winter storm. And there were the polar bears of Churchill, sitting in a row and staring like bored children in a church pew.

But where was Miss Karr?

The monkey scampered out into the backyard, which looked more like a zoo. Through French doors we could see all sorts of birdcages, and dogs and rats and cats and guinea pigs capering about.

And there, beneath the shade of an arbutus tree, sat Miss Karr behind a small easel, painting. She was a stolid-looking woman in her early forties, dressed in a shapeless, stained smock. On her head she wore an odd kind of hairnet with a band around her forehead. The monkey leapt up onto her shoulder and pointed back at the house.

Miss Karr turned and stared. She hurriedly put down her paintbrush, stood, took her painting off the easel and slammed it face down on a table. Then she stomped towards the house, the monkey clinging to her shoulder.

"Does she look angry to you?" Kate said worriedly.

I nodded. "Yes, I'd say so."

Miss Karr strode into the studio and glared at us.

"Who are you?" she demanded.

"Miss Karr," I said nervously, "my name's Matt Cruse and—"

"Yes, yes," she said, giving an impatient wave.

"And I'm Kate de Vries," Kate said. "Mr. Otto Lunardi asked—"

"Parasitic little weevil," Miss Karr muttered darkly.

I glanced at Kate, hoping she wouldn't contradict Miss Karr.

To my relief, she said, "That's a very fine Javanese monkey you have."

Miss Karr grunted. "You know your animals, I see. This is Haiku. I found him two years ago in a curiosities shop in Chinatown."

"Hello, Haiku," Kate and I chimed in at the same time.

Miss Karr stared hard at us, wiping her hands on a rag.

"I'm sorry if we interrupted your painting," I said.

"It's nothing," she said tersely. "Stand over there. In front of the backdrop."

She was referring to an enormous piece of canvas violently painted with swirling blacks and greys and whites, like weather you'd do anything to avoid. Kate and I glanced at each other, then promptly did as we were told.

Miss Karr stepped behind one of her cameras, peered through the viewfinder, then busied herself adjusting bamboo blinds to sculpt the light in the room.

"Miss Karr," Kate said, "I'm a huge admirer of your work. I particularly like—"

"I particularly like people who *don't* flatter," Miss Karr cut in.

Kate swallowed visibly. I doubt that she was used to being spoken to so curtly.

"I know why you're here," Miss Karr said. "Now, stand close together. Closer! You make a very handsome couple."

Kate cleared her throat. "We're not really a couple, Miss Karr. We're just—"

"Yes, yes," the photographer said impatiently. "Matt Cruse, point and stare off into the distance. You're contemplating a long and dangerous space voyage."

"Like this?" It seemed best to humour her, so I furrowed my brow and tried to pretend the backyard was the shores of Mars.

"And Miss de Vries," the photographer instructed, "look longingly at Mr. Cruse. Goodness knows when you'll see that brave astralnaut again."

"I'm going with him, actually," Kate said, sounding a bit put out.

"Pretend you're not," said Miss Karr sternly.

Click went her camera.

"Now," said Miss Karr, "Miss de Vries, you are going to swoon, just like a heroine in a penny dreadful."

"I'm sure I've never *swooned*," Kate said indignantly.

Miss Karr ignored her. "Arm up, throw one hand across your brow, let's have that other hand clutching your heart. And, Matt Cruse, move in close as if to catch her in your arms when she faints away completely."

Miss Karr was certainly eccentric, but I found it rather fun to play at these clichéd parts. Kate, on the other hand, did not seem to be enjoying herself.

"Miss de Vries," said Miss Karr, looking up from her camera, "you are supposed to look distraught. That is not distraught. That's 'My tea is cold and is there no marmalade for my crumpet.' Can we have something a bit more hysterical, please?"

"Think of Miss Simpkins," I suggested.

"Think," said Miss Karr, "how disappointed you'll be if I don't come on this space voyage."

Kate looked utterly horrified, and at that moment Miss Karr clicked the camera.

"That was quite good," the photographer said.

"Miss Karr," said Kate, sounding desperate, "you really must come on the expedition. It's a historic moment for our nation. Only you can capture it in words and pictures to show the world."

Miss Karr gave a snort. "Why bother with outer space? It can't be photographed."

"I'm surprised to hear you say that, Miss Karr," I said, suddenly remembering something I'd read in one of Kate's books. "Didn't people once tell you the Canadian forest couldn't be photographed? But you showed them how wrong they were."

Kate nodded eagerly. "And didn't you say recently, Miss Karr, that there was nothing more you wanted to photograph? Well, maybe not on Earth. But outer space would present you with a new challenge to master!"

I thought I caught a glimmer of a smile on Miss Karr's face, but it was quickly replaced by a stern frown.

"Matt Cruse, get down on one knee as if proposing to Miss de Vries."

"Is this really necessary?" I asked, feeling uneasy.

"I pretended to swoon," Kate pointed out to me with a mischievous grin.

The monkey scowled at me. I got down on one knee. I didn't want to do this, for it seemed too momentous a thing even to play-act. Kate peered down at me with great satisfaction, like she was hoping I'd quote love poetry, or at least yip like a puppy.

"Look her right in the eye, Matt Cruse!" the photographer instructed me. "This one's going to take some convincing."

I was starting to feel very uncomfortable. I wondered if Miss Karr, like my mother, had already sensed Kate's steely character.

"This is great fun," said Kate.

"Take her hand, Mr. Cruse. That's it. Now look at her beseechingly. Very good. Miss de Vries, what would you say to this fellow?"

Kate gave me a glacial stare.

Click went Miss Karr's camera.

"You'll have a battle getting a yes from her," Miss Karr cackled, clearly enjoying herself immensely.

"It won't be a battle at all," Kate said breezily. "I've decided I'm never going to marry."

I laughed nervously.

Kate turned to me. "You think I'm joking, Mr. Cruse? I've been thinking about this a great deal."

"Is that right, Miss de Vries?" I said, as though this were just polite conversation. I glanced awkwardly at Miss Karr, embarrassed she was seeing this. She was watching with great amusement. Haiku hopped up and down giddily.

"Absolutely," said Kate. "I reject the whole institution of marriage. Did you know, not so long ago, women were considered the legal *property* of their husbands. Like a comfy armchair, or a *rug*."

"That's changed," I pointed out.

"In the letter of the law. But once a woman marries, she's just a wife. I'd cease to be my own person."

"I can't see you being anyone's person but your own, Miss de Vries," I said, and tried to give a pleasant chuckle. I honestly wasn't sure if Kate was serious or still play-acting for Miss Karr's benefit. If she was, she was overdoing it, I thought.

"Men make all sorts of promises," Kate went on, "but once they're married they expect the woman to stay at home and cook and fetch their slippers and pass them their pipe . . ."

"Not all men smoke pipes," I said quickly, meaning me.

"There's too much I want to achieve," Kate said. "It's hard enough as a woman. As a wife it's completely impossible. Miss Karr, what would you say on this matter? *You've* achieved great things."

Miss Karr nodded, looking amused. "I doubt any man would have allowed me to work and live the way I have."

"Precisely," said Kate. "I mean to live my life on my own terms! I won't marry."

"I'll come," said Miss Karr.

Kate and I both looked at her in confusion.

"To outer space," Miss Karr said. "I'll come on your expedition."

"You will?" I said.

"You've piqued my interest. And you're right. What a challenge to capture outer space in words and pictures. I wouldn't miss it, especially not with you two aboard."

I didn't dare tell her that I might not be coming.

"What wonderful news, Miss Karr!" said Kate. "Thank you so much!"

"I have one condition," she said. "Haiku comes too."

"I'm sure that won't present a problem," Kate said without a moment's hesitation.

"Good," said Miss Karr. "Now go outside and tell Mr. Lunardi I won't set my guinea pigs on him. I'll just need a moment to get Haiku changed and into his pram, and then I'll take you all to lunch at the Empress."

10 / The Race Narrows

DRENCHED TO THE SKIN, I ran, my burning legs spattered with mud from the rain-churned field.

It was day nine of training—only four days to go—and I was on the final stretch of the obstacle course. We were down to forty-two candidates now, and everyone was a little leaner—and a lot fiercer. We were pushing ourselves hard. We knew that most of us wouldn't make it to the end of the week.

"Come on!" yelled Eriksson from the sidelines in his rain-slicker. "You can do better than that!"

Shepherd and Bronfman had the lead, as usual, but not by so much this time. Every night after dinner, I'd been doing extra laps on the track. It was the last thing I wanted to do at the end of the day, but I needed to build my endurance, and I thought it was working. Tobias was keeping pace with me now, though I could tell he was flagging.

We reached the timber wall, the final and most dreaded obstacle. Twenty sheer feet with only a rope to help us over.

"Can't believe I gave up smoking for this," Tobias wheezed.

He grabbed the rope and started up, but the wood was slick, and he was exhausted. He didn't even make it halfway up before slipping down into the mud.

With every second, Shepherd and Bronfman were pulling farther ahead. I looked back and saw Reg Perry and Tim Douglas coming up fast.

Tobias gripped the rope for another try, but I shoved him out of the way and started hauling myself up. I didn't look back. I didn't want third place. I wanted first, and I knew I had a shot at it. This morning we'd done more underwater trials, and even though I was a bit better, I was still clumsy and slow. Tobias was by far the best. He was my friend, but he was also my competition. I needed an edge over him.

I scaled the wall, rappelled down the other side, and sprinted after Shepherd and Bronfman. Shepherd had the lead, and Bronfman was slowing. Maybe he thought he could slack off now. I gave it my all, and though I didn't catch up with Shepherd, I skimmed past Bronfman and heard his shout of annoyance as I crossed the finish line.

When Tobias came in sixth, I went over to him.

"Sorry about pushing you," I said.

He was hunched over, catching his breath. He waved a hand. "S'okay," he panted. "I was just slowing you down."

I thought he looked a little hurt, but I didn't regret what I'd done.

Day eleven, and I swung my aching body out of bed before I was even fully awake, the morning bell ringing in my ears. Like everyone else in the dorm, I sat for a moment, squinting at the notice board and the white piece of paper pinned in the middle. Wearily we all stood and made our way over. Bronfman was there first.

"Looks like you can sleep in, Cruse," he said.

I felt like I'd been punched in the stomach. I couldn't speak. I staggered over to the board.

There were two names on the paper, but neither of them was mine.

Bronfman slapped me on the shoulder, laughing. "Should've seen the look on your face, kid."

"You're an idiot, Bronfman," said Tobias.

"Hey, it was just a joke," the test pilot said, grinning. "Don't get your knickers in a twist."

I should've been angry, but all I felt was relief.

"Just some questions we'd like you to answer," said Grendel Eriksson, handing each of us a booklet as thick as an atlas. "Nothing too difficult."

"What's that?" Tobias asked, pointing across the room.

Suspended from a complicated set of scaffolding was a narrow metal tube. Attached to its outside were all sorts of wires and mechanical arms and hosing. There was a small hatch at one end of the tube, and a wheeled set of stairs pushed up to it.

"That's where you'll answer the questions," said Eriksson.

"One person goes in the tube?" I asked.

"Five people go in the tube," Eriksson said with a wicked smile.

It was day twelve, and we were down to thirty-six candidates. Our group had only five people now: me, Tobias, Shepherd, Bronfman, and Reg Perry.

"When you finish your questions, you can come out," said Eriksson. "In you go. Don't forget your pencils."

My stomach curdled. It was hard enough to see how one person would fit in that tube, much less five.

"Don't like small spaces?" Shepherd asked me.

"Doesn't bother me," I lied. And to show him I wasn't afraid, I climbed up the steps first.

The hatch was tiny, and I had to crawl through on my hands and knees. The tube had no windows, just a single, very dim light. I instantly regretted going in ahead of the others, for I'd have to move to the very end. The space was so cramped, it was hard to twist myself into sitting position. My knees were almost at my forehead. Tobias came next, then Shepherd, Bronfman, and Perry, all of us squishing tightly together.

Eriksson's face appeared outside the hatch. "If there're any problems, just sing out." And then he sealed us inside.

"This'll take hours!" Tobias said, flipping through his booklet. "It's eighty pages!"

"Best get at it," said Shepherd calmly, putting a piece of chewing gum in his mouth.

I did not feel calm. My heart pounded and it was hard to keep my panic reined in. Was this what our spaceship would be like? It couldn't be so small, could it? Maybe I wasn't cut out to be an astralnaut after all. I closed my eyes, but that only made things worse, plunging the world into blackness. I opened my eyes and stared at the metal beneath my feet, focusing on the rivets holding the plates together. Beyond the metal plates was the room, and the building, and beyond it the whole wide world. Somehow this thought helped ease my claustrophobia.

I got to work. The first page was multiple-choice questions, fairly simple logic problems. As I finished those, a mechanical drone came from outside, and the tube tilted—not a lot, just enough to slide us all to the right, pressing us against one another even more. Reg Perry, at the low end, got the worst of it.

"Can you get your elbow out of my armpit, Bronfman?" he said.

"Nowhere else for it to go," Bronfman replied.

The tube levelled off, then rotated suddenly. We all pitched forward, banging our heads on the wall. We shuffled on our bums, readjusting ourselves.

"How're we supposed to work like this?" Tobias demanded.

"That's the point," said Shepherd implacably, turning to the next page of his booklet.

I worked steadily for maybe ten minutes before noticing the sweat trickling down my flanks. I glanced over and saw everyone's forehead slick with perspiration.

"Hot in here," said Perry.

"Open a window, would you, Blanchard?" said Bronfman. "And feel free to jump."

"Bronfman, you smell bad," Tobias said.

"That's the sweet smell of success," the test pilot retorted. "I'm on page twelve, by the way."

I was only on page eight. My sweaty hand was smearing my answers.

"We'll run out of air at this rate," Perry said, a trace of alarm in his voice. "Is anyone else feeling dizzy?"

I did, but wasn't about to admit it.

"They're testing us," said Shepherd. "They want to see how we cope."

"This thing's got to be ventilated," said Tobias.

As if on cue, there came a loud hiss, and I could feel the tube cooling.

"That's better," said Perry.

But it got colder and colder, and before long I was shivering, the sweat icy against my skin. I tried to keep working, but my fingers were growing numb.

A deafening bang against the tube made me drop my pencil. Then came a second bang, and a third, from different parts of the tube. The bangs kept up. Soon my head was ringing. I saw Shepherd take the chewing gum from his mouth, break it in two, and stick it in both ears. He kept writing.

The banging went on for some time, and after the banging came a high shrieking sound that was even worse. When the shrieking finally stopped, the tube got very hot again and started swinging back and forth. I was used to the pitch and roll of airships, so the movement didn't bother me too much, but I saw Reg Perry dragging his hand across his sweaty forehead and looking a bit ill.

"Yee-haw!" said Bronfman. "This is my kinda ride!"

"Put a cork in it, Bronfman," said Perry.

"Can't take the heat, get out of the kitchen," Bronfman said, pumping his legs to make the tube swing higher.

I was worried Perry might take a punch at him, but at that moment the light went out. The tube suddenly seemed much, much smaller.

"Great," said Tobias. "How're we supposed to do the blinking questions?"

There was a tiny flare of light. Chuck Shepherd was holding a slim battery-powered torch. Its beam was very small and lit only the page of his booklet. He kept scribbling.

"You're a regular Boy Scout, Shepherd," I said.

"Always prepared," he said.

"Can you lean that light over here a little, Captain?" said Bronfman.

"No can do, Lieutenant," said Shepherd.

There was nothing to do but wait and sweat, and try to ignore the ripe smell that was building inside the tube. To my relief, the light came back on after five minutes, the swinging stopped, and we could all get back to our booklets.

"Damn it," Tobias muttered.

"What's wrong?" I asked.

"These math questions. Six pages of them. There's no way I can do these."

I was well into that section. Math had never come easily to me. At the Academy I'd struggled to master it, and now I mostly got by—but I could certainly handle the questions on this test.

"Just skip ahead," I told him, and kept working.

I wanted to beat him. I wanted to beat everyone. Shepherd and Bronfman might fly ornithopters, but I bet I'd spent more time aloft than both of them put together. The sky was my domain. And I certainly had more right to the stars than an underwater welder. I realized I was glad Tobias was having trouble—and it made me feel suddenly ugly. I remembered how I'd shoved him out of the way on the obstacle course.

"Here," I said, looking over. "Maybe I can help."

I started showing him how to solve some of the problems. Tobias was smart; he'd catch on quickly enough.

"What's the matter with you, Cruse?"

I looked up to see Shepherd staring at me in disgust.

"You've got an edge over him," the Aero Force captain told me. "You think you're gonna get on that spaceship by being a nice guy?"

Bronfman sniffed, as if he couldn't believe my stupidity.

Head-splitting screeching noises started up inside the tube, and I could feel the temperature drop swiftly. The tube began rotating back and forth in little erratic jerks. It was nearly impossible to read the questions.

"I don't know how much more of this I can take," muttered Perry.

"Just holler and Eriksson'll spring you," Shepherd said.

"More room for us," quipped Bronfman. "But I bet you find your name on that bulletin board bright and early."

"I've had just about enough of you, Bronfman," Perry said.

"Can never have too much of a good thing," said the test pilot.

"Bronfman," said Tobias, his teeth chattering, "you're so full of yourself I'm surprised you don't explode."

"Pipe down, all of you," said Shepherd. "The sooner you finish, the sooner you get to leave."

"Maybe there's a faster way," I said. I was so cold that I was surprised my brain was still functioning. "There're five of us. We divide the questions into five, and each does a chunk. We all finish at the same time. And we get out sooner."

"Sounds like cheating to me," said Bronfman, shivering, but I thought he seemed interested.

"Why's it cheating?" I said. "All Eriksson said was that when we were done, we could come out. He didn't say we couldn't work together."

"They want to see how we fly solo, Cruse," Shepherd said.

"To hell with that," Tobias said. "I'm in."

"Me too," said Perry.

"What about you, Bronfman?" I asked.

He stole a glance at Shepherd, and then shook his head. "Nice try, kid, but I trust my own answers, not yours."

We divvied up the rest of the questions three ways and got down to it. The tube swayed and jerked, grew hot and then cold again, and deafened us with its noises, but somehow we managed to finish the booklet.

Finally Reg Perry slapped the inside of the metal tube. "Hey! We're done in here! Let us out!"

Seconds later the hatch opened and Eriksson looked in. "That was quick. Who's done?"

"Me, Cruse, and Blanchard," Perry said.

"Interesting," said Eriksson, stepping back to make way.

It really did give me an amazing amount of pleasure to crawl over Shepherd and Bronfman on my way out.

"Big mistake, Cruse," the Aero Force captain murmured.

"Hey, watch your knees, Cruse!" Bronfman said.

"See you fellows later," I said. "We'll save some dinner for you."

Day thirteen, the last day of training, and my body was so sore I could barely sit up in bed. My eyes went to the piece of paper on the notice board. I feared my name really would be on it this time. Maybe Shepherd was right. Had we cheated inside the tube yesterday?

As usual, Bronfman was first to the board. He stared at it so long I wondered if he saw his own name there.

"Who got the chop today?" Shepherd asked, walking over.

"It's a death threat," said Bronfman.

"You're hilarious, Bronfman," I said.

"No joke," he said.

We were all over there in a trice. The typed note was brief

```
    Quit this dangerous enterprise before
              disaster befalls you.
      The heavens were not made for man.
```

There was no signature.

I felt a chill. Whoever had written this, they knew about the astralnaut program. They knew where our secret training facility was, and how to get inside.

Eriksson strode into our dorm with his clipboard. "Congratulations, gents, no one got cut today—what's this?" He had seen the note on the board, and angrily ripped it down. "Mr. Lunardi'll want to know about this," he said, and disappeared.

"Who'd write stuff like that?" Tobias asked.

"Babelites," I said, for I was suddenly sure.

"Who're they?" Perry asked.

"I had a run-in with them." And I told them about how they'd tried to use my ship to blow up the Celestial Tower. It was a good story, and even Bronfman kept his mouth shut till the end.

"How come I never read about this in the papers?" he said.

"They hushed it up," I said. "That tower's their new symbol of national pride. They don't want anyone knowing how close they came to losing it."

"Huh," said Bronfman dubiously, but he looked a bit uneasy.

"You told any of this to Lunardi?" Shepherd asked.

I shook my head.

"Might be a good idea," he said. "These fellows sound like halfwits, but they're halfwits with guns."

I nodded, and then quickly got dressed and made my way downstairs to find Mr. Lunardi.

It was unusually quiet in the cafeteria at breakfast—not just because there were only twenty-four of us left, but because everyone was nervously waiting to hear from Mr. Lunardi. I'd already been to his office and told him what I knew about the Babelites. He'd listened carefully. Then he thanked me very much and said he'd be speaking to us all shortly.

Now we all looked over as he strode in.

"Gentlemen," he said, holding up a note and whisking it about dismissively, "you've all seen these pinned up in your dorms. Doubtless they're the work of the Babelites." He smiled. "Some of you may have heard of these poor fellows. They think heaven is just above our heads. They're afraid we might anger God if we go to outer space. I would never dare anger God, gentlemen, but his creation is vast, and I don't believe heaven has such an exact location. The Babelites have been making all sorts of threats against the Celestial Tower in Paris. Most of them have been toothless, but, as you may have heard from Mr. Cruse, one of them was very dangerous indeed."

"How'd they find us?" said Bronfman. "I thought this place was supposed to be secret."

"I'm actually surprised it wasn't found out sooner," said Lunardi. "All it takes is one careless comment."

"How'd they get into the building, though?" Reg Perry asked.

"We've already taken measures to make sure it can't happen again," said Mr. Lunardi. "I'm doubling our security staff and changing all the locks."

"Sounds like some of them have pretty serious firepower," one of the other trainees said.

"I've just been on the telephone with the Ministry of Defence," said Mr. Lunardi. "They're confident the Babelites can't have had enough time to organize any significant threat over here. Likely these notes are the work of a single disgruntled fellow. He may not even be connected with the real Babelites."

The thought was reassuring. I looked around to see how everyone was taking this. Some of the trainees were nodding, relieved.

"Now, if anyone has misgivings," Lunardi went on, "you're free to step down from the program. I know some of you have families, and other responsibilities. The decision's yours. But remember who you are, gentlemen. You've all made it to the final trials. You're hammered from strong stuff. Your eyes are on outer space. Progress. The future of our nation and our world! Will we let a handful of lunatics deter us?"

"Hell, no," said Bronfman, and some of the other fellows laughed.

Reg Perry, I noticed, still looked a little unsure, as did Tobias. Shepherd was as inscrutable as always. He wouldn't be stepping down, and neither would I. I trusted Mr. Lunardi to take care of us.

Lunardi scanned the cafeteria and smiled. "Now, you have tomorrow off. Rest, relax, visit with friends and family if you can. I look forward to seeing you Monday for the final tests."

11 / A Cycle in Stanley Park

"**C**OME ALONG, MARJORIE!" Kate called back over her shoulder, "just once more around the park!"

Miss Simpkins was far behind us now, wobbling on her bicycle as she tried to keep up. She waved for us to slow down. Kate just waved back cheerfully and continued on.

"She'll never catch up," she said happily. "I adore my bicycle."

"Great invention," I said.

We pedalled along the broad boardwalk towards the regal span of Lionsgate Bridge. The weather was perfect, the breeze off the water just fresh enough to cool my sweat. It was Sunday afternoon, my day off before the final trials, and I'd rented a bike in Stanley Park. I had spent the morning with my mother and sisters, and Kate and I had arranged to meet now, as if by accident.

"What you said the other day to Miss Karr," I began cautiously, "about never getting married. You weren't serious, were you?"

She glanced over. "It makes perfect sense from my point of view."

"You don't think it would be . . . lonely?"

"I'm sure it would, sometimes. But if you want to achieve

your goals, it's sometimes necessary to make sacrifices."

"I don't really like the idea of being a sacrifice," I said.

"Well, it's not like I'm going to burn you at the stake or anything," Kate said.

"You'll just keep me around in a cage," I muttered. "Like one of your specimens."

She grinned. "Well, you are quite an *appealing* specimen."

"You don't mean any of this," I said impatiently. I checked over my shoulder and couldn't see Miss Simpkins any more. "Let's turn off here."

Kate peered down the narrow forest path. She raised an eyebrow at me. "I don't think that trail would make for easy bicycling."

"It'd wear us out," I agreed. "We could always have a rest."

"In the shadows behind a large tree, perhaps?"

"Most likely," I said.

Kate and I hadn't been properly alone since we'd left Paris, and I was desperate to hold her and kiss her. Maybe I could get her to admit she wasn't serious about never marrying.

"It's not a good idea," Kate said playfully. "You obviously haven't heard of Mimsy Rogers."

"Who?"

"Earlier this summer, she said she was just going off to have a bicycle in Stanley Park. A little while later some family friends were hiking in the forest and they spotted Mimsy's bicycle against a tree. A few paces on, they saw someone else's bicycle against a tree, and a few paces after that, they saw Mimsy Rogers in a passionate embrace with Michael Wright. It caused quite a scandal."

The words *passionate embrace* made my heart beat harder. "When have *you* ever cared about causing a scandal?" I asked.

"There's nothing I'd like more than a good kiss in the woods," Kate said, "but I don't have time right now. I've got to be somewhere at four, and I don't want to be all rumpled."

"Tea with James Sanderson, maybe?" I asked.

"No. It's a secret."

We pedalled on along the boardwalk in silence. I tried not to let my disappointment—or jealousy—show. I didn't know when we'd have another chance to be alone—I couldn't imagine we'd have any aboard the spaceship. Assuming I even made it onto the ship . . . My thoughts drifted uneasily to the final trials that awaited me.

"I really want to be on this expedition," I said.

"You *will* be," she said.

Maybe I should've been flattered by her confidence, but I felt irritated. She really had no idea. "It's not that easy," I said. "There're still over twenty candidates, and they're all good."

"Not as good as you."

"I wish. I'm weak in some areas. In the suit, especially."

I told her about the underwater training, and how even after three sessions I was still clumsy. She said nothing for a moment, and I wished I'd held my tongue. Maybe she didn't like hearing about my shortcomings. Kate had very high standards. I didn't imagine she'd be very tolerant of failure.

"If people try hard enough, they usually get what they want," she said.

I glanced over at her, annoyed. "Easy for you to say."

"What do you mean?"

"Well, they just *invited* you. You didn't even have to prove yourself."

"Prove myself?" she said, glaring. She reached over and tried to shove me off my bicycle.

"Hey!" I said, swerving out of reach.

"So all the reading and studying and discovering I've been doing, that doesn't count as *proving myself*?"

She veered over to have another go at me, but I was ready this time, and braked. She overshot and teetered off her bike. Luckily she landed on the soft wood chips beside the boardwalk. I dropped my bike and hurried over to her.

"Are you all right?" I asked, holding out my hand.

She ignored my hand and got up herself, dusting her skirt off. "Mr. Lunardi and Sir John invited me because of what I'd already accomplished," she said, looking at me coolly. "I've *already* proven myself. Now *you* have to prove yourself."

"I will," I said. "Like I've always done."

"Well, make sure you do, because Miss Karr likes you— for some *bizarre* reason—and if you don't come, she might change her mind again."

"Is that the only reason you want me to come?"

"No, just one of them."

We got back on our bikes, though our conversation shrivelled up after that. I was too angry and hurt to rush in and patch things up. Let Kate do that, I thought. But she too was silent.

"I didn't mean to insult you," I said finally. "It just seems easy for you, that's all."

"Well, it's not. Men always think they're more deserving than women. It's just like Mrs. Pankhurst said."

"I'm tired of Mrs. Pankhurst," I muttered.

"And she's tired of you too." Then Kate smiled. "Sorry for trying to push you off your bike. The look on your face was very satisfying, though."

When we neared the main road leading back into the city, Kate checked her pocket watch.

"I should get going," she said.

"Where?" I persisted. What was it she'd rather do than spend the rest of the afternoon with me?

"You don't want to know," she said. "And it's nothing to do with you."

"You won't tell me?"

She shook her head.

I was near crazed with curiosity by now. "I'm coming."

"Don't," she said.

"I'm coming."

"Suit yourself."

Pedalling hard, she took the city road out of the park.

"What about Miss Simpkins?" I asked.

"She knows the way home."

Kate was very quiet as she led us downtown. We turned onto Rostrum Street with all its smart shops and fine ladies and gentlemen, and nannies pushing rich babies in their prams. Kate coasted to a stop in front of Wittmer's department store and tipped her bike against the wall. She looked into the shop window.

"Now listen," she whispered. "You might want to stay on your bike."

I was confused. "Why?"

"Just get ready to leave when I say." Her eyes narrowed and slid slyly from side to side.

"Kate, what's going on?"

I looked around suspiciously, but noticed nothing unusual. Kate stared hard at the fur coat in the window, the front of her blouse rising and falling rapidly with her breathing.

The art gallery clock chimed the hour.

From the wicker basket on her bicycle, Kate produced a hammer.

"Is that a hammer?" I asked stupidly.

"Yes," she said. "The biggest I could find. Watch your eyes—" And with that she swung the hammer at the window.

"What're you doing?" I exclaimed.

"Making a statement," she said, as glass shattered and sprayed everywhere. Twice more she swung the hammer, and the sound of breaking glass wasn't coming just from Kate's window. Up and down the street, hammers flashed in the gloved hands of elegantly dressed women. The sidewalks were instantly awash with glass. Nannies screamed and wheeled their prams out into the street. Cars began honking. I thought I heard a policeman's whistle, and then came the shouting of shop owners rushing to their doorsteps.

Kate dropped her hammer on the sidewalk and seized her bicycle. "We're off!" she cried, her cheeks flushed. She hopped on and scooted away.

Stupefied, I followed. There was a traffic jam now, as dozens of women on bicycles fled the scene. A couple had already been seized by gentlemen, and there was much shouting and screaming.

Kate glanced back at me, and I don't think I'd ever seen her eyes brighter. "What would your mother think of me now?" she asked.

Suddenly a policeman stepped out in front of us, and a man from behind shouted, "That's her! And the young fellow too! Grab them!"

Kate tried to swerve around him, but the policeman grabbed her handlebars and then mine.

"Hold up there!" the officer shouted. "You'll be coming with me to the station, the both of you."

"Would you like some of my bread?" Kate asked.

"I'm not hungry," I said.

"It's not a bit stale. I always thought they only gave stale bread, but it's quite fresh. Really, I've been most impressed by how courteously—"

"We're in jail, Kate."

We were crammed into a holding cell in the basement of the Lionsgate police station. The police had clearly rounded up a great many window smashers, for we had no shortage of company. It was as merry a scene as you were likely to find in a jail cell. Apart from the bewildered drunken man cowering in one corner, it was all ladies in their white blouses and long skirts and summer hats. There must've been over twenty. Some of them were cheerfully chanting slogans and singing bits of inspiring hymns.

"A bit quieter if you don't mind, ladies," moaned the drunk. "My head's hurting something awful."

"Look," Kate said to me, "I tried to tell them you weren't my accomplice, but they didn't believe me."

Apart from the drunk, I was the only man in the cell, and some of the ladies were making a fuss of me.

"What a noble young man!"

"Our brother in arms!"

"I think it's commendable you're supporting our cause," said a woman in a big flowered hat.

"I'm not really," I said.

"Not many men would link arms with us for equality and justice. Mrs. Pankhurst would be very proud of you, young man!"

I smiled weakly.

"I must say, I did enjoy it," Kate said. "I'm sorry I didn't give you a chance with the hammer."

"That's all right," I said. "I'm not quite ready to become a window-smashing lunatic."

"All we want is the right to vote, Matt, same as men. But they won't listen to us, so we have to make ourselves heard." Kate grinned. "I think they heard that, don't you?"

"I can't believe the trouble you've caused me," I said.

"Look, I did tell you not to come. Anyway, you've done nothing wrong. It's a simple misunderstanding. Once my father arrives to get me out, he'll be able to sort—" Her voice trailed off. "No, no, he can't do that."

"What?" I said.

Kate looked desperate. "If my father sees you here, he'll know we were together, and that would open up Pandora's box."

"Can't you just tell him we ran into each other on the street?"

She snorted. "He wouldn't believe that. I could tell he suspected something at the garden party. He thinks we're having a . . . liaison."

"They're having a liaison!" the woman in the big hat said to her friend. "'They've found love in a jail cell—"

"There's no liaison!" I said.

Kate pulled me deeper into the cell. "Daddy can't know you're here. When he comes, um, just cower back here."

I stared at her in mounting anger. "You're joking."

"And maybe turn your face to the wall."

"You're going to waltz out of here without me?"

Kate spoke in a taut whisper. "My parents are going to be upset enough as it is. But if they think I'm sneaking around with you too, they might not let me go on the expedition."

I was almost shouting. "And what about me? If I don't show up for my final trials tomorrow, they'll kick me out. I'll be finished!"

"Call your mother," Kate said. "She can get you out."

"I don't want her to know!"

"My father knows!"

A great flash came from the other side of the bars, and I turned, blinking, to see a wiry press photographer beaming at us over his camera.

"That's lovely, thanks very much, ladies—oh, and gentleman. Don't worry, sir, you made it into the picture too. Tomorrow's early edition, if you're interested."

Kate and I stared at each other in stunned silence.

"Well," she said. "Now that we're in the paper together, I suppose Daddy can get you out too."

"Thanks," I said. "Thanks very much."

12 / The Final Trials

"**T**HIS IS YOU, is it not, Mr. Cruse?" asked Sir John McKinnon, the Minister of Air. He pointed to the photograph on the front page of the *Lionsgate Times Herald*. There I was, beside Kate, amongst a large group of jailed suffragettes, some of whom looked very pleased to have their picture in the paper.

"It is, sir, but I can explain."

It was first thing Monday morning, and I'd been summoned to Mr. Lunardi's office. He sat behind his desk, glowering. Captain Walken stood nearby, his face grave.

"I hope it's a very good explanation, Mr. Cruse," said Sir John.

I told them, as simply as I could, about the window-smashing incident, and how my presence was just an unhappy coincidence.

"You had no idea what Miss de Vries meant to do?" Sir John asked.

"None, sir."

"The young lady's very strong-willed," said Captain Walken "We saw that when the *Aurora* was shipwrecked."

"If I'd known she was a suffragette," said Sir John, "I'd never have invited her. Our government doesn't look kindly on anarchists. Smashing windows! What a load of nonsense!"

I took a deep breath. "But her cause is right, sir."

"What's that?" Sir John snapped.

It was too late to go back now. "Women should have the right to vote, sir."

"Outlandish," said Sir John. "I won't hear of it."

I looked from Mr. Lunardi to Captain Walken, wondering what they were thinking. I worried I'd just set myself apart from both of them. It was a very lonely feeling, but I'd said what I believed and wouldn't try to take it back.

"I'm sure," Mr. Lunardi said carefully, "that we all have our own views of the suffragettes. But let's put them aside for now. Politics has no place on our expedition."

"It's not that simple," said Sir John. "Miss de Vries's name and photograph are in the paper. If we publicly announce she's part of our expedition, there will be an outcry. I won't have her besmirching the Canadian space program. She's out, gentlemen."

I was about to object, but Captain Walken caught my eye and silenced me with a small shake of his head.

"I think that would be a great shame," Captain Walken said to Sir John. "Miss de Vries can be headstrong, certainly, but I've never met a young lady who's smarter or braver."

Mr. Lunardi nodded. "At such short notice, it'll be difficult, if not impossible, to find someone of her knowledge and abilities."

"We can delay the launch," said Sir John. "I don't see what choice we have."

"We do have a choice and it's ours to make," said Mr. Lunardi, standing and pacing, hands thrust into his pockets. "I'll be frank. I wish Miss de Vries hadn't got her picture in the paper, but I don't want to replace her for it. She's perfect for this expedition, and I know you feel the same."

"The Government of Canada—" Sir John began, but Mr. Lunardi cut him off.

"I'm an equal partner in this venture, and I don't want second best here. I despise compromises for appearance's sake. My ship is ready to launch, and I don't think anyone, including the Prime Minister, would want us to delay and risk being beaten by another country."

It was quite a speech, and I was awfully impressed—and grateful.

Sir John gave a harrumph and gazed out the window. "Very well, we'll keep her on, but I'll be writing her a very stiff letter this morning, forbidding her from any more suffragette shenanigans." The Minister of Air looked at me. "And what of Mr. Cruse here?"

"He's blameless," said Mr. Lunardi. "I'll make sure the paper prints as much in the evening edition."

"Thank you, sir," I said, feeling completely wrung out.

"You're free to go, Mr. Cruse," said Mr. Lunardi. "And good luck today."

Captain Walken came out into the hallway with me. "That young woman has a habit of getting you into trouble," he said with a chuckle. "I can still see the two of you on the island after the *Aurora* was shipwrecked. She'd dragooned you into searching the jungle with her, and you two came out after the typhoon hit, soaked to the skin. I don't think I'd ever seen a lad look more miserable."

"It was the ship, sir—seeing her so tattered and torn."

The captain gave me a kind look. "When I wasn't much older than you, I had a rather ill-advised romance. I was like you, Matt, from a humble family, but her people were wealthy. It caused no end of trouble."

I'd never known this about him, and I feared what he would say next.

"Everyone told us no good could come of it," Captain Walken said.

"What happened, sir?" I asked hesitantly.

"I married her," he said, and grinned. "We celebrated our thirtieth anniversary this year."

I grinned back. "I like the ending to that story."

"But put her from your thoughts now and get some break-fast, Matt. You've got a long day ahead of you."

"Gentlemen," said Captain Walken as he stood on the pool deck, "here is your situation, and it is a dire one. The hull of your ship has been breached and you are outside to replace the damaged metal plate. But time is of the essence; the ship is losing pressure and oxygen, and you only have half an hour. What's more, you're working on the dark side of the ship, and your helmet-mounted lamp is your only source of illumination. Work swiftly; every second counts."

Ten of us were getting suited up, just waiting to put on our helmets. I knew the captain wasn't simply being dramatic. We were being timed, and if I did poorly this morning, I hadn't a hope. My stomach was in knots.

"Good luck, Matt," Tobias said beside me.

"You too."

"Hey, Cruse, what's that on your back?" Bronfman asked.

"What is it?" I asked, worried that something was wrong with my suit.

Some of the other fellows were looking over at me and laughing, but I couldn't see what they were looking at, or reach it with my stiff arms. Tobias turned me around—and snorted. He peeled off a piece of paper and handed it to me.

Votes for Women, it said.

I couldn't help chuckling. "Good one, Bronfman."

He frowned at me, as if he wasn't sure whether I was being sarcastic. But I was honestly glad of the joke.

"Good luck, Cruse," Shepherd said, as an assistant put his helmet over his head.

"Thanks, Shepherd," I said in surprise.

"You're going to need it," he said.

I looked over at Tobias and shook my head. "I thought he was actually being nice there for a second."

"Don't worry about him," Tobias said with a wink. "Remember: you're a shark."

And then there was no more time to talk, for the helmet was coming down over my head. I took one last breath of free air. The clamp snapped tight.

We all took our places under the cranes, and the winches

lifted us up and swung us out over the water. Overhead, the rows of lamps shut down one by one, and then I was sinking fast, my helmet lantern boring a column of lonely light into the dark water. I touched down, felt my suit inflating to make me weightless, and got to work.

This was my fourth dive, and though I still battled feelings of panic, I was a bit more practised at moving under water. My pulse beat like the ticking of a clock, reminding me I only had thirty minutes.

I reached my segment of ship's hull, a curving metal wall about ten feet high. In the pitch darkness, it took me a minute to find the damaged plate—and my heart sank. It was high up. I carefully climbed the metal rungs protruding from the hull. Four bolts needed removing, so I pulled the socket wrench from my tool pouch and began. It was slow, exhausting work, but it went smoothly. Soon the last bolt fell to the pool floor, followed by the damaged plate.

I took some deep breaths. I didn't feel panicky. I was starting to like the weightlessness, though I still hated being enclosed in the suit.

Now to install the new plate. I'd seen it earlier, tilted against the hull on the pool bottom. I climbed back down the rungs, grabbed it, and made my way back up. This part was much harder, for I somehow had to hold the plate in place while driving the first bolt home. Wedging my boots into two footholds, I grasped on a handhold above the plate, holding the plate in place with my body. With my one free hand, I gripped the socket wrench. I was already soaked with sweat.

It would have been impossible to handle something as small as a bolt in my gloved hand. Luckily Lunardi's team had invented a new kind of socket wrench, one with a hollow shaft, bolts already loaded inside, one behind the other, ready to screw in.

One went in, then the second. I was making good time. I readjusted my grip on the wrench—and dropped it. I made a grab for it, but it had already fallen out of the circle of light from my lamp.

Clumsily I pushed myself down the hull, jerking my helmet lamp in all directions. I couldn't see the wrench anywhere. Without it I couldn't finish the job. My minutes were ticking away. My visor started to fog from my panting. Without the wrench I would never make it to outer space with Kate. I was staggering about in despair when I felt someone grip my shoulder. Looking up, I saw Tobias. He was holding my wrench up for me.

"Thank you," I wheezed inside my helmet.

He pressed the wrench into my hand and I gripped it tightly. Then he stepped back, signalled with his hands, and floated up as his suit inflated. He was already done, and I had only two more bolts to screw into place.

I hauled myself up the hull once more. Got the third bolt in. But before I could do the fourth, my suit inflated and I was lifted up through the water, the wrench still in my hand, my task unfinished. I'd run out of time.

Strapped into our parawing packs, we perched on bench seats, facing one another across the cramped airship cabin as we climbed to eleven thousand feet. Earlier in the day we'd sprinted through a series of other tests, but this was the last.

"Five minutes," Eriksson shouted above the engine noise. "The landing zone's much smaller this time around. We're looking for accuracy and speed here."

We'd already done three jumps during the training program, but I'd had even more practice at the Academy. I was good with the wings; I understood the air and knew how to ride the wind. But I was still nervous about this jump. I felt tired in every muscle and joint of my body, and I figured I needed to do well, very well, to make up for my poor showing in the pool. Even so, I wasn't sure it would be enough. The two Aero Force test pilots were also experienced parawingers, especially Shepherd. I'd hoped I could at least be best at this one thing, but I'd seen Shepherd come in swift and steep as a falcon. I didn't know if he was as good as me, but he was close.

I looked over at Tobias. I knew he was anxious. He managed with his wings, but it didn't come naturally to him. I could see his right hand in his pocket, rubbing the bit of space rock for good luck. His eyes moved restlessly around the cabin.

"What're you scribbling now, Eriksson?" he asked.

Our group leader didn't even look up.

"Let me look at that clipboard," Tobias said. "I don't know about the rest of you, but I want to know what they're saying about me."

"You'll find out soon enough," Eriksson said.

"How many of us are going to outer space?" I asked. "Just give us a number. Can't hurt now."

"Sorry, gents."

Tobias reached across and yanked the clipboard from Eriksson's hands.

"Hey, Blanchard!" Eriksson grabbed for it, but Tobias tossed it to me.

Laughing, I tossed it on to Perry, who kept it going while Eriksson scrambled after it.

"This is confidential information!" he exclaimed.

The clipboard landed in Shepherd's lap and he calmly picked it up and held it out to Eriksson.

"Thanks, Shepherd."

"We already know *we're* going to outer space," Bronfman smirked.

Tobias looked at me, his mouth twitching. "Someone never got the modesty talk from Mommy," he said, and I wondered if the altitude was making him giddy.

But I couldn't stop my laughter from joining his, and before long half the other fellows were chuckling too.

"Pull yourselves together, men," said Eriksson, still looking indignant. "We're almost over the drop zone. Double-check your harnesses."

As Eriksson stood, I saw, pushed back underneath the bench seat, a small crate. I suddenly felt very sober.

"What's that?" I asked. "Under your seat."

"Hmm?" Eriksson glanced down distractedly. "Don't know."

"If you don't know, who does?" I said.

"Just some extra gear, likely. What's the problem, Cruse?"

"Someone should know what the box is," I said, my heart kicking against my ribs. There must have been a tone of command in my voice, because Eriksson stared at me.

"Cruse is having a little case of nerves," Bronfman remarked.

"You think there's something in there?" Tobias asked me, frowning.

"Cruse is right," said Shepherd. "Who brought that crate aboard?"

None of the other trainees knew anything about it. Eriksson went up front to ask the two pilots. I saw them both look back and shake their heads.

"You think that little thing's a bomb?" Bronfman demanded.

I swallowed. "I'm going to find out." I stood and pulled the crate carefully out from underneath the bench. It was marked PEARSON'S AIR CHANDLERY. I opened the clasp and pulled back the lid. Nestled in wood shavings were two replacement running lights for the ship.

"You're a hero, Cruse," sneered Bronfman.

I felt embarrassed, but I wasn't sorry I'd done it. I would never forget that experience aboard my aerotug.

Tobias clapped my shoulder. "Better safe than sorry," he said.

"All right," said Eriksson, "thank you for that little bit of drama, Cruse. Now let's get to it, shall we? Blanchard, you're out first, Cruse next . . ."

He ran through the jump order and then opened the cabin's hatch. He pointed.

"Your landing site is that field. It's about two miles due north. You're going to have to do some flying to get there. Go!"

I watched Tobias's face clench, and then he jumped.

"Cruse, go!" shouted Eriksson.

I jumped, shaping myself to the wind as I fell, nose to my target. I had ten seconds of free fall before I deployed my wings. Below me I could see Tobias. I watched for his wings to burst from his pack. They didn't. I counted one second, two—

Something was wrong.

I saw his hand reach back, fumbling with his pack.

Folding back my arms, I angled my body and streaked down towards him. I collided hard against him, but managed to hold tight. His eyes were huge with fear.

"Won't open!" he shouted.

I pulled myself around to his front and looked for his ripcord. It must have torn clean off, for I couldn't see it anywhere. That cord triggered a spring-loaded pilot chute that would fly up and drag out the parawings.

The ground was coming up fast. Tobias was clinging to me with all his might. I had to make a decision. I could open my wings and hope they were strong enough to carry both of us—but I knew there was almost no chance Tobias could hold on to me, especially during the violent deceleration. Only one other choice . . .

"I'm going to try to trigger your chute!" I shouted at him. I needed to get around to his back, but he wouldn't release his grip on me. "Tobias, let go!"

He clung to me like a drowning man.

I hated to do it but there was no other way. I punched him in the face. His grip loosened and I dragged him around in mid-air so I could get at his pack. I tore it open. I saw the cylinder that contained the pilot chute—the spring mechanism was missing altogether. I clawed open the cylinder's hatch, reached in with two fingers, and yanked out the top of the pilot chute.

Still holding on to it, I kicked myself free of Tobias and opened my arms and legs wide to slow myself down. Tobias fell faster, drawing out the pilot chute to its proper length. I tumbled out of the way as the chute opened and, a split second later, dragged the wings out of Tobias's pack. There! He was flying!

I pulled my own ripcord, and my harness straps bit into me as the wings soared. Without the free-fall wind it was suddenly very quiet. But I got a shock when I looked down and saw how close the ground was. Tobias and I had fallen too far, too fast. We needed to lose a lot of speed to avoid breaking our legs—or worse. Our only hope was to steer ourselves through a series of sharp turns.

I looked up and signalled to Tobias. He wasn't very good at turns, and I could only hope he'd be able to follow my lead. Desperately I scanned the area for our landing site, and realized we weren't going to make it. But with a bit of luck we'd get a soft landing in a bordering field.

I started my turns, pulling hard on my lines, willing myself to lose speed. It was all happening too quickly. Below me, trees were coming up fast, and then I was soaring over a fence into a field and corn was crackling beneath me as I landed, dumping the air from my wings before tripping and rolling over and over. I heard the rustle of Tobias's wings as he careened into the field, cutting a swath through the cornstalks.

I scrambled up, jubilant that I had no broken bones, and staggered over to Tobias. He'd pushed himself up on his hands and knees, his face ashen. But he was alive, and he didn't seem to be injured—aside from the bruise I'd made on his face.

He got to his feet and grabbed me by the shoulders, shaking me, his eyes blazing with disbelief. "I thought I was going to die!" he shouted.

"Me too," I said. "I thought we both might. Those were good turns you made up there."

"You saved my life!" he said, and hugged me with surprising strength for someone who'd nearly died. "When you first knocked into me I thought you were some enormous bird!

'Lighter than air,' isn't that what they used to say about you?"

I nodded, laughing. "They did. They did say that."

Someone had sabotaged Tobias's parawing pack. There was no question. When we examined it later, it turned out the ripcord had been snipped and the pilot chute's spring mechanism torn out.

Grendel Eriksson had not returned to the training facility.

Our airship had returned to its airfield and the pilots said they'd seen Eriksson get into a motorcar and drive off. Mr. Lunardi was furious. He believed Eriksson was working alone, and vowed he would be caught swiftly and brought to justice.

Three of the other candidates dropped out that evening, Tim Douglas and another two fellows. They'd had enough. I didn't blame them. Tobias had nearly died, and who knew what might happen next. I just hoped Mr. Lunardi was right— that Eriksson was acting alone and that he'd soon be behind bars.

That night on the terrace, everyone was pretty quiet, stunned that we'd had a Babelite in our midst the entire time.

"I knew he was sadistic," said Reg Perry, "but I never thought he was a killer."

"I hope he took his fecking clipboard with him," Tobias muttered.

I slipped away to call Kate from the pay telephone, but it was Miss Simpkins who answered. She told me Kate was not at home, and that I'd best not call again. I wanted to shout at her, but she hung up too quickly.

I needed to talk to my Kate. I needed to tell her what had happened to me today. And I needed to hear what had happened to her after the jail incident. Were her parents going to let her go on the expedition?

As for me, I had no idea whether I'd be going. Mr. Lunardi and Captain Walken had congratulated me heartily for saving Tobias's life, but I wasn't at all sure that would help me.

I wouldn't find out till tomorrow night.

13 / The First Astralnauts

THE GRAND BALLROOM of the Hotel Lionsgate was packed. Reporters jostled with photographers and newsreel cameramen, and the toast of the town were there in their evening finery. Lunardi had wanted a big event and he'd got one. Tonight he would announce the first voyage into outer space—and introduce the world's first astralnauts.

I'd arrived with Tobias, and we meandered about, tongue-tied, eyes skittering around the room.

"This is agony," I said. "Lunardi might've told us beforehand."

"Maybe he only told the people who got chosen," Tobias said glumly.

That was a terrible thought. I searched for the other finalists, trying to see if they looked happy and relaxed. I spotted Shepherd and Bronfman, together as usual, but even Bronfman seemed subdued.

"I don't think anyone knows," I said.

"It's more than a bit cruel," said Tobias, and he wandered off to find a drink.

I could barely stand still. The mayor was here, and various magnates, and the chancellor of the university. Across the room I caught sight of the French ambassador. He was smiling and chatting, but when I saw him snap at his assistant, I could tell he was anxious. No doubt he was worried that his Celestial Tower was under threat.

I'd been keeping an eye out for Kate, and when I saw her enter with her parents, I felt a double jolt of joy and nervousness. I didn't know whether I should go to her. Fortunately, she spotted me, and soon left her parents to move through the crowd. She was looking very fine in a burgundy evening dress with white opera gloves.

"Hello," she said. She looked ill at ease, and didn't even offer me her hand.

I looked past her and saw Mr. and Mrs. de Vries watching us with severe expressions.

"I tried to telephone," I said. "Is everything all right?"

She gave a nod. "My parents are still letting me go. Sir John wrote me a blistering letter, though. Sounds like he came close to cutting me."

"He wasn't happy. Lunardi and Captain Walken spoke up for you."

"And you?"

"Of course I did!"

She gave an apologetic smile. "I hope you didn't get into too much trouble."

"They knew I was just an innocent victim of a criminal mastermind."

"Do you know yet, if you're going?"

I shook my head. "We all find out at the same time."

From deep within the room came the sound of an animal

shrieking. I peered into the crowd and saw a small, furry shape dancing about on someone's shoulder.

"Is that Haiku?" I asked.

Kate squinted. "I think you're right, but—he's not on Miss Karr's shoulder . . ."

Haiku's screeching grew all the louder as the crowd fell silent, trying to see what the commotion was.

"Somebody get this bloody monkey off me!" roared a man.

"Leave him alone!" came a powerful woman's voice that I recognized instantly as Miss Evelyn Karr's. "What are you doing to the poor animal?"

Finally the crowd parted and I could see that Haiku was having a temper tantrum, beating his little fists against a gentleman's head.

"Isn't that—?" I began.

"Yes," Kate said, aghast, "it's Sir Hugh Snuffler."

"Why is Haiku attacking him?"

"Animals despise Sir Hugh," Kate explained.

"But he's a zoologist!"

Kate shrugged. "He can't walk down a street without a dog biting him or a bird defecating on his head. Even indoors he's not safe. I've seen it myself. He was giving a lecture once, and a skinny little rat ran across the stage, stopped, and then ran back and *hurled* itself at his pant leg. One of the most amazing things I've ever seen. But what on earth is Sir Hugh doing *here?*"

Miss Karr reached Sir Hugh and plucked Haiku off his shoulder. The moment the monkey was in her arms, he became meek and quiet, his brown eyes huge, as if he'd been the one beaten about the head.

"Madam," bellowed Sir Hugh, "your monkey has mussed me!"

"How dare you!" Miss Karr bellowed back. "You've obviously frightened him. Poor Haiku," she said soothingly to her monkey. "There now, that disagreeable man's gone."

"I hope Haiku's better behaved on the ship," Kate said.

Mr. Lunardi had not been happy when Kate told him the monkey was coming, but even he hadn't dared to argue with Miss Karr.

"Ladies and gentlemen!"

We all turned to the stage as Mr. Lunardi strode out like a circus ringmaster, arms held wide.

"Welcome, and thank you for coming on such short notice. For weeks the newspapers have carried rumours about an astralnaut training program in our city. I am happy to tell you they are all true. The Lunardi Corporation, in partnership with the Government of Canada, has created a vessel that will take us into the heavens. And we have just selected the astralnauts who will embark on the first ever voyage to outer space!"

There was a moment's stunned silence, and then the audience erupted into thunderous applause.

"This is history in the making, ladies and gentlemen," said Lunardi. "And I don't think I need remind you that all over the world, others have been striving to do the same, so far without success. We Canadians shall be the first!"

There was another burst of applause. I found the French ambassador in the crowd. His face was pale with outrage. He seemed to snarl something at his assistant, and the two turned and walked towards the exit.

"Aboard our ship," Lunardi continued, "we will carry some of the world's most eminent experts, whom I would like to introduce to you now. To chronicle our maiden voyage in words and pictures is the celebrated photographer and writer Miss Evelyn Karr. Miss Karr, please join us."

The crowd parted, keeping well clear of Haiku's reach, as Miss Karr stomped across the ballroom and took her place on stage, towering over Mr. Lunardi. The applause grew all the more enthusiastic when Haiku leapt onto the airship magnate's shoulder and gave him a vigorous handshake.

"Now then," Mr. Lunardi continued, "this expedition would have been quite impossible without the phenomenal scientific knowledge of Dr. Sergei Turgenev. He has, shall we say, paved the road to outer space for us, and he will serve aboard our ship as chief science officer. Dr. Turgenev, please."

Leaning on his cane, the Russian scientist walked to the stage and wearily raised his hand to the crowd, in a gesture more of resignation than triumph.

I could see that Kate was getting agitated, clearing her throat and rustling her gloved hands against her dress, waiting for her name to be called.

"Of course," Mr. Lunardi went on from the stage, "we have little idea of what awaits us in outer space, but we must be prepared for extraterrestrial life."

I looked over at Kate and smiled encouragingly. Her cheeks were glowing, her eyes bright.

"And so," said Mr. Lunardi, "to observe the flora and fauna of the heavenly ether, our expedition will be joined by the illustrious zoologist Sir Hugh Snuffler."

My breath snagged in my throat. I turned to Kate, whose face was suddenly quite pale.

"Mr. Lunardi never mentioned anything about this," she hissed to me over the applause. "If I'd known, I'd have . . ."

"Gone anyway," I said.

"I'm furious," she muttered.

"And working with Sir Hugh," Mr. Lunardi was saying now, "will be Lionsgate City's very own Miss Kate de Vries, who specializes in high-altitude life forms. Sir Hugh, Miss de Vries, if you'd be so good as to join our team on stage."

Kate was breathing again, and she began making her way to the front, wearing a smile that might have looked more at home on a wax dummy. I caught a glimpse of Sir Hugh as he passed, still patting his mussed hair and not looking at all pleased. I wondered if he was as surprised as Kate.

They made it to the stage and stood on opposite sides of Mr. Lunardi. Haiku had spotted Sir Hugh, and even from a distance was shaking his tiny fist and making threatening swipes at him.

"Ladies and gentlemen," said Mr. Lunardi, "I present to you the specialist team aboard the first voyage to outer space!"

I watched Kate on stage as she waved and smiled at the

audience. Cameras flashed. She seemed so far away, and I felt like I was peering through a telescope at stars I had no hope of ever reaching.

"And who," said Lunardi, "you're now wondering, will pilot these brilliant minds to outer space?"

The whir of newsreel cameras was the only noise to be heard as a hush fell over the audience.

"It gives me great pleasure to introduce to you the commander of the expedition, as fine a pilot as ever sailed the skies, Captain Samuel Walken."

Captain Walken strolled onto the stage and waited for the applause to die down. "These past two weeks," he said, "a group of truly exceptional gentlemen has been undergoing rigorous trials. By the end we narrowed the candidates to twenty. But only three will be joining this first expedition."

Three! I'd never thought it would be so few. What chance could I have? Across the silent ballroom Tobias and I caught sight of each other and moved together. My insides were roiling.

"There's no way," Tobias whispered to me. "The underwater stuff's all I was good at."

"These then," announced Captain Walken, "are the astralnauts who will form our crew. From Halifax, Mr. Chuck Shepherd!"

Shepherd gave no whoop of joy, just strode purposefully towards the stage as if he'd never had any doubt he'd be called. The crowd parted around him, applauding wildly.

"I'd have chosen him too," I murmured.

"Makes perfect sense," Tobias said, his eyes fixed on the stage, where Lunardi was shaking Shepherd's hand. Camera bulbs exploded enough light for a fireworks display.

One down, two to go.

"From Victoria," Captain Walken said, "Mr. Tobias Blanchard!"

It was my shout of pleasure that drew everyone's eyes, for Tobias himself was mute. I grabbed him by the shoulders. "You did it!" I said.

He nodded, dazed.

"You're an astralnaut!" I said. "Go on!" And I gave him a little shove.

Even though it meant there was one less place for me, I was glad for him. The way he moved weightlessly under water was a marvel. He had the fire too, kindled by that bit of space rock he kept in his pocket. Maybe I'd be searingly jealous of him later, but right now, I felt only delight to see him walking up onto the stage and shaking everyone's hand.

"And finally," Captain Walken called out, "the last member of our crew . . ."

I took a deep breath.

" . . . from Saskatoon, Mr. Joshua Bronfman!"

As the applause rang out, I had to remind myself to let out my breath, and smile, and clap. Bronfman was whooping and hollering and pumping his fist in the air as he jogged up onto the stage. I felt ashamed. I was glad I'd not asked my mother and sisters to be here tonight. I couldn't look at Kate, in case she was watching me with pity in her eyes. I'd failed, and she'd think less of me now. I thought less of myself.

I had tried to be sensible, had realized that my chances were slim. I was still clumsy in the suit, I fought claustrophobia. I was the youngest, and wasn't as strong as some of the other men. But I was good in the air, very good, and I'd hoped that would be enough to see me through.

As the photographers and reporters pressed closer to the stage, bombarding the astralnauts with flashbulbs and questions, I made my way towards the exit. I knew I should stay and congratulate everyone, but I just couldn't face it. I passed Kate's parents and they scarcely acknowledged me.

I was crossing the lobby when someone grabbed my arm from behind.

"I don't understand!" said a breathless Kate, as I turned to face her. "How could you not be chosen?"

"I wasn't good enough," I said simply.

A few people were exiting the ballroom, so Kate took me by the hand and led me down a quiet hallway.

"They made a mistake," she said. "I'll talk to Mr. Lunardi—"

"You'll do no such thing. Those three will make excellent astralnauts."

"But . . ." She looked completely dispirited. "I never imagined you wouldn't be on the ship with me!"

"I'm sorry," I said. "I tried as hard as I could."

All my life I'd been used to trying my best, knowing that determination and hard work were my only ladder to a loftier life. It had worked so far. I'd done well aboard the *Aurora*; I'd been accepted into the Academy; I'd fought pirates and salvaged ghost ships, and survived. But this was the first time I'd met with total failure. I felt stunned and . . . *lesser.*

She took my hands. "You'd be every bit as good as those three."

I smiled at her loyalty, but knew in my heart she was wrong. I'd been bested. That was all there was to it.

Through her left glove, I felt something hard.

I touched it and looked into Kate's eyes. She stared back, silent, guilty. I didn't care that there was a couple walking towards us down the corridor—I seized her glove and peeled it off her hand. On her finger was an engagement ring.

"What have you done?" I whispered.

She swallowed, and the guilt in her eyes was extinguished by a flare of defiance.

"This," she said, "is my ticket to outer space."

14 / The Astral Cable

THE SIGHT OF THE RING and the hardness in Kate's face made my stomach turn over, and I was worried I might be sick. I walked away. I heard her calling out, but didn't stop. Out through the doors and onto the street, not knowing where I was going. My stomach clenched and I made it down an alley before I retched, tears springing to my eyes.

After a few minutes I pulled myself together and ventured back out onto the busy street. Still in a daze, I bumped right into Reg Perry. He was with a group of other finalists, all loosening their ties and looking morose.

"Cruse!" Reg said, clapping me on the shoulder. "We're off to Gassy Jack's to drown our sorrows. Come with us."

I went. I sat with them at the bar, inundated by the noise and smoke, and glad of it, for I didn't want to talk or think. They bought me drinks and slapped me on the back and said, "You should've been up there, Cruse." They said, "You land dived like a falcon! You saved Tobias's life. That should count for something! What're they thinking? Really, you should've been up there, mate."

They thought I was simply disappointed; they didn't know my heart had just been clawed from my body. The clock ticked through the hours of the evening and the small hours of morning, and when I arrived home in a cab at an ungodly hour, my mother said nothing. She had heard the news on the radio. Silently she made up a bed for me in her sewing room back behind the kitchen.

I wasn't drunk, but pretended to be, for all I wanted was to sleep and forget. But sleep would not come, leaving me to see again and again that ring on Kate's finger and the defiant look in her eyes, and to know that I'd lost her now for good.

When finally sleep did take pity and tug me under, it seemed mere seconds before my mother was gently shaking my shoulder.

"Matt, there's someone to see you. Get dressed."

I squinted at the sun-filled window. It must've been late morning. I pulled my trousers and shirt on, hoping it was Kate; dreading it was Kate. I walked out to the parlour and saw Captain Walken talking to my sisters.

"Ah, Matt," he said. "Good morning."

"Good morning, sir."

"Sylvia, Isabel, let's give them some privacy," my mother told the girls.

"Thank you, Mrs. Cruse," said Captain Walken. "It's lovely to see you again."

"And you, Captain Walken."

I ran a hand through my sleep-tousled hair, knowing I looked bedraggled. He'd probably come to try to cheer me up. He was a big-hearted man, and I didn't think ill of him for not choosing me.

"I wanted to talk to you last night," he said, "but I couldn't find you."

"I left early."

He smiled. "But stayed out late, I hear."

"Some of the other fellows sort of swept me along with them."

The captain nodded. "A hard night for you."

I cleared my throat. "Maybe I wasn't cut out to be an astralnaut."

"Not so, Matt. Not so. It was very difficult to pick only three. It's the size of the ship that limits us, not the quality of the men."

He was being kind. "I think you made the right choices, though. They're all excellent."

"They are," he agreed. "Unfortunately, Mr. Bronfman celebrated a bit too much last night. In his drunken exuberance he broke his leg."

"He didn't," I said, aghast.

"Quite badly. He'll be in a cast for some time."

"But when does the expedition leave?" I asked.

"Immediately. You're next in line."

My heart leapt. "I am?"

"You've not gone and made other plans, I hope?"

I chuckled. "No, sir."

"We leave tomorrow morning for the launch site."

My mother appeared in the doorway, her eyes wet.

"You heard," I said.

She nodded, and I went to hug her. "I'm going to outer space!" I said.

"And what about these Babelites?" She glared at me.

"It'll be fine, Mom. Captain Walken'll keep an eye on everything."

She smiled through her tears. "I'm sure he will."

"There's one more thing I wanted to talk to you about," said the captain. "I assume you heard that Miss de Vries is engaged to James Sanderson."

My mother turned to me in dismay. "Matt, is this true?"

I nodded. "I found out last night."

Captain Walken looked at me closely. "Is this likely to interfere with your performance aboard my ship?"

The thought of seeing Kate right now was almost too painful to bear, and I felt my enthusiasm curdle. But I hardened my heart. I wasn't going to let her ruin this for me. I'd worked for it more determinedly than I'd ever worked in my life.

I looked the captain in the eyes and shook my head. "No, sir."

"Did you have any idea she meant to get engaged?" my mother asked.

"It was a . . . surprise," I said slowly.

"I think very ill of her now," said my mother darkly.

I sighed. "We'd made no promises to each other, Mom."

"Still, I think it a very sly thing to do. I'm sorry, Matt. But you're well rid of her."

I nodded. "Maybe you're right."

But I didn't believe my own words.

The sun had yet to crest the horizon and the morning still had an invigorating chill when I arrived at the aeroharbour. It was all activity around the *Bluenose,* a sleek air schooner that would take us to our launch site. Judging by the supplies and provisions they were loading aboard, the trip would not be a short one. The location of our launch site and spaceship was still a secret. After the latest Babelite plot, Mr. Lunardi was taking no chances. Armed security guards were posted all over the landing field, and my papers were examined by two sentries before I was allowed up the gangplank.

Leaving my bags with the ground crew, I went aboard and found my way to the starboard lounge. It was a luxurious ship, intended for private charters, and it was very well appointed with armchairs and sofas and writing tables. Shepherd and Tobias were already there, and Tobias came towards me with a big smile on his face.

"They just told us you were coming!"

"I guess you heard about Bronfman," I said.

"I was there!" Tobias said. "He tried to skate down the banister of the grand staircase!"

I winced. "There's quite a curve to it."

"Yeah. You can imagine what happened."

"Damn foolishness," said Shepherd. He cut an imposing

figure in his grey Aero Force uniform. He looked at me with his cool, appraising eyes. "Bronfman should've been here."

"Not with his leg in a cast," said Tobias.

I hated benefiting from Bronfman's misfortune, but I couldn't help that, and I'd be a fool to let it stop me coming. All I could do was work my very hardest to make sure I earned my place aboard ship.

Through the windows, I saw a fine motorcar pull up with many trunks stacked on the roof. The driver opened the passenger doors and Mr. and Mrs. de Vries stepped out, followed by Kate—and James Sanderson.

I couldn't hear what they were saying, but I saw Mr. de Vries shake his daughter's hand—which seemed a rather stiff farewell, considering she was embarking on a long journey that was hardly free of danger. Mrs. de Vries placed her hands lightly on Kate's shoulders and kissed her on the cheek. James, on the other hand, seemed very eager to wrap his arms around Kate and lean in for a kiss on the mouth, which Kate hastily deflected to her cheek. My teeth clenched and ground, as if sharpening themselves for an attack. I wanted them very sharp.

"Who's that?" Tobias asked beside me.

"That," I said, my jaws tight, "is Miss de Vries's fiancé, James Sanderson."

"Isn't he heir to the Sanderson fortune?" Tobias asked.

"Yep."

"Interesting," said Tobias, giving me a strange look.

Outside, another motorcar drew up and Miss Karr emerged,

with Haiku hopping about on her shoulder. She spoke at length with the de Vrieses, and I guessed she was promising Kate's parents that she'd keep a strict eye on their daughter. Mrs. de Vries looked a bit uncertain, and her eyes kept drifting to the monkey, who was gleefully chewing on part of Miss Karr's hat. Everyone made their final farewells, and I saw James push some kind of letter into Kate's hands. Then Miss Karr and Kate headed up the gangway.

I felt my stomach shift; I wasn't sure I was ready to see Kate yet.

I hurried out of the lounge and headed aft, but the passageway was jammed with porters wrestling with Kate's steamer trunks. I headed back the way I'd come, rounded a corner—and ran straight into her.

She stared at me. "What are *you* doing here?"

"You don't sound very happy to see me."

"But—"

"Bronfman broke his leg. I'm his replacement."

"That's brilliant!" she said.

"Bit hard on old Bronfman."

"Matt, I'm so glad you're here."

"Are you?" I said coldly. "That was a touching send-off with your fiancé."

I heard Miss Karr's loud voice around the corner. Kate grabbed my hand and pulled me through a doorway into a dark room, and I felt her lips on mine and her arms around my neck, pulling me to her. I was so surprised and excited that I kissed her back, though I was furious with her and wanted to bite her as much as kiss her. Panting, I pushed her away and fumbled on the wall for a switch. The lights came on. We were in a women's lavatory, but I didn't care about that just now. I glared at Kate. I had never felt so angry and hurt in my life.

"After all your talk about never getting married," I said, "you go and get engaged! How could you?"

"Listen to me," she whispered. "This engagement does not mean a thing."

I gave a bitter laugh. "Of course not. You've only promised yourself to be another man's wife."

"Don't be ridiculous," she said. "I scarcely know him. I have no intention of marrying him."

"Then why'd you get engaged?"

She waggled her ring finger. "Isn't it obvious? I told you already. This is my ticket to outer space." She looked me straight in the eyes. "I had no choice."

I snorted. "You have as much choice as anyone. More."

"Not after the jail incident."

"Whose fault was that?"

"I know." She nodded ruefully. "But after my father saw us together in the cell, and then the photo in the newspaper . . . My parents don't trust me any more. They think I'm going to ruin my chances of marrying well. They said I couldn't come unless I agreed to marry George Sanderson."

"It's *James*," I snapped.

"James. George. Whichever."

"So you have no intention of marrying him?" I demanded.

"None. Matt, you know there's no one I care for more than you."

"Well, I'm not sure I care for you any more," I said. I didn't mean it, but I was humiliated and I wanted to hurt her.

I walked away without looking back.

We set sail, and not long after departure we were all summoned to the dining room, where a celebratory breakfast was laid out for us. We sat down at the long table like a big and rather odd extended family: Miss Karr and Haiku, the doleful Dr. Sergei Turgenev, Sir Hugh Snuffler, looking particularly puffy and self-important, Kate and me, Tobias and Chuck Shepherd, and Captain Walken. And sitting at the head of the table was Mr. Lunardi, lifting a flute of champagne.

"Ladies and gentlemen, to outer space!"

"Outer space!" we all cried, glasses raised high.

"And let me say once again," Lunardi continued, "how delighted I am to have each and every one of you on the expedition."

I wished I hadn't been fourth choice. I glanced at Shepherd, who didn't look particularly delighted with his fellow astralnauts. Sir Hugh, who was seated as far away as possible from Miss Karr and her monkey, cleared his throat.

"I must say, though, Mr. Lunardi, I had second thoughts when I found out I wasn't to be the only"—he paused, looking across the table at Kate—"*zoologist* coming."

"As did I, Sir Hugh," said Kate, with the kind of smile that the Grim Reaper might wear to greet you.

Miss Karr, I noticed, was busily recording something in her notebook, always the journalist. I could just imagine the kind of dispatches she'd be writing.

"The only reason I'm here at all," said Sir Hugh, "is to put a stop to the kind of sloppy, amateur observation that gives the sciences a bad name."

"Or," Kate retorted, "is it the refusal to consider new ideas that gives the sciences a bad name?"

Mr. Lunardi beamed. "This is *precisely* what I was after! Sir John, you see, had some reservations about inviting both of you. But not me. You, Miss de Vries, have made fascinating discoveries, but they're controversial, and you're still young, and a woman, and that will make many people distrustful. But you, Sir Hugh, have a reputation that's esteemed worldwide. No one doubts your word. But you do belong, shall we say, to an old school of thinking that might be just a touch closed-minded. Now," Mr. Lunardi continued, waving away Sir Hugh's indignant objection, "with *both* of you aboard, we'll have the most rigorous scientific debate at all times. And any discoveries you jointly make will be all the more credible to the world. Do you see the beauty of it?"

Kate and Sir Hugh stared at Mr. Lunardi in silence.

"No," said Sir Hugh. "I'm afraid I don't."

There was a flash, and Miss Karr gave a delighted cackle as she lowered her camera. "Your expression was priceless, Sir Hugh. Wonderful."

"Miss Karr, I hope you won't be snapping pictures of us all the time," Sir Hugh said irritably.

"That's why I'm here," the photographer replied.

"Mr. Lunardi," Chuck Shepherd said from down the table, "you've kept us in suspense a good long time. Can you tell us now where we're going?"

"I can, Mr. Shepherd, and I'm sorry we've kept you all in the dark. But I think you can understand our need for secrecy, especially after recent events. We're sailing for an equatorial island in the Pacific, three days' journey. That is where we've built our launch site, and our ship."

"Bit far away from everything," said Miss Karr, her eyes alight with curiosity.

"Indeed, but absolutely necessary, as you'll see when we get there."

"What about the ship?" Shepherd asked. "If I'm going to fly it, I'd like to know how it works."

I glanced over at Tobias and he rolled his eyes. Shepherd made it sound like he'd be doing everything single-handedly. Still, I shared his impatience. During training, they'd told us nothing about the ship itself, or how it would take us to outer space.

"Ah, the ship," said Lunardi. "I could tell you, but so much better to let you see for yourselves. The ship is really quite . . . unexpected. Indulge me just a bit longer, all of you; I want to see the looks on your faces."

"Is there anything else you *can* tell us?" said Shepherd with a wry smile.

"I can tell you about your new uniforms," said the airship magnate. "You'll see them after breakfast. They're very sharp. Insignia of an arrow against the moon. No need to wear your military uniform any more, Mr. Shepherd. This is a civilian expedition, after all."

I watched Shepherd carefully to see how he'd take this mild rebuke. He wouldn't be very happy to part with his captain's uniform. I'd known him long enough to notice the temperature drop in his blue eyes. But he just nodded placidly and said, "Yes, sir."

We set to our breakfast. It was quite something to see everyone congratulate Kate on her engagement, and to watch how she beamed and held out her hand so they could admire her ring. I tried not to look, for I worried I might start snarling.

"It's a fine ring, Miss de Vries," said Miss Karr. "But didn't you say you'd never marry?"

"Did I?" said Kate. "Dear me, that must have been some silly girlish thing I said a long time ago."

"Just last week, actually."

"Is that all?" said Kate. "Well, I obviously didn't know the power of true love."

I chewed hard on my sausage, imagining it was James Sanderson's finger.

"Well, congratulations again, my dear," said Miss Karr dryly. "I hope you'll be very happy. You'll certainly be very rich."

Kate merely smiled. I felt Miss Karr's gaze settle on me

like a lead weight, but I wouldn't meet it. Instead I stared out the window at the wispy cirrus clouds.

"I was wondering, Mr. Lunardi," said Tobias, "when you first got interested in outer space?"

The magnate smiled—but I thought I caught a trace of sadness in his eyes. It was the first time I'd seen a lapse in his boundless energy and good cheer.

"Well, it's the way of the future, isn't it? It's what we humans must do if we're to keep exploring." He didn't seem entirely convinced by his own reply, and after a moment he went on. "My boy Bruce took a great interest in the planets and stars. I didn't appreciate it at the time; I was only intent on seeing him make his mark in business. But here, take a look at this."

From his breast pocket he removed a piece of paper, which he passed around the table. It looked like it had been folded and opened many times. When the paper reached me I saw it was a scientific drawing of the solar system. The planets were all drawn to relative size, with the constellations forming a border. In the bottom corner, Bruce had printed his name very neatly in small letters.

"It's a fine drawing," I said.

"I think so too," agreed Mr. Lunardi. "He did that when he was only ten. He made hundreds of sketches, without my ever knowing. Maybe he knew I'd just say there was no point staring into outer space. But it turns out his vision was clearer than mine."

I hadn't known Bruce very well, or for very long, but I did remember how he'd told me he didn't know what he wanted to do with his life. It made me glad to think he really had known.

"To Bruce," I said, lifting my glass. "I wish he could be travelling with us."

"Thank you, Mr. Cruse, that's very kind of you," said his father.

"Has anyone seen Haiku?" asked Miss Karr, her eyes searching the dining room.

At that moment there was a tremendous din from the kitchen. Pots bonged, cutlery clattered, and there was a barrage of cursing in various languages. Then came an ominous silence.

The door of the kitchen flew open. Striding out carrying an enormous soup pot was Chef Vlad Herzog, a murderous scowl on his face. The soup pot was lurching and banging in his arms. He stopped at the head of our table and lifted the lid slightly. Two small brown hands gripped the rim, and a furry head popped up.

"Whose monkey might this be?" he roared.

"Haiku!" exclaimed Miss Karr.

Chef Vlad clanged the lid back down.

"Release him at once!" said Miss Karr, shooting to her feet.

"Ha!" said Chef Vlad. "Release him, you say? Release him so he can lay waste once more to my kitchen? So he can squat on my omelette?"

I caught sight of Sir Hugh looking down at his omelette with dismay.

"Release him at once, you disagreeable man!" said Miss

Karr, rolling up her sleeves as if she meant to box with the chef.

"Perhaps Haiku could wear his leash, just for the rest of the meal," Mr. Lunardi suggested peaceably. "Just so he doesn't come to any harm in the kitchen."

"Haiku never misbehaves!" Miss Karr insisted. Nonetheless she produced the monkey's leash.

"Madam," Chef Vlad said, still holding the lid tight, "if your monkey so much as *peeps* his adorable little head into my kitchen again, I will *cook* him. Do you understand this? Little *Achoo,* or whatever silly thing you've named him, will be all *crispy.* I will serve him with maybe an orange sauce and *leeks!*"

Chef Vlad then paused as if considering this properly for the first time. "I've never attempted such a thing, and it would be challenging, and yet—"

"Release him!" Miss Karr said sternly.

Chef Vlad pulled back the lid with a flourish and Haiku leapt out into his mistress's waiting arms. Looking resentfully back at Mr. Vlad, he piteously chittered his tale of woe to Miss Karr.

The chef winked at me. "Monkey *à l'orange*—it would not be so bad, eh, Mr. Cruse? I see real possibilities."

"Mr. Vlad, why aren't you in Paris?" I asked. When last I'd seen him, he was the chef of Paris's most famous restaurant, the Jewels Verne, atop the Eiffel Tower.

Mr. Vlad's cheeks filled with air and he gave an exaggerated sigh. "Paris is charming for a time, Mr. Cruse. It is like one of their delightful little pastries. It sits there looking plump and smug and *delicious,* but let it sit too long and it becomes soggy and *repellent.* There is no energy in Paris, no dynamism. An artist like myself must move on. Also, I set fire to the French president."

"You don't say."

"Yes. I could not stay a moment longer."

"What exactly happened, Mr. Vlad?" Kate inquired, barely able to hide her grin.

"The President's moustache was excessively long, and I was preparing crème brûlée and he came between me and my blowtorch."

"It was an accident, though," I said hopefully.

"No, no," said Chef Vlad. "We were having a difference of opinion about the thickness of the sugar crust. He had some very vexing views on the matter." His eyes strayed to a window, as if recalling the scene, and he smiled. "It was regrettable, but these things occur from time to time. There was a question of a prison sentence, so I left town rather quickly. I had the good fortune to meet Mr. Lunardi while fleeing— and he said he would like to offer me another position."

"Chef Vlad is coming with you to outer space!" Mr. Lunardi told us with a smile.

"Hooray!" Kate said. "I was wondering what we'd eat."

"Miss de Vries, how lovely to see you again," said Chef Vlad with a little bow. "Yes, I am to be your chef. The first chef in outer space. And now, if you'll excuse me, I must find someone else to put in my pot."

We were all quite pampered aboard the *Bluenose*. Mr. Lunardi refused to give us duties of any sort. He promised there'd be a great deal of work awaiting us on the island, and urged us to rest now and enjoy Chef Vlad's fabulous meals.

On the second day, we left the Hawaiis in our wake and continued southwest towards the equator. It was strange to think that I'd first met Kate on an almost identical journey, some two years ago. But it made me sad, and bitter too, for I felt so far away from her right now. She spent a lot of time in the port lounge with her camera, scanning the skies with her field glasses, probably hoping to sight an aerozoan or a cloud cat.

I avoided her. *She* needed to make things right, not me. But I got the feeling she was avoiding me too. I was miserable.

On the morning of the third day, I woke early. I knew we'd be arriving that afternoon, and all night I'd dreamed about our ship, and what awaited us in outer space. I dressed eagerly and headed down to the dining room for breakfast. I was the first to arrive. Covered serving dishes had already been set out along the sideboard. I took a plate and was helping myself to some scrambled egg when I felt warm fingers stroke the back of my neck. The simple touch sent a deep electric current of pleasure through me. I took a slow breath, not wanting the moment to end just yet.

"Please don't be angry with me," Kate whispered in my ear.

I turned. She was looking very apologetic and tentative—

and it was so unlike her that I almost smiled. But I didn't want her to think I'd forgiven her. Yet.

"I never thought I could be so angry," I said.

We were still alone in the dining room, but it wouldn't be for long. I continued moving along and filling my plate, in case anyone came in suddenly. Kate did the same.

"I'll break off the engagement when I get back," she said quietly.

Just hearing the word *engagement* made my heart ache. Right now James Sanderson was engaged to my Kate. I might never be engaged to her, and the thought of this other fellow claiming the privilege made my blood steam.

"Will your parents let you?" I asked.

"They can't force me to marry him. Anyway, people break engagements all the time. With a bit of luck I can probably rig it so it looks like his fault."

I glanced over at her. "You really are a very devious person."

"If necessary, yes. I've heard James is a notorious flirt, so there's a good chance he'll do something naughty while I'm away. Then I can act all heartbroken and say he's wounded me terribly, and I can refuse to marry him."

"Why don't you just frame him for murder?"

She frowned, considering this. "Too much work. Now you and I have a tricky job ahead of us. For this to work, everyone on the expedition has to believe I *want* to be engaged, and that you and I are just *acquaintances*. We've got to watch Miss Karr in particular. She suspects something. If she hints at anything in one of her newspaper dispatches, we're sunk. There'll be a scandal and my parents will lock me up forever."

"Might not be a bad idea," I muttered.

Kate ignored me. "So you can't flirt with me or pay me any undue attention. Ignore me as much as possible."

"Easy," I said, annoyed by her bossiness. "I'll be too busy flying the ship."

"And you have to stop glaring at me," Kate added.

"I don't glare at you!"

"You do. I catch you looking at me sometimes and it's positively homicidal. You'll give the game away if you keep doing it."

"This isn't a game to me," I said.

"I know," she said, "and I'm sorry, Matt. I really am. There was just no other way."

I said nothing. I'd known for a long time how determined Kate was, but I hadn't thought she'd ever be quite this ruthless. She'd made promises she had no intention of keeping. She'd lied. She'd hurt me.

How did I know she wouldn't hurt me again—and worse—to get something she really wanted?

The cry of "Land ho!" brought me to the windows of the starboard lounge. I stuck my head out into the balmy breeze. The island had no dramatic mountains or volcanoes like some of the others we'd passed. Waves broke against its outer reef in a jagged white line and rolled serenely onto the sandy beach.

As we drew closer, I saw numerous buildings clustered together near the coast. The largest was some four storeys tall and had a flat metal roof. Above the island I glimpsed something that made me squint. A golden, vertical seam flickered in the sky. Some kind of atmospheric trick, maybe, a refraction of the sun's rays in the tropical moisture.

"Do you see that?" Tobias said, sticking his head out the window next to mine.

I nodded. The golden line seemed to be coming from the tall, flat-roofed building, and stretched higher and higher until I could see it no longer.

I pulled my head back inside the ship. Everyone was in the starboard lounge now, Kate and Sir Hugh, and Miss Karr and all the others, gazing out the windows at the island —and the strange golden line glimmering in the sky.

"What is it?" I asked, pointing.

"I've never seen anything like it," Kate said. "Is it some kind of rainbow?"

I noticed that Mr. Lunardi, Dr. Turgenev, and Captain Walken weren't looking out the windows, but at the rest of us, smiling at the astonishment on our faces.

"That," Mr. Lunardi said with immense pride, "is the astral cable."

"What's an astral cable?" asked Tobias.

"It's the track upon which our ship will travel," Captain Walken told him.

"You mean like a train track?" Shepherd said, peering out at it.

The Russian scientist limped closer to the window. "More like elevator cable."

"But how high does it go?" I asked Captain Walken.

He grinned. "When I tell you, you may not believe me."

"All the way into outer space?" Kate gasped.

Captain Walken nodded. "Twenty-five thousand miles."

I looked at him in disbelief. "But . . . what holds it up?"

Captain Walken nodded at Dr. Turgenev. "Maybe you should tell them, Sergei, since you invented it."

Dr. Turgenev gave a weary shrug. "Is very simple. Cable is attached to Earth, here on island. At end of cable in outer space is counterweight. Very big object. Earth turns, cable turns, counterweight keeps cable taut. Yes?"

"Centrifugal force!" I exclaimed.

"Correct, Mr. Cruse."

"How did you get the counterweight up there in the first place?" Shepherd asked.

"Rocket," said Dr. Turgenev with a sigh.

Mr. Lunardi stepped in. "We've been messing about with rockets for years. We have a launch site on the other side of the island. I can't tell you how many we shot off. They all blew up, or crashed back down. The ocean's littered with them. But once I got Sergei involved, we made a big leap forward. We got them to stay up for longer. Then one day, they stopped coming back down altogether."

I caught sight of Tobias gazing up into the sky, as though he might see one plummeting home.

"So you used a rocket to get the astral cable into outer space?" I asked.

Dr. Turgenev nodded. "Inside rocket is astral cable on big spools. Rocket goes up, pays out cable. Rocket runs out of fuel in outer space, but stays attached to end of cable."

"So the rocket *is* the counterweight?" asked Kate.

"Yes, same thing," said the scientist.

"The counterweight is in geosynchronous orbit," Mr. Lunardi explained excitedly. "It stays in exactly the same spot over the earth at all times. Do you see? It's our ladder to the heavens."

"Jack and the beanstalk," I murmured, shaking my head. When I was a little boy, I'd wondered if I could climb to the stars, if only I had a ladder tall enough.

"That's right," said Mr. Lunardi. "And you'll be going to the very top."

"Twenty-five thousand miles?" asked Sir Hugh.

"To the counterweight, yes," said Captain Walken. "That's as high as we can go at the moment. The ascent should take about eight days."

"And this trip's just the first of many," said Mr. Lunardi. "We plan to build a proper space station up there. And from that we can launch expeditions deeper into the solar system, and beyond!"

Everyone was quiet for a moment. It was almost too much to take in all at once.

"I hope your cable's well tied down," said Miss Karr bluntly, and Haiku jumped up and down as if sharing her concern.

"Very well tied down," Lunardi promised her. "It's welded to an anchor deep in the earth. And it's wound through a system of pulleys to reduce the strain."

"What's it made of?" Shepherd asked.

"Who's to say it won't snap like a thread?" Sir Hugh asked uneasily. "Has it been inspected by the proper authorities?"

"Is it some kind of alumiron alloy?" I said. "Like the French are using for the tower?"

Lunardi shook his head. "There's no metal on Earth strong enough to withstand the kind of strain our cable's under."

"Then what?" said Sir Hugh.

"It's metal from another world."

"How?" Kate asked, sounding as surprised as I felt.

"You've heard of the Badlands Crater, perhaps?" Mr. Lunardi said.

Tobias was nodding excitedly. "They say it was made by a meteorite, millions of years ago."

"Exactly," said Mr. Lunardi. "They found metal that had never been seen on Earth before. It's light, flexible, and, when made molten, can be spun thinner than spiderweb, only a thousand times stronger."

"It's this," said Tobias, pulling his bit of space rock from his pocket.

"Let's have a look," said Mr. Lunardi, hefting the lump in his hand. "It is indeed. The very stuff."

As the *Bluenose* came in to land, I stared out at the glinting astral cable in awe.

"All the way to outer space," Kate said softly beside me.

I wished I'd been there to see it: the rocket blasting off from the island and searing up into the sky, unspooling the golden cable behind it. A ladder dropped from the stars.

I could imagine the land crew seizing the end of the cable and hurriedly welding it to the anchor deep within the island's rock. And then they must have stood back and stared up at the metal thread as it stretched, straight as a navigator's line, into the tropical sky and the high cirrus clouds until it disappeared from view. And they must have looked at one another, maybe a bit afraid, wondering just what they'd done, marvelling that they had tethered heaven to Earth.

15 / The *Starclimber*

SHE HUNG THERE like a giant metal spider upon her thread, all fifty silver feet of her, towering over us in the hangar. She was cylindrical, bulging slightly in the middle and tapering at both ends. Slender vertical fins were spaced evenly around her flanks. Judging by the rows of portholes, she had three decks, and at the summit a glass-domed bridge.

"We call her the *Starclimber*," Lunardi told us proudly as we all stood gazing up at her.

Until I'd seen the astral cable, I'd imagined our vessel would look pretty much like an ordinary airship—pressurized, of course, with new engines that could rocket us beyond the sky. But this was an altogether different kind of ship, with no need for lifting gas or rudders or propellers.

The *Starclimber* was suspended over a wide shaft, out of which rose the astral cable. It didn't look like a cable at all. Thin as a ribbon it was, and no wider than my hand. It ran through the very centre of the ship, from stern to bow, and continued on through the centre of the hangar roof, into the depths of space. The back of my neck tingled at the thought that something right before me was connected to the heavenly ether.

"How does it actually climb the cable?" I asked.

Lunardi smiled. "We spent months trying various methods. We settled on a simple friction grip." He held his two hands up, palms flat, and pressed them together firmly. "Rollers grip the cable from opposite sides and crawl up its length. Look here." He pointed at the sets of muscular metal spider legs that protruded from the ship, two at the bow, one at the stern, and locked around the cable.

Tobias looked at me and swallowed. "That's all that's holding us to the cable?" he said.

"No, no," said Mr. Lunardi. "These legs are just the external rollers. The astral cable runs through a sealed shaft inside the ship. You'll see it when you go inside. It's like a thick column in the very centre of every level. Now, on the inside of that column are more rollers, gripping the cable so tightly there's no risk of slippage. It's quite incredible."

It *was* incredible—but a stubborn part of me wondered if it could really work. Miss Karr was jotting things down in her notebook; Sir Hugh looked faintly queasy.

"Where does the ship get her power?" Shepherd asked.

"Ah, yes," Dr. Turgenev said ruefully, "this was big problem for us. Amount of power needed for ship is huge. Aruba fuel too heavy, and takes up too much space. Battery is not powerful enough —"

"The solution lay with the cable itself," Mr. Lunardi cut in impatiently. "The metal, we discovered, was an excellent conductor. So we use it to deliver a constant supply of electricity to the *Starclimber*."

"It's got no generator of its own?" asked Shepherd, frowning. "What if you lose power down here on Earth?"

"We have an abundant supply," said Mr. Lunardi.

I remembered the ranks of wind turbines I'd seen on the island's windward shore, and the blustering smokestack of a coal-burning generator.

"And what if the cable breaks?" Kate asked politely, as if she were inquiring about the possibility of rain.

For the first time since I'd met him, Dr. Turgenev actually chuckled. "If cable breaks we have bigger problem than no electricity. But cable will not break. We try to break it. We hit it and cut it and heat it. Cannot be broken."

For a moment we all stared at the ship in silence. I looked at Captain Walken, who'd known all about it well before the rest of us. No unease showed in his face, and that reassured me.

"I thought I was here to fly," said Shepherd with obvious disdain. "This isn't a ship; it's an elevator."

"Don't be deceived, Mr. Shepherd," said Captain Walken. "It may have a different means of propulsion, but it's no less a ship."

Shepherd grunted. "It runs on a track. It's like flying a streetcar."

The captain raised an eyebrow. "I believe there will be enough challenges in space to satisfy even you, Mr. Shepherd."

"Yes, sir," said Shepherd, but he seemed unconvinced.

For the first time, I wondered how well he was going to take orders. I didn't like the way he looked at the captain, as though he knew better.

"By voyage's end you may change your mind, Mr.

Shepherd," said Mr. Lunardi. "But for now, your training isn't quite done. We leave in a week, and you all have a great deal to learn. Now, to work!"

"Not fast enough, Cruse," Shepherd said, looking at the pressure gauge. "We're already dead."

We were up in the *Starclimber*'s glass-domed bridge, running through an emergency depressurization drill, and I hadn't got the back-up system working in time. Tobias glanced over from his control panel. His look was sympathetic, but also a bit weary, for this was our third try and it was late in the afternoon.

"Sorry, everyone," I said, "I thought I had it that time."

Shepherd said nothing. Whenever I made a mistake, he never lost his temper or insulted me. In some ways I wished he would, because then I could defend myself. But how could I when all he did was calmly state the facts?

It was the last day before our launch. For the past week, Shepherd, Tobias, and I had worked dawn to dusk, getting acquainted with the ship. The controls were unlike anything I'd seen. There were no rudder or elevator wheels. There were no levers to valve hydrium or dump water ballast. Instead, there were a bewildering number of control panels, with more lights and switches than I'd ever seen. Even Shepherd had looked subdued when he'd first set eyes on it all.

Every day the *Starclimber* bustled with activity as everyone learned about the ship and their various duties. Chef Vlad was kept busy in the kitchen, practising with the new pumps and dishware that would be necessary once our gravity failed. Dr. Turgenev showed Sir Hugh and Kate how to use the laboratory and all its equipment. We all practised wearing magnetic space shoes, to help us move about the ship when we became weightless. We also got a lively lesson on the space toilets, which involved complicated straps and funnels and levers to turn on the suction. Miss Karr assured us that Haiku was quite capable of using the space toilets as well—much to everyone's relief.

As for us astralnauts, day by day, all the buttons and switches began to make sense. We pored over blueprints and technical diagrams, peered into ducts, and traced bundles of multicoloured cable through the ship's innards. We got so we could move about the *Starclimber* with our eyes closed. It was a lot to learn in just seven days, and I'd never worked harder, wanting to prove that I belonged aboard. But I could never quite forget I wasn't first choice, especially when I fouled up a drill—like now.

"All right, gentlemen," Captain Walken said. "Reset your controls and let's go again. We need to get this right."

The drone of powerful engines drew our eyes skyward. The hangar roof was retracted and I saw a big airship pass overhead. On its flank and fins was the insignia of the Aero Force. Two ornithopters dropped from the ship's belly, wings flapping, and circled the astral cable like gulls.

"What's the Aero Force doing here?" I asked, as the ship came in to land on the island.

"I'm sure we'll find out," said Captain Walken, but I

thought I saw a shadow of annoyance cross his face. Then he looked back at us with a wink. "Now then, let's do this drill for the last time, shall we?"

When the four of us left the *Starclimber*, Mr. Lunardi was walking across the hangar floor to meet us. At his side was a silver-haired military man. Judging from the colourful rows of insignia on his uniform, he was high ranking.

Shepherd saluted sharply and said, "General, sir!"

"Ah, Captain Shepherd, delighted to see you. A shame Bronfman's not joining you."

"Yes, sir."

For just a second the general's eyes settled on me before turning back to Shepherd. "Still, I'm relieved to know we have a man of your calibre aboard. Excellent."

"Gentlemen, this is General Lancaster," said Mr. Lunardi, sounding just a bit too cheerful. "The Minister of Defence thought we could use some help."

"I wasn't aware this was a military operation," Captain Walken said coolly.

The general laughed. "And it's not, Captain Walken. We're just here to lend a hand. Just to make sure things are tickety-boo."

It seemed such a childish turn of phrase that I had trouble holding back a smile. But the general's expression was severe when he next spoke.

"I'll be frank, gentlemen. The Minister's worried your security's slack."

"We've stepped it up," said Mr. Lunardi.

"Not enough for my liking," said General Lancaster. "Grendel Eriksson's still at large, and our spies are hearing rumblings about new Babelite activity. We'll be guarding the astral cable and the ground station. Your power plants in particular—they'd be a prime target. My team will also make sure nothing suspicious gets loaded onto your ship. If the Babelites have any designs on the *Starclimber*, we'll be ready for them."

This didn't seem like a bad thing to me, but I could tell that both Captain Walken and Mr. Lunardi were still ill at ease.

"Well, we're very grateful to you, General," said Lunardi.

"Not at all. The Minister considers it a matter of national security. And on that subject, I do have some other news to share with you. Perhaps it's best done in private."

"Of course," said Mr. Lunardi, leading the way to his office.

Once we were all seated, the general launched right in. "About four weeks ago, our astronomers on Mount Steele made some unusual sightings. It turns out they weren't alone. There was a special meeting in Zurich recently, and quite a few astronomers reported strange lights moving in the night sky."

"I think I've seen them!" I blurted out.

"You have?" Tobias said in surprise.

"At the Paris Observatory," I said, and told them about the

blue and green lights I'd watched through the telescope. Of course I didn't tell them I was with Kate at the time.

"That sounds very like what our scientists reported," said the general. "They don't know what they are. If they're just meteorites, they're no concern of ours. But if they're some kind of spaceship, we want to know."

Lunardi was shaking his head. "Can't be. No one else is even close to getting a ship into space."

"I didn't say it had to be from Earth," the general said.

I looked at Tobias and felt a prickling of gooseflesh across my neck.

"Let me show you something," said the general. From an attaché case he pulled a sheaf of photographs and laid them out on Lunardi's desk. "These are photos of Mars taken over a two-year period. Classified, of course. You see these networks of lines?"

"The canals," said Shepherd. "I've read about them."

"They're not really canals, though," said Mr. Lunardi. "Just canyons."

"We're not so sure any more," said the general. "Look at this one on the upper left. And now look at it two years later."

"It's a bit longer," said Tobias.

On paper the difference was small, no more than an inch, but with a shiver I realized just how big that distance really was. "That must be a thousand miles," I said.

"Fifteen hundred," said the general. "And straight as an arrow. This doesn't look like any natural canyon, gentlemen.

It's possible it was built by intelligent creatures—creatures that must be incredibly advanced."

"Advanced enough to make spaceships," Shepherd said.

The general nodded. "Maybe. That's what we want to find out. These flashing lights are a mystery and we need you to solve it for us."

"General," said Mr. Lunardi, "as you know, we have three scientists aboard and we mean to collect as much information about outer space as possible. If we make any sightings of these lights, you can be sure we'll share them with the world."

The general gave a gruff laugh. "But we want to know *first*. We want to know what we're facing up there."

I shifted uneasily. Why did he seem to assume they were a threat?

"I'll be frank," the general went on. "This expedition might be more dangerous than you thought. Alien vessels. Babelites. The Minister of Defence has some misgivings about how some of your astralnauts might perform in a tough situation."

I felt a surge of anger, but held my tongue. It was painfully obvious the general was talking about me, and maybe Tobias too.

"I'm sorry if the Minister has misgivings about my crew," said Captain Walken. "I myself have none."

"I'm glad to hear it," the general said. "But if any extreme situation were to arise, I'd like Captain Shepherd to report directly to me."

I felt the barometer plunge in the room. I wasn't quite sure what was happening, but it seemed as if the general wanted Shepherd to have some special authority. Was he even suggesting that the test pilot should be captain? I looked at Shepherd, but his face betrayed nothing. I couldn't help wondering if he'd had some inkling of this ahead of time. He certainly hadn't seemed very surprised to see the general.

I'd never seen Mr. Lunardi look more grave.

"I'm afraid that's simply not acceptable, General," he said. "As you yourself acknowledged, this is a civilian expedition. And I don't think I need remind you that Captain Shepherd has no military rank aboard the *Starclimber*. He reports only to Captain Walken."

There was a brief, chilly silence, but then the general smiled agreeably.

"As you wish, Mr. Lunardi. I never meant to undermine the good captain's authority. Very well. We're only here to lend a hand and keep everything tickety-boo. Nonetheless, we need you to be our eyes up there, and the Prime Minister himself wants it to be a priority of the expedition."

The Prime Minister hadn't been mentioned before now, and it felt like a warning.

"Of course, General," Mr. Lunardi said.

"Good evening, gentlemen," said the general. "And good luck tomorrow."

Shepherd stood and saluted as General Lancaster left the room.

"I'm sorry about that, everyone," said Mr. Lunardi. "Sir

John mentioned there might be some additional security, but I hadn't realized it would be quite so vigorous."

"They'll take good care of us," said Shepherd.

"I've no doubt," said Lunardi dryly. "As for this business with the lights, I remain skeptical. But you'll need to make sure you keep a special watch out."

Tobias looked at me. "Did you think the lights were spaceships?"

I shook my head. "I couldn't tell."

"If they're up there, we'll find out soon enough," said Shepherd.

"We will indeed," said Captain Walken. "Now I suggest we all get an early night. We launch at seven sharp."

16 / Liftoff

THE HANGAR ROOF was already open to the luminous dawn sky. There were virtually no clouds, and the wind was light. Tobias, Shepherd, and I were overseeing the final cargo, double-checking our lists to make sure nothing had been left out. General Lancaster's men were out in full force, inspecting everything inside and outside the ship. I was glad of my uniform, for it made me look more confident than I felt. The uniform was armour.

Near the gangway, Chef Vlad was loudly complaining to a soldier about the way he was loading the food. Mr. Lunardi came over to soothe the volatile chef, while Captain Walken and Dr. Turgenev made their final inspection of the *Starclimber*'s exterior. Miss Karr was busily setting up her camera equipment near the gangway, Haiku leaping about excitedly on her shoulder. Kate and Sir Hugh were arguing about whether to bring a large specimen cage.

"We're ready to board," Captain Walken finally announced.

"This is a great moment," said Mr. Lunardi. "To my brave astralnauts, and our illustrious passengers, I wish you a glorious and safe journey. Godspeed."

As everyone filed up the gangway, Miss Karr's camera flashed again and again, commemorating the occasion.

"History in the making!" she said, though I thought there

was a hint of mischief in her voice. "It reminds me of those glorious images of people boarding the *Titanica*."

"Come now, Miss Karr," the captain said genially, "I won't hear such superstitious stuff aboard my ship. I think we have enough photos now, don't you. Let me help you with your tripod and let's get you settled on B Deck."

I was the last to board, for it was my duty to shut the main hatch. I heaved the great circular door closed on its vast hinges, and it locked snugly. All sounds of the outside disappeared abruptly: the noise of the ground crew in the hangar, the birdsong, the powerful crash of the surf through the open roof.

It was like putting the space helmet over my head that very first time, and I felt a sudden flare of panic. I'd just been cut off from the world. I could see it through the porthole, could see Mr. Lunardi giving me the thumbs-up before walking off to the radio room. But the world was somehow no longer mine. I wouldn't see it again, or breathe its air, until we returned to harbour in three weeks—if we returned at all. I thought of the mysterious lights, the possibility of ticking crates in our cargo hold.

I took several deep breaths and looked across at the rack that held our four spacesuits. Across the chest of each was stitched a name. *Walken. Shepherd. Blanchard. Cruse*. I touched my suit. Were it not for a split second of foolishness, Bronfman's name would have been on it.

"If you're ready, Mr. Cruse, we've got a ship to take airborne."

I turned to see Captain Walken, waiting for me in the airlock doorway, smiling.

"Yes, sir."

"I'm delighted to have you on my crew again, Mr. Cruse," he said.

His simple words reassured me greatly. For years I'd dreamed of serving under his command again, and here I was, a second officer on the first voyage to the stars.

Together we climbed the spiral staircase, past B Deck and A Deck to the glass-domed bridge atop the ship. Shepherd and Blanchard were already buckled into their seats, going through their checklists. I took my position.

"Check all hatches, please," said the captain.

"All hatches closed," I confirmed, looking at the indicator lights on my panel. "We are airtight."

"Battery," Captain Walken said.

I saw Tobias check his voltometer. "We have full charge, sir."

Though the *Starclimber*'s motors were constantly supplied with electricity from the ground, the ship also had a large backup battery that gave us enough power for six hours.

"Thank you, Mr. Blanchard. Start the ventilation system, please, Mr. Shepherd."

It was a pleasure to be under Captain Walken's command once again. I'd never forgotten his calm authority at the helm, nor his unflagging politeness.

My ears popped as the air pumps pressurized the *Starclimber*'s interior. Even though we would be rising to heights that might have no air at all, and virtually no pressure, we'd be kept comfortable inside. On Shepherd's console to my right, I saw a sequence of green lights flare, telling us that the proper mix of oxygen and nitrogen was being fed through the ducts. Dr. Turgenev's team had devised an ingenious system of using liquid oxygen. Stored in special tanks, it took up much less space than gas, and was enough to last us three weeks.

"We are fully pressurized, sir," said Shepherd. If he secretly felt that he should've been captain, he was doing an excellent job of hiding it.

"Air scrubbers?" asked Captain Walken.

We breathed in oxygen but we exhaled carbon dioxide, and if there was too much of that, our air would be poisoned. They'd come up with a lithium hydroxide filter system that removed the carbon from the air and recirculated the oxygen.

"Filters are functioning, sir."

"Engine temperature, Mr. Cruse?"

The numerous motors that controlled the ship's rollers had already been activated and were warming up. I checked the row of gauges.

"All motors are primed, sir."

"Emergency descent system, please," said the captain.

Built into the ship's hull near the bow were two hydrium balloons that could be rapidly inflated in case our rollers failed on descent.

"Explosive bolts charged, and hydrium pressure is optimum," reported Shepherd.

"Thank you. Mr. Blanchard, would you test the radio?"

As incredible as it sounded, we'd be able to communicate with the ground station even when we were twenty thousand miles away. The astral cable was our antenna.

"Transmitter and receiver working just fine," said Tobias, a set of earphones over his head. "And we have radio contact with the ground station."

"*Starclimber,*" came Mr. Lunardi's familiar voice over a speaker. "Do you read me?"

"We read you, Ground Station," said Tobias.

"Please tell Mr. Lunardi we are airtight, pressurized, and fully charged," said Captain Walken, and Tobias relayed the message.

"Excellent. You are cleared for liftoff, *Starclimber,*" said Mr. Lunardi.

"Mr. Cruse, engage the rollers, please," said Captain Walken.

I took hold of a large lever, pulled it hard towards me, and locked it. Above the dome I saw the flexed spider legs quiver slightly as they tightened their grip on the cable. I knew that all the rollers within the ship had also taken hold. I felt a small but eager vibration pass through the *Starclimber's* frame—and my body too, for I was straining for the takeoff. My pulse raced.

Captain Walken looked overhead to confirm that the hangar roof was fully open, and then, with a simple nod of his head, said, "All ahead dead slow, Mr. Shepherd."

I glanced over at Shepherd enviously. He was first officer,

and he had the privilege of guiding the world's first spaceship out of harbour on her maiden voyage.

"All ahead dead slow, sir," Shepherd repeated, easing the throttle forward.

Behind me, within the cable shaft, I heard the ship's rollers hum as they began to turn. With scarcely a shudder, the *Starclimber* moved.

We were rising!

Until this moment, some small part of me hadn't quite believed it would work. How could it? You couldn't dangle a thread from outer space and just climb it! There was nothing holding it up. No steel trusses, no bolts. It simply wasn't possible.

Yet it was—and we lifted.

We rose through the hangar and into the sky. Out of the panoramic windows I saw the tops of the tallest palms drop away. There was the coast, and the water ablaze with the rising sun. The Pacificus stretched to all horizons.

"We're aloft!" Tobias cried into the radio. "Ground Station, we are aloft!"

"We see that, *Starclimber!*" returned Mr. Lunardi, and even over the speaker I could hear his voice was hoarse with emotion. "We see you, and you are a beautiful sight to be sure!"

I watched the altimeter and saw the needle climbing. One hundred feet, one ten, one twenty. The noise of the rollers filled the bridge like the reassuring thrum of airship engines, yet it only emphasized the strangeness of this utterly new form of flight.

"It feels so odd," I said. "To be moving up without moving forward."

"It is uncanny," Captain Walken said.

"I keep waiting to slide back down," said Tobias.

But the rollers' grip was true, for there was absolutely no sensation of slippage. There was virtually no sway to the ship either. All its movement was vertical. Up was its only direction and desire.

Two hundred feet . . . two fifty . . . three hundred . . .

A pair of Aero Force ornithopters circled us from a distance, and beyond them I saw the general's airship hovering, keeping watch. We were still rising no faster than an elevator, but it was an amazing feeling.

"Five hundred feet, sir," I said, after checking the altimeter.

The captain nodded. "Throttle back, Mr. Shepherd, please."

He gradually brought the *Starclimber* to a full stop, and we hung there on our astral cable. I must say it made me feel strange all over, because I'd never been utterly motionless in the sky like this. It seemed to defy every natural law. I couldn't help peering out the windows to make sure we weren't falling.

"Ground Station, this is *Starclimber*," Tobias said into the radio. "We're stationary at five hundred feet and awaiting further orders."

"*Starclimber*, you look grand from here," said Lunardi. "Run another complete check and report back, please."

Once more the four of us methodically went through all the ship's systems to make sure they were working properly.

"Everything's fine up here, Ground Station," Tobias radioed minutes later.

"Excellent. You're clear to continue your climb, *Starclimber*. Report back when you've reached ten miles, please."

"Full ahead one-third, please, Mr. Shepherd," Captain Walken said.

He set the ship in motion once more. The pitch of the engines increased. We'd taken her out of harbour dead slow, but now I felt a slight weight in my stomach as we picked up speed.

"We're at forty aeroknots, sir," I reported.

"Make turns for eighty, Mr. Shepherd," the captain said.

I marvelled that Shepherd could look so composed as he pushed the throttle forward and we shot upward. The heaviness in my stomach intensified. Outside the windows, the ornithopters fell out of sight as though they'd been yanked down with strings. We were now going as fast as an airship—only straight up.

The captain grinned. "Let's give her a workout, Mr. Shepherd. Take her to full speed."

"Full ahead, sir."

As Shepherd pushed the throttle almost to its farthest point, I felt my body pushed down hard against my seat.

"One hundred twenty aeroknots, sir!" I said.

"Fast enough for you, Shepherd?" asked Tobias.

"I've been faster," he said, nodding out the window at the two ornithopters, which had caught up with us and were swooping around the cable. But Shepherd had a smile on his lips, and I could tell he was actually enjoying himself.

"Those fellows won't be able to keep up for long," said the captain with a chuckle, for sky sailors tended to think ornithopters an inferior form of flying. "We're climbing at ten thousand feet a minute."

Sure enough, the ornithopters, after one last flapping surge, sank swiftly below us. Shepherd watched them go.

"Come on, Shepherd, admit it," Tobias said, "you're impressed."

"It's an impressive machine," he said. "Just isn't my idea of flying. My granny could fly this thing."

"Maybe we should've brought her, then," said Tobias.

I bit back my laughter. I didn't want to appear unprofessional, right now of all times.

"Well done, gentlemen," said the captain. "A smoother first launch I couldn't imagine. We're on our way to the stars. At our current speed, we should reach cable's end in eight days."

It was amazing how quickly the sensation of speed disappeared. Apart from a vague heaviness in the stomach, you could almost forget you were hurtling through the sky at great speed. The captain turned to me.

"Mr. Cruse, why don't you go below and see how our passengers are faring?"

"Yes, sir."

Now that the *Starclimber* was underway, a crew of only two was needed on the bridge, and we'd be beginning our shifts soon. I started down the spiral staircase.

The ship was remarkably steady. There was hardly any of the rocking or pitching of an airship. My footsteps felt a bit leaden with gravity's drag, but my spirits were lighter than air. Nothing could match the delicious feeling of setting sail on a long voyage.

I passed A Deck, which was entirely taken up with our sleeping quarters and a single lavatory. I'd be sharing a cabin with Tobias. It was certainly small, but no more cramped than crew quarters aboard the *Aurora*. There were two bunks, each fitted with restraining straps (for when gravity failed us), and a chest of drawers for our belongings—that was it. The porthole was large, mercifully.

As I continued down to B Deck, I could hear the sounds of Chef Vlad already at work in his kitchen. Pots clanged, a knife whacked against a cutting board, a whisk scratched against a metal mixing bowl, and Mr. Vlad muttered ominously to himself all the while in Transylvanian. It was just like old times aboard the *Aurora*. The *Starclimber* was properly coming to life.

B Deck was the largest of the ship's levels, for the *Starclimber* was widest amidships. Apart from the kitchen, adjoining pantry, and lavatory, which had all been built in a semicircle around the central shaft, B Deck was a wide-open area: lounge, dining room, and observation deck combined. Floor-to-ceiling windows were generously spaced along the curving hull, letting in dazzling sunlight and a sweeping view of the Pacificus. Kate was already on her feet, field glasses around her neck and nose pressed to the reinforced glass, gazing out in wonder.

Miss Karr was examining the numerous cameras that had been mounted on tripods all around the deck so that she could take pictures of virtually anything outside the ship. Haiku leapt about excitedly, chittering advice. Dr. Turgenev was nowhere to be seen, so I assumed he must already be below on C Deck in the laboratory, using his complicated machinery to test the atmosphere as we climbed. Sir Hugh was the only one sitting, turned away from the windows and writing busily.

Mr. Lunardi certainly hadn't spared any expense on the ship's furnishings. There were leather armchairs and ornate tables and velvet sofas and shaded reading lamps. A hand-painted mural of the solar system adorned the walls between windows. At first glance, the room didn't look very different from the first-class lounges on his luxury airships. But every stick of furniture was bolted to the metal floor, and all the chairs and sofas were fitted with restraining belts. Spaced all across the deck, walls, and ceiling were handholds and footholds so we'd be able to move about more easily when we were weightless.

"How's everyone feeling?" I asked.

"It's incredible!" said Kate. "I was a bit woozy just at the very beginning, but I'm fine now. How fast are we going, Mr. Cruse?"

"One hundred twenty aeroknots, Miss de Vries." I pointed at the odometer mounted on a nearby bulkhead. "And that tells us the distance we've travelled."

"Almost four miles already!" Kate said. "That's about twenty thousand feet!"

Sir Hugh glanced up at this, and I thought his brow seemed shiny. He quickly looked back down at his papers.

In an airship, such a swift ascent would have left us gasping on the floor. But here, in our pressurized, heated *Starclimber*, we noticed no changes at all. I looked at Kate, field glasses to her eyes, scanning the sky. I'd hardly seen her this past week, and I longed for her touch—even the brush of her fingertips against mine would be enough. But there was no chance of that here.

With a sigh, she lowered her field glasses and moved to another window. "I just don't understand why I haven't seen one by now."

I knew she'd been hoping to sight a cloud cat, and prove to Sir Hugh they existed once and for all.

"Maybe it's the wrong time of year, Miss de Vries," I said. I'd become quite used to calling her Miss de Vries by now. "It was September when we saw them, remember."

"You're not still fretting over your flying cats, are you?" said Sir Hugh from his armchair.

Kate's eyes narrowed. "Sorry to disturb you, Sir Hugh. I thought you were *napping.*"

"Not napping, Miss de Vries, writing. I'm working on a scientific article refuting all this nonsense about mysterious life in our skies."

"Surely you should wait a while, Sir Hugh," said Kate.

"I've seen all there is to see in the skies, believe me."

"Maybe they're frightened of the cable, or the ship," I said, hoping to head off any angry words between them.

"They weren't frightened of my grandfather's balloon," Kate replied. "Or the *Aurora*. They're curious. They'd be drawn to us."

"Who's to say they haven't cleared off," I said. "There's been an awful lot of activity around here over the last couple of years. Machinery and rockets and noise."

"I didn't realize we'd be going so fast," Kate said irritably. "I need more time. Can't you ask the captain to slow down?"

"We're bound for outer space, Miss de Vries," I said firmly, practising my own aloofness. "It was never Mr. Lunardi's intent to linger down here."

She looked at me as if she wasn't quite sure whether I was play-acting. I felt pleased by her discomfort. Let *her* see what it's like to feel bewildered and uncertain. Smiling to myself, I moved to another window.

If I gazed straight down I could just make out our ground station—a series of grey rectangles amidst the island's startling green. The coastline was outlined by a beautiful turquoise. Farther away the water became darker and darker blue until it was almost inky.

The *Starclimber* was approaching a bank of cumulus cloud, and I was looking forward to passing through it. For a few moments the windows were enveloped in white mist, brilliant with the sun's light above. Our ship gave a little shudder and then broke through into blue sky.

"Stop the ship!" Kate said suddenly.

"What's wrong?" said Sir Hugh.

"I see one!" said Kate, staring through her field glasses. "Please stop the ship!"

"One what?" said Miss Karr.

"A cloud cat!"

"You're sure?" I asked.

"Yes, yes!"

I went to the ship's phone and pulled it to my mouth. "Cruse here. Request we stop ship. Miss de Vries has made a sighting."

"One moment, Matt," came Tobias's voice from the other end, and I could hear him conferring with Captain Walken. "It'll take us a bit to make a full stop. Stand by."

Through my feet and legs I felt the ship slow, and within thirty seconds we'd come to a complete stop. I checked the odometer: just a shade under six miles. Everyone was crowded around the windows now: Miss Karr and Sir Hugh, even Dr. Turgenev had limped up from his laboratory to see what was going on. Sir Hugh had his own pair of field glasses around his neck. He didn't seem too steady on his feet, and I could tell he didn't like looking out the window. He dabbed his forehead with his handkerchief and cleared his throat.

"Is that it?" said Miss Karr, pointing.

I spotted it too, a distant silhouette of wings against the cloud. "It's coming closer! It's huge!"

"It's just like my grandfather wrote," Kate said triumphantly. "He thought they were birds, but when he drew closer . . . Miss Karr, is your camera ready?"

"I'm *always* ready," snapped Miss Karr, quickly positioning one of her cameras and peering through the viewfinder.

"It should pass right by us!" said Kate breathlessly. "Take as many pictures as you can! Sir Hugh, I think you'll find this exceedingly interesting."

An electric tingle worked its way down my back. I remembered that first, incredible time I'd beheld one of these creatures. They seemed impossible, part bird, part panther, as dangerous as they were beautiful.

With my naked eye I could still see only its silhouette against the bright sky.

Miss Karr took one picture, then another.

"Wonderful," said Sir Hugh, peering through his field glasses.

"You see it?" Kate said, delighted.

"Very clearly," he said. "It's a wonderful whopper swan."

"What?" Kate seized her own binoculars and stared.

"Take a good look, my dear," said Sir Hugh. "I think you'll find your cloud cat has feathers, and a rather prominent bill."

As Kate stared, all the rest of us strained to see the winged creature as it passed within fifty feet of us. I exhaled. It was indeed a very large swan.

"Unusual to see them so far out over the sea," said Sir Hugh smugly, "but not unheard of. They're high flyers too. However, twenty-nine thousand feet is certainly the highest altitude I've heard recorded. I shall write a note for the *Royal Zoological Journal*."

"Sorry for the false alarm, everyone," said Kate with admirable composure.

"You see, my dear," Sir Hugh said, "it's not enough just to see something once; one has to look again, and again, to be sure. *That's* good science."

Kate said nothing. Her face was rigid, her cheeks so red you might have fried eggs on them. I felt a wrenching sympathy for her, but couldn't do anything to comfort her without seeming too familiar.

I went to the ship's phone. "Cruse here. It was a whopper swan."

I heard Tobias chuckle. "All right, thanks, Matt. Let us know if you see any budgies or woodpeckers."

With scarcely a shudder, the *Starclimber* resumed its silken ascent, accelerating into the sky. We all stayed at the windows, even Sir Hugh, staring out in amazement, for the view seemed to change by the second.

"You can see the curve of the earth now!" said Miss Karr.

Sure enough, the blue horizon of the Pacificus was starting to slope gently away on either side.

I checked the odometer. "Seven miles!" I said. "No one's ever been this high!"

"And no one's ever seen a view like this," murmured Miss Karr, taking several pictures. "Earth, sea, sun, and stars, all at once."

Our speed was mind-boggling. Every thirty seconds we were another mile higher. Our island below became smaller and smaller. The upper dome of the sky began to lose its colour, the blue giving way to whiteness.

"Stars!" Kate said, pointing.

Beyond the gauzy veil of the morning sky I could just make out the pinpricks of stars. They became brighter with every breath I took. Then, before my eyes, the upper sky began to dissolve into darkness. It was as though we'd stolen into night, and left the earth still in daylight. Below, the bright blue curve of the ocean, and above, the stars, beckoning us towards outer space.

17 / The End of the Sky

SIR HUGH WAS IN HIGH SPIRITS during lunch, droning on about famous zoological frauds. Kate spooned soup into her mouth, her eyes on the table. I could tell she was still humiliated by her mistake this morning. There was nothing I could do to comfort her properly, so I kept quietly offering her food.

"Some more bread, Miss de Vries?"

"No, thank you, Mr. Cruse."

"Perhaps some salt for your soup?"

"Thank you, I'm fine."

"Some pepper?"

"No, Mr. Cruse, not at this time, but thank you for asking."

"My pleasure. Can I offer anyone else some pepper?"

Captain Walken and Tobias were still on duty on the bridge. My shift would start after lunch. I wasn't looking forward to being paired with Shepherd, but I'd have to get used to it.

". . . the poor fool spent five years insisting that dragons lived on Borneo," Sir Hugh was saying.

Miss Karr was listening to the zoologist, but her dark eyes smouldered with dislike. Shepherd actually looked interested. Haiku had jumped up onto the chandelier above the table, and would occasionally shake a tiny fist at Sir Hugh as the man yammered on.

"The locals called it the Komodo dragon, you see, and had all sorts of outlandish stories about how it breathed fire. Now, this fellow made some sightings and was certain he had a major discovery on his hands. Do you know what his dragon turned out to be, Mr. Shepherd? Nothing more than a very large lizard, a rather slothful thing too. That's why—and I stress this with my students every year—one must look very long and hard at nature, or it can trick you."

It was obvious this story was meant for Kate's benefit. She said nothing, but I couldn't stand his arrogance any longer.

"You know, Sir Hugh," I said, "Miss de Vries isn't the only one who's seen the cloud cats. I've seen them too. They're real."

"I have no doubt you saw *something*," the zoologist said dismissively. "But I'd wager it wasn't what you thought, dear boy."

Dear boy. There was nothing I hated more than being talked down to. I wanted to hurl a bun at his fat head, but held back. I caught Shepherd looking at me with a hint of amusement in his cool eyes, as if wondering how I'd react.

"I know what I saw, Sir Hugh," I said, as calmly as I could. Miss Karr, I noticed, had started taking notes in her book. I hoped she was writing down things like "boastful ass" and "insufferable nitwit."

Seeing that he was being quoted by a journalist, Sir Hugh carried on enthusiastically. "That's why amateurs must be discouraged," he said. "They lack the proper knowledge and powers of observation. And I must say, in my long experience, women are not the equal of men in this regard."

"This is despicable talk, Sir Hugh," Kate said.

"There's no sense railing against the natural order of things," said Sir Hugh calmly. "Mrs. Pankhurst and her suffragettes might as well try to stop the rotation of Earth. Men are simply better suited to scientific investigation. Now, there's nothing wrong with women just because they don't excel at these things; I dare say they have skills we men lack. Why, threading a needle, for instance, is a very difficult business, and I've never met a man who could do it better than a woman."

There was a loud splashing sound as a narrow stream of yellowish liquid curved down from the chandelier into Sir Hugh's soup. Everyone watched, mute with amazement. The last few drops of liquid splish-splashed into the soup, then silence.

"The monkey has urinated in my soup!" cried Sir Hugh.

"It might've been worse," remarked Miss Karr.

Shepherd had pushed back from the table and was doubled over laughing. I don't think I'd ever seen him laugh before, but a monkey peeing in someone's soup was obviously his kind of humour. I couldn't stop my own grin.

"Is it impossible for you to control that beast?" Sir Hugh roared. "This isn't the first time he's harassed me. He needs to be locked up."

"Barbaric!" said Miss Karr. "Haiku isn't some specimen, nor is he a pet. He is a person—not a human person, thank

God, but a person nonetheless—and if there were any justice in the world, he'd have the same rights as you."

"Do I have the right to go urinating in people's soup?" demanded Sir Hugh.

"I really don't see what all the fuss is about, Sir Hugh," said Kate with a polite smile. "As a man of science you should know that urine is sterile. It's only when it's left to stand that it accumulates bacteria. So, if I were you, Sir Hugh, I'd eat my soup *quickly*."

Before the furious Sir Hugh could make a response to this, Dr. Turgenev appeared at the top of the stairs, his spectacles askew.

"I am very excited," he said glumly as walked towards the table. He didn't seem to be leaning as heavily as usual on his cane. "I have momentous news."

"What is it, Dr. Turgenev?" I asked.

He sighed deeply. "Sky has ended."

"How do you mean?" Shepherd asked.

Dr. Turgenev sat down. "I have all morning been studying atmosphere. Up to sixty miles, composition is unchanged—oxygen, nitrogen, hydrium. But after sixty miles, big change occurs."

"What happens?" Kate asked.

"All gone." Dr. Turgenev nodded twice, which, for him, was a sign of huge excitement.

"Nothing at all?" Kate said, and she looked quite upset. "No gases of any kind?"

The scientist shook his head. "Maybe few stray atoms of

oxygen or hydrogen. But mostly nothing. Zero air pressure. This is outer space now."

"Already?" I said, jumping to my feet and rushing for the windows. Everyone else followed.

I was almost disappointed, for we'd been watching the view all morning, and it was not so different now. The distant islands of the Pacificus were small brown wrinkles against the ocean. Earth's curve was a bit deeper now, and ringed in luminous blue light. And beyond that was the great star-speckled blackness of outer space.

But we weren't just looking up at it any more.

We were *in* it.

I peered up and saw the sun, almost directly overhead the *Starclimber*, blazing away in the blackness. It was a strange and thrilling sight.

"Look at the stars!" said Kate. "They're not twinkling."

I stared, for she was right. Their searing light was unwavering.

"Earth's atmosphere distorts light," explained Dr. Turgenev. "That is twinkle. No twinkle in outer space."

"I did like the twinkle," murmured Kate.

"But if we're really in outer space," said Miss Karr suspiciously, "shouldn't we all be floating around?"

Dr. Turgenev shook his head. "Not yet. Gravity does not disappear all at once. It weakens every mile from Earth. Right now we have only seventy-five percent gravity."

We looked about at one another, surprised.

"I hadn't even noticed," I said.

"I had," Dr. Turgenev said, taking a few steps. "My limp is not so bad."

"I *do* feel lighter, now that I think about it," said Miss Karr, giving a few experimental hops. "And Haiku has been extremely bouncy."

"When do we lose gravity completely?" Shepherd asked.

"I am predicting five days," said the scientist, and then he gave a weary sigh. "This is momentous trip. Already we make great discoveries. I have lunch now."

As he walked back to the dining table he glanced at Sir Hugh's bowl with a frown.

"Soup is very yellow," he said.

The moon was bigger and brighter than I'd ever seen.

It hung directly above us, and through the glass dome of the bridge, I watched as the astral cable stretched silver and sparkling towards it, as if anchored there. I knew it wasn't, of course, but somehow I found the thought reassuring. It still made me nervous—that the only thing keeping the *Starclimber* aloft was a metal counterweight spinning through outer space.

"Wouldn't mind going there one day," Tobias said, nodding up at the moon.

"What about your fear of heights?" I asked.

He shrugged. "Well, you know what Dr. Turgenev said. There's no up or down in space, anyway."

It was close to midnight. All day we'd been working short,

staggered shifts on the bridge, but this was the first time Tobias and I had been paired together. We were junior officers, and I think we both felt a bit nervous without Captain Walken around—or even Shepherd, who seemed so confident that you automatically assumed he'd never make a mistake. At the beginning of our shift, Tobias and I had looked quickly at each other, as if to say, *They're putting us in command?* But we didn't say anything. We just got straight to work.

It wasn't that the *Starclimber* was difficult to fly. Once in motion it almost flew itself. But the ship needed constant minding, to make sure all her systems were functioning properly. The motors and cooling fans, the pumps and valves. We checked regularly on the temperature and pressure, the level of carbon dioxide in the air. We scanned the heavens for anything dangerous, especially moving lights. We were pilots and lookouts and mechanics, all.

We didn't talk much, except to pass along necessary information. Everything was new enough that basic tasks still took most of our attention. I didn't know about Tobias, but I had an excited feeling in my stomach the whole time. I was on the very first spaceship, and one of her pilots too.

Travelling at night towards the stars, it occurred to me yet again how very far away they were, and how you could travel your whole lifetime and never reach even the closest one. But knowing you couldn't have something didn't stop you from wanting it. I wondered if Kate was to be my star, if I'd spend my life gazing upon her, but never reaching her.

"There's something between you and Kate de Vries, isn't there," Tobias said.

I checked some gauges. "We're just acquaintances."

He snorted. "You're sweethearts."

"We're not," I said, startled. I'd thought my play-acting was getting pretty good.

"Oxygen's steady at twenty percent," Tobias said, marking the ship's log. "It's the way you look whenever she mentions her fiancé. My cat looks like that before he hacks up a hairball."

"Miss de Vries and I are only—"

"Oh, put a cork in it, Cruse," he said, laughing.

I sighed. I liked Tobias very much, and didn't want to lie to him. "I'm trusting you to keep this secret."

"So why is she engaged to this Sanderson fellow?"

I told him our whole story as we worked. It felt good to talk.

"Well, she's a daredevil for sure," chuckled Tobias. "So she's going to break it off when she gets back?"

"I just hope she can manage it," I said.

"Will she marry you then?"

I let out a slow breath. "I don't know. I hope she'd say yes it I asked her."

Tobias looked over in surprise. "You're not sure?"

"With Kate, I'm never sure of anything."

"But she loves you, doesn't she?"

"I . . . think so. But now she's saying she doesn't want to get married to anyone, ever. She thinks it'd mean giving up too much." I groaned, shaking my head. "Even if she did say yes to me, her parents wouldn't approve. I'm not even sure my own mother would."

"Well, you're in a heck of a jam," he said. "Still, she's very beautiful."

I glanced over at him warily. "Don't start getting any ideas about her. The last time someone took a fancy to Kate, things went very badly for him."

"What happened?"

"He got shot."

"*You* shot him?"

"Well, no, but he did get shot."

"I can see you have a jealous streak," Tobias said.

"Volcanic."

"Well, you don't need to worry about me, buddy. I'm a wipeout with girls. I always say the wrong thing, or spill a drink on them. Or sit on them."

"You *sat* on a girl?"

His eyebrows shot up defensively. "She was really small—I didn't see her. Anyway, I'm a complete disaster."

"You just haven't met the right one yet," I said. "I'm sure there's a girl out there who likes having drinks spilled on her."

"*Thanks,* Matt," he said, then, "We need to check the battery charge."

When Captain Walken and Shepherd came to relieve us at midnight, I didn't feel ready for sleep. Tobias went to our cabin to turn in, but I continued down to B Deck. In the kitchen, I poured myself a glass of water and carried it out into the darkened lounge.

We were now two thousand miles above Earth, a perfect dark semicircle beyond the ship's windows. Gravity's hold had slipped even more since lunch, and I felt awfully light. I set down my water glass and gave a little hop. I lifted much higher than I should have. I wondered if I could hit the ceiling. Flexing my knees, I sprang. Up I shot, much faster than I'd anticipated, and banged my head on a light fixture.

"Ow!" I dropped back down, landing as softly as a cat.

"You're very entertaining," whispered a voice from the darkness.

I jerked in surprise as Kate leaned forward from the shadow of an armchair.

"Sorry to startle you," she said. "I couldn't sleep. The view's better down here."

She was wrapped in a red velvet dressing gown, her hair down, her feet bare. I checked to make sure we were alone.

"If anyone sees us together like this, it'll cause a scandal," Kate said.

I wasn't sure I'd entirely forgiven her for what she'd done. But I'd missed her terribly these past days, and pretending to be just polite acquaintances had nearly driven me crazy. I bent over her and kissed her on the mouth. She reached up and put her arms around my neck, her fingertips in my hair.

"I should go," she murmured, but she didn't.

I drew her onto a sofa beside me. We kissed some more, then sat in silence, staring out the window at the stars. It should've been like that time together in the Paris Observatory, but it wasn't. Everything had changed.

"I hate that ring on your finger," I said.

"Me too." She gave me a mischievous smile. "It is very pretty, though."

"Don't get too fond of it."

"You're becoming a very accomplished actor," she told me. "There were a few times when I looked at you and thought, 'He really doesn't care for me at all.'"

"No," I said, but secretly I was pleased. "Anyway, I'm not that good an actor. Tobias knows."

She looked alarmed. "How? Was it something I said?"

I shook my head. "Apparently, it's the way I look when you talk about Sanderson. Don't worry, he won't tell anyone."

"It's Miss Karr I'm most worried about," said Kate.

"I thought you liked her," I said.

"I like her very much, but she suspects something. Those bright eyes of hers. Scribble, scribble, scribble. Who knows what she's writing down? If she mentions anything romantic about us in the newspaper, I'm finished. I'll be considered a hussy. I might as well go live in the Himalayas with the yetis."

"Well, there was nothing in today's dispatch," I said. "I was on the bridge when she read it to Ground Station. She did say quite a lot about Sir Hugh, though."

"Did she mention how Haiku peed in his soup?"

"No. But she did say Sir Hugh had the bearing of a peacock."

Kate giggled. "He won't like that."

I grinned. "He won't know till he gets back to Earth."

"I wanted to strangle him at lunch," she said. "I actually imagined how his fat neck would feel in my hands."

"You did a good job hiding it," I said.

Kate gave a big sigh. "I keep thinking about what Dr. Turgenev said. If there's really no oxygen, no *anything,* it's hard to see how there can be life of any sort."

She seemed downcast, so I said, "I wouldn't give up on outer space just yet. Strange things tend to pop up when you're around."

"I hope so. I can't bear it if Sir Hugh's right." Her eyes brightened. "Oh look, another shooting star."

I caught sight of a tiny bright diamond moving through outer space. We'd seen hundreds of shooting stars that morning. Even though I knew they were just meteoroids burning up in the atmosphere, I couldn't help thinking of what General Lancaster had said about other spaceships. I wasn't the only one who'd been watching them very closely. I'd seen Shepherd's eyes lock on to them and follow them until they'd flickered their last.

I frowned. "We're not in the atmosphere any more."

Kate looked confused.

"It's the friction against the atmosphere that makes them glow," I explained. "That one's too high to be a shooting star."

"Are you sure?" Kate said.

I stared hard as the light abruptly angled upward.

"*And* they don't change course," I said, running for the ship's phone. It was Shepherd who picked up on the bridge. "It's

Cruse here. Can you see a light moving off your starboard side, about four o'clock?"

I waited for a moment, tracking it myself through the window.

"We see it, Cruse."

"It just changed course."

His voice grew muffled as he talked hurriedly with Captain Walken. Then he came back to me. "Cruse, get Dr. Turgenev to see this. And wake Miss Karr too. We want photos."

"Will do." I hung up and turned to Kate. "I need to wake Dr. Turgenev and Miss Karr. You should go."

"It just changed colour!" Kate exclaimed, pointing.

Sure enough, the moving star was now blue.

"It's like the one we saw in Paris," I breathed.

Kate squeezed my hand. "How far away do you think it is?"

"Could be a hundred miles, could be a million." Even after three years of crow's nest duty, judging distances across the sky was no easy feat. There were so few reference points.

Then, in the blink of an eye, the light was gone.

"Where'd it go?" Kate cried.

My eyes tracked across the dark ether, trying to anticipate where it would reappear. I kept thinking of it as a star, even though I knew it couldn't be. Stars did not move.

"There!" I said. The blue light was stationary now, but seemed to glow more intensely. "I'm waking the others."

I took a few steps, then stopped and turned back. I realized the star wasn't motionless at all. It was moving—only this time, straight for us. It started to pulse. And it was clearly swelling in size.

I rushed to the phone. "It's coming right at us!"

"We see it, Mr. Cruse," came the captain's voice. "I'm sounding the alarm."

The light was the size of a golf ball now. The ship's alarm began its slow wail. I heard cabin doors opening on A Deck.

"What's happening?" said Tobias, rushing down the stairs.

Dr. Turgenev was close behind.

I pointed. "I think it's headed our way."

Miss Karr hurried down and went straight for her camera.

"What is it?" Tobias said.

It was the size of a billiard ball now, the flashing light so bright it scared my eyes. The entire lounge was bathed in an eerie blue glow.

"Do not look directly at light!" warned Dr. Turgenev as he pulled down the polarized blinds we used to screen out direct sunlight.

I didn't know what the captain's plan of action would be. Slow down? Or accelerate? It would be like trying to dodge a cannonball. I knew the *Starclimber* was rising at full speed, yet the light was still coming right for us. I felt so powerless I wanted to shout.

"Good God!" said Sir Hugh as he came down the stairs.

Chef Vlad was here now too, shaking his head.

Even with the blinds, the light made you squint. Everyone

was cast in blue. The thing was the size of a tennis ball now. In between flashes, I thought I caught an outline of something wedge-shaped. The size of a basketball now . . .

"Hold tight!" I shouted, even though I knew it was pointless. The impact would be colossal. We'd be obliterated instantly.

Sir Hugh threw himself into a seat and buckled up, as did some of the others. But Miss Karr didn't budge from her camera, taking picture after picture, and I marvelled at her bravery.

Just when it seemed the light was about to engulf us entirely, it veered and was gone, leaving behind a faint tremor in the *Starclimber,* and the sensation of something large and immensely fast having sped by. I rushed across B Deck to the opposite windows.

There, slanting heavenward, was the blue light, already quite tiny again, and still pulsing before it disappeared from sight.

Chef Vlad served coffee, and we all sat hunched forward in our chairs, cradling our mugs, talking and talking about what we'd just seen. Captain Walken had brought the *Starclimber* to a standstill, and he and Shepherd were now with us in the lounge.

"Dr. Turgenev, what do you make of this?" the captain asked.

"Seeing was very difficult," the scientist said dejectedly, polishing his spectacles on his rather threadbare dressing gown. "Maybe meteorite."

"But it changed direction," I said.

The scientist shrugged. "This I did not see. Is possible it is in deteriorating elliptical orbit." With his finger he drew a shrinking spiral in the air. "It circles around Earth, but to us it looks like it moves up and then down, yes?"

I nodded. It seemed a reasonable enough explanation. After it had passed our ship, I'd watched as it climbed high and then angled back towards Earth.

"That doesn't explain the light," Shepherd said.

"Or the blue colour," I said.

"This is harder to explain," said Dr. Turgenev. "Maybe some kind of phosphorescent ore."

"Rock doesn't flash," said Shepherd.

"I have no explanation for this," said the scientist simply.

"The flash was quite regular," Kate said. "I don't know if anyone noticed."

I hadn't, and I was very impressed that she had.

"Three seconds bright," she said. "Two seconds dark. I counted."

"Sounds almost like a ship's running lights," said Shepherd, looking at Captain Walken.

"What are you suggesting, Mr. Shepherd?" said Sir Hugh with a nervous laugh.

Shepherd ignored him. "Miss Karr, did you get any pictures?"

"Lots," she said. "But I've no idea how they'll turn out. That light might've overexposed my film. Even if it hasn't, all we'll see is a very bright light."

"But no one else has a spaceship," said Sir Hugh impatiently. Then he looked at the captain. "Do they?"

"Not on Earth, Sir Hugh," said Captain Walken. "But there's been some speculation that they may come from another planet."

"Like Mars," said Tobias.

Sir Hugh rolled his eyes. "Oh, not the old Martian canal hoax again!"

"I agree with Sir Hugh," said Dr. Turgenev. "Is much more likely this is space rock. Maybe type we have not seen before."

"Thank you, Dr. Turgenev," said Sir Hugh.

Shepherd's cool eyes were far from convinced. "Unless you can show me a rock that flashes blue light, that thing was a ship. And it took a nice long look at us. General Lancaster needs to hear about this."

"You have my permission to radio him the details," said Captain Walken, and I could tell from his tone of voice that he was reminding Shepherd of his place. "Whatever we saw," he continued, "my chief concern is whether we'll have another close encounter with it."

Dr. Turgenev shook his head. "If it is meteorite, no. By time it makes another orbit, it will be below us."

"But what about the cable?" I said, repressing a shiver.

"Good point, Mr. Cruse," said the captain. "Could it withstand a collision?"

Dr. Turgenev shrugged. "I think no. But let us remember that cable is very thin. Probability of being struck is teeny."

"I hope so," said Tobias.

I saw Kate take a breath. "No one's raised the possibility that it was alive."

Sir Hugh snorted. "Ah, Miss de Vries, once again leaping to conclusions." Wrapped up in his plush royal blue robe, he seemed even puffier than usual. Miss Karr's description of him as a peacock seemed remarkably appropriate.

"I haven't made *any* conclusion," said Kate firmly. "But I think we should consider the possibility."

"My dear," said Sir Hugh, "didn't you hear what Dr. Turgenev said earlier? Nothing could survive outside these walls."

"Life exists in all sorts of difficult places," Kate said. "There are organisms that can live in ice, and boiling water, even acid."

"You're talking about extremophiles, perhaps," said Sir Hugh, with a dismissive wave of his hand. "But they tend to be microscopic. And even they need some kind of food supply. What do you expect would nourish something up here?"

"I don't know yet," said Kate. "But it's something to investigate."

"Feel free," said Sir Hugh. "Perhaps you can self-publish a pamphlet like Dr. Ganev. He claimed he saw life bouncing about on the moon. Do you know what his little moon-people turned out to be? Moisture inside his telescope."

"Could anyone make out the shape of it?" Kate asked, ignoring the zoologist.

"It was too quick," said Tobias. "I was nearly blinded."

Kate turned hopefully to me.

"I might have seen its outline," I said, "before it got too close, but I'm not sure. Oval-shaped."

"I thought so too!" said Kate. "And smooth. It didn't seem like rock."

"It was a *rock*, Miss de Vries," said Sir Hugh.

Kate's nostrils narrowed. "Aren't *you* the one leaping to conclusions, Sir Hugh? It seems you've already decided there's no chance of life in outer space. *I'm* willing to keep looking."

"I'm sure we all will, Miss de Vries," Captain Walken said. "That's one of the reasons for our journey. We may see our blue light again. Though I hope, for all our sakes, not at quite such close quarters."

Captain Walken returned to the bridge with Shepherd, and the rest of us carried our mugs to the kitchen and then headed up to our cabins. Kate went on ahead with Miss Karr, for they were sharing adjoining rooms. I wondered if Miss Karr had noticed that Kate had not been in her bed when the alarm sounded.

As I tried to get to sleep, my head was noisy with thoughts. Part of me hoped that Kate was right, and that outer space was no empty wasteland but home to all sorts of new life. But for the first time I felt the true vulnerability of the *Starclimber*. We were fragile, with only a thin metal shell between us and astral ether. We were far from home, and could be broken so easily.

18 / Raptures of the Heights

"**W**HO'S IT GOING TO BE, do you think?" I said. I was down in the airlock with Tobias, checking the astral suits and the life-support machinery.

"Shepherd, probably."

"Probably."

But we didn't know for sure who the captain would choose for the first spacewalk. All we knew was that slowly, day by day, gravity had weakened, and according to Dr. Turgenev, it would disappear altogether sometime today. As soon as it did, a single astralnaut would be going outside to make history.

It was ten in the morning, day five of our expedition, and we were fifteen thousand miles from earth. If I pressed my face against the porthole and looked straight down, I could just make out the indigo-hued curve of our planet—like a small ball I could hold in one hand. It gave me a pang to see it so far away, and to know that we'd get farther still, for we were still three days from cable's end.

There'd been no more sightings of the blue light, but it was never far from my thoughts—or Shepherd's, I knew. When not on duty, he'd taken to scanning the heavens, and had had Miss Karr teach him how to use the cameras in case he saw anything. He still thought the light was some kind of ship, and every day he radioed a report to General Lancaster at Ground Station.

Kate was disappointed there'd been no more sightings, for she still held out hope there was life in outer space. Miss Karr too grew more restless, saying that she was bored with the view and that she'd photographed space in every way possible. She'd taken to prowling about the ship with one of her smaller cameras, sneaking candid pictures of us. In her daily dispatches home she was starting to comment on the stale air aboard ship, the cramped quarters, and how certain passengers seemed to take up more than their fair share of oxygen. Sir Hugh seemed content enough, though he too complained about the stuffiness, and about Haiku. The little monkey harassed him at every turn—and was a notorious farter to boot. None of us were thrilled, but it drove Sir Hugh quite mad.

As for me, I was growing impatient too—and I could tell Tobias and Shepherd were as well. As nervous as I was about making a spacewalk, I wanted to get out there, to know what it felt like. But I doubted I'd be the first to go.

"Looks good to me," said Tobias, after checking the last astralnaut suit.

I replaced a helmet on its peg. Everything was incredibly light now. We had to be careful walking, for we tended to lift off with every step.

I heard footsteps, and Shepherd appeared in the hatchway.

"We just got some news from back home," he said. "The

captain wanted me to pass it on. The Celestial Tower's been destroyed."

I felt his words like a blow to my stomach. "Was it the Babelites?" I asked.

"They don't know yet. The thing just collapsed."

I'd worked on that tower for two weeks. Nothing had seemed more solid. And the French had been so confident. I thought of all those posters plastered about Paris, the promises that they'd be in outer space within a year. How could all those dreams be reduced to a mountain of twisted wreckage?

"Were many people killed?" I asked.

"Not that many," Shepherd said. "That's the good news."

"It could've been much worse," I said. "It was already two miles high when I worked on it."

Tobias was shaking his head. "Didn't Dr. Turgenev say it'd never make it?"

I nodded. "Sounds like it couldn't bear its own weight."

"Or the Babelites gave it a push," said Shepherd.

I didn't know which was more worrying: an accident caused by the Babelites, or one caused by the mistakes of so many brilliant scientists and engineers working together.

"We're lucky the general's keeping an eye on things for us," said Shepherd.

I didn't like the general, but I had to admit it was a comfort to think the Aero Force was guarding the astral cable back on Earth.

Tobias looked uneasy. "You ever wonder if the Babelites were right?"

Shepherd turned to him sharply. "What're you talking about?"

"Not about God getting angry," said Tobias awkwardly. "But . . . maybe we're not supposed to be up here at all."

"If you felt that way, why'd you come?" Shepherd asked calmly, but I didn't like the edge to his voice.

"I'm just speaking my mind, Shepherd," said Tobias in anger, his eyebrows compressing together.

Shepherd shook his head. "I didn't expect superstitious talk from my fellow astralnauts."

"It's not superstitious," I said, feeling my own temper rise. "I know what Tobias means. What we're doing is dangerous, and no one's done it before. We don't know what to expect up here. Anything could happen. And I don't like hearing about the tower coming down either."

"Makes me wonder if anyone really knows what they're doing," said Tobias.

"Doubts have no place aboard ship," Shepherd said. "It's bad for morale."

"So's pretending to be captain," Tobias shot back.

Shepherd said nothing, but there was a flash of fury in his eyes that was nearly as violent as a blow. My whole body tensed.

"You two are on duty in five minutes," Shepherd said, and left the airlock.

Tobias grimaced. "Stupid of me. But it's true enough. The way he talks to us."

And it wasn't just the way he treated *us*. We'd both noticed how Shepherd seemed to chafe under Captain Walken's command. He was always civil, and obedient, but I got the sense he didn't respect the captain. That bothered me— made me angry too. Shepherd, despite all his skill, would never make as good a leader as Captain Walken.

I clapped Tobias on the back. "Don't worry. Let's head up."

We climbed the stairs to B Deck, our feet scarcely touching the steps, we were so light now. In the lounge, Miss Karr was sitting before her typewriter, clacking out her latest dispatch. Kate was engrossed in a big book. Sir Hugh was writing away. Haiku was perched on a side table, slyly looking at Sir Hugh. I kept my eye on him. He was obviously plotting. Then, with a flick of his wrist, he threw something. I watched it sail through the air and over top of Sir Hugh's head. The zoologist didn't notice. Haiku sat very still, pretending to pick his nose, and then made a second throw. This time he hit Sir Hugh square on the head.

The zoologist's hand flew up and came away smudged brown. His face wrinkled in revulsion.

"Where's that damn monkey!" he cried.

"What's the matter?" said Miss Karr, looking up.

"You said he was toilet trained!"

"He is."

"He's throwing his feces at me! I'll have his head!"

Sir Hugh looked about in fury, spotted the monkey, and heaved himself out of his chair in pursuit. And then an amazing thing happened—

Sir Hugh left his chair and kept going, soaring weightlessly across the room. Haiku, seeing Sir Hugh coming for him, launched himself off the table, and with a squeal, flew across the room. Miss Karr, who'd been in the midst of standing, floated straight up towards the ceiling.

Haiku grabbed hold of a floor lamp and scampered beneath the shade as Sir Hugh went careening past, thrashing his arms and legs and bellowing like a sea lion. He collided with the window, and I winced, even though I knew the glass could withstand it. He ricocheted off and bounced, upside down, against the ceiling.

"Help!" he bellowed.

"We have zero gravity!" Dr. Turgenev announced, coming up the stairs behind me from C Deck.

"We know!" I called back.

A great clash of cookware came from the kitchen, followed by some serious cursing in Transylvanian.

"Why does no one warn me of this!" Chef Vlad roared through the doors.

"I told him earlier," Dr. Turgenev said with a shrug. "But I do not think he was listening."

"I've been looking forward to this," Tobias said, pushing off across the room. He was so accustomed to working under water that weightlessness was quite familiar to him. Laughing, he somersaulted in mid-air, tumbling over and over. I was envious of his agility in the air.

"Help!" Sir Hugh wailed again.

"Use the handholds on the ceiling, Sir Hugh," I called out, but it seemed beyond him.

Miss Karr, on the other hand, had already given herself a firm push off from the ceiling and had drifted back down to the floor, where, with Kate and Tobias's help, she got herself reseated and buckled in.

"Is Haiku all right?" she asked, searching with her eyes for him.

"He's swinging from the lamp," I said. Haiku was spinning gleefully round and round the lamppost.

"Cruse, lend a hand, will you," said Sir Hugh crossly.

I gently launched myself and sailed diagonally up to the ceiling to help Sir Hugh. "Just give yourself a little push now, Sir Hugh," I said when I reached him.

It took us a couple of tries but eventually we floated down to the floor together, and I slipped my feet into two nearby footholds. I manoeuvred the zoologist into an arm-chair and fastened his seat belt.

"Well, this is quite unusual," he said. His legs and arms kept drifting up, and he stared at them askance before pulling them back down to their proper positions.

Kate was already becoming quite adventurous, soaring across the room, pushing off from bits of furniture when she stalled in flight. Her long auburn hair undulated about her face. I turned to see Dr. Turgenev floating too. For the first time since I'd met him, he was truly smiling. He had no more need of his cane, and he seemed a completely different person.

I was handing out the magnetic overshoes when Captain Walken floated deftly down the spiral staircase.

"Excellent," he said. "I see you're all getting your space legs. Mr. Blanchard, suit up, please. You're to be our first man in outer space."

Floating side by side in the airlock, Tobias and I breathed pure oxygen through our face masks. We needed to do this for half an hour, to purge our blood of nitrogen. Even within our pressurized spacesuits, any nitrogen gas left in our bodies could expand and give us what divers called "the bends." Tobias knew all about it. A mild case could give you itchy skin, rashes, pain in your joints. A serious case could paralyze or kill you. We were all suited up except for our helmets. I wasn't going outside, but would stay behind in the open airlock to spot Tobias.

"I can't believe I'm going first," he said, shaking his head.

"After you, no one will ever be first again," I told him.

"Well, let's hope I'm up to it." His voice sounded hoarse.

"Of course you're up to it. That's why the captain chose you."

"He just needed someone fresh," said Tobias. "It would've been Shepherd if he hadn't just come off shift." He grinned at me. "Still, I wish I could've seen his face when the captain told him."

"It's right you're first," I said. "No one was better than you in the pool."

Tobias's face clouded. "I keep thinking of the Celestial Tower."

I nodded. It had been hovering over my thoughts too.

"Do you think it was the Babelites?" he asked me.

"All I know," I said, "is that they can't touch us. We're safe. Every bolt on this ship's been gone over four times. And we've got good old General Lancaster down there, making sure everything's 'tickety-boo.'"

Tobias chuckled and imitated the general's voice. "Tickety-boo."

I looked at the wall-mounted clock and removed my mask. "We're ready."

I floated over to the two great spools of umbilical tubing mounted on the ceiling. I took the end of one and locked it into the back of Tobias's suit. The umbilicus had been specially redesigned and strengthened so that it was both oxygen line and safety tether. This line would be the only thing connecting Tobias to the ship. I turned around so Tobias could hook mine up for me.

"Stay away from the stern," I reminded him. The astral cable carried an immense voltage, enough to electrocute a man. The *Starclimber* itself completed the electric circuit, so the cable above the bow was safe to touch.

I picked up his helmet and lifted it over his head. "Good luck," I said. "You're a shark, remember. One very lucky shark."

He winked, but his face was pale. I lowered the helmet,

locking it into place and double-checking the clamps. Then he put on my helmet for me.

Drifting over to the control console, I flicked the switches that would start the flow of oxygen into our suits. My ears popped at the reassuring hiss. I turned on our radios. Unlike the underwater practice suits, these ones were fitted with small transmitters and receivers that would let us communicate with each other.

"Can you hear me?" I said.

"I hear you," Tobias replied.

"Are you ready?"

"Ready."

Before we could open the outer hatch, we needed to make sure the airlock was the same pressure as outer space. I pulled a lever, and even through my helmet could hear the pumps busily sucking the atmosphere out of the airlock. The needle on the pressure gauge gradually fell, from fourteen pounds per square inch . . . all the way to the bottom.

"We're at zero," I said. "I'm going to open the hatch."

I manoeuvred myself in front of it and locked my feet into the floor cleats. I took hold of the wheel, as I'd practised under water many times, and turned. It moved surprisingly easily. Then, with a careful tug, I swung the hatch inside, all three hundred pounds of it, as though it were light as tin.

There, right before me, was outer space, nothing separating us.

Just me and the stars and a billion miles in between.

Without tinted windows to dull them, the stars looked

brighter than ever—and more numerous than I'd ever imagined.

Everything seemed so still, though of course we weren't really still. Even though the captain had stopped the *Starclimber*, we were in fact moving. As we clung to our astral thread, we turned with the planet at thousands of miles an hour. The thought made me feel a bit woozy, but luckily I had to look away so I could fasten the hatch securely against the airlock's inside wall.

Tobias drifted over to the open portal and put his hands on the rim. For a moment he gazed out into the star-pricked vastness. Then, without another moment's hesitation, he stepped outside.

"I'm out!" he said.

I positioned myself within easy reach of the controls and the umbilicus spool. I kept a close watch on the spool, making sure it rolled out smoothly. Tobias floated away from the ship, angled slightly forward, ten feet . . . twenty feet . . . thirty feet. It was the most uncanny thing to see him, his arms and legs spread wide, hanging there against the heavens. I stopped paying out the umbilicus.

"I've got you at forty feet, Tobias," I said.

I saw him reach the end of his tether and jerk back slightly. It was made of the same material as the land-diving cable and had plenty of bounce in it.

"You're looking grand, Tobias!" I said. "The first man to walk in space!"

I knew that inside, on B Deck, Miss Karr was busily taking

pictures. Everyone would be pressed to the windows, watching, and I felt a hot flush of envy. I wished I could have been out there for Kate to see.

"Not much of a spacewalk yet," I heard Tobias say. He bent his knees slightly and did a somersault. "Now the problem is stopping," he said as he continued to twirl neatly round and round.

"Try the air pistol," I suggested.

We'd been kitted out with a tiny pistol that clipped onto our suits. Inside was a cartridge of compressed air. One squeeze of the trigger would release a minuscule squirt—but in the vacuum of space, it was supposed to have enough force to shove you in the opposite direction.

I saw Tobias unclip his pistol and point it. "Let's see if Mr. Isaac Newton was correct," he said. "Every action has an equal and opposite reaction. Here goes."

Newton was right. Tobias squeezed the trigger and he instantly reversed direction.

"How are you feeling, Tobias?" I asked.

"Just fine," he said.

"You see any blue lights?"

"No blue lights, but the view is absolutely amazing! I can see Earth below us. It's no bigger than a tennis ball! I can see the Pacificus and the Hawaiis. Pretty sure I can see Van Diemen's Land too! Give me a few more feet, will you, Matt?"

"I'll uncoil you to sixty," I said, and measured out the line.

Using the air pistol, Tobias jetted out to the end of his tether, swooping and putting on a bit of a show. I could just imagine Miss Karr eagerly capturing this on film and noting details for today's dispatch: *Tobias Blanchard, our first astralnaut, cavorts in space* . . .

He was amazingly acrobatic. With a twitch on his lifeline he came sailing back towards the *Starclimber*, and managed to land boots first against the hull, just above the hatch. I craned my neck to see him, standing straight and tall, holding a loop of his tether in both hands like the reins of some stellar chariot. Sunlight blazed off his reflective visor. He was an astral god, plunging through space towards his home planet.

"This is fantastic!" he said. "I had no idea there were so many stars. I swear we only see half of these from Earth! You can see things in them, you know, there're so many, you can see shapes, and faces . . ."

He sailed out again to the end of his tether. I worried he was travelling with a little too much force this time, so I eased him out some more line, not wanting him to get tugged back too sharply. I couldn't quite banish the image of the umbilicus snapping—and Tobias sailing eternally out into space.

I checked the clock in the airlock. Captain Walken had given us orders that the first spacewalk was to be no longer than thirty minutes. We were already halfway done—

"Matt, there's something out here."

I turned back to the hatch, and was shocked when I couldn't see Tobias. I poked my head out and saw that he'd propelled himself higher, almost level with the ship's bow.

"What do you see?" I asked.

"Some kind of rock, I think."

"Is it stationary?" I asked.

"I think so. I think it's quite close."

I wondered if he was right. Distances out here were almost impossible to estimate. It might be something very small, inches from his nose, or a planet, a million miles away.

"If you give me about twenty more feet, I can get closer."

"Careful, Tobias." With some unease, I unwound the spool.

"Here we go," Tobias said. "It's definitely some kind of rock. Oblong shape, kind of flat. Should I bring it back to the ship?"

"I think our scientists would be thrilled to have a space rock," I said, thinking of Kate's reaction. Finally, something for her to examine.

"Let's see . . ."

High above me Tobias unhooked the specimen bag attached to his hip and with both hands held it open and brought it down over something I couldn't see, for his body was blocking my view. He cinched the bag tight.

"It's pretty big," said Tobias over the radio. "Doesn't weigh a thing out here, though!"

"You should be heading back inside now, Tobias," I said.

"I can see Orion so clearly. Practically make out the scratches on his club."

I laughed. "Just make sure he doesn't whack you one."

"And the moon!" he exclaimed. "It's just on the other side of the ship!"

"Looks close, does it?"

"It *is* close. I had no idea we'd be getting so near it!"

I was no astronomer, but I knew the moon was still very, very far away.

"It's incredible, Matt. I can see everything, every crater. One good push and I could get there."

Suddenly Tobias seemed to be getting smaller. I pulled my head back inside the hatchway and, shocked, saw the spool unreeling line, fast. Tobias had obviously given himself a big push with his air pistol and was sailing out deeper into space.

"Tobias, our half-hour's up. You need to come back now."

"I just want to get a bit closer to the moon, Matt."

"Tobias. That's a long trip, and not for today."

"I hadn't counted on the sounds," said Tobias.

"What sounds are those?" I asked.

"From the stars," he said. "There's a definite music they make. You can't hear it inside the ship, but out here, it's really clear. It's beautiful."

Every sky sailor had heard about the raptures of the heights, when someone sailed too high or lost their way over the sea, and was overwhelmed by the endless vista before them. It took the form of euphoria, a feeling that anything was possible. I started worrying that Tobias was intoxicated by the heavenly ether.

I locked the spool so it wouldn't pay out any more umbilicus.

"Hey!" came Tobias's voice, and he sounded angry. "Why're you stopping me?"

"Tobias, time's up," I said firmly. "Captain's orders, mate."

"Matt, the moon's just up ahead. I know there's a lot more line left on that spool. Come on!"

"Can't do it, Tobias." I started to reel in the line, but met with resistance. He was fighting me with his air pistol, trying to inch his way closer to the moon.

I wedged myself against the cleats and started turning the umbilicus wheel with all my strength.

"Matt, let it go!" shouted Tobias. "I can always unhook my tether."

I went cold all over. I stopped turning the wheel. "Tobias, don't do that."

"I might never get a chance like this again—"

"Later. But come back in now. Miss Karr wants to interview you and get your picture for the papers. A lot of people back home are waiting to read about the first man in space."

I heard his breathing over the radio, laboured. "It's all so big . . . shouldn't be out here . . . don't belong . . . I'm cold . . ."

I tried to keep the panic from my voice. "We'll have a nice mug of coffee waiting. I'm going to reel you in now. Help me out."

There was no answer. I listened hard, straining to hear the sound of his breathing.

"Tobias?"

I started turning the wheel to reel him in, and this time there was absolutely no resistance. My stomach lurched. It felt like there was nothing at the end of the line. What if he'd cut himself loose? I turned harder, and then my frantic brain remembered how everything was weightless now. Too late, I saw Tobias come soaring down past the open hatchway, arms and legs splayed, motionless. I'd brought him back with too much force, and now he was headed beyond the stern and—

"Tobias, watch out for the cable!"

But I got no reply. He made no attempt to use his air pistol. I reeled him in with all my might, trying to shorten the line and keep him from colliding with the high-voltage cable. He wasn't ten feet away from it when he reached the end of his line. He snapped back and began rising towards me. I reeled in some more.

I made a bad job of it. Twice he banged against the hull before I could get him close enough to grab him. It was a clumsy, exhausting business, my feet jammed into their cleats. Seizing him under the arms and pulling, it took all my strength to haul him back inside.

"Tobias!" I shouted. "Tobias, let me hear you!"

"I'm fine, I'm fine," he said, sounding half asleep.

He bobbed about. I couldn't make out his face through the mirrored visor. As quickly as I could, I swung shut the outer hatch.

I pulled the lever and heard the fans furiously pumping air back into our chamber, pressurizing it. While waiting, I managed to get Tobias belted down to the bench.

"I'll have you out in a second," I said to him.

"I must've just blanked out for a minute," he said groggily, starting to fumble for his helmet clamps.

"Not yet!" I pushed his hands away and kept an eye on the pressure gauge. When the needle touched 14.7 pounds per square inch, I unclasped Tobias's helmet and lifted it from his head. His pale skin glistened with sweat, and his eyes seemed huge, like he'd seen more than he could comprehend.

I pulled off my own helmet. "You all right?"

He nodded miserably. "I messed up."

"You did not mess up," I told him. "It's all new, and you did it first. No one could've done better."

He grunted, but I could tell he didn't believe me. I felt terrible for him. We obviously hadn't realized how mesmerizing outer space was. I'd had just a taste peering out from the airlock—but what must it be like to be surrounded by the vastness of it, and spreading your wings above Earth?

The inner hatch opened and Captain Walken floated in.

"Seems you were a bit too comfortable out there, Mr. Blanchard," he said.

Tobias sighed. "I was just . . . I wasn't prepared for it. It's completely overwhelming. I'm sorry, sir."

"Not at all, Mr. Blanchard. You did beautifully. Well done." Captain Walken gave me a nod. "Good work, Mr. Cruse."

"Thanks, Matt," Tobias said. Colour was returning to his face. "Should've listened to you sooner. I feel totally shattered."

"Come have something to eat," said the captain, nudging Tobias towards the inner hatch. "Mr. Vlad has lunch waiting upstairs."

It was our first meal in zero gravity.

Gone were the plates and bowls and glasses. We buckled ourselves down to our seats at the dining table and ate from little containers with slotted lids. You had to push back the slot so you could stick in your fork and spear a bit of food, then quickly close the slot so the rest of the food didn't float away. There were sealed cups with special valved straws jutting out so we could sip our water or tea. Everything had a magnetic bottom and stuck to the surface of the metal table.

The food, as always, was delicious. Everyone was here except Captain Walken, who was keeping watch on the bridge. He'd started the *Starclimber* moving again, back on course to cable's end.

We all listened, enthralled, as Tobias told us about his spacewalk. Miss Karr busily took notes for her newspaper dispatch. Whenever she paused, she let go of her pencil and let it hover.

"I don't think the tests really prepare you for it," said Tobias. He looked over at me. "Not even close. You'll see when you get out there."

"Astral psychosis," Dr. Turgenev said.

"What's that?" I asked, alarmed by the sound of it.

"Is just theory," he said. "Space is alien environment to humans. Very traumatic for us. We need to study this now."

"You said you heard music," I reminded Tobias.

He frowned as if he'd forgotten, then looked embarrassed. "You're right, I thought I did."

"Sounds like another hallucination," said Shepherd, who probably thought Tobias had done a poor job altogether.

"Although," Kate said, "Pythagoras did think the movement of the stars and planets made a kind of perfectly harmonious music. He called it 'the music of the spheres.' He said it was inaudible on Earth, but presumably not in the heavens."

Miss Karr beamed. "I like that," she said, making a note of it.

There was something beautiful, but also eerie, about the idea of music in outer space. It reminded me of the myth of the siren's song that would trick mariners into jumping overboard to reach it. The music of the spheres had almost drowned Tobias. I hoped I would be strong enough to resist its pull.

"Pythagoras lived over two thousand years ago," remarked Sir Hugh, "when they believed many quaint things."

"What a dry little life you lead, Sir Hugh," Miss Karr said.

Sir Hugh tilted his chin. "Not at all, Miss Karr. I merely prefer to restrict myself to the *real* wonders of the world, and not the imaginary ones."

"Is no sound in outer space," said Dr. Turgenev simply. "I am sorry, but music is impossible. Sound is wave and must pass through *something* to make vibration. Is nothing up here to carry sound."

Sir Hugh smiled smugly. "Thank you, Dr. Turgenev, for your voice of reason."

Kate said nothing, but I knew she was disappointed.

"Is there any more news about the Celestial Tower?" Tobias asked Shepherd.

"Dreadful business," murmured Miss Karr.

Shepherd nodded. "We got word during your spacewalk. The French are saying it was a bomb."

"Good God," said Sir Hugh.

"How could the French let it happen?" I said, stunned. "After that first attempt, they must've tripled security!"

"Whatever they did, it wasn't enough," said Tobias.

A heavy silence fell over the table. I wondered if everyone was thinking the same terrible thought as me. If it could happen to the Celestial Tower, it could happen to us. I noticed that Shepherd's eyes were moving from one person to the next, as if studying our reactions.

"We don't have anything to worry about," he said with complete authority. "The French obviously didn't know what they were doing. But General Lancaster and our Aero Force are taking good care of us."

"Tickety-boo," said Tobias softly.

At that moment Mr. Vlad clanked out from the kitchen in his magnetic shoes. In one hand he held a dusty brown bottle with an impressively faded label.

"Mr. Lunardi gave me a very fine champagne," he said, swaying back and forth. "He gave me express instructions to open it after the first spacewalk."

"I think we could all use some champagne, Mr. Vlad," I said.

"I will uncork it carefully, so no one loses an eye, hey?"

"Wait—" I said, but was too late.

As he yanked out the cork there was a loud *pop*, and champagne spurted across the room in a huge golden arc, instantly forming itself into a thousand perfect sparkling spheres.

"Ah yes, I forgot," the Transylvanian chef remarked. "Drinking this may be somewhat of a problem now."

"Not so," said Dr. Turgenev, and he unbuckled himself and pushed off, sailing through the air and capturing a globe of champagne in his mouth.

It was quite an amazing manoeuvre, and all the more remarkable because it was the doleful scientist who'd done it.

"What fun!" said Kate, shooting off in pursuit, her braided hair hovering above her head like a cobra waiting to strike.

"To outer space," I said, launching myself after some champagne. "And the first man to walk in it. To you, Mr. Blanchard."

"Congratulations, Blanchard," said Shepherd, giving Tobias a cool nod. If he was consumed with jealousy, he did a good job of hiding it.

"Thank you very much," Tobias said. "The two of you'll be out there soon. And I'm sure you'll behave yourselves better than I did."

It was a very merry time as we all sailed about the lounge trying to catch the champagne. Miss Karr clanked over to one of her cameras and flashed off picture after picture. Tired as he was, Tobias perked up after gulping a bit of champagne. Sir Hugh, refusing to unbuckle himself from his seat, used a long straw to suck in bits of champagne that floated within easy reach. Miss Karr tried the same technique, but grew impatient and slipped out of her magnetic shoes to join us in the air.

Haiku had figured out that his flatulence could give him an extra push in mid-air, and he was now farting enthusiastically as he chased after champagne. But before long he was hanging upside down from the ceiling, flailing his arms about like an opera singer and singing an aria of delight, which after several minutes dwindled into a kind of parched whimpering.

"Look at him, he's completely sloshed," said Miss Karr. "You silly little monkey. That'll teach you."

Soon most of the champagne had been devoured.

"Where's this space rock you brought aboard?" Kate asked.

"It's down on C Deck," I said. "I strapped it to one of the lab workbenches."

"This will be worth examining," said Dr. Turgenev.

Something flashed beyond the window, and my breath caught. I floated closer to the glass, and saw only the astral cable, catching the sunlight. But something about it bothered me, and it took me a few seconds to realize why.

I shouldn't be seeing the cable at all.

Normally it was all but impossible to spot from inside, since it ran directly beneath the ship. But right now the cable very gently curved out from the stern on its way earthward.

"Dr. Turgenev," I said quietly, for I didn't want to alarm anyone yet. I drew his attention to the astral cable. "What do you make of that?"

The Russian scientist gazed at it. I watched his long face, trying to guess what he was thinking, but having no luck.

"There should not be curve," he said finally, and though he spoke softly, I felt my whole body tense.

Before I could ask any more, the ship's phone rang.

I was closest and picked up. "Cruse here."

"Mr. Cruse," said the captain. "Could you ask the entire crew to come up to the bridge. Dr. Turgenev as well, please. We have a problem."

19 / The Sky Is Falling

I'VE JUST HEARD from Mr. Lunardi at Ground Station," the captain said when we reached the bridge. "He says the astral cable's losing tension."

"We have seen it bulging behind us," Dr. Turgenev said.

"What does this mean?" Tobias asked in alarm.

The scientist removed his spectacles and polished them on his shirt. His hands, I noticed, were trembling.

"Is only one explanation. Counterweight is falling."

Falling. The only thing in the universe that was keeping us aloft was now falling. I caught myself holding my breath, as though I could suffocate my fear. I forced myself to breathe out. I looked over at Tobias, who I knew dreaded heights, and saw my own fear amplified in his eyes.

"Could it be sabotage?" said Shepherd.

"You mean the Babelites?" Tobias said.

"A bomb on the counterweight," I breathed, seeing a terrible image in my head. An explosion ripping through the rocket. The severed cable whirling earthward, carrying us with it.

Dr. Turgenev shook his head. "No, no. If bomb, we fall quickly. This is very slow. And remember, cable has been up for two months already, and tension was fine, no problems."

"Is it us?" I said. "Our weight on the cable, dragging it down?"

"No, no, we plan for this of course," said the scientist. "Counterweight more than balances our mass . . . unless . . ." He tapped his fist against his chin as though trying to hasten his thoughts. "Yes, yes, here is explanation. Rocket never went high enough."

"You mean the counterweight never reached its proper altitude," said Captain Walken.

"Correct," said Dr. Turgenev.

"Why wouldn't the rocket go high enough?" Shepherd demanded.

"This I don't know," said Dr. Turgenev, jetting to a locker and pulling out a thick binder. He started quickly paging through it.

"Just how fast is this thing coming down?" Shepherd asked.

"Moment, moment," said the scientist, sounding harried.

Shepherd's eyes grew colder still. "We need to make decisions now."

"My decision's already made, Mr. Shepherd," said the captain. "We're returning to Earth at full speed. Tobias, radio Ground Station and let them know. Mr. Cruse, reverse the rollers, please. Mr. Shepherd, stand by at the throttle."

We all snapped to it, strapping ourselves down in our seats so we could work more easily. My hands flew over the control panel. I'd rehearsed this moment many times, but had always imagined it would come when we'd reached cable's end and were making our triumphant return to Earth.

"We're ready, sir," I said, after double-checking.

The captain nodded. "Mr. Shepherd, full speed, please."

Behind us in the central cable shaft, I heard the rollers whir to life. Up here in zero gravity, there was no sense of motion, up or down. Only the ship's vibration told me we were moving at all. It gave me some small comfort to know we were heading home—but was it fast enough?

I glanced over at Dr. Turgenev. He was poring over his sheaf of notes, writing frantically.

"Stop!" he cried suddenly. "Stop ship!"

Captain Walken gave no such order, but looked attentively at the scientist. "What's the matter, Dr. Turgenev?"

"We will not make it."

"To Ground Station?" Tobias said.

Dr. Turgenev shook his head.

"Are you sure?" the captain asked.

"This is five-day journey. In just two days counterweight will accelerate as it drops out of geostationary orbit. Cable crashes. We crash. We die. I am very sure of this."

"We've got no other choice," said Shepherd. "Captain, I suggest we accelerate to flank speed."

As much as I disliked Shepherd trying to take charge, I was with him on this one. I wanted to race for home and chance it, even if it might end in our deaths. What else was there to do?

"We do have choice!" said the scientist.

"Let's hear it, please," said Captain Walken, his patience showing no signs of cracking.

"We can reach counterweight in two days. Now—"

"You want us to climb higher?" Tobias exclaimed, echoing my own surprise. It seemed madness to crawl farther into space when we were already falling.

"Climb higher, yes," said the scientist, thumping on his thick binder. "I think we will have time!"

"Time for what?" the captain asked.

"To save counterweight! I think I know reason for problem. Rocket shuts down engines too early."

"Why would it do that?" I asked.

"Did it run out of fuel?" Shepherd asked.

Dr. Turgenev was shaking his head. "No! It had enough fuel. I do not know why it stops. Maybe some timer malfunction. Maybe simple as blown fuse. But important thing is, fuel is there. And if fuel is there, we can ignite rockets."

"And send it to its proper altitude," I said after a moment, understanding.

"Correct!" said the scientist.

"Will that work?" asked Tobias.

"I think maybe yes," said Dr. Turgenev.

"Maybe isn't good enough," said Shepherd.

"Maybe's all we've got right now," said Tobias.

"Can the cable withstand the stress of a relaunch?" the captain asked.

"Yes," said the scientist.

I watched the captain, already knowing what his decision would be but dreading it all the same—it seemed to run counter to all instinct.

"Mr. Shepherd, full stop," said the captain.

Shepherd looked at him, his hand resting on the throttle but not moving it. No words passed between the two men, but I could see the power in both their gazes, and it scared me. Slowly, Shepherd pulled back on the throttle and brought the *Starclimber* to a standstill.

The captain gave a curt nod. "Thank you. Dr. Turgenev, are you certain we can reignite these rockets?"

"Yes, yes. Inside there is simplified control panel we use for tests."

"How do we get inside?" I asked.

"Is no airlock," said Dr. Turgenev. "But there is hatch can be removed."

The captain gave orders to reverse the *Starclimber*'s rollers once more, and then we began to climb for cable's end, this time at flank speed.

"Would shedding weight help?" I asked. "There must be things we could jettison."

"Throw off monkey and we are fine," said Dr. Turgenev, and gave a dry little laugh. "That is joke. To lighten mood. No. Throwing overboard makes no difference now. We are weightless up here, yes? Damage is already done. Counterweight will continue to fall until we stop it. We must hurry."

"Once we get there," said Shepherd, "how much time will we have to relaunch it?"

I waited nervously as Dr. Turgenev's pencil flew across his notepad. He muttered as he worked. "At full speed . . . and assuming counterweight falls at exponential rate . . . we have maybe four hours. After that, counterweight's velocity is too much, and we are too late to stop it."

There was a moment of heavy silence. It didn't seem like much time. I thought of all the things that needed to be done, that needed to happen, if we were to survive. In my mind it was like a high ladder with many rungs, some of which were splintered and weak.

"We'll need blueprints of the rocket," the captain said.

"These I can draw up," said the scientist.

"As detailed as you can, please. I want to know every inch of her."

"The control panel too," said Shepherd. "I want to see every button and switch of the launch procedure."

"We could build a mock-up," I suggested. "We've probably got enough spare parts."

"Good," said the captain.

"What about the hatch?" Tobias asked. "Is it complicated?"

The scientist squinted, remembering. "Six bolts."

"It's like the *Starclimber*'s cargo bay door," I said. "We could practise on that."

"For this to work," said Shepherd, "it's got to be run like a military operation."

Captain Walken looked at him sternly. "It will be run like a civilian operation, and will be done flawlessly. Now, we have some forty-eight hours to practise. By the time we reach the counterweight, we'll be ready. I want everyone as agile as possible. After that, we'll get started practising on the cargo bay door in two-man shifts. Mr. Blanchard and Mr. Cruse, I want you to work with Dr. Turgenev on a mock-up of the control panel. Dr. Turgenev, we'll need to know what parts we might need to replace. Mr. Shepherd, suit up, you're going on the next spacewalk. I'll be spotting you. Then we'll switch places. Mr. Cruse, would you please go below and tell everyone what's happening. Be as reassuring as you can."

"Yes, sir."

I made for the stairs, practising my brave face. It felt like a mask.

In just half an hour, everything had changed.

If we ever wanted to see Earth again, we had to race away from her with all speed. We had to perform a spacewalk, open a hatch that was never meant to be opened in outer space, and reignite engines that had mysteriously shut off. And now I had to go and convince Kate and everyone else that all would be well.

I took a deep breath as I floated down towards B Deck. I decided a smile would be too forced, so I just tried to look confident. But in my head, I couldn't stop hearing the ship's clock, ticking away our hours and minutes and seconds.

Space engulfed me.

Seeing it through the hatch was one thing, but I was out in the thick of it now for the first time. Any sense of up or down, east or west, evaporated. I didn't look at the earth, or turn so

I could see the ship. All I could see was stars and blackness, and I forced myself not to look away. I wanted to stare it right in the face and not be afraid. I breathed smoothly, trying to slow my pulse. Everything seemed very still, but I knew I was spinning with the planet at thousands of miles an hour, and that far above me, the counterweight that held us aloft was slowly but surely falling.

I should've panicked, but for some reason I didn't. I was suddenly very calm. My chest rose and fell evenly. I'd been so worried that I would come apart when I did my spacewalk. If Tobias had been overwhelmed, what chance did I have?

But I could do this.

"You're at fifty feet, Mr. Cruse," came the captain's voice inside my helmet. "Ready to get to work?"

I felt a slight backward tug as I reached the end of my line. I looked back at the *Starclimber*. My umbilicus undulated from the airlock, and I could see Captain Walken in the hatchway. The sun burnished the ship's silver flanks. *Starclimber* really was a magnificent thing, and despite everything, I felt proud to serve aboard her.

"I'm ready, sir."

"I'm timing you now."

In thirty minutes, I had to manoeuvre myself down to the cargo bay hatch, secure myself to the hull, and see how many times I could remove and replace one of the hatch's bolts.

It was late afternoon, and Shepherd and the captain had already made their first spacewalks. I was the last of the astralnauts to venture out. We'd stopped the *Starclimber* for

Tobias's spacewalk—but not any more. We couldn't afford the time. We'd need to train while the ship was rising at a hundred and twenty aeroknots an hour, and us with it.

It had been only six hours since we'd learned about the counterweight, and we were all furiously busy. Inside the *Starclimber,* Tobias was putting together a mock-up control panel; Dr. Turgenev was assembling any blueprints we had, and drawing the others from memory. Shepherd was in charge of logistics and was mapping out the entire procedure, action by action, minute by minute.

I sighted the cargo bay hatch. It was beneath the airlock and off to one side, closer than I liked to the astral cable and its deadly current. Now to get down there. I fired off a little burst with my air pistol, and right away I saw how tricky it was to use effectively. Unless you pointed it just right, you could veer off in the wrong direction, or spin yourself upside down.

I flailed about for a while, hoping that Kate wasn't seeing this—or Miss Karr. I didn't really want any pictures of me looking like a great drunken ballerina. How had Tobias managed it? My time was ticking away. I decided to get to the ship's hull as fast as I could; there were hand- and footholds there. I gave a little tug on my umbilicus to get me going, and steered with the air pistol. I thudded against the ship, and managed to grab a handhold before I bounced off.

"You're at twenty minutes, Mr. Cruse."

Just ten minutes left! And I wasn't even at the cargo hatch!

My legs and torso floated up away from the ship, which

wasn't very helpful—but there was no way of getting them back down, so I had to traverse the hull using just my hands. Though I weighed nothing at all, by the time I reached the hatch I was soaked with sweat, and my visor was misting up. I was just reaching into my tool belt for a wrench when the captain's voice sounded in my helmet.

"Time's up, Mr. Cruse. I'll reel you in now."

"I've only just reached the hatch, sir," I said, my voice heavy with disappointment. I knew the captain and Shepherd had screwed in two bolts on their first walks.

"Don't be discouraged, Mr. Cruse," the captain said, as I released my grip on the ship and started floating back towards the airlock. "You'll soon have a feel for it."

Aboard the *Aurora*, they'd said I was lighter than air, I was so agile in the sky.

So why did I feel leaden in outer space?

Back inside, we pressurized the airlock and removed our helmets. The captain was looking at me curiously.

"You were humming out there, Mr. Cruse."

"Was I, sir?" I said, surprised.

"From the very start. Quite a symphony."

He hummed a bit for me, and it was the strangest thing, for I instantly recognized the sound. I realized it had been playing in my head from the moment I'd stared into the deeps of space and felt calm. At first it was just a single clear note that quickly faded out, then came back, accompanied by a hundred violins being stroked in unison. There were other sounds as well, too odd to come from any earthly orchestra, but beautiful and eerie, and beyond them a kind of deep, penetrating pulse that I'd felt through my bones.

"I heard music out there," I confessed.

He smiled. "As did Shepherd. And I myself."

"You never mentioned it, sir!"

"I wanted to see if we'd all hear it."

"It's funny," I said. "I don't hear it when I'm spotting from the airlock."

The captain nodded. "Maybe you need to be completely out in space before you hear it."

"What do you think it is?"

He shook his head. "A pressure on the inner ear, perhaps? An auditory hallucination? Or maybe it truly is music of the spheres."

"I like that theory best," I said.

"Me too," chuckled Captain Walken. "Me too."

As we left the airlock, I noticed Kate working alone in the laboratory. *Laboratory* was a fancy word for the space, since it was really just a small area of C Deck amidst the clutter of ship's machinery and vents and cables and stacks of spare equipment.

She was buckled to a seat at the workbench, intently swabbing the space rock with a wet brush. The rock was securely strapped down to the table. It was larger than I remembered, a bit bigger than a basketball, though irregularly shaped, with quite a rough exterior. It had a dark, slightly porous look, flecked with what could have been quartz.

"You're hard at work, Miss de Vries," said the captain.

Kate looked up. "Well, there's not much point sitting around, worrying."

She'd been very brave earlier when I told them what was happening. Most everyone was. Chef Vlad had nodded gravely, said "Soup," and floated back to his kitchen to make some. Miss Karr gave a wry laugh and muttered something about "big boys with their big, big toys," but then added that she had no doubt we'd fix things. Sir Hugh, however, had launched into an angry tirade, saying he'd never have come if he'd known this sort of thing could happen, and he was going to write a very severe letter to Mr. Lunardi. Kate had wanted to know what she could do to help, and hadn't seemed happy when I told her there was nothing at the moment.

"How was your first spacewalk?" she asked me now.

I cleared my throat. "Well, it was—"

"Excellent," said Captain Walken. "I couldn't ask for a better team of astralnauts."

Feeling grateful, I said nothing.

"What are our chances of surviving this?" she asked. "Please be honest."

"Our chances are very good," said the captain. "Very good indeed."

Her eyes were on my face, not the captain's, watching. I hoped my expression didn't betray my own fears. I didn't want her to be frightened, but I'm not sure she believed me.

"What is it you're doing exactly, Miss de Vries?" I asked, eager to change the subject.

"Just preparing some slides," she said, and daubed her wet brush on a glass plate. She carefully placed a thinner glass on top, and slid it beneath the lens of her microscope.

"If you'll excuse me, I've got to return to the bridge," said the captain. "Mr. Cruse, see if you can find some more toggle switches and indicator lights down here for the mock-up console, please. Mr. Blanchard said we were still short."

"Yes, sir," I said. I'd been prepared to go with him to the bridge, for I knew how much there was to be done. I wondered if he was giving me permission to have a moment alone with Kate.

The captain floated up the stairs and was gone.

I moved closer to Kate. Her head was bent over her microscope, her slender fingers turning the focus knobs.

"There really is music of the spheres—"

"Get Sir Hugh," she said abruptly, looking up from her microscope.

I pulled back. "What?"

She twisted around and gave me a push that sent me sailing towards the stairs. "Go get Sir Hugh! Hurry!"

Her tone was so urgent that I didn't dare argue. I jetted up to B Deck. As I sailed around the circular lounge, looking for the zoologist, I saw his spectacles floating in mid-air, and a little farther on his favourite pen, and then various sheets of his notepaper, fluttering like giant snowflakes.

One of the unexpected things about weightlessness was

how things had an odd habit of travelling around on their own. It wasn't at all unusual to find a pair of underwear drifting through the lounge, or someone's toothbrush turning up in the kitchen. It was as if outer space had liberated these things from their boring, immobile lives and given them a giddy freedom.

I found Sir Hugh strapped into an armchair, fast asleep, his arms and legs floating straight out from his body.

"Sir Hugh," I said, shaking him gently. "Miss de Vries would like you to have a look at something."

"I'm very busy," he grumbled, still half asleep.

"It's important, I think," I said more loudly.

Sir Hugh sighed deeply. "Oh, very well. Give me a few moments."

He unbuckled himself. I drifted closer to lend him a hand, but he waved me away.

"I'll be quite all right on my own."

Of all the people aboard the *Starclimber*, he was the clumsiest in zero gravity. With tiny shuffling steps of his magnetic shoes he started working his way towards the stairs. Too impatient to wait, I hurried back down to C Deck.

"You've found something, haven't you," I said to Kate.

She was peering into the microscope, as if afraid to break her gaze in case what she saw might vanish.

"It's here," she said softly. "There's life."

When she looked up, her face shone with an almost uncontainable excitement. "Look!" she said, jabbing her finger at the eyepiece.

Floating on my stomach, I grabbed the edge of the workbench and lowered my head to the microscope.

Jewels. That's what they looked like to me, some round, others long and diamond-shaped, many beaded together like glistening necklaces. The colours startled me, for somehow I didn't imagine that something so small could explode with luminous blues and deep purples, like things from the sea. Beautiful they were.

"Where did these come from?" I asked.

"The surface of the space rock," she said, practically panting in her exhilaration.

"And they're alive?"

"I thought they were moving a bit at first. Our air may have killed them, or at least our air pressure. They wouldn't be used to it."

"But what *are* they?"

"They look a bit like diatoms to me. Tiny unicellular organisms. Yet they're quite different from anything I've seen on Earth, crystalline almost. The way they link together in patterns reminds me of plankton."

"Little fish in the sea?"

"Not fish. Plankton are drifters." Something seemed to occur to her. "You know those early scientists, who wondered if outer space was liquid? Maybe they weren't so far off! Maybe it's like a vast sea and what I've just discovered is some kind of astral algae!"

"It's incredible!" I said.

"And if there's plankton drifting around out there, maybe there's other life that *eats* the plankton!"

She looked so thrilled, I wanted to hug her, but just then I heard Sir Hugh's magnetic feet clanking down the stairs.

"Is there anything interesting about that bit of space rock?" he asked.

"Quite interesting, Sir Hugh," Kate said pleasantly. "You'll want to take a look."

When he was finally buckled down at the workbench, he put his eye to the microscope. He spent a great deal of time adjusting the knobs and clearing his throat. Kate looked at me overtop Sir Hugh's balding head and gave a huge grin.

"Your slide is dirty, Miss de Vries," the zoologist declared.

Kate's mouth fell open. "It's not in the least dirty!"

"You prepared this slide yourself?" he asked.

"Yes, from a swab of the surface of the space rock."

"Either your solution or the slide itself was already tainted with some microbial matter."

"I took every precaution," said Kate indignantly.

"You've got some old algae debris here," Sir Hugh said dismissively. "That's all."

"Very well, then, Sir Hugh, please take your own sample and prepare a slide. I think you'll find exactly the same thing."

"We shall see, Miss de Vries. I will undertake a proper investigation."

I saw Kate's eyes narrow to arrow slits and was worried she was going to say something colourful, and possibly unladylike, but at that moment the *Starclimber* gave a shudder.

"Did you feel that?" Kate asked, eyes wide.

I nodded, holding my breath, waiting. I heard a dull *thud* against the hull, and the ship shook again.

"What was that?" demanded Sir Hugh.

"I'm going to find out," I said, and jetted up towards the bridge.

20 / Astral Fauna

BEYOND THE GLASS DOME of the bridge, countless space rocks tumbled slowly past the *Starclimber,* blazing in the sun's light.

"Continue dead slow, Mr. Shepherd," the captain said.

"We're in some kind of asteroid field," Tobias told me, staring out tensely. "You got back inside just in time, Matt. You wouldn't want to be out there now."

They were all around us, so thick and numerous that I couldn't see any end in sight. I winced as another one deflected dully off our hull. If the *Starclimber* were breached, how could we go outside to mend her without being struck ourselves?

"Can she withstand this?" I asked Dr. Turgenev.

"Small knocks okay," he said. "And we are lucky so far. Rocks are in same orbit as us. If they had greater velocity, we would be pulverized."

I stared nervously up at the astral cable and the fragile-looking spider arms that gripped it. A rock bumped against one of them, but deflected off without harm.

For half an hour we crawled through the asteroids, and then half an hour more, and still there seemed no end to them.

"If this keeps up," I said, "we won't make it to the counterweight in time."

"Cruse is right," said Shepherd. "Permission to take her ahead one-third, Captain?" His hand hovered above the throttle.

"No, Mr. Shepherd. I won't risk a collision at greater speed."

"We're not leaving ourselves much time, sir."

"That'll be all, Mr. Shepherd."

I felt rebuked too, for I'd been the first to worry aloud about our headway. Infuriating as the situation was, the captain was right. We could do nothing but inch along the cable—or risk a devastating impact. I was sweating. Every second we lost here was a second less to relaunch the rocket.

"It's strange," said Tobias. "How they're all the same, I mean."

I nodded. "They all look like the one you brought aboard."

As I peered out at them, one suddenly exploded. A plume of dust glittered, brilliant as ice crystals.

"What happened there?" Shepherd exclaimed.

"It just blew up!" I said, staring. But it hadn't blown up so much as *erupted,* for the asteroid was still largely intact, except for a missing chunk. A second geyser of dust and vapour erupted from the asteroid, and shards of rock pattered against the glass dome. Hovering amidst the asteroid debris was something round and pale in the stellar light.

"What is that?" I said, pointing.

There was something about its texture that made my skin crawl. It didn't look like rock; it looked . . . fleshier. Then it abruptly revolved and knocked against the glass dome.

I gave a shout, for what I beheld looked like a severed,

upside-down head, about the size of a human's and shockingly grotesque. It was all jaw—a gaping maw, churning against the glass. It moved so quickly, I wasn't even sure if it had eyes, though I caught sight of two long dark slits beneath its lower jaw.

"Look at its teeth!" exclaimed Tobias.

The creature was darting about so rapidly, battering the dome, that it was impossible to get a clear fix on it. But its teeth seemed to be needle thin, and so long that they spanned the entire space between its parted jaws.

Beyond the glass there was another explosion, and I saw a second asteroid fracturing, releasing a silvery sphere near the ship.

"These aren't asteroids," I said, suddenly sure. "They're eggs."

"We're in the middle of some floating hatchery," Shepherd agreed.

All around us now, these dreadful things were hatching, and a great cluster of them suddenly butted against the dome. I felt the *Starclimber* shiver.

"They look almost like viper fish!" Tobias muttered.

But they didn't have the bodies of fish at all. There were no scales, no fins or tails.

I marvelled at their strength and persistence. Then I had an idea.

"Try dousing the running lights!" I said. "And the bridge lights too. Maybe it's attracting them."

"Good thought, Mr. Cruse," said the captain, and he jetted over to the light switches and flipped them off.

The bridge went dark; only the instrument panels emitted a soft glow now. Almost at once, the astral hatchlings turned away from the glass and began jetting off in other directions. I heard some thumping against the lower decks, where the cabin lights were still on.

"That seems to do the trick," said Captain Walken. "You should go below, Mr. Cruse, and turn off the remaining lights."

"Tobias's space rock," I said in horror, suddenly remembering. "We've got one on board!"

I was already pushing off for the stairs. Kate was down there.

"Go with him!" Captain Walken told Tobias.

When we passed through B Deck, I saw Miss Karr at the windows, taking pictures of the astral creatures hounding the ship.

"Bit of wildlife for you, Miss Karr," I said.

"They move so quickly!" she complained. "I'm not sure I'm getting them properly."

"Turn off the lights, please, Miss Karr," Tobias called out to her.

Then we were down on C Deck. Sir Hugh was staring out the porthole from a distance, looking very green. Kate turned and gave me a huge smile.

"I knew it!" she cried. "I knew there could be life up here! It's positively *teeming!*"

"We're going to be teeming too," I said, "unless we get rid of that egg, fast."

"What egg?" demanded Sir Hugh.

"The rock is an egg!" I said, pointing.

"Are you sure?" Kate asked.

I had to admit it looked perfectly harmless right now, on its best rocklike behaviour. For a moment I wondered if I was mistaken—but I wasn't taking any chances.

"I think I'll clear off until you get this sorted out," said Sir Hugh, already clanking towards the staircase.

I took a breath and looked at Tobias. I hadn't actually had time to think of a plan. All I knew was that I wanted this thing off the ship as fast as possible.

"Is there anything we can put it in?" I asked Kate.

"As a matter of fact, yes," she said, very pleased with herself. "Sir Hugh thought it was pointless, but I brought a rather nice specimen case."

She floated over and pulled it out from beneath one of the workbenches.

"That's big enough," Tobias said.

"Let's get it into the case," I said, "then into the airlock."

"What are you going to do with it?" Kate demanded.

"Chuck it off the ship," I said.

"You can't just get rid of it!" Kate said, aghast. "It's an invaluable specimen."

"Maybe you haven't seen its teeth," I said. I didn't have time to debate with Kate right now.

"We'll need someone inside the airlock," Tobias said, "to open the outer hatch."

"Someone," I echoed.

Neither of us volunteered.

Inside the airlock. With the egg. Who knew how long before it hatched, or how strong Kate's specimen case was. My eyes drifted to the portholes, and the astral hatchlings battering themselves against the ship.

On the lab workbench, the space egg trembled.

"Hurry!" I said, fumbling with the buckles on the restraining straps. "Get that case open!"

The buckles were very fiddly. I wedged my feet into two footholds so I could use both hands. I loosed the first strap, but as I unbuckled the second, the egg cracked. Two big shards floated off. Through the fissure, I caught sight of a pale swirl of movement.

"Get it inside!" Tobias shouted.

Wincing in revulsion, I seized the egg and moved it towards the open case. But the egg gave a sudden sharp hiss and flew out of my hands, spewing debris and a horrible smell. It struck the ceiling hard, knocking off a few more shards. I pushed off from the floor, reaching out to grab it.

"Get the case up here!" I cried. We were running out of time. The thing was almost out of its shell.

The moment I reached the ceiling, another blast of noxious gas hit me in the face, along with a hunk of exploding shell. The force was enough to send me tumbling backward. My eyes stung, and I blinked furiously to clear away the tears. I grabbed a handhold on the ceiling to steady myself. Where was the egg?

I heard Kate cry out in alarm: "Behind you!"

I spun to find myself face to face with a huge silvery head, a few pieces of shell still clinging to it. Its mouth was closed in a long curving line, like a malicious, tight-lipped smile. The narrow eyes had no lids. It did not seem to breathe. The thing floated motionless. All over its body were little fleshy slits, like wounds that had never healed.

Perfect little red spheres dotted the air between us, and I realized it was my own blood, pulsing from the wound on my forehead. I was petrified, afraid even to exhale for fear the thing would attack. Very slowly its mouth parted and stretched wide. I saw the sharp white surfaces of its teeth. A big drop of my blood drifted close to its jaws and was immediately inhaled. Then, with a terrifying wheeze, the creature sprayed the blood back in my face.

Below me, Tobias shot up, the open case held over his head and aimed straight at the hatchling. It must have sensed his approach. One of the fleshy slits on its body dilated and released a jet of reeking gas, and then it shot sideways. Tobias crashed against the ceiling.

Across the room, the creature collided hard with a porthole and ricocheted backward, straight for me. I gave a cry and tried to swim out of the way, but it struck me in the shoulder, knocking me against the wall. I punched the thing away from me, but it seemed to have regained its senses. It spewed multiple jets of gas so that it revolved to face me once more. Its jaws were pulled back farther than seemed possible. Its teeth looked like blades.

"Matt, here!" cried Kate.

In her hand she held the air pistol I'd brought back from my spacewalk. She sent it flying towards me, and I seized it, hoping it still had some puff in it.

I fired. The recoil sent me slamming against the wall, but also blasted the creature away from me. It collided with the spiral staircase, then shot straight up to B Deck.

"Oh no!" I panted.

From the lounge I heard a shriek, and wasn't sure if it was Miss Karr or Sir Hugh. I jetted upstairs, Tobias and Kate right behind me. When I arrived on B Deck, the hatchling was careening around the lounge. Haiku was sending up a terrible high-pitched squeal. Miss Karr clutched a camera to her face, trying to get pictures. Sir Hugh had removed his magnetic shoes and was thrashing frantically in mid-air, going nowhere. His academic papers swirled loosely about him. The hatchling streaked towards him and stopped mere inches from his face. Sir Hugh bellowed. The hatchling seemed to bellow back, releasing a jet of stinking gas that sent Sir Hugh spinning backwards head over heels.

"Drive it towards me, Matt!" shouted Tobias, who had the case with him.

I swallowed and flew straight towards the hatchling, air pistol outstretched. But it evaded me easily, shooting across the lounge and into the kitchen. I heard an explosion of cursing from Chef Vlad, and a great clanging and banging. Then silence.

"Mr. Vlad!" I cried, hurrying towards the kitchen. I feared the worst. But before I reached the door, it swung open and the chef floated out, holding an enormous pot tightly shut against his body. His hair and eyes were wild, but he was smiling.

"My soup pot is very useful, eh, Mr. Cruse?"

"Well done, Mr. Vlad!" Kate said.

The pot gave a violent shake, and then was still.

"Let's get it into the case," I said.

We arranged ourselves carefully, and pushed the opening of the specimen case snugly against the pot before sliding back the lid. I was expecting the hatchling to come hurtling, but it listlessly floated out and into the specimen case. We closed the case door tightly.

"It looks exhausted," said Kate, sounding almost sorry for it.

Mr. Vlad peered at it carefully. "I am thinking maybe this could be interesting to cook."

"Sorry, Mr. Vlad," I said, picking up the case, "we're getting rid of it."

"You're not serious!" Kate cried.

"Completely serious," I said.

"But it's safely caged."

"We can't risk it, Miss de Vries." I was getting tired of this argument, and worried that she was making me look weak in front of the others.

"But this creature is of huge importance!" she insisted.

"So are the humans aboard ship."

"Your forehead's still bleeding," Tobias told me, taking down a first-aid kit and sending it my way.

"Mr. Cruse, I *want* this specimen!" Kate said, and I felt like she was speaking to a servant.

"I am an officer aboard this ship," I told her, my voice raised in anger, "and right now we have more pressing things to think about than your specimens. I won't discuss it any more, Kate."

She stared at me in mute shock, her cheeks reddening. The expression on her face was not one I'd seen before, and I must say I enjoyed it—until I realized I'd just called her Kate in front of everyone.

They were all watching us, silent.

"How *dare* you speak to me in that way!" Kate said, and I didn't think she was play-acting.

"But I quite agree with Mr. Cruse," piped in Sir Hugh. "We should get rid of it immediately."

Kate whirled on the zoologist. "So you can say it never existed?"

"Nonsense," Sir Hugh said.

But Kate's temper was in full force now. "Oh, I know you, Sir Hugh. You're not really interested in the truth, you're just interested in being *right!* If we get rid of this specimen, what proof do I have?"

"I'll take some pictures of it right now," said Miss Karr, looking at me. "If I can just have a moment?"

I stared at the hatchling and noticed that the hiss of its venting gas was more of a high-pitched whistle now. It was still moving, though sluggishly, nudging against the case. Its body didn't seem as round as it had when first hatched. It looked like a ghastly shrunken head I'd seen once in a museum.

"What's happening to it?" Tobias asked.

"It's in distress," Kate said.

It made a few more feeble whistling sounds, and then was still. Its face was such a mystery to me that it was hard to tell if it was conscious or not. Then, before my eyes, it crumpled, as though an invisible fist were squeezing it.

"The air pressure," I said. It seemed so obvious now, I was surprised it hadn't occurred to me sooner.

"Yes," said Kate. "That must be it."

"What do you mean?" asked Miss Karr.

"It's used to a vacuum," Kate said. "Zero pressure. But this is fourteen pounds per square inch. I bet that's why it had so much trouble hatching. Remember the ones outside? They just blasted out of their shells. This one could barely crack it. Our atmosphere crushed it to death. Poor thing. Still," she added, unable to suppress a smile, "I now have a specimen to bring back."

"I'm glad things worked out for you, Miss de Vries," Miss Karr said.

"They usually do," she replied.

I felt quite disgusted by her. I'd always known her work was important to her, and that she had a selfish streak, but I hated to think she'd risk endangering the lives of others for the sake of a specimen.

The ship's phone rang in my hand. "Cruse here," I said.

"Everything all right down there?" the captain asked.

"We're fine now, sir."

"Well done. We're clear of the hatchery now."

I looked out the windows and saw the last of the space eggs falling past us. From the ship's central shaft came the sound of the rollers accelerating. I felt the welcome vibration pass through the ship's girders and rivets and I blew out a big breath of relief. We were back on course to the counterweight, and at flank speed to make up for lost time.

I just hoped we wouldn't be too late.

21 / A Message from Earth

"**W**E NEED TO PICK UP the pace, Cruse," said Shepherd. What he meant was that *I* needed to pick up the pace. We were both outside the *Starclimber* in our astral suits, clinging to the cargo hatch, trying to remove its six bolts. We were each doing three. Shepherd was already on his third; I was still on my second.

"Ten minutes left," came the captain's voice from the airlock.

It was noon on day six. We were less than twenty-four hours from the counterweight. Captain Walken had decided it would take two astralnauts to get aboard and reignite the rocket engines, so we'd started drilling in pairs. All of us were working on four hours' sleep or less. I'd taken enough spacewalks now to feel much more agile in my suit. I could use my air pistol well, and scuttle nimbly about the ship's hull. But Shepherd was still faster, and better at using tools.

In my head were the faint strains of the music of the spheres. There was no explaining it, how it was made, or where it came from, but I knew now that it wasn't a hallucination. We'd all heard it. Once you'd accepted it, it lost some of its eerie intensity and seemed to play more softly in the back reaches of your brain.

"I'm all done," said Shepherd. "I'll do yours."

"I'll do it," I said, and finally got my second bolt off.

"Five minutes," came the captain's voice.

"Faster if I do the last one," Shepherd said.

"I'll do it," I told him again, but he ignored me. I saw him floating over from his side of the hatch. The thought of him finishing my work filled me with a sudden, pounding rage. I was sick of his disapproval. Never fast enough. Never good enough. I reached up to push him away.

"Back off, Shepherd!" I said.

I must have shoved harder than I thought, because he gave a grunt of surprise and sailed away from the ship—

—straight down towards the astral cable, pulsing with high voltage.

"Shepherd, look out!" I shouted.

He fumbled for his air pistol, but I grabbed hold of his umbilicus as it snaked past, and gave it a jerk. Not five feet from the cable, he snapped back towards me and came sailing up to safety.

"Mr. Cruse, report please," came the captain's voice in my helmet.

"Sorry, Shepherd, I'm sorry," I said, horrified by what I'd done.

"I'm bringing you both in," said the captain.

Shepherd said nothing as we were reeled back towards the *Starclimber*.

"This is most unlike you, Mr. Cruse," said the captain.

We were inside the pressurized airlock and I'd made my

report of what had happened. I was deeply ashamed of myself, but there was no point trying to hide anything.

"I'm sorry, sir, I lost my head."

The captain looked at me thoughtfully. "We're all under a great deal of strain. But you're no stranger to that. You've been in situations few sky sailors could survive. I know I can expect your best."

"Yes, sir," I said.

"That'll be all, gentlemen."

"With respect, sir," said Shepherd, "I don't think Cruse should be considered for the counterweight job. He's not fast enough. And I don't think he can handle the pressure of outer space."

"That's my decision to make, Mr. Shepherd, and I'll be making it closer to the time."

"Yes, sir, but if it turns out I'm part of that team, I want a partner I can trust."

My face burned. I felt like a whipped dog.

"Mr. Shepherd," the captain replied, "I think you are too used to flying solo. Mr. Cruse is as trustworthy as any man on this ship."

Shepherd looked past the captain as he spoke. "Sir, he's an impressive young man with a great deal of potential, but he's too young, and he's only here because a better man made a mistake."

Captain Walken made no reply for a moment. "Mr. Shepherd," he said finally, "I know you and Mr. Bronfman were friends and that you respected his abilities. But if we're to succeed at this, we've got to trust one another. Am I clear?"

"Very clear . . . Captain," he added, after just a moment's hesitation.

"Excellent. Now, both of you take half an hour break, and then report back to the bridge. There's still a great deal more to do."

When I reached B Deck, everyone was at work. Kate floated over her specimen case, busily taking notes, while Miss Karr clacked away at her typewriter. Sir Hugh hovered about, peering at the dead hatchling from various angles.

I was tired, and should've tried to steal a quick nap, but I knew I'd just float there on my bunk, fuming about what had happened and the corrosive things Shepherd had said. I needed a distraction right now, and decided to stay in the lounge.

"I imagine you'll be writing about this creature in your daily dispatch, Miss Karr," said Sir Hugh.

"Of course," she said. "The world will want to know about this. I have to admit, I didn't think we'd find any life in outer space."

"Is that right?" said Sir Hugh with a chuckle. "A bit short-sighted, don't you think, Miss Karr? As I always tell my students, if zoology has taught us anything, it's that life can adapt to virtually any conditions. And this creature here is a perfect example of that."

Sir Hugh looked expectantly at Miss Karr, as if waiting for

her to type his priceless words that very instant. But Miss Karr merely gazed back at him like a falcon sighting prey. I glanced over at Kate, expecting her to make some sarcastic remark, but she was staring open-mouthed at Sir Hugh, clearly too stunned to speak. Did Sir Hugh really think anyone would believe such a complete turnaround?

"I suspect," Sir Hugh carried on, as though lecturing to one of his classes, "that these creatures have a completely different metabolism than what we're used to on Earth. They clearly require no oxygen, no hydrogen, no water to survive. They manage to make energy from other means. How, I don't know yet, but I will delve into this matter and make a complete study of the morphology and biology of this wonderful creature. I have no doubt the scientific world will be turned on its head when I publish my paper."

"Gosh, Sir Hugh," said Kate pleasantly, "won't that be a little awkward for you? Especially after that big article you published last spring, saying only nitwits and simpletons believed in life in outer space?"

Sir Hugh cleared his throat. "Well, my dear, when presented with new data, scientists must not be afraid to revisit past ideas. No, no, we forge ahead into the future and share our new learning with our peers. And that is precisely what I will be doing when I write about this new discovery of mine." He looked over at Miss Karr. "You may quote me, Miss Karr. I don't mind in the least."

"How is it *your* discovery?" Miss Karr asked tartly. "Any more than anyone else's aboard ship?"

"It was actually Miss de Vries who made the first discovery," I pointed out. "The microscopic life on the egg."

Kate gave me a smile, and I couldn't help smiling back. I was still annoyed with her, but I couldn't bear Sir Hugh being such a hypocrite about everything.

"Ah yes," said Miss Karr, typing away. "The astral plankton, I'll make a note of that. Now, do we have a name for the creature that hatched? A name will make it stick much better in the reader's mind."

"Well," said Sir Hugh, "when naming a new species, one has to take several factors into account, of course . . ."

"Etherians," said Kate at once.

"Etherians?" said Sir Hugh. "It's not exactly scientific, my dear."

"Please don't call me 'my dear,' Sir Hugh," said Kate. "You may call Mrs. Snuffler 'my dear' if she'll tolerate it—but not me."

At this Miss Karr gave a merry cackle. "I like your spirit, Miss de Vries. Well done. And I like your name. *Etherian.*"

"After Kepler's heavenly ether?" I asked.

Kate nodded.

"I'm using it," said Miss Karr, clacking away. "It's perfect. Mark my words, Sir Hugh, this name will stick."

Sir Hugh, I noticed, was looking sweaty at this point. With some revulsion he glanced at the dead hatchling in its case.

"It's an ugly brute," he said, as if hoping to change the subject. "Lucky it didn't get its teeth into us, hey?"

"They're not teeth at all," said Kate. "If you look closely, you'll see they're more like baleen."

"Yes, of course, of course," said Sir Hugh hastily.

"What's baleen?" I asked.

"It's what some whales have," said Kate, "instead of teeth."

I drew closer for a better look. What I'd first thought were needle-sharp teeth were actually thin blades of a dense, stringy material, stretched between upper and lower jaw.

"In whales, it's made from the same thing as hair, amazingly enough," Kate said. "The plankton gets caught up in it, and then the whale whisks them down its throat. So you see, Mr. Cruse, this creature isn't dangerous to us at all."

I looked up, feeling foolish. "They sure looked like teeth to me."

"I wouldn't be surprised," said Kate, her eyes bright, "if this creature fed on the kind of organisms I discovered on the egg. I wonder if they float free in space, just like plankton in the sea! Of course, I'm still waiting for Sir Hugh to verify my findings. He thought my slides were 'dirty.'"

"Yes, yes, I'll check that, of course," Sir Hugh said. "Fascinating stuff, lots of work ahead. Now, if you'll excuse me." He shuffled off on his magnetic shoes towards the lavatory.

"Poor old Hughie," said Miss Karr, when he was out of earshot. "It's all been a bit much for him, hasn't it?"

"I don't feel sorry for him in the least," said Kate.

"Nor I," said Miss Karr. Her hands hung over her typewriter. "Do you think I should describe him as *insufferable* or *conceited*?"

"Either is excellent," said Kate. "But you're the writer,

Miss Karr." She turned to me. "Mr. Cruse, I want to apologize to you. I behaved like a spoiled child earlier, and I'm very sorry."

"It's quite all right, Miss de Vries," I said. But I wondered if she'd have been so apologetic if she didn't have her specimen.

"I was just so overwhelmed by the hatchling, I wasn't thinking clearly."

"It's been a trying time for everyone," I said, thinking glumly of my own outburst with Shepherd.

"How does it move about, though?" Miss Karr asked. "It doesn't have any limbs I can see."

"Jet propulsion," Kate said. "You see those little slits all over its body? It expels some kind of gas through those."

"A very smelly gas," I added, for a sour odour still lingered in the lounge.

"It's a brilliant system of locomotion," said Kate. "In outer space, fins or flukes would be quite pointless. There's nothing to push against. So it produces its own propellant and off it goes. Space really does seem a kind of sea, don't you think, with all sorts of things drifting around."

"We're still in the shallows," I said, remembering the immensity of space beyond Earth.

"The shallows," said Kate, her eyes twinkling. "I like that very much. Maybe what we're finding so far are the creatures that stay close to shore. Little things. Maybe in the great deeps, we'd find bigger things, the size of squids and whales!"

I thought of the enormous, pulsing blue object that had streaked our ship on our first night out. Kate's suggestion that it was a living creature didn't seem so outlandish any more—certainly no more than a Martian spacecraft.

"What I'd really like to know," said Kate, "is what laid all those eggs."

Miss Karr's fingers froze above her keyboard, and a silence fell over the lounge.

It was a sobering image. I hadn't thought that far ahead. But of course those eggs had come from *something*.

"In most aquatic animals," said Kate carefully—and I felt gooseflesh erupt all over my neck—"in all egg-laying animals in fact, the hatchlings are a *fraction* of the size of the adults, and often undergo dramatic changes."

"Is that right," said Miss Karr, looking distinctly uncomfortable.

"Hullo?" came a muffled but urgent voice from the toilets. "Hullo?"

"Is that Sir Hugh?" said Miss Karr.

"Hullo? Could someone lend a hand? I seem to be stuck!"

We all looked at one another. Kate was trying very hard not to laugh, and then laughed anyway.

"Could someone—a gentleman, mind you—come and give me some assistance? Quickly!"

"I'll go," I said. I floated back behind the kitchen to the lavatory. Before leaving Earth, we'd all been given lessons on the space toilets. They were complicated, with straps and restraint bars and levers that you pulled to flush everything into outer space.

Even before I opened the door, I could hear the powerful

sound of the toilet's suction. I drifted inside. Sir Hugh was strapped onto the toilet, struggling mightily against the seat with both hands, while his bottom was slowly but surely being sucked deeper into the bowl.

"It's got hold of me!" Sir Hugh cried. "This bloody thing won't let up! Help, Cruse, I'm liable to be sucked right out!"

I quickly reached over to the flush lever and flipped it off. The loud sucking sound ceased, and Sir Hugh and I were left together in silence. It was rather close in the small lavatory.

"Sir Hugh," I said, "you aren't supposed to flush until you're off the seat."

"I'm sure I didn't," he said, as though I'd insulted him. "The bloody thing has a mind of its own. I don't know what happened." He was undoing the restraint straps and trying to push himself up off the seat. "Um . . . I seem to be . . . I'm wedged, you see. If you'd be so kind."

When you see a fellow with his tartan underpants down around his skinny ankles, and know his bum has been sucked into a toilet bowl, it's hard not to feel a bit sorry for him, even if he is a pompous monster. I slipped my feet into some floor cleats, grabbed his hands, and pulled.

There was a rather rude slurping noise, and then Sir Hugh's large red bottom popped out of the toilet seat. He sailed over my head and collided with the wall.

"I'm fine, I'm fine!" he said, trying to hoist up his underpants and trousers as he thrashed around overhead.

"I'll just slip out now, if that's all right, Sir Hugh," I said, trying to keep his legs and feet off me.

"Yes, all right," he muttered, still struggling with his clothing. "Uh, thank you, Mr. Cruse. Most kind. I can take it from here."

With relief, I closed the door behind me, hoping I'd never have to see Sir Hugh's bum again.

When I reported for bridge duty, Shepherd was already there, listening intently with Tobias as Captain Walken talked to Ground Station. Twenty thousand miles away, Mr. Lunardi's voice came crackling over our speaker.

"I'm sorry I had to deliver this news, Samuel," he said. "I know you've got enough to deal with right now. But General Lancaster's taking it very seriously, and thinks you should too."

"Thank you, Otto," said the captain. "You'll be hearing from us soon."

"Good luck, Samuel."

"*Starclimber* out," the captain said, and removed his headset.

"What's going on?" I asked, looking around at everyone.

The captain rubbed his temples. "Apparently the Babelites sent the Aero Force a message. They say—there's a bomb aboard the *Starclimber*."

I felt numb, but not very surprised, for I'd worried almost constantly about just such a thing happening.

"There can't be a bomb aboard," said Tobias. "It's just a stupid hoax!"

Shepherd shook his head. "The general wouldn't tell us if he thought it was just a hoax."

"Every inch of the ship was checked," I said. "Every bit of cargo. There's no way they could sneak a bomb aboard."

"Unless one of us brought it aboard," said Shepherd.

I stared at Shepherd, open-mouthed with disbelief.

"You're suggesting one of us is a Babelite?" said Captain Walken.

"I'm suggesting it's a possibility," he replied.

The captain shook his head. "Everyone's been carefully screened."

"Like Grendel Eriksson?" Shepherd retorted. "Right under our noses the whole time. I don't have that much faith in Mr. Lunardi. We should think about this very carefully."

"So who've you got in mind, Shepherd?" Tobias asked, his eyebrows angled dangerously. "Miss de Vries? She's a suffragette, after all. Practically an anarchist. Or how about Miss Karr? Or maybe her bloody monkey?"

"I was thinking more of you, Blanchard."

"You're not serious, Shepherd!" I said.

"Enough of this!" said the captain.

"Hear me out, sir," said Shepherd, his eyes fixed on Tobias. "Of all the people aboard, he's not known well by anyone else."

"Neither are you, Shepherd," I said.

"The Aero Force has a record a mile long on me. But who can really vouch for Blanchard? He's not sure we should even be in outer space—he's said as much to me."

Tobias was red-faced. "If I was secretly a Babelite, I'd hardly be talking like that, would I?" he shouted.

"Why are you getting so angry, Blanchard?" Shepherd asked calmly.

I should've leapt to Tobias's defence, but all I could think about was what Tobias had said towards the end of his spacewalk. *Shouldn't be here . . . don't belong.* I hadn't mentioned it to anyone because I thought it was just his mind wandering. But now I stared at him, looking like he was ready to take a swing at Shepherd—and I wondered. I wondered if he could truly be a Babelite. Back in Paris I'd flown for two weeks with one, and had never had a clue.

"Enough!" said the captain once more. "This is a waste of our time, gentlemen. We can't afford to be distracted. Mr. Blanchard is no Babelite, nor is anyone else aboard. The idea is absurd."

Hearing the captain's fierce certainty made me feel ashamed of my doubts.

"We're going to ignore the Babelites' threat," said Captain Walken, "and that's an end to it."

"You're making the wrong decision, sir," said Shepherd.

My breath caught in my throat. I couldn't believe Shepherd's insolence.

The captain's voice was hard. "Mr. Shepherd, you'd do well to remember there can be only one captain aboard ship."

"With respect, sir, I think we got the wrong one for this expedition."

I'd served under Captain Walken for three years and I'd never seen the ferocious face he wore now.

"Be very careful what you say, Mr. Shepherd. I am a tolerant commander, but one thing I will not tolerate is mutinous talk. I will overlook it this once, as you are clearly under strain, but let me hear no more of it. Do you understand?"

Shepherd stared back at the captain, then looked down. "Yes, sir."

"Then let's get back to work, gentlemen."

"And we have liftoff!" Dr. Turgenev said. "Is simple, yes?"

Tobias and I drifted back from the mock-up control panel we'd built in an empty stretch of B Deck behind the kitchen. We'd all been taking turns practising the ignition sequence, and this was my third run-through.

"How fast were we that time?" I asked Shepherd, who held a stopwatch.

"Seven minutes," he said. "We need to shave it down to six."

"One lousy minute," grumbled Tobias.

"One lousy minute could make all the difference, Blanchard," he said.

Tobias glared at him, and I worried there might be another flare-up. It was four in the morning and we were all worn out, but there was no chance of a decent rest. According to Dr. Turgenev's calculations, we were six hours away from the counterweight. The moment we reached it, we'd all have to get to work. The captain hadn't yet told us who the two astralnauts would be.

The timeline was seared into my memory by now. Forty minutes for suiting up and doing the pre-breathe in the airlock.

Thirty minutes to get from the airlock to the counterweight's hatch. Thirty minutes to open it. Twenty minutes to get inside and set up in front of the control panel. Six minutes for the ignition sequence. Thirty minutes to get back to the ship. And thirty minutes for the *Starclimber* to reverse away from the counterweight at top speed so we didn't get incinerated by the rockets.

"We need everything to go like clockwork," Shepherd said. "If something happens, or someone messes up along the way, we might not make it."

It was too terrible to think about—the counterweight, unstoppable, taking us with it on its fatal plunge earthward. We'd just need to be faster—at the control panel, at the hatch, and at all the spacewalks between *Starclimber* and counterweight.

Shepherd looked pale and a bit pinched, and kept rubbing his forehead.

"Are you all right?" I asked.

"Fine," he said. "Let's reset and go again."

I started flipping switches, and by accident ripped one right out of the console. I tried to snap it back into place, but without any luck.

"Don't worry," said Tobias. "That one's not important."

"They're all important if you flip the wrong one," said Shepherd.

Tobias was about to say something, but Dr. Turgenev cut him off. "Mr. Shepherd is correct. Very important not to be clumsy with controls."

I stared at all the small switches and dials and buttons, and realized something.

"We *will* be clumsy, though," I said. "All of us."

"What are you talking about, Cruse?" said Shepherd.

"I'll show you," I said, and jetted down to C Deck and the airlock.

When I came back to the lounge, I was wearing a pair of spacesuit gauntlets. I reached for the controls with my huge, stiff fingers. It was impossible to grasp some of the switches, they were so thin and close together.

"He's right," said Tobias. "There's no way we can do it in the gloves."

Dr. Turgenev was nodding. "Is very good to know, Mr. Cruse. I had not thought of this."

I glanced over at Shepherd, stupidly hoping he'd look impressed. He didn't. He seemed irritated.

"We can use needle-nose pliers," he said.

"That'll work," said Tobias. "But it'll take longer."

"Six minutes," said Shepherd.

"You've got to give us more time," Tobias insisted.

"I can't invent more time," said Shepherd. "You'll do it in six—unless you want to sabotage the whole thing, Blanchard."

"Oh, right," said Tobias, his temper flaring, "I was forgetting I'm a Babelite. And Cruse is too young and can't take the pressure. Is there anyone you *do* trust, Shepherd, you arrogant git?"

Shepherd's normally placid face darkened with fury, and he pushed himself at Tobias.

Hurriedly I put myself between them. "Stop it!" I shouted. "This is what they want! *Exactly* what the Babelites want. They want us to fall apart and start attacking each other. They don't need to put a bomb on our ship to make us fail. Just make us start doubting each other."

Dr. Turgenev gave me an approving nod.

"All right. Fine," said Tobias, breathing hard.

Shepherd said nothing for a moment. "We can add on a few minutes for the ignition sequence," he said. "I'll steal it from somewhere else. So let's put on our gloves and tool belts and get it right. The clock's ticking."

After running through the sequence a few more times, Tobias had to report for bridge duty. I had an hour before my shift, and was headed back to my cabin for a rest. Floating along the A Deck corridor was an envelope. It was hardly unusual to see things floating about—sometimes very unusual things at that. I'd once found Sir Hugh drifting along A Deck in his pajamas, fast asleep. I suppose he'd forgotten to strap himself into his bunk.

I grabbed the envelope and saw Kate's name written on the outside. Not just her name, but the words *My darling Kate*. The handwriting was not mine.

I shouldn't have, but I did: I stuffed it into my pocket and hurried inside my cabin. I had the place to myself. I turned on the light and pulled out the letter. The envelope had been slit open, so Kate must have read it already. Hovering near the ceiling, I extracted the piece of cream-coloured paper, unfolded it, and began to read.

> Dearest Kate,
> I wanted you to have this letter to open after you embarked, so you might have some reminder of me on your historic expedition. Here is a photo of me that is not bad, and might help keep you company on those lonely nights in outer space.

Swallowing back my jealousy, I glanced at the small sepia portrait of him in a fine suit. He was looking at the camera, head cocked as though having some very stimulating and original thoughts. The camera made him look smarter and more handsome than he was. I went back to the letter.

> My darling, I just wanted to say again that you have made me the happiest of men by agreeing to marry me. I must confess that I've admired you from afar for years. I'm terribly sad that you have to go away so soon upon our engagement, but I know how important this expedition is to you, and wouldn't prevent it for the world, my sweet.

His endearments made me feel quite ill. He wrote with a passion I hadn't expected. It was clear he was besotted with her.

> Let me also say, dear Kate, that I have the highest regard for your professional ambitions. I myself have

long been fascinated by the mysterious and unknown.
How wonderful to know I have found a soulmate
with whom to explore these tantalizing realms. Rest
assured that no interest of yours could repel me, and
I look forward to joining you on your secret nighttime
excursions.

Nighttime excursions? The fellow still actually thought Kate
was skulking around robbing graves! I cursed myself for talking to him at the garden party and filling his head with wild
notions.

Now, to the most important part of my letter. You
asked me a question the night before your departure.
You wanted to know if I'd let you carry on with your
studies and scientific pursuits once we were married.
You wanted to know if you could lead the life you've
always wanted. And my answer is yes! You may do
whatever you please. I will not try to discourage you,
but do everything I can to help. You will have all the
money and time you wish. You have my promise. I
wish I could embrace and kiss you right now, my
sweet, and I eagerly await your return so we can
come to know each other more intimately.

Your James.
xxoo

My pulse pounded in my ears. She'd told me she had no intention of marrying Sanderson, so why even bother asking him that question? I realized I was crumpling the letter in my hands, ripping it to shreds. My cheeks were wet. The *Starclimber* and all our lives were in peril, but all I could think about right now was Kate and James Sanderson. It seemed to me that he'd offered her absolutely everything she had ever wanted—and that Kate meant to take it.

22 / The Counterweight

"I THINK SHE MIGHT marry him," I told Tobias.

We were alone on the bridge, and I'd just finished telling him about Sanderson's letter. I needed to tell someone before my fury and anxiety swelled like nitrogen bubbles in my bloodstream.

"But she doesn't even like him," Tobias said.

"No, but she loves what he's offering—the chance to do whatever she wants for the rest of her life."

It was coming on nine o'clock in the morning, and we were travelling at flank speed. Our main duty was as lookouts now, for we were supposed to reach the counterweight around ten o'clock by Dr. Turgenev's reckoning. We were some twenty-one thousand miles from earth. We'd switched on the bow-mounted searchlights and they blazed a column of light along the astral cable. The captain had told us we should be able to see the counterweight from quite a distance, but we weren't taking any chances. A collision was the last thing we needed. Tipped right back in our chairs so we could stare straight up, Tobias and I took ten-minute shifts at lookout, so our eyes wouldn't weary.

"I don't understand," Tobias said. "She's rich already. She doesn't need Sanderson's money to do what she wants, does she?"

I shook my head. "It's not just the money. If she breaks off this engagement, even if she makes up some fantastic story, her parents aren't stupid. They're going to know she's tricked them. They might cut her off for good. No more money, no more university, no more Paris. Just drinking tea and sewing little doilies in Lionsgate City. But if she goes through with the marriage, she's guaranteed *everything* she wants."

"Not everything," said Tobias. "Not you."

I sighed. "That's what worries me. What if she can do without me?"

"Come on, Matt, what does Kate want more? You or her work?"

"You've seen what she's like. She was ready to keep that etherian hatchling aboard, even if it ate people."

"She's pretty determined," Tobias admitted.

We sat for a moment in silence. I was waiting for Tobias to leap in with something brilliant that would put all my worries to rest. I looked off to starboard and saw the star I'd named for Kate, twinkling tauntingly, reminding me how very far away it was.

"Look, I'm no expert on these things," Tobias said, "but it seems pretty simple to me. Ask her to marry you."

I looked at him, horrified.

"Isn't that what you want?" Tobias asked.

"Yeah, but I'm not sure I want to get married yet."

"The engagement can go on for years," Tobias said. "One of my cousins was engaged for five years while he got established. Just propose to Kate. If she loves you, she'll say yes. But if she says no, and makes up some excuse, then you'll know it's never going to work out. You'll just get your heart broken. In the long run, it's best to know now, don't you think?"

I thought for a few moments, then said, "You're right, Tobias. Thanks."

He shrugged. "What do I know about girls? I just sit on them. Anyway, if you're going to ask her to marry you, you might want to do it soon, because we might be dead before long."

I laughed at myself. "Yeah, sorry, I'm thinking about all the wrong things."

It seemed ridiculous to worry about Kate right now, but she was such a big part of my life, I could never shut out thoughts of her for long. I glanced at the ship's clock and took over from Tobias as lookout.

"Shepherd and the captain are going to be making the spacewalk," Tobias said. "Don't you think? We're on duty, they're resting up."

"Makes sense," I said. Part of me was relieved. It was a huge job, and our lives depended on its success. I'd become much swifter after all the practice runs, but I still worried I'd make a mistake, especially if paired with Shepherd. He was good, but he was no team player, and his lack of confidence in me undermined my own.

Directly overhead, something sparkled in the ship's searchlights.

"Look!" I cried.

"Is that it?" said Tobias.

It was like a small metal moon, still a ways off, but growing slowly and steadily.

"Yeah, that's it," I said, checking the pictures Dr. Turgenev had drawn for us. Taped to our control panel, they showed what the counterweight would look like from various distances as we approached. "We're at sixty miles, I'd say."

"I'll go wake everyone," said Tobias.

"Dead slow, please, Mr. Blanchard," the captain said.

We all stared up through the glass dome, the four astralnauts and Dr. Turgenev, watching tensely as the *Starclimber* crawled towards the underside of the counterweight. Now that we were closer, we saw how truly immense it was. Its stern loomed over us, its four protruding rocket engines each the size of the *Starclimber*. From the very centre of the stern ran the astral cable.

"There is room, there is room," said Dr. Turgenev as the *Starclimber* eased up between the four rocket engines, closer to the ship's hull.

I felt my shoulders tensing as the great singed columns of the engines slid past the windows, for it seemed very tight; but according to the blueprints, the *Starclimber* was designed to fit between them.

I looked over at Shepherd and saw him squinting and rubbing at his left brow.

"And full stop, please," said the captain, when our flexed

spider arms were within twenty feet of the counterweight's stern. "Dr. Turgenev, how much time do we have?"

The scientist had been furiously jotting notes. "Two hundred five minutes, give or take a few minutes."

"We're in good shape," the captain said. "Our best time in trials was a hundred and eighty minutes. Mr. Shepherd and I will be making the walk. Mr. Blanchard, I want you in the airlock spotting us and guiding us back when the time comes. Mr. Cruse, I want you up here at the helm. As soon as we're in the airlock, you put the *Starclimber* into reverse at flank speed."

"Yes, sir."

"Let's head to the airlock, Mr. Shepherd."

Shepherd was blinking a lot, one hand to his face as though shielding his eyes from the sun's glare. He was very pale.

"Are you all right?" I asked him quietly.

He waved me away. But he was clumsy as he sailed towards the stairs, and he overshot, colliding with the wall.

"Mr. Shepherd, are you unwell?" the captain asked.

"Just a headache," he muttered, his voice sounding thick.

The captain floated over to him. Shepherd kept blinking as if having trouble focusing. A tremor of fear passed through me. We needed Shepherd strong. As much as I disliked him, he was our best astralnaut.

"How bad is the pain?" the captain asked.

"It'll pass."

"Does the light hurt your eyes?"

"Some. Not much."

"Catch," said the captain, tossing a pencil in his direction.

Squinting, Shepherd grabbed for it, but missed by a foot.

"You're having a migraine, Mr. Shepherd. My wife's a sufferer. How long have you had this condition?"

"Not a condition, sir," said Shepherd. "I've had maybe three my whole life."

The captain didn't look convinced. "How long do they last?"

"They come on real slow, and mostly go away without amounting to much." Without warning he turned and retched, his vomitus drifting in the air.

The captain placed a hand on his shoulder. "You're not going out." He turned and looked from Tobias to me.

He would pick Tobias. I'd improved, but my friend was still more agile in outer space. That was the right choice.

"You're coming with me, Mr. Cruse," the captain said.

"Me, sir?" I said, astounded—and afraid.

"Cruse can't do it," Shepherd said, gripping his temples.

"Mr. Cruse is more than capable," said the captain. "Mr. Blanchard, you'll remain spotter. Mr. Shepherd, I suggest you get some rest; you're in no fit state to be on duty. Dr. Turgenev, you know the controls as well as we do. We'll need you to reverse the *Starclimber* and take us down before the rockets ignite."

"This I can do." The scientist nodded, but looked nervously out at the enormous engines.

I imagined them spewing flame, creating enough heat to melt the ship to slag.

"We've already lost a few precious minutes," said the captain. "Mr. Blanchard, Mr. Cruse, to the airlock."

It was a kind of torture to know our seconds were ticking away, and to have to sit still, breathing tanked oxygen in the airlock. I tried not to think about everything we needed to do in the next three hours. I looked over at the captain.

"You'll be glad to return to the *Aurora* after this, sir," I said.

"She's a grand ship. But this is my last voyage as captain."

I was stunned. "I didn't know that, sir."

"No captain likes to talk of retiring."

I felt a keen disappointment. I'd always hoped that one day I'd work as an officer aboard the *Aurora,* under Captain Walken's command. But right now, it was also comforting to imagine him retired, safe at home. It meant we would live through this.

"Well, sir, it's hard to imagine a more dramatic finish for your career," I said.

He chuckled. "Indeed. We'll be quite the heroes when we return home."

"You'll probably be happy to have your feet on the ground," Tobias said, and added, "I know I will."

"It's no easy thing to give up the sky," the captain said. "But I made a promise to my wife. She and the children have seen me off on far too many long voyages. It's been hard on them, and me too. So I promised to retire early, to see more of them all. I'm finally ready to be at anchor."

It made me think of the life I wanted for myself—always sailing off somewhere. Was it foolish to think I could fit Kate into it, if she'd even have me?

"But you don't regret it, do you, sir?" I asked. "The airborne life?"

He smiled. "Not at all. It's been grand. Now, let's get our helmets on, gentlemen. We're ready."

We jetted out from the airlock, between two of the counterweight's storm engines. It was like travelling through a metal canyon, and we took special care to keep our umbilicuses from getting tangled. I breathed a sigh of relief when we were through and into open space.

Slowing myself with my air pistol, I gazed up at the counterweight. I hadn't seen it properly before now. It was truly enormous, rising up like the Eiffel Tower and looking bizarrely out of place in the heavenly ether. Incredible that it had been able to blast off from Earth. Carefully I manoeuvred my body, and with a pulse of compressed air, guided myself up beside the counterweight's hull towards the access hatch.

I had no watch, and every moment out here was so absorbing that I lost all sense of time. Tobias was our clock, calling out every five minutes; and the gaps between some times seemed an age, and other times little more than a few heartbeats.

"We're at the hatch," the captain said, when we'd secured ourselves to the hull.

"This is very good," came Dr. Turgenev's voice now. He'd managed to rig our radios so he could communicate with us from the bridge and give us directions once we were inside. "You are three minutes ahead of schedule."

"Off to a good start," the captain said.

The hatch wasn't exactly like our own cargo door, but not far off. It was the handholds that were the problem. They were in different places, and it took me a while to get into a proper working position. As I readied my tools, the music of the spheres played in some secret part of my mind, soothing me. I worked steadily, without talking, without thinking of anything except the next motion of my body. I thought I was doing really well—until I heard Tobias's time call and realized I was nearly behind schedule.

I looked over to see Captain Walken working on his last bolt; I was just finishing my second. I tried to hurry, and very nearly lost my wrench.

"Steady, Mr. Cruse," said the captain. "You're doing well."

I fought my frustration and kept going. Never did I forget that time was streaming past, even though I couldn't tell how quickly or slowly. When my last bolt finally drifted off, I almost cheered.

The captain pulled on the handle and I pushed. The hatch popped in and folded back on its hinges against the hull.

"We have the hatch open," the captain reported.

"You are five minutes behind. This is not bad," said Dr. Turgenev.

My limbs felt shaky with fatigue. This was the longest any of us had been out at one time. Dew had started to form and freeze along the outer edge of my visor.

"We're going inside," the captain said.

I felt the tight grip of claustrophobia. The hatchway was small, and it was pitch black inside. The captain went first, and I followed, checking our umbilicuses once more. I was grateful for our helmet-mounted lamps, which cast powerful beams of light.

Entering the counterweight was like stumbling upon something from another civilization, a cathedral or a factory, some immense space filled with things you'd never seen before. The inside was a vast spoolworks, an intricate arrangement of gears and colossal cylinders welded into place, one above the other, carrying tens of thousands of miles of astral cable. Now most of the spools were empty, but a hundred feet above me, near the counterweight's peak, I saw several cylinders still wound with tight rows.

"I see some cable," I said, with huge relief. Dr. Turgenev was right. The counterweight had never gone high enough, had never paid out its full length of astral cable. It was still there, just waiting to be deployed.

"Yes, is good," said Dr. Turgenev, sounding unsurprised.

His matter-of-factness reassured me. Maybe our plan was possible after all.

"Now," he said, "please find control panel."

From the blueprints, I knew that the panel wasn't far from the access hatch. A spindly catwalk had been built around the inside hull, and my beam of light picked out a massive control panel about twenty feet along.

I kept checking back over my shoulder as we moved towards it, making sure our umbiliuses ran clear. It would be all too easy for them to get tangled up on something in here.

"We're at the panel," the captain said.

There were no proper footholds, so we had to make do gripping on to the railing with one hand and floating before the controls. Our lamps illuminated the familiar array of switches and buttons, dials and lights, organized into different sections, each labelled with a capital letter. I'd rehearsed this so many times, I'd memorized the entire ignition sequence. But I was very glad Dr. Turgenev would be talking us through it, for I was tired and I didn't want to make a mistake. From our tool pouches we each took a pair of needle-nose pliers. We'd all practised managing different banks of controls.

"Please find section F," Dr. Turgenev told us.

"I have it," said Captain Walken.

"Press white button to test battery," the scientist instructed.

"The indicator light flares green," the captain reported back.

"Good. We still have charge. In section G is gauge with four-digit number. You see it?"

Captain Walken leaned closer and read the number to Dr. Turgenev.

"Ah," the scientist said. "This explains great deal. This number is seconds of rocket burn. Rockets shut off five seconds too early. Must be defective fuse. Now to check fuses. Please find section A."

My eyes went to the proper place.

But I saw no row of fuses.

"Do you see fuses?" came Dr. Turgenev's voice again.

"I just need a second. . . ." My eyes darted everywhere, and I felt a flash of panic. In my mind I could see the mock-up we'd built; I could see the fuses. But there was nothing right now in front of me. Was I hallucinating?

"They're not here," I said.

There was a brief silence. "You are sure?" said Dr. Turgenev.

Captain Walken floated closer. "I confirm that," he said. "The fuses are not in section A. Is it possible they're somewhere else?"

"Yes, please look," said Dr. Turgenev. "I work from memory only . . ."

I started searching through section B, and in section C found a row of fuses.

"There're six," I reported. Our mock-up had only four. "Are these the ones?"

"Yes, yes, must be," said Dr. Turgenev, but he sounded flustered.

A terrible wave of doubt broke across me. He'd been working the whole time from memory, under terrible stress. If he could forget one thing, what else could he forget?

"Please to check fuses now, starting from left."

Two of the fuses had blown, and I started to replace them. We'd practised all this in the trials, but my gut told me it was taking too long.

"Now fuel gauge in section D. Please read me weight of fuel."

That was on the captain's side. The pause that followed was too long.

"The needle shows empty," came the captain's voice in my helmet.

"This is not possible," said the scientist.

"It's on empty, Dr. Turgenev."

I felt like I might throw up. No fuel. Without fuel there was no rocket burn. Without rocket burn the counterweight would continue to fall out of orbit, taking us with it. All our hope and work was to come to nothing.

"The fuel's weightless up here," said Tobias from the airlock.

"Yes, he is right!" said Dr. Turgenev with a slightly hysterical laugh. "Of course! Gauge was not meant to be read in outer space. I am fool! No problem now. Is fuel, I am sure."

I let out a long breath. My pulse slowed.

"So now," said Dr. Turgenev, "we have good chance for reignition."

"*Chance?*" I said in surprise.

"Is small possibility engines are too cold to ignite," the scientist replied.

"You didn't mention that earlier," Captain Walken said.

"Small possibility, *very* small possibility," said Dr. Turgenev urgently. "Now find please section B. Do you see dial?"

"I've got it," I said. This, I knew, was the timer to ignite the engines. We needed thirty minutes to get back to the *Starclimber,* and another thirty minutes for the *Starclimber* to get safely clear.

"Turn all the way to right until number says 60," Dr. Turgenev told me.

The manoeuvre was tricky with the needle-nose pliers, but I gripped hard and managed to turn the dial. The numbers flickered up: 20 . . . 30 . . . 40 . . . 50 . . . and there it stuck.

"It's stopped at 50," I said.

"It goes to 60," said Dr. Turgenev.

I tried again. "It must be jammed," I said.

Captain Walken came over and tried, with no more success. "I don't want to force it."

"No, no, do not force!" said Dr. Turgenev. I heard him clear his throat. "Fifty minutes only . . ."

Captain Walken and I turned to each other. I couldn't see his expression through his mirrored visor, but I got the feeling he was thinking the same thing as me.

"Is that enough time?" I said quietly.

"It'll have to be," he said. "The ship needs thirty minutes to get to a safe distance. That means we need to get back in twenty. We can do it. Dr. Turgenev, we need to keep going, please."

"Find ignition button in section A," the scientist said. "Push until green light comes on. And remember, once you see green light, there is no stopping."

I found the ignition button. I pushed it hard.

There was no sound in outer space, but I could feel, through my feet, a stuttering vibration, like an engine struggling to start in cold weather.

Whrrrr . . . whrrrrr . . . whrrrr . . .

"Do you have green light?" Dr. Turgenev asked urgently.

"I have no green light," I said.

I pushed again, felt the same feeble shaking through the catwalk.

"I have no green light!" I said again.

I kept pushing.

Everything was too cold: the wires, the batteries, the mechanics. The rocket was built to launch from Earth, not from the frozen ether. Suddenly the vibration at my feet strengthened, and this time did not falter. The indicator light flared green.

"I have a green light!" I cried out.

"Go!" shouted Dr. Turgenev.

We had only twenty minutes, so would need to be all the faster now. Immediately, Captain Walken and I pushed off the catwalk towards the hatch. I was closest. I swam through first, and was fairly blinded by the sunlight and starlight blazing off the counterweight's silver hull.

I looked back at the hatch, waiting for Captain Walken to emerge. He jetted through, but was suddenly jerked back. In alarm I saw that part of his umbilicus was still inside the counterweight.

"I'm snagged on something," he said. "Go on ahead, Mr. Cruse. I'll sort this out."

He turned himself and started back inside. With a burst of my air pistol I followed him.

"Mr. Cruse, return to the ship!" he said sharply when he caught sight of me.

He was already manoeuvring himself up towards a complicated mesh of gears beside one of the empty cylinders. In the combined blaze of our headlamps, I saw his umbilicus caught amidst the machinery. It must have drifted up and got tangled while we were at the control console.

"You have only fifteen minutes to return to ship," Dr. Turgenev said over my radio.

"Mr. Cruse, you are directly disobeying an order," said the captain.

We'd both reached the spot where the umbilicus was caught. My throat went dry when I saw it. It was trapped between the teeth of two meshing gears. The captain reached for the umbilicus, and I held onto him, helping anchor him as he tried to pull it free. It wouldn't budge. He tried once more, and this time the gears moved, but meshed even tighter, pinching the umbilicus.

"Ten minutes," said Dr. Turgenev.

"Mr. Cruse—" said the captain.

My words came out in desperate gasps. "Sir, I am —not going—back alone."

"If I pull any more, I may sever the umbilicus. I'm stuck, Matt. You need to return."

"We'll cut you loose," I said, taking my knife from my hip pouch. "We'll cut your umbilicus a few feet from your suit.

You grip the end tight, you won't lose your air and pressure."

I was lying, and we both knew it. No matter how hard he squeezed, his oxygen and heat would find a way out. How fast was the only question.

"Cut it," said Captain Walken.

He measured a length of umbilicus from the back of his suit and held it in front of him, clamping it in his fist. I started sawing. The material was thick and resilient, and it seemed to take forever before I heard a hiss and saw a line of escaping vapour. The captain squeezed tighter. I sawed harder.

"Five minutes!" cried Dr. Turgenev. "You must return to ship!"

At last I cut all the way through. The ship's end of the umbilicus started whipping around, venting oxygen into space. There was now absolutely nothing connecting the captain to the *Starclimber*.

"Grab hold!" I told him. I needed one hand for my air pistol, so we linked our free arms as firmly as we could. I jetted us back towards the hatch.

Glancing back to check my own umbilicus, with horror I saw it looping out behind me, dangerously close to the gears. It was too late to slow down, so I just gave us another burst of speed, sure I'd feel a great backward jerk as we snagged. But we made it through the hatch and were outside.

"Tobias! Start reeling in. I've got the captain."

We were unwieldy, the two of us locked together, and with the air pistol it was almost impossible to move us in a straight line. We tumbled down past the counterweight's hull, went too far, and my umbilicus brought me up short, almost jerking the captain free of my grip.

"You all right, sir?" I knew that with every second he was losing more and more oxygen and air pressure.

"Yes," he said, but his breathing was laboured.

Now to get through the counterweight's engines and to the *Starclimber*'s airlock. Tobias was very slowly reeling me in—he couldn't do it too quickly or he'd send us slamming into the engines. With little bursts from my air pistol I lined us up. I could see the airlock dead ahead, could see Tobias waiting for us in the hatch.

We passed between the counterweight's giant engines, and I was startled to already feel their heat as they warmed up.

"We are out of time!" said Dr. Turgenev.

"We're almost there!" I shouted. We were endangering the entire ship now, but I could *see* the airlock. "Don't leave without us!"

"We cannot wait long!" said the scientist.

"We're coming!"

I felt the captain's grasp weaken and he slipped off my arm, started to drift away. I dropped my air pistol and just managed to grab hold with both arms. I saw the trail of his oxygen, venting from his severed cable more rapidly now as his grip faltered.

"Bring us in, Tobias!" I shouted. "Fast as you can!"

"Hold tight!" he said.

The tug on my umbilicus spun me around and I hurtled

backward towards the *Starclimber*, praying I wouldn't lose my hold on the captain. Without my air pistol I had no way of steering, and with a jarring *thud*, we scraped the side of one of the rocket engines and deflected off, tumbling now. There was another great *thump* as we hit the *Starclimber*, and it knocked the wind out of me. Then I felt a sharp tug on my line and there was Tobias, leaning out and grabbing me.

He pulled the captain and me inside, and shut the hatch behind us.

"We're all in!" I shouted into my radio. "Dr. Turgenev, we're all inside. Reverse!"

"Beginning descent," he replied. "We are nine minutes behind."

Through the porthole, I saw us slide down past the counterweight's engines. They were already glowing orange. I hoped we weren't too late.

"Pressurizing airlock," said Tobias.

"Need air," gasped the captain, teeth chattering inside his helmet.

I grabbed hold of the stump end of the captain's umbilicus and squeezed hard, trying to hold in whatever remained of his oxygen and air pressure. I watched the pressure gauge in agony.

"We're almost there, sir, almost there," I said. "Just a few more seconds, you're doing fine."

The moment the airlock was at proper pressure, I

unclamped his helmet and yanked it off his head. His face was grey, his lips blue with cold, and he was struggling for breath. Tobias placed an oxygen mask over his face.

By the time Tobias and I had removed each other's helmets, the captain was breathing easier, and some colour had returned to his face. He removed the oxygen mask and looked at me.

"Mr. Cruse, I'll be in your debt till my dying day." He gave my arm a squeeze. "Thank you for disobeying orders. . . . Just don't make a habit of it."

"No, sir," I said, grinning.

Captain Walken seemed to recover miraculously, and we quickly got out of our suits and jetted up the stairs to the bridge. Shepherd was still there, strapped into one of the pilot's chairs, looking wretched. Dr. Turgenev was at the helm, the throttle pushed to flank speed. Overhead the counterweight still seemed uncomfortably close, its four rocket engines glowing red-orange now.

"Three minutes to ignition," said Dr. Turgenev. "This is not so far away as I would like."

We were already at top speed, and all I could do was watch, willing the counterweight to get smaller and smaller.

"Good work out there, Cruse," Shepherd said to me quietly.

I couldn't have been more surprised. "Thanks," I said. It wasn't an apology exactly, but it was probably the closest thing I'd ever get from Shepherd.

"One minute . . ." said Dr. Turgenev.

I had no idea what to expect. Would the *Starclimber* be shaken off its cable? Would the cable be able to withstand the strain? Would it snap free back on Earth?

"Ten seconds," said Dr. Turgenev.

I finished the countdown in my head and watched as the engines erupted with flame. It seemed to engulf the entire counterweight, for all I could see was a great sphere of fire hanging in the ether.

"We have ignition!" cried Dr. Turgenev.

A huge shudder ran through the *Starclimber.*

The ball of fire seemed to be shrinking with unbelievable speed.

"It is working!" cried Dr. Turgenev. "It climbs! Cable is unspooling!"

And suddenly the flame disappeared and all I could see was the tiny dot of the counterweight, now incredibly far away and climbing heavenward.

"That was five-second burn," said Dr. Turgenev.

"That's it?" Tobias said.

"That is all we need, yes," he said, looking at his clipboard. "That will take counterweight to proper altitude. We are fine now."

"We did it!" I said, feeling limp with relief. "It actually worked!"

Dr. Turgenev rubbed his forehead. "I had very big doubts."

"*Big* doubts?" I said weakly.

The scientist shrugged. "I am pessimist," he said.

23 / The Final Stretch

WHEN I WOKE, the sun was blazing through my cabin porthole, and I knew it must be late afternoon. I felt the *Starclimber*'s reassuring vibration through the bunk and knew we were climbing towards the cable's summit. Even though I was weightless, my entire body felt heavy and sore with fatigue.

I'd done it.

I hadn't thought I could. Since the very start, I'd worried I didn't have the right stuff. But I'd made a three-hour space-walk, starting off bone-tired. I'd helped get that hatch open, muddled through the ignition sequence, and gotten the captain back to the ship in time. I wasn't the best, and I wasn't first choice, but I'd done it—and that felt good enough.

I floated there in my cabin, in the sunshine, for just a moment longer, enjoying it. Then I pulled on my uniform and hurried up to the bridge.

Tobias and Shepherd were on duty.

"Hey, Matt," said Tobias. "Did you get a good rest?"

"I'm sorry. I slept like the dead. Have I missed my shift?"

"I figured you could use the sleep," said Shepherd.

I stared at him in surprise, but he didn't look up from his control panel.

"Thanks very much, Shepherd," I said. "Is your head okay?"

"It didn't last long, this one."

"We had some more good news," Tobias told me. "General Lancaster radioed earlier. They caught Eriksson, and he confessed there was no bomb. Turns out I'm not a Babelite after all."

"I'm very glad to hear it," I said, grinning.

"We'll reach the counterweight in twenty-two hours," Shepherd said.

The calm of the bridge right now seemed dreamlike after the frenzied rush of the past forty-eight hours. It had all worked out. I could scarcely believe it. But even though we'd escaped disaster and death, something still clouded my thoughts.

Kate's letter.

"You should get something to eat," Tobias said. "You're on duty in half an hour."

I drifted downstairs to B Deck. Captain Walken, Miss Karr, and Dr. Turgenev were just buckling themselves up at the dining table.

"Ah, Mr. Cruse," said the captain. "Join us."

"How are you feeling, sir?" I asked. I shouldn't have been the one sleeping late, when it was the captain who'd had the brush with death.

"Remarkably well," he said. "You got me back just in time. Another minute or so and it would have been very different."

"You're quite a hero," Miss Karr said to me.

"Heroics are nothing new to Mr. Cruse," Captain Walken said.

I felt my cheeks warm with their praise. I wasn't at all sure that what I'd done was heroic. Someone like Shepherd might have said I'd endangered the entire ship by bringing the captain back—and in some ways he'd be right. What I did was selfish, for the thought of losing the captain filled me with such fear and sadness, I couldn't bear it.

We'd just started our meal when Sir Hugh and Kate floated up from the laboratory to join us. They were having a very intense conversation with lots of scientific words I didn't understand. I think they were talking about the etherian specimen.

"Hello, everyone," said Kate distractedly. Her eyes lighted on me briefly, and she added, "Well done, Mr. Cruse. I hear you saved the day."

"Thank you, Miss de Vries."

And then she went back to talking to Sir Hugh.

I'd been hoping for more, somehow. I knew Kate couldn't throw her arms around me and tell me how worried she'd been, and how glad she was that I was safe, and what a hero I was. Maybe she wanted to but was just play-acting her part as James Sanderson's fiancée. Or maybe she was just engrossed in her etherian specimen.

Over the past two days, even as we'd been frantically preparing our rescue procedure, she'd been busy in the laboratory. Her concentration and dedication were amazing. Whenever I passed by, she'd be taking notes and peering at things under microscopes and arguing with Sir Hugh about this or that procedure. She seemed to have pushed all thoughts of danger from her mind—and maybe that was for the best. But I couldn't help wondering if she'd also pushed all thoughts of *me* from her mind.

"The substance is completely unique," Kate was saying to Sir Hugh. "I'm wondering if some of its molecules even exist on Earth. But it did exhibit some of the same characteristics as luciferins."

"One of the enzymes that produces the firefly's glow," said Sir Hugh. "Interesting. I shall be very happy to mention that in a footnote."

Kate paused for a moment. "A footnote?"

"Yes, in my article."

"A *footnote* in *your* article," said Kate, her voice suddenly chilly.

"A very generous footnote, yes," he said.

Kate's nostrils narrowed. "Sir Hugh, I was under the impression we'd be writing this article together as equal partners."

The eminent zoologist pursed his lips and shook his head. "No, no. I shall write my article, and you are free to write your own, of course."

"Ha!" said Kate, looking around at the rest of us. "That's a trick, you see. Sir Hugh is very well known, and any journal will publish his paper before mine, and then he can take sole credit for the discovery."

"Rubbish," said Sir Hugh, but I thought he looked fairly guilty.

"I think Mr. Lunardi meant for the two of you to work together," Captain Walken said. "And present your findings to the world as a team."

"As co-authors," Kate said, staring hard at Sir Hugh.

"This is standard scientific decorum," said Dr. Turgenev.

The monkey launched into a barrage of angry chittering.

"I think Haiku feels the same," said Miss Karr.

Sir Hugh glanced nervously at the animal. "Very well," he said. "Miss de Vries, you and I shall write the paper together."

"Thank you, Sir Hugh," she said, her expression triumphant, and the two continued with their polite scientific chat.

I was actually starting to feel jealous of Sir Hugh. As much as Kate loathed him, she was spending a great deal of time with him lately. He got all her passion. I desperately wanted to talk to Kate, about the letter, about the turmoil in my heart, but I'd have to wait until we could be alone.

"And how are you, Miss Karr?" I asked, trying to distract myself.

"Never better," she said. "Strange as it might sound, this crisis was just the thing for me."

"It'll make for quite a newspaper dispatch," I said.

"Oh, I didn't mean that," she said. "It's finally jolted me out of my funk."

"Funk?" said Kate, who must have been listening with one ear.

"For the past two years or more," she said. "Haven't taken a picture worth a damn. Everything bored me. Including myself."

"But you've accomplished so much!" Kate said.

Miss Karr gave one of her merry cackles. "Don't look so distressed, Miss de Vries. I'm a good deal older than you, and most things lose their lustre eventually. That's why I came on this trip—one of the reasons anyway. I was hoping a new view might shake me out of it. But it didn't."

"I'm sure your photographs are remarkable, Miss Karr," Captain Walken said. "Once you develop them back on Earth, you'll be very pleased."

"Oh, the photographs will be fine," she said dismissively. "But it's the photographer who needs to change." She smiled as if she had a secret she wasn't willing to share quite yet, then turned her lively eyes on Kate.

"So, Miss de Vries, has all this danger given you a new hunger for life too? You must be pining after your Mr. Sanderson more than ever."

"Terribly," she said, managing to look pale and wistful. "I've been quite beside myself."

Miss Karr nodded. "You're very wise to marry."

Kate looked as surprised as I felt.

"I thought you took a very dim view of marriage, Miss Karr," the captain remarked, amused. "I read somewhere that you called it little better than slavery."

"I think Mrs. Snuffler would take exception to that," said Sir Hugh indignantly.

"Slavery, if you marry the wrong person," Miss Karr said firmly. "But having a soulmate would be a very fine thing. I made some bad choices in my life. When I was younger, I withheld my love where it was wanted, and gave it where it was not."

We were all listening, rapt, even though I felt a bit awkward to be hearing such personal things. But Miss Karr had always been plain-spoken, and she didn't seem in the least embarrassed. I stole a glance at Kate, but she didn't return my gaze.

"And after that, I stupidly turned away from love altogether. It took a while, but when I'd smothered those feelings, they were gone for good. I thought they'd just interfere with my work. That's where I think you've been so smart, Miss de Vries. You've said yes to love, and I'm sure you'll be very happy with James Sanderson."

"Yes, I expect I shall," Kate said brightly. "Thank you very much for your kind words. Now, if you'll all excuse me, I must get back to the laboratory."

I was on duty until midnight, and after that I came down to B Deck, hoping Kate would be there. But no one was in the darkened lounge. I floated round and round the circular deck like some lovesick whale, willing Kate to come to me. If she loved me, she would come. She would know I needed to be with her. I waited till one in the morning, and then decided to wait just a little longer.

When I woke up, bumping against the ceiling, it was nearly six o'clock. My shift on the bridge would be starting in just a few minutes.

I was about to hurry upstairs and scrub my face with a damp washcloth when I heard some noise from C Deck. I swam over to the staircase and saw lights, so I jetted silently down. Kate was already up and at work, head bent over a microscope.

"Marry me," I said.

Kate twisted around with a gasp. "You scared me!"

I'd scared myself. I hadn't planned what I was going to say, and the words had just leapt out. But there was no taking them back now. Kate stared at me, her pretty mouth agape.

"What did you say?"

I swallowed. "Will you marry me?"

Her eyes slid away from mine. "Please don't ask me that," she murmured.

"Why not?"

She laughed nervously. "I'm already engaged; I can't be engaged to two people at the same time, can I."

"Shouldn't be a problem for someone of your talents."

"And just what's that supposed to mean?" she said angrily.

"You're avoiding my question," I countered. I was still bobbing about in the air, making little swimmy motions with my hands to stay upright, and I felt extremely undignified. I wished I'd strapped myself down before starting all this.

"I've already told you," she said. "I'm not sure I mean to marry *anyone*."

"So you can end up like Miss Karr?" I whispered. The ship would soon begin stirring, and I was nervous now that someone might overhear us from upstairs.

Kate tilted her chin up. "I have the greatest admiration for Miss Karr."

"She pushes a monkey around in a pram!"

"She's an amazingly accomplished woman who pursues her own ambitions."

"Yes, I know how important that is for you. Maybe important enough to make you marry James Sanderson."

Kate growled in exasperation. "I've told you already, I've no intention of marrying the fellow."

"Oh, really?" I said, and then let the hammer fall. "Then why'd you even bother *asking* him if he'd let you continue your work once you two married?"

She stared at me, speechless. Then her nostrils narrowed. "You read my letter."

I nodded.

"How did you get a hold of it?"

"It was floating in the hallway outside your room."

"That was very rude of you to open it."

I gave a savage laugh. "How naughty of *me*! Almost as bad as *deceiving* people to get what you want."

"I haven't deceived you!" she protested.

"No? Were you really planning on breaking off the engagement, or did you just lie to me so I wouldn't make a fuss?"

Her face went pale. "Is that really what you think?"

She looked almost hurt, but I didn't trust her any more, so I said, "Yes, that's what I think."

"I'm very sorry to hear that," she said coldly.

We glared at each other for a moment, and then I heard metallic footfalls, and Sir Hugh came clanking down the stairs.

"You're up early, Miss de Vries," he called out. "Oh, hello, Mr. Cruse."

"That does seem very interesting work, Miss de Vries," I said to Kate as I retreated. "I look forward to hearing more about it. Good morning, Sir Hugh."

And I left the laboratory, floating weightless, but my heart was as heavy as planet Earth.

24 / Etherians

RISING FROM THE COUNTERWEIGHT's summit, the Canadian flag fluttered with surreal slowness in outer space.

"That's quite a sight," Shepherd said, floating next to me in his astral suit.

Far below us, the earth was the size of a golf ball held at arm's length. It seemed incredible that we were still connected to it by such a narrow strand of thread. The music of the spheres played softly within my mind.

We had reached cable's end at noon. Mr. Lunardi had radioed us a congratulatory telegram from the Prime Minister, and another from the King. We were the first humans in outer space, and had journeyed higher than anyone had ever been—twenty-five thousand miles above Earth.

We'd drawn straws for the privilege of raising the flag on the counterweight, and Shepherd and I had won. I should've felt a huge sense of pride and accomplishment. We'd done our country proud. But I was still too dejected after my conversation with Kate that morning.

"How're you two making out up there?" Tobias asked from the airlock.

"The flag is up and looking beautiful," I said.

"Wish we could see it from down here," Tobias said. The *Starclimber* was berthed like last time, right underneath the counterweight, its view blocked by the rocket engines.

"I took some nice pictures," Shepherd said. Miss Karr had equipped him with one of her cameras, and it floated from his suit on a tether. "We're coming in now."

We began our descent to the *Starclimber*. Off to our left hung the moon, much larger than the earth. It really did look close enough to reach with a big push. I thought of Tobias, and his dreams of one day setting foot on it.

"You planning to stay on as an astralnaut?" I asked Shepherd.

"Maybe," he said. "My days as a test pilot are numbered."

I looked over at him in surprise, but his mirrored visor told me even less than his usual inscrutable expression. "The migraines?" I asked.

"When the Aero Force finds out, they'll move me to a desk job."

"But you can tell when they're coming on, can't you?"

"Doesn't matter. It's a weakness and they'll give me the boot."

"Doesn't seem fair at all," I said. "I can't see you in a desk job."

"That's why I tried out for the astralnaut program. Thought it might be a way to keep flying high."

I realized this was the longest real conversation we'd ever had. Maybe behind his mirrored mask, out here in the deeps of space, Shepherd felt free to talk, even with Tobias listening from the bridge. I suddenly wondered if that cool, composed face of his was a kind of mask too. He hadn't revealed much about himself to me, except his infuriating arrogance and perfectionism. For the first time I felt sorry for him. The migraines were going to cost him his beloved job—and in his mind they were a shameful weakness. Try as he might, he'd never be perfect.

"Well," I said, "the captain's still letting you make spacewalks."

"He's a decent man," said Shepherd. "We'll see what happens when we get back to Earth. Lunardi may ground me."

"I think he'd be making a mistake," I said.

"What about you, Cruse?" he asked. "You staying on?"

Reflected in Shepherd's visor was a small, intense green light. I swivelled myself round. The light was no larger than a candle flame, and moving slowly across the heavens.

"Look!" I cried, pointing. "Do you see it?"

"I see it," he replied.

"Tobias, we've spotted a green moving light," I reported.

"I can't see anything from down here," came his reply. "Hang on, I'm going to connect us to the bridge."

Shepherd had the camera to his face and was taking pictures. I tracked the light across the heavens. Over the radio I could hear Tobias telling the captain what was going on. Then I lost sight of the light as it passed behind the counterweight. My gaze settled on the other side, waiting for it to reappear. It didn't. I waited another few seconds. I should've seen it by now, unless—

"It's coming straight for us!" said Shepherd.

Green light emanated from behind the rocket's hull like an aura, growing brighter.

"Do you have a distance, Mr. Shepherd?" said the captain.

"Hard to say, sir—"

An immense green mass streaked over our heads. There was no turbulence, no blast of wind from its wake. But the sheer size and nearness of the thing sent a tremor of fear through me. Heart pounding, I whirled clumsily, half blinded by the light.

"Where is it?" I cried.

Shepherd had a hand to his visor, shielding his eyes. He pointed.

Silhouetted against the moon was a long, dark shape. No green light glowed from it now. The thing was tapered like a wedge. From this distance it was the size of my gloved thumb. It seemed to be waiting, and I couldn't shake the feeling that it had intent. I couldn't look away.

"It's stationary right now," I reported. "In front of the moon."

"Its size?"

"It must be huge, sir."

"It's got to be a ship," said Shepherd. "It's too big to be anything else."

"Mr. Cruse, Mr. Shepherd, I want you back inside," said the captain.

"Yes, sir," I said.

"I'll start reeling in," said Tobias.

The shape suddenly pulsed green. I counted three seconds before it pulsed again, then another three. I felt the gentle tug on my safety line and used my air pistol to position my body towards the ship. Shepherd was snapping off more pictures. The thing was still motionless, flashing regularly.

Then we had to pay close attention, for we were manoeuvring beneath the counterweight and between its massive engines, and then into the *Starclimber*'s airlock. Minutes later I was glad to be back aboard the ship, though, given the size of the mysterious object, I couldn't see how we'd be any safer inside than out.

We were imprisoned in the airlock until the pressure was high enough, and the needle moved with maddening slowness. I kept wondering what the thing was doing out there—just hovering, watching us? Or getting ready to ram the ship and pulverize us?

"I'm going to reverse the *Starclimber* so we have a clear view," came the captain's voice in my helmet. "We're blind where we are right now."

Through the porthole I saw the counterweight's engines slip past, and then we were back out in the open.

The moment the pressure needle touched 14 psi, we yanked off each other's helmets, opened the interior hatch, and jetted out onto C Deck, still in our suits. Kate and Sir Hugh were working in the lab, oblivious.

"You'll want to see this," I said to them as we passed, and we all carried on upstairs.

In the lounge, Miss Karr and Dr. Turgenev had already pulled down all the polarized blinds, and were staring out the window at the strange silhouette pulsing against the cratered face of the moon.

"Miss Karr, as many pictures as you can," Shepherd said, and hurried up to the bridge.

"It's changing," Kate said.

She was right. It had shrunk in length and now looked roughly square.

"What's it doing?" said Sir Hugh, squinting.

"Turning," I said. "And . . . coming at us."

In just a few heartbeats the shape had doubled in size.

"Why aren't we moving?" Sir Hugh demanded. "We have to get out of here!"

"It can outrun us," I said, remembering the incredible speed with which it had streaked overhead. I wondered what the captain's plan of action would be.

"What on earth is it?" Miss Karr muttered, taking one picture after another.

"It's no meteorite," said Kate.

"Agreed," said Dr. Turgenev.

The thing's green light filled the lounge as it grew in size. We were helpless, our hands raised to shield our eyes, despite the polarized blinds.

"It's stopped flashing!" said Tobias.

Kate had her field glasses around her neck and lifted them to her face. I seized a spyglass that was floating near the window. Now that it wasn't blinding us any more, I might get a decent look at the thing. A faint green aura still hung about it as it streaked towards us. Was it some kind of ship, after all? It was hard to focus on it, it was moving so swiftly. My eyes skittered across its dark flanks, searching for a glint of metal.

"It's not a vessel," Kate said quietly. "Or a machine."

Through my spyglass, I saw an eye.

It was a very long, narrow oval, and it didn't have the hard quality of metal. It had translucence, and conveyed a kind of consciousness.

I lowered the spyglass.

"It's alive," breathed Tobias.

The creature filled almost the whole window now, and was still closing on us. I tried to make sense of its blunt, sloping head. Two eyes angled far back on either side, and above them was a deep crease, which I assumed was a mouth, but I wasn't sure, for the thing had so many deep gouges and creases. I had no idea which was its back and which its belly, because it had no limbs at all—no dorsal fins or flukes or tail. The steep angle of its eyes gave it a terrifying look. And then it opened its jaws.

"Good God!" cried Sir Hugh.

"It's the same species!" cried Kate. "It's an etherian! This must be an adult!"

Between its cavernous jaws stretched vast blades of baleen. I knew the hatchlings could only consume astral plankton, and I couldn't help wondering what an adult might inhale through its baleen. Even if it had no interest in us, there was no ignoring the terrible power of its head and flanks. It could shatter the *Starclimber.*

"It's going to ram us!" cried Sir Hugh. "Why isn't the captain doing something?"

Tobias looked at me anxiously, then jetted towards the ship's phone to call the bridge.

"I don't think sudden movements are a good idea," Kate said. "They tend to trigger an animal's fight response."

"Wait," I said, "I think it's slowing down . . . it's definitely slowing down!"

The etherian couldn't have been more than a hundred feet from us now, and was filling all the windows of the lounge. It was at least the size of the *Starclimber*. Without warning a single pulse of green light exploded from its body.

Haiku was flinging himself around the lounge, shrieking in terror.

A second green pulse engulfed us.

Then a third.

"Five seconds between pulses!" said Kate.

"Why's it doing this?" Tobias said.

Kate turned to Sir Hugh excitedly. "The male firefly flashes every five seconds when trying to attract a mate."

Miss Karr looked up from her camera, alarmed. "It wants to mate with us?"

"Bloody hell," muttered Tobias.

The ship's phone rang and I snatched it up. It was Shepherd. "We've got one on our other side."

"There's another one!" I called out, jetting across to the opposite windows. Kate and Tobias came with me.

Far away, a blue light flashed rapidly.

"It's not us they're interested in!" said Kate. "It's each other! They're communicating! Sir Hugh, it's bioluminescence, just like *Photinus pyralis!*"

"Like what?" I asked.

"Fireflies," she said. "The male flashes every five seconds, the female every two, when trying to attract a mate."

The blue light was growing in size, pulsing urgently.

"Green one is moving now!" shouted Dr. Turgenev from across B Deck.

Through my window, I saw the etherian gliding slowly out from beneath the *Starclimber,* and for the first time I realized how truly vast and long it was. It was like something made from the moon itself, ancient and silent and mysterious. Its mottled black and grey flanks had an armoured look, and were scored with countless furrows, some quite fine, others deep fissures.

"It looks like it's been mauled," Tobias said.

"No," said Kate. "Scars from micrometeoroids. Look how straight they are."

"This is right," said Dr. Turgenev, floating over with Miss Karr. "Every day, creature would encounter many such impacts."

"It looks a bit like a blue whale," said Tobias. "I saw one once. They can be a hundred feet long."

The etherian was twice that, and I shook my head in wonder as I stared. The ancient mariners must have felt like this, when they leaned far out over the railings of their vessels to take their first look at the great denizens of the oceans.

And Tobias was right. Peering down now, you might, just for a second, mistake it for a whale, for along its back were countless blowholes. As I watched, one of them twitched and dilated. A geyser of gas vapour shot out and the *Starclimber* shuddered violently with the impact. The etherian pivoted deftly, adjusted itself with another little burst of gas, and then glided slowly in the direction of the growing blue light.

The creature was completely out from beneath the ship now, and I saw that the tapered end of its body glowed pale green.

"That's where it makes its light!" said Kate excitedly, pointing. "That tail segment, there!"

As if to prove her right, it gave a green pulse that made us all squint and laugh.

This was what Kate and I had seen from the Paris Observatory, all those weeks ago. I glanced at her, wondering if she was realizing the same thing. Her face was close to mine at the window, and I could smell the familiar scent of her hair and skin. But her eyes were on the etherians, and it made me sad, for everything seemed so different and ruined between us now.

I could see the massive dark outline of the blue etherian as it drew closer. Flashing, the green one glided swiftly out to meet it, about a mile from the ship. Their pulsing lights subsided to a dim, erratic stutter as the two creatures circled about each other.

Then, suddenly, their tails erupted into flashes of colours we hadn't seen before—dazzling purples and reds and oranges. It was all so joyful that I had to laugh, echoing the delight of everyone at the window, to see this ecstatic display of colour in the dark of space.

Haiku too seemed enchanted with the cosmic fireworks. Before this, he'd been shaking his fist at the creatures and making strange yipping sounds. But now his old man's face tilted and became thoughtful, eyes curious.

Tobias chuckled, watching the etherians. "These two seem pretty keen on each other."

"It's some kind of courtship ritual!" Sir Hugh exclaimed.

I glanced at him and saw not the pompous oaf who wanted to keep Kate down, but the young, curious man who'd always loved nature and wanted to study it his whole life. His face shone.

The etherians' flashing became fiercer and more rapid until they were swirling around each other, grazing flanks. Then, as we all watched, spellbound, they touched the narrow ends of their tails together and seemed to fuse, then began rotating as one. The combined light from their lanterns blazed as one single turquoise star.

Sir Hugh cleared his throat. "Perhaps this isn't entirely appropriate for all present."

"I'm quite all right, thanks," said Kate, sounding fascinated. "I imagine the male's fertilizing the female's eggs right now. If it's similar to a firefly's cycle, the female should lay her eggs in several days. Thousands of them, if what we saw earlier's any indication."

Miss Karr fired off more pictures.

Around and around the two etherians slowly twirled. I quite admired their abandon.

"They seem oblivious to us," said Sir Hugh. "I wouldn't

have thought they'd be willing to mate so close to alien creatures."

"I wonder how long it takes them to grow to full size," Kate said.

"It *would* be useful to see some intermediary forms," Sir Hugh agreed. "Do you think perhaps there's a larval stage involved?"

"If it follows an insect model," Kate replied thoughtfully. "But there's also the shark model to consider."

"Indeed," Sir Hugh said, and he seemed genuinely interested in her opinion. "Of course, it's too early to make any conclusions. Fascinating stuff."

"Look, they're separating," said Kate.

With twin blasts from their vents, the two etherians had parted. They circled each other for a time, and then jetted off together into the depths of space. They moved so fast, they almost seemed to dissolve into the darkness.

"Did you see that?" I said. "Their speed!"

"Incredible," said Miss Karr.

"Is possible for them to achieve enormous velocity," said Dr. Turgenev. "Is no friction to slow acceleration."

"They could travel between worlds," I said. These were just the shallows. I wondered what awaited the creatures in the deeps.

"How far do you think they'll go?" Miss Karr asked.

Kate shook her head, still staring out the window into the distance. "I suppose they can go wherever they want. Maybe out of the solar system altogether. Imagine that. They've probably seen planets we don't even know exist."

I imagined the two etherians skimming the surface of the moon, moving so quickly that its gravity couldn't drag them down, and then sailing onward together, towards the red planet, and beyond, to colonize the shores of other worlds.

25 / A Reef in Space

WE WERE HOMEWARD BOUND.

Now that we'd begun our descent, we needed someone in the stern to be the ship's eyes. Below C Deck was a tiny lookout post, and the thick window gave a view straight down at Earth. It was a funny kind of upside-down crow's nest, to be sure, but lookout was a job I was well acquainted with, and I must admit, I liked the quiet and calm.

Two powerful floodlights were mounted on the *Starclimber*'s stern, illuminating the spidery traction arms and the astral cable that ran between their rollers like a golden thread. It stretched down towards Earth, growing thinner and thinner till it disappeared into the blackness. I kept a careful watch out for etherians and their eggs.

It was night over the Pacificus, but the earth's eastern curve glowed faintly with the coming dawn. The west coast of North Americus was silhouetted like a map, and I could actually see the pinprick glimmer of cities, the brightest of all coming from Lionsgate City.

I felt a pang of yearning. I wanted home; I wanted my sky. But there was apprehension mixed up in it too. My worries felt heavy enough in zero gravity, but once back on Earth they'd become much, much heavier. Kate would have to return to her family—and what if she couldn't get out of her engagement? What if she didn't *want* to? I had a quick, sickening image of her in a wedding dress, James Sanderson smug beside her.

The *Starclimber* began to shiver like an airship in light turbulence. I pulled myself closer to the porthole and peered along the astral cable. It glittered in the floodlight—something I'd never noticed before. I squinted. There was something on the cable's surface. My first thought was ice. But that was impossible. There was no water up here to freeze.

I picked up the ship's phone. "Cruse here. There's something on the cable."

"We're already slowing down," said Tobias. "We feel it too."

Speed was virtually impossible to discern up here. With only the distant Earth as a reference point, it always seemed we were motionless. Only the pitch of the ship's rollers told me we were moving at all—and right now, decelerating from a hundred and twenty miles an hour.

"Whatever it is, I think it's getting thicker," I said in alarm.

"We see it now too," said Tobias.

It would take the ship about thirty seconds to come to a full stop. We were shuddering like a motorcar over gravel. I watched the traction arms, afraid they'd get damaged. In the distance, I thought I made out shadows massing around the cable. How far away, I couldn't tell. Maybe it was just one of the many illusions cast by the ghostly half-light of space. I glanced away, blinked, and when I looked back there was something looming towards us.

"Stop the ship, stop her!" I yelled into the ship's phone. "There's something dead astern!"

Colour exploded from the darkness of space, a phantasmagorical jungle lashing against the porthole. I recoiled with a cry. The ship was still moving, crashing through a dense tangle of bizarre foliage. A brittle symphony of tinkling sounded against the hull. I could barely see the astral cable, or the traction arms, shaking violently as they tried to keep their grip. In horror I watched as one of the arms snapped and dangled limp, buffeted by branches and tendrils. Sparkling clouds of astral dust dazzled my eyes.

Finally things stopped smashing against the ship, and I knew we'd come to a standstill. I was shivering with a cold sweat. No alarms sounded. That was good. We hadn't been breached. We were still airtight.

"Make way, Mr. Cruse, I'm coming down."

It was Captain Walken, manoeuvring himself into the crow's nest beside me.

Together we stared out the porthole.

"This wasn't here when we came up," I said, dazed.

Bristling from the cable were all manner of strange growths. There were clumps of pink spongy material that looked like the human brain. Jutting up amongst them were crooked, crystalline tendrils of brilliant crimson and purple, some as long as ten feet. Clinging to the cable were colonies of enormous barnacles with jagged craters. As I stared, a few gaseous bubbles emanated from them, floated up, and were quickly inhaled by the branchlets of an unusual orange plant with sharp leaves that were angled at the sun.

Days ago, there had been nothing, and now, a coral reef bloomed in outer space.

"I think what we have here," Sir Hugh told us in the B Deck lounge, "is a remarkable colonizing event."

Everyone had crowded down into the crow's nest to have a look, and now we were all discussing what was to be done. The *Starclimber* was still motionless.

"Outer space must be teeming with microscopic life," said Kate. "They're drifters mainly. And we've given them something they've never had before—anchorage."

"They seem to like it," said Tobias.

"I wonder," Kate mused, "if it's the electricity in the cable, stimulating their growth."

"Also heat," said Dr. Turgenev. "There is significant heat loss through cable."

"That could easily be a factor," said Sir Hugh. "Like algae in warm water."

"But why wasn't any of this here when the *Starclimber* came up?" Miss Karr asked. "The cable's been here for two months, hasn't it?"

"Yes, but is only electrified as ship travels up it," Dr. Turgenev explained. "Ship completes circuit, you see?"

"So this all grew in a matter of days," Kate said excitedly. "It's remarkable!"

"I appreciate its scientific importance," said Captain Walken. "But my chief concern is whether we can move through it. Dr. Turgenev?"

The scientist shrugged. "Damaged traction arm can be repaired once we get back to Earth. Remember, external rollers are supplementary grip only. As long as internal rollers function, we are fine."

"We need to assess those internal rollers," Shepherd said.

"Difficult," I said. The shaft was no more than three feet across, and taken up entirely with the roller mechanics.

"We'll need to go outside and shine some light into the cable shaft," said the captain. "See what kind of shape they're in."

"The ship's still holding on, though?" said Sir Hugh nervously.

"Yes, yes, of course," said Dr. Turgenev. "But we are still weightless. Once gravity takes hold, we need excellent grip to make safe descent."

This was a sobering thought. As we got closer to Earth, the *Starclimber* would get heavier. It would want to accelerate and plummet.

"We'll need to clear it all away," said Shepherd. "Some of those barnacles on the cable look wickedly sharp."

"How much of it is there?" Tobias asked.

"We won't know till we go outside," I said.

"Must we disturb it?" Kate asked, frowning.

"It depends if you want to get home, Miss de Vries," I said. She didn't seem to understand how serious this could be.

"We won't get much done, floating around and swatting at the stuff," said Shepherd. "We need some way of gripping on so we can get some leverage."

Everyone thought about this for a moment.

"I know," said Tobias. "The spare roller grips. You could clamp a set onto the cable, wherever you want to work, then tether it to your suit harness. That should hold you steady. Pretty easy to rig up. Half an hour, tops."

I nodded in admiration. "That sounds good."

"Excellent, Mr. Blanchard," said Captain Walken. "Can you get two ready, please. Mr. Cruse and Mr. Shepherd, start your pre-breathe."

"We forget something very important," said Dr. Turgenev suddenly. "We cannot have astralnauts touch cable."

I looked at Tobias and let out a breath. Of course Dr. Turgenev was right. We'd be electrocuted instantly.

"I'll radio Ground Station and ask them to shut down the current," said Captain Walken.

"Is that wise?" asked Miss Karr.

"Our batteries can take care of the ship for six hours," I told her. "Ground Station can turn off our power for a few hours without any problems."

I'd meant to be reassuring, but I can't say I liked the idea of our power being flicked off from twenty thousand miles away. What if nothing happened when they flicked it back on?

"Can you bring back some samples, please?" Kate asked Shepherd.

I noticed she didn't ask me.

"Yes," agreed Sir Hugh. "That would be most valuable indeed."

"I'm sure we can manage it," Shepherd said.

Mr. Vlad poked his head out from the kitchen. "And perhaps an extra smattering of something for me. I would very much like to try working them into a new recipe."

Shepherd and I glided away from the *Starclimber*, our homemade cable-gripping rigs trailing from our suits. It was now mid-morning above the Pacificus. The sun was behind us and provided all the light we needed. We had an excellent view of the cable directly beneath the ship, enveloped in a coral reef in the midst of an endless black ocean.

"Seems to trail off after about fifty feet," I said to Shepherd over my radio.

Why it had formed right here, I had no idea; I was just relieved it didn't stretch out for hundreds of miles. With little bursts from our air pistols we carefully propelled ourselves closer. It was difficult to see the cable itself, the astral vegetation was so thick and bristly. We came to a stop a foot or two from the outer tendrils.

"Let's see how strong these things are," said Shepherd.

From our tool pouches we extracted pry bars. Very lightly I tapped the end of mine against a vermilion tendril. Soundlessly a large section snapped off and twirled like a baton through space.

"Brittle," I said.

Shepherd smashed a few tendrils. "Should be able to clear this away pretty fast," he said confidently.

"It's the barnacle things that worry me," I said.

"My concern as well," came Captain Walken's voice from the bridge. "But first, inspect the internal rollers, please."

It seemed a shame to cut down the beautiful crystalline flora, but there was no other way to get to the ship's stern. In ten minutes we'd cleared a path. I remembered to push a few tendrils into the small specimen pouch clipped to my belt.

"We're at the stern," Shepherd reported to the captain. "Could you confirm the power's shut off?"

"The power is off, Mr. Shepherd," said the captain. "You're safe to make contact."

I examined the cable, the gold ribbon no wider than my hand. Seeing it up close, I felt a spasm of dread. This was all that kept us tethered to Earth. It looked like something you could snip with a sharp pair of scissors.

All along its surface sparkled pale astral barnacles, some no bigger than blisters, others the size of my fist. Sea barnacles, I knew, used strong cement to fasten themselves. I hoped these ones wouldn't be so hard to dislodge.

Holding my breath, I gripped the cable. Through my thick glove I could actually feel a faint warmth, the residue of the powerful current it had carried just moments ago.

"I'll take a look inside the shaft," I said.

"I'll get started cleaning up," said Shepherd.

Using the cable as a guide, I pulled myself up to the

opening and peered inside. My helmet lamp illuminated the complicated system of rollers that gripped the cable as it passed through the *Starclimber*'s centre. I could properly see only the first set of rollers, since they blocked my view of those behind.

"How does it look, Mr. Cruse?" Captain Walken asked.

"I'm seeing some scoring on the treads," I told him. "But they don't look too bad."

"Any cracks or tears?"

"No. There's a bit of debris in there, ground-up astral flora, but I can't see any broken machinery."

"Very good, Mr. Cruse. Proceed with the cleanup."

I turned myself around. About ten feet down, Shepherd had already clamped Tobias's rig onto the cable, and was sitting astride it, facing the ship. He was hooking the tethers from the rig to his spacesuit harness, front and back. The back one was tricky, but he got it after a couple of tries.

It took me about five minutes to get my own rig fastened, closer to the ship. I decided to sit on the opposite side of the cable from Shepherd, so we could clear both surfaces at the same time.

Setting to work with my pry bar, I knocked away the spindly stuff first, then the spongy stuff, leaving the barnacles to last. There were plenty of them.

Dr. Turgenev had promised that the cable could take all our scraping and chopping. But I still felt hesitant as I chipped away at the sloped sides of the barnacles. I didn't want to break anything.

"These things are really glued on," Shepherd muttered across from me. "Hang on . . . I think I've got it . . ." He gave a grunt as one of the barnacles shot off. "There we go," he said with satisfaction.

I pried hard and one of mine popped off too.

"How are you two making out?" Tobias asked from the airlock.

"Good progress," Shepherd said, which I thought was optimistic, since there were fifty feet of barnacles to clear.

We continued to work away. I'd soon cleared about a foot of barnacles, and noticed that the cable underneath looked strangely tarnished. Probably it was just discoloured by the barnacles. I bent closer.

The normally smooth surface was pockmarked.

Panic bloomed within me. I stared at the cable, and a bit of it sparkled. It took me several seconds to realize the light wasn't coming *from* the cable, but *through* it. There was a tiny pinprick hole in the astral cable, and starlight was blinking through from the other side.

"Shepherd," I said.

"I think I can get this whole bunch off at once, Cruse," he said.

I looked over in horror to see him with his pry bar wedged deep into a big barnacle cluster, ready to lever it up.

"Shepherd, wait!"

Too late. He brought his force down on the pry bar, and the entire colony of barnacles snapped off as one and went sailing into space.

"What's wrong?" he asked.

"There's a hole in the cable."

"Mr. Cruse, can you repeat that please?" came Captain Walken's voice.

"The barnacles, their glue, or whatever it is, it's corrosive. It's—"

"Damn it," murmured Shepherd, peering at the stretch of cable he'd just exposed between us. "It's like it's been scored with acid."

I now saw little fissures in it, like cracks in ice.

"Mr. Cruse, is the cable intact?" the captain asked urgently.

"It's intact, but badly damaged," I said, not recognizing my own hoarse voice. "We pried off some barnacles and the surface underneath is splintered . . ." I wasn't thinking clearly any more. "We're going to need Tobias out here to do some welding, it . . . it doesn't look at all strong—"

"Return to the ship now!" said Captain Walken. "Mr. Blanchard, bring them back in."

"Hold up, Blanchard," said Shepherd. "We've got to get out of our rigs."

We both started fumbling with our harness tethers. But I couldn't keep my eyes off the cable. It had always seemed terribly thin to me, but now, pitted and cracked, it looked frail as cobweb. I thought of the counterweight whirling about the earth, and the ground station anchored in the earth's bones, and the tremendous strain upon the taut cable in between.

And as my eyes skittered nervously along its surface, I saw

one of the whisker-thin fissures begin to stretch out across the cable's width.

"It's breaking!" I shouted.

Shepherd looked down just as the cable split, and we both instinctively reached for it with our gloves, clumsily trying to hold it together. For one impossible moment it seemed to work. We gripped the cable from opposite sides with our hands, holding heaven to earth.

But then a gap opened, at first no more than a finger's width—and it was almost comical, for the gap seemed such a little thing. As if you could mend it with needle and thread . . .

Then the two ends began to slide away from each other, for the *Starclimber* was bound to the counterweight, which was moving much faster than the earth, and it had broken free.

Shepherd and I were still tethered to the cable, me on the ship's side, Shepherd on Earth's side.

"Your straps!" I shouted. "Just cut them!"

I reached my hand out to him, but he was already too far away.

I saw his umbilicus racing out from the airlock to keep up with him. He fumbled for his knife.

"Shepherd's getting left behind!" I shouted.

He was already so far away from me.

"His umbilicus is running out!" I heard Tobias yell.

"Shepherd, hurry!" I gasped.

"Help!" he cried out, his voice hoarse with terror.

I saw his umbilicus stretch taut, then recoil, looping back on itself, the end ripped clean out of Shepherd's suit. His oxygen spewed into outer space. His silver suit crumpled as it lost all pressure.

"Stop!" I shouted madly. "We've got to go back for Shepherd!"

"Matt, get inside!" commanded the captain. "He's gone!"

I heard Shepherd call out again for help, his voice crackling with static.

"I'm sorry, I'm sorry," I said.

"Matt, I'm going to reel you in—are you ready?" Tobias barked. "Are you ready?"

My shaking fingers couldn't manage my harness tethers, so I just unclamped the entire roller rig from the cable. I thought I heard Shepherd's voice once more over the radio, but I was sobbing and could not make out his words. I felt the tug on my umbilicus, drawing me back towards the *Starclimber*. I couldn't see Shepherd any more, but I could not stop myself imagining what was happening to him, his body losing heat and oxygen and going cold as ice, and colder still as he was dragged homeward.

26 / Cut Loose

AS THE AIRLOCK PRESSURIZED, I started shaking so badly inside my suit that I thought I was going to fly apart. Tobias placed his hands on my shoulders. I couldn't see his face, and he couldn't see mine, but his steady grip calmed me. Gradually my trembling eased.

"His umbilicus ripped right out," I panted when Tobias removed my helmet. "He couldn't get out of his harness fast enough."

"I should've made the straps easier to undo," he said, looking sick.

"It happened so fast. The cable snapped and he was already out of reach, like he was being dragged. There was no way of stopping it."

"It's really broken?" Tobias said.

"It's really broken."

When we got up to B Deck, Kate and Miss Karr and Sir Hugh were in the lounge, chatting, and I realized they didn't know what had happened yet. For them, everything was still all right, and I shut my eyes and wished I could be them, even for just ten seconds.

Captain Walken and Dr. Turgenev floated hurriedly down from the bridge, both looking grave.

"What's happened?" Kate demanded.

"Where's Mr. Shepherd?" Miss Karr asked.

"The barnacles ate through the cable," I said.

"You mean it's broken?" Sir Hugh said, his voice rising.

"Yes," said the captain.

"Well, can it be fixed?" asked Miss Karr. "And where is Mr. Shepherd?"

"Mr. Shepherd—" I began, and could not speak. I felt like a fist had tightened around my throat. Tears sprang to my eyes and drifted away through the air in tiny spheres.

"Oh no," Kate gasped, her hands flying to her mouth.

"Mr. Shepherd died outside," the captain said. "When the cable broke he was dragged away from the ship. His lifeline snapped."

"How horrible," whispered Miss Karr.

"Poor man," said Dr. Turgenev.

"Did he have any family?" Sir Hugh asked. "He never talked much about himself."

"I know he was engaged," I said, choking out the words.

For a few moments no one could say anything. I kept seeing Shepherd's spacesuit collapsing, hearing his voice dissolve into crackles over my radio.

"And what's to become of the rest of us?" Sir Hugh asked quietly.

"This moment," Dr. Turgenev said, "we are still attached to counterweight. Only now, counterweight is not attached to Earth. It has flown free."

"Will it stay in orbit?" Kate asked.

Dr. Turgenev shook his head. "It has great deal of velocity and will soon break out of orbit."

"And take us with it," I said numbly.

"You mean . . . deeper into space?" Miss Karr asked.

"Correct," said Dr. Turgenev. "Eventually out of solar system altogether."

Sir Hugh's face lost all its remaining colour, and his chest began to rise and fall unevenly, as though he were sobbing.

"We need to get off the cable," said Captain Walken.

Sir Hugh looked horrified. "But then nothing will be holding us up!"

"We don't need holding up right now," I said, starting to feel more in control of myself. "We're still weightless."

"Why can't we get ourselves back onto the other half of the cable?" said Sir Hugh. "That's what we should be doing!"

"This would be unwise," said Dr. Turgenev. "It will be dragged swiftly back to Earth. With us riding it, it falls out of control all the faster. No. Captain is correct, we need to get off cable."

"Will we keep orbiting around the earth?" I asked the scientist.

"We are at twenty thousand miles now," he said. "No longer in geosynchronous orbit. Even as we speak we accelerate into decaying orbit."

"Decaying?" said Miss Karr, sounding fed up. "Dr. Turgenev, I'd like a little more plain talk here. Meaning what?"

Dr. Turgenev started polishing his spectacles with great

ferocity. "Meaning, eventually we get pulled back into Earth's atmosphere at enormous velocity and burn up like shooting star."

"No . . ." moaned Sir Hugh, his large hands gripping his head.

"How long will we have?" Captain Walken asked.

"Perhaps several days, but battery will run out long before."

I swallowed. I'd not thought of that. Severed from the ground station, we were no longer getting electricity. At the end of six hours, we'd be without light, or heat, or the power to pump oxygen through the ship. We'd freeze to death and suffocate before Earth pulled us back to her.

"Can we radio Ground Station for help?" Kate asked.

"The cable was our antenna," I said. "We've lost contact."

"Start shutting off everything that's not necessary," said Captain Walken. "Lights, any machinery we don't absolutely need. Mr. Blanchard, come with me, please. We need to move the *Starclimber* off the cable."

The two of them jetted up to the bridge, and I was left with the others. We silently floated about, switching off all the lights on B Deck. Dr. Turgenev and Kate went down to the lab to turn off any scientific apparatus that wasn't essential.

I heard the ship's rollers humming, and felt queasy, for I knew exactly what was happening. I saw it all in my mind's eye. The severed end of the astral cable was disappearing up into the *Starclimber*'s central shaft, past the rollers in C Deck, past B Deck and A Deck. And now the cable was coming out through the bow, where the spidery external arms had their final grip on it before it slipped through into empty space. It hung above the glass dome for a moment, forever out of reach, and then swiftly disappeared. My heart pounded.

Nothing held us now.

We were all alone, adrift.

Chef Vlad emerged from the kitchen and pressed little cups of brandy into our hands. I took a sip through the straw and felt a numbing, reassuring heat along my throat.

"Thank you," I said.

"Medicinal purpose only," he said, patting my back. "We need food. No, no, do not argue with me. I know about food and how and when people need it. I will make food for us now!"

In the lounge, Dr. Turgenev had a pencil and slide ruler, and was frantically doing calculations on a notepad. Sir Hugh was strapped into an armchair, his eyes tightly shut, as though hoping he'd open them to a new and better day.

"Well," said Miss Karr with a sardonic smile, "we've come through one scrape. With all the big brains around here, I'm sure we'll get through this one too."

We all nodded and said yes, yes.

But we didn't talk much after that. I think we were all too scared to voice our fears, in case they swelled and billowed and filled the room to bursting. The captain had turned the heat down, and already it was getting chilly, so we went up to our cabins briefly for extra clothing.

Aside from the cold, the ship felt not one bit different, but this wasn't reassuring at all. It made it worse, because you could almost convince yourself we were still making our normal descent earthward, but only for a second—and then it was like learning the crushing truth all over again.

The captain and Tobias came downstairs to join us. There was little need for anyone on the bridge right now: there was no way of piloting the *Starclimber*. Tobias looked pale. He accepted a cup of brandy and took a big swallow.

I noticed a small leather-bound book in Captain Walken's hand.

"There's no prayer yet for loss of life in outer space," he said. "The closest I could find was for the sea."

He opened the book and we all bowed our heads.

"Lord God, as we commit the body of our brother Charles Shepherd to the deep, grant him peace and tranquility . . ."

The prayer was brief and beautiful, but I can't say I found it comforting. I didn't like thinking of his body, all alone out there.

After a moment's silence, Captain Walken looked up at us. "Now then, we need to find a way back to Earth."

I was amazed at how easily he said it. It wasn't a question, but a confident statement of fact. Going home was within our grasp, he was telling us; all we needed to do was bend our wills to the task.

Just then, Chef Vlad appeared from the kitchen and summoned us all to the table to eat. Captain Walken looked like he was about to object, but then he smiled and nodded. Like obedient children, we drifted to the dining area, buckled ourselves to our seats, and let Chef Vlad put food before us. It smelled delicious.

I picked up my cup of water. "To Mr. Shepherd."

"To Mr. Shepherd," the others said solemnly.

It felt good to eat, and was surprisingly comforting: to chew, to swallow, to feel something basic satisfied inside you.

"Dr. Turgenev," said the captain. "I see you've been making notes. Do you have any ideas?"

"Ship was designed only to climb cable. So we did not make engines. Why make engines, since cable was unbreakable?"

"Well, it bloody well wasn't, was it," puffed Sir Hugh. "A little barnacle just ate it!"

"Unbreakable on Earth," said Dr. Turgenev. "We test and test it . . ." His voice trailed off, as if he couldn't quite believe this terrible thing had happened.

"I'm sorry, Dr. Turgenev," said Sir Hugh. "That was uncalled for."

Hovering over the table, eating tidbits from Miss Karr, Haiku let loose with an explosive fart that jetted him halfway across the lounge.

"Miss Karr," said Sir Hugh, "it's a shame we can't harness your monkey's flatulence to get home."

Staring at the drifting monkey, I had a brainstorm. "That's it!" I said. "Jet propulsion, like the etherians!"

Tobias was looking at me like I'd cracked, but then I saw the light come on in his eyes.

"We've got no rocket engines," I said, "but we do have compressed gas. There's an emergency tank of oxygen in the airlock."

Captain Walken was nodding, a smile lifting the corners of his mouth. "Carry on, Mr. Cruse."

"Open the valve, out it shoots—and off we go!" I said.

Kate's eyes were wide. "Surely that can't be enough to get us back to Earth."

"We're weightless," I told her. "There's a lot of force in that canister. Dr. Turgenev, what do you think?"

"It is crude form of propulsion," he said.

"It's the only one we have," I replied.

The scientist looked glum. "We cannot control thrust, or duration. Once valve is opened, gas will vent until gone. It will be single big push."

"But, could it get us home?" Captain Walken asked.

Dr. Turgenev rocked his head from side to side. "I don't know."

I could tell he was getting interested in the problem, and watched him with a mixture of dread and hope.

"Let me see tank. Go get for me."

At once I glided down to the airlock, unstrapped the emergency tank, and floated it back up to Dr. Turgenev. He peered at it overtop of his spectacles, making a few notations on his notepad, murmuring numbers to himself. He looked very unhappy and my heart sank.

"Yes, yes," he said, "I think, given current speed, this would give us enough thrust to make re-entry."

"Thank heaven for farting monkeys," said Miss Karr.

"How would we rig it?" I asked. "We can't just point the tank out the hatch and turn it on."

"We'd need to fix it to the outside hull," said Captain Walken. "Very securely."

"I can weld it," Tobias said. "We've got the equipment aboard."

"We forget something," said Dr. Turgenev dolefully. "Please remember that Earth's atmosphere is thick, yes? Very dense. Remember shooting stars? That is rock, burning up as it hits atmosphere."

"I don't understand," said Kate. "We always meant to re-enter the atmosphere. No one talked about burning up before!"

"On the cable we'd be going pretty slowly," I said. "Only a hundred twenty-five aeroknots an hour."

"And that is not problem," Dr. Turgenev said. "But now we make re-entry at maybe, uh, seventeen thousand aeroknots an hour."

"That much?" gasped Sir Hugh.

Dr. Turgenev angled his hand towards the table. "If we re-enter too steep, heat is too much, and we burn up. *Pfffft!* If too shallow—" he levelled off his hand, grazed the table, and deflected off it—"we skip off atmosphere like stone hitting water. We must make sure angle of ship is just right. But is impossible, because there is no way of steering *Starclimber.*"

This silenced everyone. I hadn't thought about steering. It wasn't as if a rudder would help us in outer space.

"The etherians have vents all over their bodies," said Kate. "Isn't there any way we could do the same kind of thing?"

"This is very complex system of thrusters," said Dr. Turgenev. "I do not think we have time or resources up here."

"The toilets!" she exclaimed.

"The girl's come unhinged," said Sir Hugh. "It's no wonder, the pressure we're all under—"

"I am *not* unhinged," Kate said impatiently.

"No, no, she's right," I said, understanding. "The toilets flush out waste. It's like a little controlled explosion. It could give us a push."

"We have two toilets," said Kate, beaming. "A Deck and B Deck, and they're more or less on opposite sides of the ship, aren't they?"

Captain Walken nodded. "Would those be enough to adjust our angle, Dr. Turgenev?"

"This is very crude," he replied doubtfully, pursing his lips.

I wouldn't let my hopes cool so swiftly this time. By now I knew the tortuous way Dr. Turgenev thought things through.

"Maybe yes, it works," said the scientist. "We would have to flush toilets great deal. What we must do is this. We must angle ship where she can best take heat during re-entry."

"The stern," said Captain Walken. "She's thickest there, apart from the porthole. Tobias, can you weld something over that?"

Tobias nodded. "A couple of layers of spare hull plate maybe."

"Good," said Dr. Turgenev. "We make re-entry stern first, at angle of . . . hmm . . . I need to make more calculations for this."

"So that means we'll want the oxygen tank at the ship's bow," I said.

"Dead centre," said the captain. "The dome's summit. There's alumiron plate around the cable shaft."

"It must point straight as arrow," Dr. Turgenev told Tobias. "We need true course. You can do this, Mr. Blanchard?"

"Yeah. I'll need help, though."

"I'll lend a hand," I said, starting to feel truly hopeful.

"Er, forgive me," said Sir Hugh with a bitter chuckle. "Even assuming we can re-enter the earth's atmosphere, what then? We'll just plummet to our deaths in a giant tin can!"

"Don't worry, Sir Hugh," said the captain. "We had two emergency hydrium balloons built into the bow, just in case the rollers gave out on descent."

"The big boys think of everything after all," said Miss Karr.

"Actually, I was against plan," said Dr. Turgenev. "I thought it needless. Mr. Lunardi overruled me."

"And we're very glad of it," said Miss Karr.

"Once we're back in the sky we can inflate the balloons," the captain said, "and they should slow our fall."

"Enough to give us a soft landing?" Sir Hugh asked.

"Soft enough," said the scientist. "Now, I must do mathematics, please."

"Dr. Turgenev, we don't have a great deal of time," the captain said gently.

"I know, I know. I work swiftly."

The *Starclimber* seemed almost unbearably small and lonely as Tobias and I made our way through space to the bow. No cable ran through the ship's centre, guiding her home. Below us turned the earth, but it moved slowly compared to us. Cut loose from Ground Station, we hurtled around the planet in our fatal orbit.

Earlier on the voyage, I had gotten tired of seeing the same view of the Pacificus from our fixed spot. I'd wished we could swoop around the earth like some cosmic bird. I was getting my wish now, at a terrible price. Asia was below us, Japan just coming into view over the eastern horizon. The music of the spheres played faintly in my head, but I couldn't help feeling it had a mocking tone.

Without Shepherd, it fell to Captain Walken to spot us from the airlock. Dr. Turgenev manned the bridge, watching us through the glass dome. Drifting behind us on tethers was all the equipment we'd need for the job ahead: the oxygen canister, Tobias's bulky arc-welding gear, and an additional pouch of tools.

"You're not to get all giddy and fly off to the moon," I said to Tobias over the radio.

I heard his chuckle. "Promise."

We'd already made a separate trip to the ship's stern, to cover the crow's nest porthole. I thought of the immense heat the ship would have to endure when we re-entered. I hoped what we had done was enough.

When we reached the dome's summit, we positioned ourselves securely, and then started to manoeuvre the equipment into place. Tobias was surprisingly deft despite his bulky gloves. Inside the *Starclimber,* he'd fixed a thick metal collar around the oxygen tank—our rocket—so he could weld it more securely to the outside hull. I did my best to hold the tank steady for him. From the corner of my eye I saw the spark of blue light from Tobias's torch as he set to work. It took all my attention and strength to keep the tank straight. It was to be our one and only engine, and if not properly fixed, it wouldn't send us on a true path home.

"Let's trade places," Tobias said. "I need to weld the other side."

When he finished, I inspected his handiwork. The tank looked as if it had been custom-designed to fit atop the *Starclimber*'s dome.

"That's a fine job," I said.

"Should hold it."

I glanced at the tank's valve. When it was time, a good turn would release a jet of compressed oxygen that would rocket our ship earthward. Back home. Back to my sky.

"We're coming in," I told the captain over my headset. "The *Starclimber* now has rocket power."

Fluttering all around us on the bridge were Dr. Turgenev's sheets of paper, each of them covered with a bewildering swirl of equations and diagrams. He'd suddenly flail about, snatch one, check something, and then go back to scribbling on his notepad or looking along his astrolabe.

I'd learned enough celestial navigation at the Academy to know what he was doing. He was finding reference points in the heavens, so that he could calculate our current trajectory around the planet. And from that he'd figure out the angle, speed, and distance of our re-entry. I shuddered at the task. We were asking a great deal of him. There was no room for even one wrong calculation. A decimal point could mean the difference between life and death.

"Very complicated," he muttered to himself. "Very complex, everything moving. We move. Earth moves. Earth rotates. Earth revolves . . ."

My face felt feverish, even though the heaters were turned to their lowest setting. Captain Walken, Tobias, and I were all on the bridge, furiously performing the calculations that Dr. Turgenev set us. There was much talking as facts and figures flew between us.

The earth, turning at 1,047 miles per hour . . .

The Starclimber, *moving at 15,000 miles per hour in an eastward equatorial orbit that was deteriorating as we accelerated . . .*

Earth's gravity pulling us in, changing our trajectory, pulling us lower . . .

The shape of our orbit changing from circle to ellipse, slinging us around the earth faster and faster with every minute . . .

Nothing was still, just as Dr. Turgenev had said. Take too long to solve one equation, and all the numbers had already changed.

"Mr. Cruse," the scientist said, snapping his fingers. "Do you have figures I gave you?"

I handed him my piece of paper. "Please check them, Dr. Turgenev, I wouldn't trust myself . . ."

His bloodshot eyes glanced over my workings. "Good, Mr. Cruse, this is very good. Thank you."

I'd struggled with math and physics at the Academy, and had never thought those wretched theorems would be of any use. I was glad now that I'd forced myself to master them.

I glanced once again at the ship's clock, ticking away the seconds, and felt like I was watching sand hurtle through an hourglass. Captain Walken had unfurled a map of the world and fastened it to the chart table, making notations. We'd picked the prairies as our ideal landing site, just to the east of Moose Jaw, Saskatchewan. It was as flat as you could hope, and the winds would be light.

"If we deploy the hydrium balloons at forty thousand feet, here," the captain told us, pointing with his dividers, "then we can free-balloon to Earth, venting hydrium as necessary."

It would be a difficult business, but we'd have plenty of space, and our landing was bound to be in a field of wheat or corn.

"What is all this scribbling here?" Dr. Turgenev said irritably.

We all turned to the scientist, who was squinting at a sheet of paper like he'd never seen it before in his life. I leaned closer to have a peek.

"Weren't those your final calculations, Dr. Turgenev?" I said, trying not to sound worried. I think we were all concerned that, under the stress, Dr. Turgenev might suffer a bout of astral psychosis. His was the only mind capable of getting us back home safely.

"This is complete gibberish," he murmured, then, "Oh . . .

yes . . . I see now. This is done. This is it. Good. We are finished. Look here."

He floated closer to the map and pointed to the steppes of Mongolia. "We re-enter atmosphere here, at angle of no greater than seven and a half degrees. Then we travel east over Pacificus and Rocky Mountains. And then, if we have not melted—little joke, ha ha—we come out over prairies. This is what will happen."

Captain Walken patted him on the shoulder. "Thank you, Dr. Turgenev."

Step by step we went through the entire re-entry procedure. There were parts where I had to concentrate very hard, to stop my mind from straying to the disasters that could crush us at each turn. I needed to focus only on what we must do, if we were to have any hope of survival. It was a sequence of daring and risky actions, held together by fraying cobweb.

"Are we all clear?" Captain Walken said.

There were a few tricky bits that we went over a second time.

"We're out of time," I said, checking the ship's clock.

Tobias glanced at the voltometer. "Our batteries are near worn out," he said.

"As long as the ventilation system keeps ticking over, that's all we need," I said.

"Not quite," Tobias reminded me. "We'll need enough power to launch the emergency balloons with the explosive bolts."

"We must align *Starclimber* now," Dr. Turgenev said. He made his way over to the astrolabe. "I stay here to check ship's position against stars and Earth. I will need several minutes to prepare. Captain, you stay here and relay my instructions via ship's phone. Mr. Cruse and Mr. Blanchard, go below and get ready to flush toilets!"

When Tobias and I emerged from the bridge, Kate was waiting on A Deck at the base of the stairs, looking furious.

"I was just about to come up and find out what's going on!" she said.

"We've been hammering out the re-entry plan," I told her.

"I'm sure you have, but you've been up there two hours and you need to tell the rest of us what's happening. You can't just forget about us down here. It's very inconsiderate!"

"I'm sorry," I said, and truly I was. It must have been terrible for them, waiting and waiting while we made our calculations. I thought for a moment she was going to burst into tears, but then her eyes grew fierce again.

"There's something else I want to say to you," she said. "About me and George Sanderson."

"James," I said. "And we're actually in a bit of a hurry."

"Um, should I go away?" Tobias asked.

Kate ignored him, glaring only at me. "You wanted to know why I asked him that question. About whether he'd let me do as I pleased when we got married. I did it because I was trying to scare him off! I didn't think he'd actually *want* to be married to someone like me. I'd just embarrass him in polite society. I wanted *him* to be the one to break it off. *That's* why I asked the question. Do you see now?"

I felt sheepish, and hugely relieved, but I was hardly going to beg her forgiveness after what she'd put me through.

"Well," I said, "too bad it didn't work."

"Yes, thanks to you," Kate said, "it seems he's quite smitten with me and my grave-robbing."

"So you're really going to break it off with him?" I asked.

"For the hundredth time, *yes!*"

"If we get home alive," Tobias said. "Sorry, just a thought I had."

"What are our chances?" Kate asked.

"We can do it," I said. "But right now we need to realign the ship."

"With the toilets," she said.

"Right. And we need your help."

"Really?" she said, smiling.

I pointed at the ship's phone in the corridor. "The captain's going to be calling out his orders, and you're to bellow them on to Tobias and me."

She seemed disappointed. "That's it?"

"You've got a good loud voice."

"I was hoping for something a little more . . . dynamic. Is there a lever I could pull or something?"

"No. Tobias, you take the A-Deck toilets, I'll do B-Deck."

"Do you mind if I do B-Deck?" Tobias asked.

"What's the difference?"

"I had a bad experience with the A-Deck toilet. Damn near sucked me in."

We started laughing and had a great deal of trouble stopping. As tears streamed down our faces, Kate stared at us disapprovingly.

"This is no time for astral psychosis, gentlemen," she said.

The ship's phone rang, and I snatched it up.

"Mr. Cruse, are you ready?" came the captain's voice.

"Yes, sir, Miss de Vries will relay your commands."

"Very good. We're about to begin."

Tobias and I went off to our respective lavatories. I left the door of mine open so I could hear Kate, and stood by the flush lever. I took a big breath. If we couldn't angle the ship properly, we couldn't make a safe re-entry. A lot was riding on this. And it all came down to two toilets.

"A Deck!" I heard Kate shout.

As I pushed my lever I heard the short burst of air escaping into the vacuum of space. Only the smallest vibration ran through the ship, but there was no porthole in the lavatory, so I couldn't tell if the ship was actually revolving.

"B Deck!" Kate bellowed, and I heard a flush from Tobias's toilet, to counter my spin.

On the bridge, I knew that Dr. Turgenev was gazing along his astrolabe, gauging our angle amidst the stars, rapidly recalculating.

"A Deck!" Kate cried, and again I flushed.

For the next five minutes, Kate shouted out Dr. Turgenev's wishes with bewildering speed, and in ever more erratic sequences. I worried that the Russian scientist had lost his mind. But finally I heard Kate give a triumphant shout.

"It's done! It worked!"

I propelled myself out along the corridor and downstairs to the lounge. The view from the windows was quite different now. We were lying almost on our side, relative to the earth, and the planet could be seen clearly below us. We sailed over the earth at a rakish angle. I could make out Italy's boot in the blue Mediterranean.

Tobias and I laughed and grasped hands and shook fiercely. Dr. Turgenev and Captain Walken both came down from the bridge looking mightily relieved.

"What happens now?" Kate asked me. "Please tell us, step by step."

"We need to open the oxygen tank," the captain said.

"Which will shoot us back towards Earth," Kate said.

"Yes. It'll get very hot as we re-enter the atmosphere, but the ship should be able to withstand it. We get down to forty thousand feet and deploy the emergency hydrium balloons, and then we just sail down to land."

"Sounds perfectly straightforward," said Miss Karr wryly.

"Shepherd would've liked this," I said. "We're actually flying the ship."

"It's one mean streetcar ride now," said Tobias.

"Where will we set down, do you think?" Sir Hugh asked.

"We're aiming for the prairies," Tobias said.

Kate frowned. "A bit far from Lionsgate City, isn't it?"

"We can always push you out early, Miss de Vries," I said.

"You're too kind, Mr. Cruse."

I liked the playful look in her eyes. It gave me a surge of energy. Three hours ago, I hadn't thought we had a chance. Now I figured we had a very decent shot.

Dr. Turgenev looked anxiously at his pocket watch. "No time to relax. We are soon in proper position to alter trajectory and begin re-entry, or we overshoot landing site. Who is going outside to turn on tank?"

In all the frenzy, I hadn't given much thought to this.

"When that valve's opened," Tobias said, "we'll shoot backward like a bullet from a gun."

"Much faster," said Dr. Turgenev. "We already move at many thousands of miles an hour. Rocket will change course suddenly, and accelerate us even more."

"Will the person outside be able to hold on?" I asked, alarmed.

"It will be big jolt," Dr. Turgenev said. "But then, once we are accelerated, it will feel like nothing at all until we reach atmosphere."

I looked from the captain to Tobias. "I'm worried about that 'big jolt.' Will the safety lines hold?"

"I'll make sure I have plenty of tethers," said the captain.

I was speechless.

"You're surprised, Mr. Cruse?" he said, smiling faintly.

"Well, sir, it's just . . . what if something were to happen to you?"

"Then I have two superb astralnauts to take command of the ship. In any event, Mr. Cruse, this task is no more difficult than any of the others. I'll be held snug during the acceleration."

"Yes," said Dr. Turgenev. "Just make sure to keep body away from valve, or gas jet will blast you to pieces."

I swallowed. That was hardly reassuring. Had I been commander, I too would've done the job myself. But I had a terrible fear Captain Walken might come to harm. I'd known him since I was twelve, and his gaze upon me was the closest I had to a father's.

"I'll suit up for my pre-breathe," said the captain.

Dr. Turgenev looked startled. "No time. We must engage rocket in thirty minutes. This is *essential.*"

I swore under my breath. Of all the calculations we'd made earlier, we'd forgotten to leave time for the astralnaut to do his thirty-minute pre-breathe.

"But it's crucial," I said anxiously. "Otherwise, there's a risk of the bends . . ."

"Fifteen minutes will have to be enough this time," said the captain matter-of-factly. "Everyone buckle up, please. Mr. Cruse, I want you on the bridge, and Mr. Blanchard, you'll be my spotter. Let's suit up."

Through the domed windows, Dr. Turgenev and I watched Captain Walken glide into view and drift to the summit, where the oxygen tank was welded. He carefully tethered himself to the hull, then looked straight down at me. He gave me the thumbs-up. I signed back.

"Ready," came his voice over the radio. "Is everyone safely buckled in?"

I checked my safety restraints, and Dr. Turgenev's too. In the airlock, I knew Tobias was strapped to his seat. In the B Deck lounge, Kate and Miss Karr, Chef Vlad and Sir Hugh were all buckled up, awaiting the rocket blast that would send us homeward. The *Starclimber* had not been built for such violent treatment, and I hoped she was up to the test.

"We're all snug, sir," I replied.

"I'm going to open the valve," he said. "Let's see if we have enough wind to sail home by, eh, Mr. Cruse?"

"It should be a swift ride," I said. "Hold tight, sir."

I worried my voice sounded choked. I kept thinking of how this was the captain's last journey, and how his wife and children awaited his return. I saw his hand lift and take hold of the tank's valve. He turned it.

A razor-thin line of compressed air shot from the valve, already impossibly long. The ship leapt, every rivet and metal plate shrieking its distress. Captain Walken flew back, his four safety lines taut. He was perilously close to the rocket jet, and he hauled back on his tethers to try to keep himself clear of its deadly path.

"Sir, are you all right?" I cried out.

"The lines are holding!" he said, sounding strained.

The stars beyond him began to shift, then slide as we accelerated.

"Tank will empty in two minutes," Dr. Turgenev said beside me.

I could not take my eyes off Captain Walken as the *Starclimber* hauled him through the ether. I was terrified he'd be torn apart in the rocket's blast, and I begged his lines to hold and keep him clear. Every few seconds I'd ask him if he was all right and he always replied with a terse "yes." Gradually the ship's screeches and groans faded to the occasional ominous creak. My eyes roved over the instruments, checking to make sure we'd not sprung a leak. We seemed to be holding together.

Suddenly the white line of oxygen ended.

"Tank is spent," said Dr. Turgenev. "We are at full speed."

I wished I could see our planet, but she was at our stern now, hidden from view of the bridge. It made me nervous not to see my destination, and I could only trust Dr. Turgenev's mathematics.

"We're at full speed, Captain," I said over the radio. "Tobias, stand by to reel in."

"Give the word, whenever you're ready, sir," came Tobias's voice.

When I heard the pinging sounds, I thought they were a rattling within the ship's vents. But then the noise came again, above my head this time, and I saw something small and glittering patter against the dome.

"Matt, we've got something striking the ship," said Tobias from the airlock. "Little rocks . . ."

"Micrometeoroids," said Captain Walken. He hurriedly unstrapped his safety tethers from the dome. "Bring me in, please, Tobias." The captain pushed off. There was a clatter against the dome as pea-sized rocks deflected off the glass.

"They're getting bigger!" I said.

All I heard over the radio was a startled grunt, and when I looked up, Captain Walken's body was limp.

"Captain!" I cried.

He made no reply.

"He's been hit!" I told Tobias. "Get him in as fast as you can!"

"I'm bringing him in!"

I unbuckled myself and flew down the stairs, all the way to C Deck. Outside the airlock, I watched helplessly through the window as Tobias hauled the captain's body through the hatch. I couldn't go in until the chamber was pressurized, so was forced to wait in torment.

"What's wrong?" said Kate, suddenly at my side.

"Captain got hit," I replied, and could say nothing more.

The captain's suit was scratched up from the micro-meteoroids, and as Tobias strapped him down to the bench, I saw that the top of his helmet had a big dent.

I caught Tobias's attention and touched my head. He nodded, and I saw him lean down to examine the captain's helmet.

The moment the airlock was pressurized I heaved open the door. I feared the worst, for the captain still wasn't moving.

"Did it puncture his helmet?" I asked.

"Don't think so," Tobias said.

Together we undid his collar clamps and eased off the helmet. My hands shook. I feared I'd see the captain's skull broken like eggshell. There was certainly a great deal of blood matted in his hair. Fresh droplets drifted up into the air.

"He's still breathing," Kate said beside me.

"It's a lot of blood," I said.

"The scalp bleeds easily," Kate said, "even from a superficial cut."

She drifted closer and examined the captain's head carefully with her fingers. "His skull's not fractured. And I think the bleeding's pretty much stopped. She took a handkerchief and pressed it firmly against his skull. "Pass me some bandages."

I pulled down the first-aid kit and helped her bandage his head. The captain twitched and mumbled something, but didn't wake.

"How is he?" asked Dr. Turgenev from the inner hatchway, his eyes red-rimmed with fatigue.

"I don't know," I said. "He's still unconscious."

"We enter atmosphere within minutes," said the scientist. "It will be very rough."

I made a decision. "Let's strap him into his bunk with an oxygen mask."

Tobias and I gently floated the captain out of the airlock and upstairs. When we passed through the lounge, Miss Karr gave a stifled gasp.

"He's not dead," I said. "Just knocked out. A space rock hit him."

"Who's going to fly the ship?" Sir Hugh demanded.

"It'll be fine, Sir Hugh," I said.

"How can it be fine?" he cried. "We have no captain!"

"Silence!" growled Chef Vlad. "We have Mr. Cruse. Trust me, we are in good hands."

In his cabin, Tobias and I strapped Captain Walken onto the bunk as snugly as we could. We set up a portable oxygen tank and fixed the mask to his face. I didn't like to leave him alone, but he was breathing peacefully, and the bleeding seemed to have stopped. He had a little more colour now. His pulse was steadier than mine.

Outside we closed his door securely. Tobias looked at me in silence. His thoughts, I was sure, mirrored my own. Our captain was unconscious and unable to help. The two of us were the ship's only chance of returning safely home.

"We can do this," I said.

He gave a nervous laugh. "I'm an underwater welder."

"You're an astralnaut," I told him, "and we're going to bring our ship home."

"We'll need some extra hands on the bridge," he said. "Dr. Turgenev."

I nodded. He was an obvious choice. He knew the ship like the back of his hand, and we'd doubtless need his mathematical expertise.

"And Kate," I added. "She's steady."

"I'd trust her in a crisis," Tobias agreed.

"We have our crew, then," I said. "Let's get ready on the bridge."

27 / Re-entry

WE HURTLED EARTHWARD.

After the initial jarring burst from our homemade rocket, there was absolutely no sensation of speed. Our flight was eerily silent and smooth, but I knew that would end when we reached the earth's atmosphere, sixty-two miles from the surface.

Even though we were much closer to the planet now, we were still weightless. Not because gravity was weak any more, Dr. Turgenev told us, but because we were in free fall, plunging towards the earth at tremendous speed.

"Exactly how fast are we going, Dr. Turgenev?" Kate asked, adjusting her harness in the seat next to mine.

The Russian scientist pushed back his spectacles. "Right now, 22,570 miles per hour, but this is just crude estimate."

"Has any man-made object ever gone faster?" Kate asked, and though her voice was bright, I could tell she was talking from nerves.

"Is certainly world record," said Dr. Turgenev, with an uncharacteristically kind smile.

"I don't think I want any more world records," Tobias said, checking his control panel.

"Five minutes until re-entry," said Dr. Turgenev, looking at the ship's clock.

Below on A Deck, Miss Karr and Sir Hugh and Mr. Vlad were strapped onto their bunks. That position, Dr. Turgenev had decided, would be safest for them. Upon re-entry, our bodies would become triple their normal weight. Miss Karr had protested, saying she'd feel like a corpse in a crypt. I sympathized, for it was dark and frigid aboard the ship now, and I would've hated lying there alone, powerless, not knowing whether I might live or die. But there was no way around it.

It was so calm now, it was hard to believe our re-entry would be as violent as Dr. Turgenev predicted. Like flying a building through a typhoon was how he described it. On Earth, the atmosphere gave us life, but right now it was like armour, trying to keep us out. Maybe it wouldn't be so bad, but on the other hand, I didn't really want Dr. Turgenev to be wrong. I wanted all his calculations to be flawless—they *had* to be. All those numbers, swirling in the air like dust . . .

I felt a great swelling bubble of hopelessness inside me, but I crushed it before it overwhelmed me. Almost all of Dr. Turgenev's calculations had been correct so far. He was a genius. He wouldn't fail us.

The four of us talked through the re entry procedure one more time, so that Kate could hear it and the rest of us could rehearse it again. We'd divided up the tasks simply, since we had no idea how difficult it would be to move and think during re-entry. Dr. Turgenev had taped various instructions to the control panels in front of us.

"We are at three hundred miles," said Dr. Turgenev, watching the ship's clock, "two hundred . . . one hundred . . ."

The *Starclimber* began to vibrate lightly. I didn't know what to expect. What was normal and what wasn't? How would we know if we were too shallow and had bounced off the atmosphere back into deep space? And if we were too steep . . . well, that was easier to know. We'd be incinerated.

The vibration became a tremble, and then a steady shake.

"This is beginning of friction in outer atmosphere," said Dr. Turgenev. "This is good news! We are in!"

"So far, so good," said Tobias.

My spirits lifted as the weight began returning to my body. My restraint straps pressed into my chest and shoulders. Beyond the windows, I could still see the darkness of space, but there was a brightening around the base of the dome.

The shaking intensified.

"I hope Lunardi built this ship strong," said Tobias.

"Lunardi builds all his ships strong," I said.

To my left I saw that Dr. Turgenev had strapped his cane to the wall, as though he fully intended to take it up when we landed, and walk off the ship—as though nothing unusual had happened. It struck me as a hopeful sign and cheered me up considerably.

But the ride was getting rougher now, and it was difficult to see straight.

I saw Kate fumbling with her hands. In astonishment I watched her yank off her engagement ring and fling it to the floor.

"I'd just like to say something," she announced, her voice quavering as the ship juddered. "I don't love George Sanderson."

"James," I corrected.

"I don't love James Sanderson either," she said. "And I have no intention of marrying him." The ship shook violently and she gulped. "I love Matt Cruse, and have for some time now! No matter what happens to us, I want everyone here to know that."

Dr. Turgenev sighed wearily. "This we already knew."

"You did?" Kate said, sounding astonished. "All along?"

"Everyone knows. Even Sir Hugh knows. It is obvious."

"Oh," Kate said, disappointed. "I thought I'd done such a . . . oh well. You all know, and that's what's important."

If I stretched, I could just reach her hand. Our fingertips touched, hooking together for a moment. Above us, the black sky, and the stars, twinkling again. She'd never told me she loved me before, and hearing these words for the first time, I was intoxicated with joy.

I gazed up through the dome. "There's your star," I said.

"*Our* star," she said.

"Do you know when I started loving you?" I said. I didn't care that the others might hear.

"Tell me," she said.

My voice rattled with the ship. "On the *Aurora*. I gave you the tour. I showed you the gas cells and said they were made from cow intestines. And you looked very serious and said, 'It must have taken a great many cows.'"

Kate looked surprised. "Really? That *exact* moment?"

"That's it."

"Hmm. It's not very romantic," she said, "but it's completely unexpected. I like that."

From somewhere below came a horrible, drawn-out screech, like a piece of metal being twisted.

"What was that?" Tobias asked in alarm.

"Hull heating up," said Dr. Turgenev.

"It *is* getting very hot in here," Kate remarked.

Sweat now filmed my back and belly. Beyond the windows, creeping around the sides of the ship, was orangey blue light. It grew brighter, and then was suddenly streaming past the *Starclimber* in great sheets and ribbons, like our own aurora borealis.

Heat.

My heart broke into a gallop. I could *see* the heat. I imagined the ship's stern glowing like something in a forge. Orange, then white. Soaking into the metal. Spreading up into C Deck and B Deck. How strong was the *Starclimber*? She wasn't built to withstand such stress. How long before she buckled and melted away altogether?

We continued to plunge backward through the upper atmosphere. My body felt cast from iron. Our chairs groaned ominously, pulling at their bolts. My restraints, creaking with strain, bit into my body.

"No matter . . . what happens . . . we're going home," I said, gripping Kate's hand.

"I'd rather . . . it wasn't as . . . a shooting star," she said.

"There are . . . worse ways . . . of dying."

Gravity clenched me tighter in its fists. I felt I could scarcely fill my lungs to breathe.

The ship shook. My body shook. The entire world was pressing down on me.

My vision started to go red.

Stay awake. Stay awake. Stay—

Everything started to fade, like a painting tipped to its side, all the colours seeping out. I feared I'd black out altogether. Tobias, his eyes closed, was grimacing, and I called out to him, but he didn't answer. Or maybe I wasn't making any noise, for my face was so heavy I could hardly move my mouth.

My vision contracted to a tunnel.

So hot. My body was afire, itching unbearably against the clothing.

Overhead the stars disappeared and the sky was suddenly blue.

I heard beeping, and it took me a moment to realize it was the ship's altimeter. I tried to find the gauge with my eyes. It was like looking through a spyglass in a small room: everything was too close. Finally I located it.

One hundred thousand feet and falling fast.

Emergency balloons! I blinked and squinted and found the lever on my panel. I was in charge of the starboard balloon, Tobias the port.

"To-bi-as!" I moaned. "To-bi-as . . ."

He wasn't moving. I turned to look at Dr. Turgenev. Both unconscious.

"Ka-ate!"

"Ye-e-s."

"Ca-an you rea-each star-board ball-oon le-ver?"

"I thi-ink so."

"Pull wh-en I sa-ay."

I saw her reaching with great difficulty for the lever. At last her hand closed around it.

I struggled for mine. My hand stretched weirdly down the spyglass tunnel of my vision. The world weighed on my eyelids, urging them to close, and rest, and surrender.

"Matt. Take hold of the lever."

Kate's voice was so clear and calm that my eyes snapped open in surprise.

The lever was in my hand.

"We're at seventy thousand feet," she told me.

The altimeter could barely keep up with itself, we were falling so quickly.

If the balloons didn't deploy—

If the compressed hydrium didn't flow fast enough—

"Fifty thousand," I said. "Forty-five . . . Now!"

My lever was stiff and I worried I was too weak, but I gave a roar and pulled it down. Kate did the same with hers.

There was a great *bang* like something exploding, then a clamouring outside the bridge. The *Starclimber* rocked, and outside the dome two long white banners unfurled into the sky, then swelled as they filled with the compressed hydrium.

"Deployed!" I shouted.

The deceleration that followed was instantaneous and brutal. My thousand-pound body was driven back against the chair, knocking the wind from my lungs. All across the bridge, things came unhinged and flew about, striking us.

Please, do not let the balloon lines snap, I begged silently.

The balloons grew, blocking my view of the blue sky. The altimeter's beeping grew less urgent. We were slowing. The balloon lines held.

The altimeter had us at thirty thousand feet and still falling, though much more slowly now. The load on my body was easing.

"Are you all right?" I asked Kate.

She nodded, but she was wheezing.

Tobias grunted and stirred.

"What has happened?" cried Dr. Turgenev, waking suddenly.

"The balloons are flying," I said. "We're slowing down."

"We're through?" Tobias said, not comprehending. "We did it?"

"We're not done yet," I said. "We've got to land this thing."

"This is your job," said Dr. Turgenev. "I am just scientist."

"Let's find out where we are," I said, unbuckling myself.

The hydrium balloons were holding the *Starclimber* more or less vertical, though we were rocking now from the wind. I staggered to the window, my body feeling incredibly heavy after its days of weightlessness.

"Can you see anything?" Kate asked. She too had unbuckled herself, and was coming over.

Below me was a sea of cloud. My heart rejoiced to be back in my sky—but we weren't yet free of danger. There was almost thirty thousand feet between us and a safe landing. I wanted to get the *Starclimber* down as quickly as possible.

We lurched through a thick layer of cumulus, getting tossed about violently. But we all held tight.

"We should be over prairies," said Dr. Turgenev.

I checked our compass. Normally I could always tell north. But after so many days in outer space, I needed to orient myself.

Down we went through the bellies of the last clouds.

"I see land!" cried Kate.

I saw water. True enough, off to the south was the brown texture of land, but directly below the *Starclimber*, and spreading off to the east and west, was water.

"Was there a lake near our landing site?" asked Tobias, surprised.

I ran around to the bridge's north side. Nothing but water.

"This is not lake," Dr. Turgenev said.

"Where are we?" Tobias demanded.

"Doesn't matter," I said. "What matters is we're getting blown away from land."

The *Starclimber* was no airship. Her shape was ungainly, and we were rocking and spinning; and it was difficult to move about the bridge.

"How do we steer?" Kate asked.

"Like a balloon," I said. "Change altitude until we find a favourable current."

It wouldn't be easy. We had no ballast. Once we dropped, we couldn't go back up. We couldn't stop our descent.

I checked the altimeter: we'd levelled off at just under fifteen thousand feet. We had some height to play with, but not a lot.

"We're going to valve some hydrium," I told everyone. "We'll drop bit by bit until we start heading south."

Each hydrium balloon had an escape valve that could be triggered from the bridge. I put Tobias on the starboard controls, and myself on the port. A pressure gauge showed the balloons at full capacity. Each control was like the trigger of a gun. We'd need steady hands to keep the ship balanced.

"Dr. Turgenev and Kate, you're the ship's eyes now. When you see us start moving back towards land, shout out!"

They took opposite sides of the bridge and pressed their faces to the glass.

"Ready?" I asked Tobias. "Now!"

We squeezed our triggers. I kept my eyes on the pressure gauge and altimeter.

"Stop!" I said. We'd fallen a couple of hundred feet. The *Starclimber* spun about as the wind shifted.

"How're we doing?" I yelled.

"We're moving to the east now!" said Kate.

That was an improvement, but not enough.

"Valve again, go," I told Tobias. "Stop!"

It was a tricky manoeuvre. Lose too much hydrium and we'd drop too fast.

A big gust hit the *Starclimber*'s flank and swung us like a pendulum. Dr. Turgenev tripped and fell. We were at ten thousand feet now, and running out of time.

"How're we doing, Kate?"

"I think you've done it! We're moving back towards land!"

"How far to landfall?"

"I can't tell, I'm sorry."

I rushed to the window. I guessed we were twenty miles off, and we were moving south at quite a clip, driven by a stiff wind. So long as it didn't change direction, we'd make landfall within minutes. The *Starclimber* swayed.

"I think now I'm going to be sick," said Dr. Turgenev, and he was, noisily, against the wall.

My stomach yawed uncomfortably, but I fought it. I couldn't be laid low right now.

Five thousand feet . . .

"We're over land!" Kate cried happily.

"Tobias," I said, "see if you can raise anyone on the radio. Tell them we're making an emergency landing!"

"Good," he said, and started calling in an SOS. I wished we had coordinates to give them.

"It looks very brown," said Kate. "I see roads and rivers and lots and lots of fields. Is that wheat?"

We were too high to tell, but what we saw was definitely farmland. Our descent was reassuringly gradual. At a thousand feet, I started looking for a likely landing site. To the south, the fields suddenly gave way to a pale brown expanse that stretched to the horizon.

"Is that . . . *desert?*" Kate said.

I seized a spyglass from its rack. "You're right, it's sand," I said. "Dr. Turgenev, I don't think this is the prairies."

He was slumped in his chair, his head between his knees. "Should be prairies," he mumbled weakly.

Static crackled over our speaker, then: "What are your coordinates, please, *Starclimber?*"

"We don't know our coordinates," said Tobias. "We've just . . . um . . . returned from outer space. Can you tell us where we are?"

"I think I see a pyramid!" said Kate.

"What!" I said.

She pointed. "Three of them, actually."

I didn't need my spyglass to spot them, rising unmistakably from the desert sand.

"We're over Egypt!" I exclaimed.

"I misplace decimal point," moaned Dr. Turgenev.

All I cared about right now was setting us down safely. We'd just cleared the last of the fields. By my reckoning we'd come down very close to the pyramids.

The crisp voice sounded over the speaker again. "*Starclimber*, this is Cairo Aeroharbour, do you have a rough position?"

"We're due north of the Great Pyramids," Tobias said, "about . . ." He looked over at me, wanting an estimate.

"Two miles," I told him.

"Two miles. Heading south. We have no power and are free-ballooning. Making an emergency landing."

"We'll dispatch a rescue crew immediately, *Starclimber*."

"Two hundred feet!" I shouted to everyone.

The wind seemed to die down altogether as we skimmed over the peak of the Great Pyramid of Cheops. There was really nothing left to do now but hope we touched down on a nice sandy patch.

"This is it!" I said. "Buckle up, everyone, this'll be rough!"

Kate pointed in alarm. "We're awfully close to the Sphinx!"

"Not much I can do about that," I said.

"But it's an invaluable artifa—"

There was a terrible *thud* and the *Starclimber* ricocheted off the Sphinx's head.

"I think you broke its nose!" Kate cried, holding tight as we swung wildly.

"Sit down and buckle up!" I told her. "Tobias, keep your hand on the balloon release. The moment we touch down, jettison them so we don't get dragged."

"Will do," he said.

I staggered into my seat. The altimeter's needle sank lower. Forty feet . . . thirty . . . twenty . . .

It seemed to take forever, but that was good. We needed a gentle touchdown.

A great jarring sent us all lurching. The *Starclimber* bounced, tilting over at a crazy angle, then banged down again for good. Sand flew against the dome. Glass shattered.

"Let fly!" I shouted, and Tobias pulled the lever. Through

the dome I saw the hydrium balloons hurtle away from the ship.

Then all was still.

"Everyone all right?" I asked.

We staggered out of our seats. Air, real air, swirled in through the cracked dome.

"We did it!" Kate cried. "We're home!"

28 / Homeward Bound

IN THE HOTEL COURTYARD Miss Karr sat painting at an easel, Haiku on her shoulder.

"I didn't know you were a painter as well, Miss Karr," I said, walking over.

"I'm not," she replied with a smile. "I tried very hard, long before I took up photography. I wasn't very good. One of my teachers said his cat could do better. So I gave up. But I'm going to try again."

I remembered something. The first time I'd seen Miss Karr, she was in her back garden at an easel. She'd stood up angrily, like she didn't want anyone seeing. I suddenly understood.

"It's the photographer that needs to change," I said, quoting her words back to her.

She nodded. "It is indeed. Come have a look."

She invited me around the easel to see. I'd expected a picture of the courtyard: the fountain or the exotic Egyptian flowers, or the minaret rising in the distance. But it was none of that.

The painting was of a luminous green forest of massive pines, and beyond it a night sky like I'd never seen. The light emanated from the stars in great auras. I felt the power of the sky and the trees, and heard the wind that stirred their great boughs.

"I like it very much," I said enthusiastically. "It's not at all like a photograph, but it's like I'm standing right there in the forest, and I can hear and smell everything."

"The soul of the forest," she said, looking at the painting with a critical eye.

"It's funny you had to go all the way to outer space to paint it."

"Isn't it?" she agreed. "Maybe sometimes you see things best when they're out of sight. Or *feel* them best anyway. I've just ordered some tea. Will you join me?"

I was glad to sit down. It was our fifth day in Cairo, but my body was still amazingly difficult to lug around. I worried that I walked like an old man. Getting used to the earth again would take some time.

The sound of running water was still marvellous to me, and I listened contentedly to the fountain. I breathed in the warm scent of flowers.

It was the smells I'd noticed first, climbing out of the *Starclimber.* Even the scent of the desert was overwhelming. The hot mineral aroma of sand, and beyond that, the fragrance of distant fields—turned earth, aromatic herbs, and water plants from the Nile. And then the pungent odour of camels, and the sulfurous fumes of the motorcars and ambulances rushing to meet us.

The *Starclimber* was badly damaged. It was amazing she hadn't been completely destroyed. The stern had absorbed most of the impact, which had almost completely crumpled C Deck, and a bit of B Deck. Safely strapped down in their cabins on A Deck Sir Hugh, Chef Vlad, Captain Walken, and Miss Karr and Haiku had escaped harm, and all walked off the ship—even the captain, who'd regained consciousness moments after our landing.

We had all been taken straight to hospital, where doctors poked and prodded us and shone lights in our eyes. Captain Walken was fine, with just a mild concussion. They kept all of us overnight, though. They'd never had patients who'd crashlanded after three weeks in outer space, and just wanted to make sure we were truly all right. As soon as I could, I sent a telegram home to my mother and sisters, letting them know I was alive and well. I didn't know how much news Lunardi had given them, but I hoped they hadn't suffered too much worry.

After the hospital, we were taken to the Cairo Ritz, where Mr. Lunardi had reserved the entire top floor for us. He didn't want us disturbed. We were disturbed anyway, by a swelling army of reporters and photographers from newspapers around the world, all wanting our stories and pictures. Mr. Lunardi instructed us not to talk to anyone. The story was ours to tell and he wanted Miss Karr to be the one to write it. She spent the next three days in a darkroom, developing all the photographs she'd taken during our trip.

As Miss Karr and I sipped our tea, and Haiku ate all the biscuits, Kate and Sir Hugh walked into the courtyard, followed by Captain Walken and Dr. Turgenev. The Russian scientist was leaning on his cane more heavily than usual. I knew they'd just come from the warehouse where the wreckage of the *Starclimber* was being stored before being shipped back to Lionsgate City. Kate and Sir Hugh had wanted to see what could be salvaged from the laboratory. Not much, judging by their downcast faces. They all sat down with Miss Karr and me, and we ordered more tea from the waiter.

"There's no sign of the etherian specimen," Sir Hugh said with a deep sigh. "Crushed to dust in the wreckage."

Kate nodded solemnly. "It was very brittle."

"It's tragic," said Sir Hugh.

"Tragic," echoed Kate. "But we do have some excellent photographs, and we discovered a great deal about it. Our article will shake the scientific world."

"I do wish we had something to show, though," said Sir Hugh. "Sometimes scientists are infuriatingly hard to convince unless you waggle the thing in their faces."

"Yes," Kate said drily. "And sometimes even if you waggle the thing in their faces and it electrocutes them, they *still* don't believe you."

"Hmm," said Sir Hugh vaguely. "Now, if you'll excuse me, I'm going to have a nap. This heat is quite enervating. I'll see you all at dinner."

As the zoologist strode across the courtyard, an exotic bird managed to poop on his shoulder.

"That's really too bad about your etherian specimen," I said.

"Oh, it's perfectly fine," Kate said lightly. "I sneaked it up to my cabin before re-entry."

"You're joking!"

"Not at all. I wanted to keep it safe."

I looked at the other astounded faces around the table. "But why didn't you tell Sir Hugh?"

"I will—in a bit. Don't look at me like that! This is my insurance."

"Insurance for what, Miss de Vries?" the captain asked.

"In case he tries not to give me equal credit for the article. I still don't trust him. When the article's published, I'll produce the specimen."

"It's devious," I said, shaking my head.

"But ingenious," said Miss Karr. "Good thinking, Miss de Vries."

Through the courtyard arches, I caught sight of Tobias. He was dressed in a flowing white robe and carrying two large shopping bags. I waved to him and he came over.

"What is this you wear?" Dr. Turgenev asked him.

"A galabya," he said. "It's a traditional Egyptian robe. I needed some more clothes."

"It looks cool," I said.

Tobias nodded. "Probably won't wear it much back home, though."

"Have some tea," said Captain Walken, pouring him a cup.

Kate stepped around behind Miss Karr's easel. "Gosh, what a brilliant painting!" she said.

"It's coming along," said Miss Karr.

Dr. Turgenev craned his neck to take a look. "Sky is not accurate," he said with a frown. "And tree is too thick. You improve with time."

"Thank you, Dr. Turgenev," said Miss Karr, her eyes twinkling.

"It's like a little piece of home," said Tobias, having a peek. "I wouldn't change a thing."

"Speaking of home," said Captain Walken, "Mr. Lunardi should be here tomorrow. He'll take us all back aboard the *Bluenose* after he inspects the *Starclimber*." He reached into his jacket pocket and took out a sheaf of letters. "We've had telegrams today from Sir John and the Prime Minister, full of bravos and patriotic hurrahs. Apparently we're to be given a tickertape parade when we return."

"I don't mind that," Tobias said.

"Not a bad send-off for retirement," chuckled the captain, sifting through the telegrams. "Let's see. The King also sends his congratulations and best wishes to all. And, oh yes, the President of France sent his sympathies for our failed mission."

"Cheeky!" said Kate indignantly. "We reached outer space first and discovered life beyond the sky! I hardly call that a failure. The last bit didn't go smoothly, I'll admit."

I thought of Shepherd—as did everyone else, judging by the silence that followed.

"What happened to the astral cable?" Tobias asked finally. "The part attached to the ground station?"

"Mostly burned up on reentry," said Dr. Turgenev. "Lowest bit drifted down into ocean."

The captain nodded. "Mr. Lunardi said it fell slow as a ribbon."

"Will this mean an end to space exploration, do you think?" I asked.

Captain Walken shook his head. "Mr. Lunardi's disappointed, but I've never known him to turn away from an idea he loves."

"We build new rocket, new cable," Dr. Turgenev said.

"The last one got eaten," Miss Karr pointed out tartly.

"You'd have to figure out some way of keeping the astral flora and fauna off it," Kate said.

"Of course," said Dr. Turgenev. "Protective coating, maybe. This is not big problem. We go up again."

I was amazed at his confidence, considering all the disasters we'd faced.

"I hope we do go back," said Tobias.

I turned to him. "After all that?"

"I think so. I want to walk on the moon, remember? What about you?"

I thought of the counterweight sailing deeper into outer space, its Canadian flag shimmering. Our little piece of Earth in the ether. Maybe other humans would come across it again one day, but not me. I shook my head.

"I missed the sky," I said.

Tobias chuckled. "Fair enough. Right now I just want to go home."

The captain and Dr. Turgenev went off to attend to business, and not long after, Tobias left to have a swim.

Miss Karr looked up from her easel with mischief in her eyes. "And what about you, Miss de Vries? You must be anxious to rush home into the arms of your fiancé."

Kate raised an eyebrow. "You knew from the start, didn't you?"

Miss Karr gave her familiar cackle. "From the second I set eyes on you two. You belonged to each other. That's exactly what I thought."

I felt my face flush. *Belonged to each other.* I loved that.

"Well, there's no point putting it off any longer," Kate said. "I'm off to send some telegrams." She gave a little shudder. "If you hear screaming, that's my mother in Lionsgate City."

"Good luck," I said.

Just as Kate stood, a porter from the hotel crossed the courtyard towards us.

"Miss de Vries?" he said. "Telegram for you."

"Thank you." She opened it and grimaced. "It's from Mummy."

Kate read it with intense concentration, her cheeks quite red by the end.

"This is horrible," she muttered.

"What's wrong?" I asked.

"My fiancé, George—"

"James."

"Apparently he went for a midnight walk in the Point Grey cemetery. He was found inside a crypt with a shovel and a wheelbarrow—and in a very indecent embrace with Mimsy Rogers. Can you believe it?"

I shook my head. "Mimsy Rogers really gets around."

Kate was in full tirade. "I can't believe what a wretch he is!"

"Why are you so angry?" I laughed.

"That's not all," Kate said. "They've eloped!"

From behind her easel, Miss Karr said, "Maybe Mimsy liked graveyards more than you."

"He pledged his undying love to me!" Kate complained. "And he didn't even last three weeks!"

"Kate," I said, "you didn't care one bit about him. You couldn't even remember his name."

She glared at me. "That has nothing to do with it. I've been completely humiliated! Rejected! And by the likes of George Sanderson too!

Miss Karr looked at Kate severely. "Enough, Miss de Vries! The fellow's done you a huge favour."

Kate took a deep breath and beamed. "I know. The timing's perfect."

She signalled the porter over to the table. "Could you take a return telegram, please? Let's see . . . 'Devastated by the news. Utterly heartbroken. Am considering becoming nun. Your loving daughter, Kate.'" She looked up at the porter. "Did you get everything?"

"Yes, miss."

"Maybe take out that last line about becoming a nun," she said.

"Best not to give your parents any ideas," I agreed.

"Please send it right away," Kate told the porter, smiling. "Thank you so much."

She lifted her tea to her lips. "This really is a delightful courtyard."

Miss Karr stood. "I think I'll take a walk in the garden. Come along, Haiku."

For a few moments Kate and I sat in silence.

"I'm sorry your wedding's cancelled," I said.

"Terrible business." She took a sip of her tea and looked at me. "I'm very, very sorry I hurt you, Matt. If I had it to do over again—"

"You'd do exactly the same thing," I told her.

She was about to protest, but then gave a little laugh. Her cheeks were flushed. "Yes, you're right. But I always knew I'd be able to make it right in the end. I wouldn't have done it otherwise, honestly. I'm not the horrible person you think."

"Marry me," I said.

She lowered her tea cup, trembling slightly, to the saucer. "Aren't you going to get down on one knee?"

I got down on one knee and took her hand.

"Will you marry me, Kate?"

"You can't propose properly without a ring," she said.

I reached into my pocket and took out James Sanderson's ring, which I'd picked up off the floor after we'd crash-landed.

"That's a nice-looking ring," said Kate with a grin.

"Cost a fortune," I said. "And now, for the third time—Kate de Vries, will you marry me?"

She leaned forward and took my face in her hands and kissed me.

"Yes," she said. "Yes, and yes, and yes. But it will be terrible."

"Probably," I agreed.

"Honestly," she sighed, "I don't know what kind of life we'll have together, with me always flying off in one direction and you in the other."

I smiled. "It's a good thing the world's round," I said.

KENNETH OPPEL is the Governor General's Award–winning author of the Airborn series and the Silverwing Saga, which has sold over a million copies worldwide. His most recent novel is *Half Brother*. He lives in Toronto with his wife and three children. Visit his website at **www.kennethoppel.com.**